DEDICATION

While writing the final chapter of this novel, my Yorkie of fourteen years passed away. I've lost pets before, but never knew I could feel so devastated. I miss you Jazzy and I will always love you.

Jazz
17 July 2008-5 April 2022

PART ONE

Fear is the main source of superstition,
and one of the main sources of cruelty.
To conquer fear is the beginning of wisdom.

Bertrand Russell, *Unpopular Essays*

Chapter One

"Circling back around." Tactical Flight Officer Carmen Bravo spoke to her co-pilot through the Bluetooth headsets. "Attempting to reacquire visual."

Carmen squinted far below, despite the fact that her human vision couldn't possibly see details that far. Her concern for the victim overrode that knowledge and she continued to scan visually and fly the craft. Darkness seemed to press in from all sides, embracing the chopper in night's comforting embrace even as Carmen's heart pounded in concern.

The padded headset into which she spoke performed double duty for reducing noise from the rotor wash while allowing for communications. Carmen tightened a strong left hand on the Bell 407 GXP helicopter's stick. At the same time, she manipulated the anti-torque foot pedals to veer right. Carmen peered through the right side of the glass cockpit searching for any detail to bring this nightmare to an end.

She loved this job, under almost all circumstances. Flying over Denver, Colorado and seeing the majestic mountainous landscape, the beauty of a late summer day, enjoying the freshness of the breeze. Today wasn't one of those times. Pursuing a child kidnapper didn't rate high on her list. That the little girl's uncle was the suspect didn't help.

"You see anything, Lopez?"

Carmen's partner took his time responding. Raphael Lopez possessed a light demeanor, always quick with a joke or a smile. His flashing white smile never failed to garner a response from his friends and co-workers. During intense work situations, like this, those jovial mannerisms rarely manifested. Carmen chanced a quick glance away from Denver's relatively quiet residential streets to shoot Lopez a measuring look. Waste of time. She couldn't hope to read his expression behind the white helmet and visor. Instead, she noticed how he worked the display controls. She could, however, clearly see the tension in his broad shoulders. Carmen redirected her focus to flying the helicopter.

"There," Lopez finally said. "FLIR is picking up the suspect pickup. Alley between Irving Street and Hooker, headed south. Might be making for the freeway."

Carmen bit off a curse. Morning rush hour loomed, promising to interfere with a dangerous chase and present even more issues. They couldn't afford a high speed pursuit through heavy traffic with a five-year-old in the car. Who was she kidding? No one wanted that kind of chase, with or without a child involved. The thought of collateral damage left a bitter taste in her mouth.

Carmen opened a channel. "Air One to ground units. Suspect vehicle traveling south in the alley between Hooker Street and Irving. Approximate speed..." She hesitated for a beat to allow Lopez time to supply the information.

"Forty-three miles per hour."

That didn't sound so bad, she thought. Until a fiberglass and plastic yellow truck charged into a steel dumpster. She repeated the information and added, "Vehicle may be in route to the Sixth Avenue Freeway."

Below, Carmen spotted multiple police units converging on the location. The distance might be great, but vehicle headlights clearly outlined the scene. Thank goodness for the helicopter's Forward Looking Infrared and Lopez keeping an eye on the readouts. With any luck, the suspect would give up or find himself blocked soon. Skies to the east began to lighten, heralding the coming day. The rising sun presented serious problems for the chase. With it came rush hour traffic. Once traffic increased, the driver could use that to his advantage. While Air One could easily keep track of the kidnapper's vehicle, patrol units would have a harder time closing in without putting the public at risk.

Carmen directed the helicopter directly over the fleeing pickup, sticking as close as possible. Her partner immediately redirected the lower belly spotlight to the vehicle's roof. As the sun rose, Carmen more easily spied patrol cars closing in from behind on the suspect. From a half a mile in the sky, she noticed a single unit coming in from the opposite direction. It originated from the south, barreling directly toward the suspect. Suddenly, the solitary patrol car decelerated. Smoke puffed into the air from tires skidding on pavement. The car stopped and an officer raced out, leaving the door ajar. Carmen kept one eye on the suspect vehicle and the other on the lone uniformed officer. A grin slowly curled her lips. She had an inkling of what was coming.

Sure enough, within moments, the female officer laid a long, black object across the alley. Then the woman jumped back into her unit and shot away from the scene in reverse. Carmen noted the officer slide in behind a dumpster, apparently awaiting the oncoming cars.

She redirected her full attention to the chase. "Lopez, how fast is the suspect going?"

Garbage and paper flew into the air from the speeding vehicle's passage through the alley. At least there wasn't anyone walking through the backstreet in this quiet neighborhood at this time of the morning. Thank God for small favors, she thought.

Lopez's voice sounded a little tinny through her headset. "Speed has increased slightly…forty-six miles an hour…oh wait. Whoops! There goes another trashcan. Looks like this one lodged under the vehicle's undercarriage. Speed reducing. Forty-two…thirty-nine."

The convoy of police units and the yellow Ford hurtled toward the spike strip. Lopez kept Carmen up to date as the speed of the chase continued to fall. It seemed the offending plastic trashcan had yet to release its hold. As they neared the spike strip, police units suddenly slowed. No doubt the intrepid female officer had communicated about the spike strip. When the truck ran over the device, Carmen found the whole scene blessedly anti-climactic. The quick-thinking lady cop pulled her vehicle across the lane to block any possible escape. She didn't need to. The pickup rolled to a stop at least six feet from the unit's passenger door.

Officers quickly closed in. As soon as ground units called the situation all clear, Carmen peeled off. It was time to head home. She said a silent prayer for the traumatized little girl and made a conscious decision to let go of the rest. Carmen knew they couldn't always come out ahead in the perils of law enforcement, but she'd take the wins when they came. Happy with the outcome, Carmen pointed the nose of her chopper into the promise of a new, glorious Denver day.

"Air One to dispatch. 10-42."

"10-4, Air One. Thanks for the assist."

"That was great, Bravo. I still can't believe we got that perp without a TC." Officer Lopez grinned at Carmen as he slapped her on the shoulder in celebration.

Considering the huge grin on his face, Carmen thought he looked as excited as she was. Probably still riding high on adrenaline. His midnight-colored eyes sparkled in excitement and his thin mustache hitched up at a crooked angle along with his smile.

Carmen returned his smile. She found it easy to meet him face to face, considering their near identical height at a little over six feet. She could still feel excitement singing in her own veins. She pushed straight black bangs away from her face as she removed the flight helmet and skull cap. Carmen stuffed the tight-fitting white cap into the helmet.

As the senior pilot of Denver's Air One helicopter unit, her days never proved boring. Assisting in the capture of a kidnapping suspect without the chase ending in a traffic collision made the job all the more rewarding. The positive outcome was the great way to start a little time off.

"I know what you mean, Raph." Carmen agreed, more than thrilled with the outcome of the pursuit. "I'm just glad that little girl is safe and on her way home."

The two officers walked away from the sun-baked helipad and into the maintenance hangar. The temperature immediately seemed to drop by five degrees. Although early, the concrete still carried heat from the previous day. Carmen grasped her helmet in her right hand and used the other to lower the zipper of her flight suit. The one-piece jumpsuit did a great job keeping her warm when flying high. Unfortunately, the dark navy color wasn't as comfortable on the ground in direct sunlight.

"So, wanna have a beer? I'm buying," Raphael offered.

"Wow, did you get promoted or something?"

"Funny, you should take that routine on the road."

Carmen couldn't hold back her laugh when she saw Raphael's disgruntled look. She chuckled and shook her head. "Thanks anyway, Raph. I appreciate it, but I have other plans and it's a little early for me."

Raphael stopped walking, forcing her to do the same. He always wanted to know more about her personal life. Even though aircraft mechanics, inspectors and other police officers wandered throughout the hangar, he didn't seem to mind if anyone overheard their conversation.

"Really, do you have big plans for the weekend? Is there a lucky lady I should know about?"

"Nah, you know I don't date. I've told you, anyone I could care about would hate what I do for a living." Carmen shrugged. "Anyway, this is going to be more than a weekend. I have so many vacation days saved up that the brass is forcing me to take some time off. Jerry Simpson will fill in while I'm gone."

For a brief moment, distaste flitted across Raphael's face. He quickly replaced it with a customary smile, but not before Carmen got the distinct sense that he wasn't happy with the replacement.

"Lucky you. So where are you headed?"

"Katie and I are going to Germany for Oktoberfest."

Raphael's eyes popped open wide in surprise. "Wow, that's quite a trip. How come you didn't tell me about it before? Did Doctor McClarin invite you or the other way around?"

Carmen trusted Raphael with her life. Partners had to in this line of work and they'd been paired together with Air One for over a year. Still, as much as she trusted him, Carmen tended to try and keep some of her off duty time to herself. Despite her reason for hesitating to answer, Raphael knew Katie as a former prominent psychiatrist who frequently testified in court proceedings. Since he knew Carmen's friend personally, his questions weren't altogether unexpected. Carmen thought Raphael might secretly have a thing for Katie.

"The trip was pretty last minute. I wasn't even sure I was going to go until last week."

"And the doc?"

"Katie invited me. I guess she didn't want to go alone. Now if you'll excuse me, Mister Nosey, I need to get out of here so I can pack." Carmen poked Raph on the shoulder and then walked away, leaving him standing in the middle of the hangar.

"Fine, but I expect you to bring me back a souvenir," he said loudly to her back. "And not some lame t-shirt either."

Carmen grinned and waved a hand in response. She found the locker room empty as she entered. Immediately, Carmen dropped her helmet onto a bench and stripped off the flight suit. The fact that few women worked in law enforcement, and even fewer possessed a pilot's license, ensured she had the room to herself. She enjoyed the quiet as she changed into jeans and a white button-down shirt. Carmen neatly hung up the jumpsuit and dropped her black boots into the bottom of the locker. She exchanged her shoulder harness for an off-duty concealed waist holster and transferred her weapon to it, then added blue sandals to her ensemble. Her red toenail polish clashed with the blue, but she didn't care. A dark shoulder bag completed her signature look.

After dressing, Carmen pulled the rubber band from her ponytail. Long dark hair dropped around her shoulders, framing and softening the angles of her tanned face. She brushed out her hair, taming the mess caused by smashing it with a skull cap for hours on end. A smile showed large dimples as she thought about the upcoming adventure. She had never visited Germany before. The history and lore drew her like a magnet. Ideas of gypsies, and traveling circuses danced in her head. She couldn't wait to see Munich locals in traditional costumes at the festival. Thankfully, no one expected her to dress in a *dirndl* and apron.

Carmen slammed the locker, grabbed her sunglasses and headed for the hangar exit. The main parking lot sat on the far side of the hangar away from the helipad. The positioning kept debris from being tossed onto objects from the chopper's rotor wash. That didn't prevent Carmen from casting an affectionate glance in the aircraft's direction as she drove away.

The Bell 407 GXP gleamed in the afternoon light as she pulled around the corner and she caught sight of her favorite transport. Newly born sunlight winked off bright metal and reflected from the glass cockpit as Carmen admired the sleek lines of the white helicopter with blue stripes.

Flying always gave her a sense of freedom. Piloting attack helicopters in Kandahar had left her feeling the same way. Unfortunately, war during her time in the Air Force didn't carry the same sense of fulfillment.

Carmen loved helping people and the police department aided her in that desire. When someone hurt, she experienced their pain like a deep ache in her heart. When she assisted in reuniting a child or a lost hiker with loved ones, she felt like she could fly without the chopper. She couldn't imagine her life without this job, though that didn't mean she couldn't use a break now and then.

Carmen's thoughts turned to the upcoming trip. The dimples reappeared. By rote, she drove her dark blue Outback from the hangar's service road toward the airport exit. Traffic picked up as she reached the main thoroughfare leaving Denver International Airport. Known commonly by the locals as DIA, Denver's airport ranked second largest in the world. The size of the place ensured tons of rushed motorists, all in a hurry at almost every hour of the day.

Horns blared as impatient drivers jockeyed for position across four lanes. Everyone seemed intent on being first through the exit gates. Of course, their antics only increased the confusion and jammed up the lanes of outbound traffic. Carmen maneuvered away from the crowd of sundry drivers and cabbies. Finally, she escaped the cacophony and headed for Gate Five. Denver police personnel used this gate to access and exit the city's maintenance facility as well as the hangar for Air One.

Carmen pressed the button on her armrest to roll down the window. She held up her airport I.D. badge as she spoke to the man seated inside the security booth. "Hi, Stanley."

Stanley scowled back in return. His thinning gray hair ruffled slightly in the morning breeze. Bushy gray brows pulled down toward washed out eyes that might once have been brown. The middle aged, skeletally thin man had never smiled in the two years since Carmen started working the air unit. Instead, he made a show of scrutinizing every detail of the plastic identification card. Once evidently satisfied with that, Stanley peered through the Outback's interior to see the orange and white checkered flag decal pasted on the rear window. The decal symbolized the car was permitted in the area.

Carmen began to run a little thin on patience. A long shift and very little remaining time to pack made her somewhat sarcastic. "Really? You know who I am, Stanley. We go through this every time I'm on duty."

Eyebrows one would expect to find on a badger drew down impossibly more. Stanley's lips compressed as he pasted them together. He held Carmen's gaze for a moment before saying, "I take pride in my work, Bravo. Maybe you should try it sometime."

"What's that supposed to mean?"

Rather than answer, Stanley grunted and slammed the tiny window closed. A second later the arm on the security gate rose.

"Of all the rude…"

Carmen quickly drove through the exit before Stanley could lower the bar again. She didn't want a new scratch on her old car. As she rolled up the window, Carmen muttered to herself. "Honestly, what did I ever do to him? I don't even really know that man."

As unpleasant as she found their exchange, Carmen knew she had to let it go. Stanley seemed to disapprove of her from day one. Carmen had no idea why and she couldn't change anything. Maybe Stanley didn't like women flying helicopters or women police officers in general. Whatever the case, Carmen had nothing to do with his problems. She decided to focus only on more positive things for the next two weeks.

Munich!

The smile returned and Carmen finished her drive home thinking about beer, *Lederhosen*, and oompah bands.

Chapter Two

Carmen lay on her right side with her hands tucked under her armpits. She had her knees bent as much as possible in the confined space. Sleeping on the last leg of the Lufthansa flight from France to Munich wasn't really possible. Near overwhelming excitement prevented that. The lights were down low and few people moved around. Thankfully, first class afforded the lie-flat seats she currently enjoyed. Conversely, every time someone strolled by on their way to the head, Carmen felt them brush against her back. She wanted to sleep. She needed to. If it weren't for the nearby sound of a buzz saw, Carmen thought it might actually be possible.

Suddenly, a potential source of the noise occurred to her. Carmen's eyes opened wide and she grinned. She sat up and peered over the partition between her and her favorite travelling companion. Katie "Katchoo" McClarin lay sprawled in the window seat. Best friend, confidant and all-around Girl Friday, Carmen loved Katie like a sister. In point of fact, Carmen loved Katie more than she did her real sister. Silently, she compared Katie with the other woman in question.

Katie had retired as a successful Denver psychiatrist after the death of her husband. A multiple car collision took Jack's life. After that, Katie closed her private practice. Before Jack's death, Katie often took clients pro bono. She cared, truly cared for others. Della Bravo, on the other hand, cared for no one but herself. Della actually thought it cute to say that she wasn't happy unless she upset at least one person every day.

Where Katie was five-feet-seven inches, blonde-haired and green-eyed, Della stood five-three and was overweight with muddy brown eyes. Katie took care of her physical appearance and kept a close watch on her weight, though she did carry a few extra pounds. Della chain-smoked and mooched money to pay her bills from any family member willing to go along.

Carmen smiled, remembering how she first met Katie. Five years ago, a man was arrested for a serial murder and turned out to be a mob enforcer with a taste for wet work. As it happened, he was also a patient of Katie's. Court-mandated therapy had him seeing the woman, and he carelessly made the mistake of communicating an active threat to another target. Katie's duty required her to forgo doctor/patient confidentiality and her information led directly to the man's incarceration. Carmen was only a beat officer at the time. She became the cliché rookie that detectives passed the suspect off to for booking. She and Katie met at the scene and hit it off like a house on fire.

Katie frowned suddenly and sneezed in her sleep. She went right back to snoring without pause while Carmen covered a yawn with her hand before stretching her arms high over head. A quick glance around told her that most of the passengers slept, or at least tried to. She cast another amused glance toward her companion and decided to stretch her legs. Carmen unbuckled her lap belt and climbed to her feet. She always felt a little wobbly walking around on a plane, but attempted to ignore the slightly weightless sensation as she struck out for the head located at the front of the cabin.

The smell of musty carpet, unwashed bodies and alcohol from the beverage service assaulted her nose. Carmen snorted in distaste and focused on her destination. She tried not to bother anyone by grabbing their seatbacks for balance as she traveled the short distance. A woman stood with her back to her while waiting for the current occupant to vacate the small lavatory. Carmen didn't relish standing in line for the bathroom, but she really had nothing else to do. Instead, she heaved a quiet sigh and resigned herself to the inevitable.

When Carmen was only a few feet from the door, it suddenly opened and a man emerged. He stopped and spoke briefly to the woman. Whatever he said, she apparently found it amusing. The unknown woman tilted her head back slightly and laughed.

The sound struck a chord in Carmen, like magic on a stormy day.

The small hairs on her arms stood up and goosebumps broke out over her scalp as she couldn't look away from the small female form. The man brushed by Carmen on his way back to his seat, but she barely noticed. All she wanted was for the woman to turn around, to laugh, so that Carmen could experience that sensation again. She could happily drown in the woman's laughter. Instead, the stranger proceeded into the bathroom and closed the door.

With that limited contact over, Carmen felt like she had just surfaced for air. The spell broken, she shook off the feeling that she'd just lost something precious and continued forward to wait her turn. Moments passed while she centered herself. She figured she must be really exhausted to react so strangely to such an innocuous thing.

When the door opened a few minutes later, Carmen didn't know what she expected. She braced herself for a resurgence of the strange feelings. Somehow, she anticipated this woman would know how she'd affected Carmen. Instead, the other passenger barely seemed to notice her. Their eyes met briefly and both offered a polite smile, as Carmen figured one tends to do on a commercial jetliner.

Stormy blue eyes met her gaze. Pink lips with a perfect cupid's bow curved upward in a polite smile. The stranger seemed small, barely reaching Carmen's chin. She wore a cotton knit red beret tilted at a fetching angle. Carmen thought the headgear rather stylish and appropriate considering their last departure point. Short blonde hair cut in a pleasingly feminine style showed off a strong jaw line. Carmen's fingers itched to reach out and stroke a perfect peaches and cream cheek. To her great disappointment, the magic didn't appear mutual. The woman passed by her in seconds and disappeared into the rear of the plane.

"What the hell is wrong with me?" She mumbled under her breath.

Carmen slammed the bathroom door closed and twisted the lock. She leaned against the sink in the tightly compressed room and closed her eyes, breathing deeply for several seconds. She had no idea why she reacted that way to some random stranger on a plane. When she had herself under control, Carmen splashed water on her face and then finished her business. No one stood waiting when she came back out. Pushing away a definite sense of disappointment, she headed back to her seat.

Katie still slept undisturbed, her snores unabated. Carmen chuckled under her breath, loathe to awaken her friend. At least not with words. She was a little bored and still slightly shaken from her earlier reactions to the mystery woman. It was time for Katie to join the party.

Carmen searched around and spotted something she could use. She unplugged the cord used to charge her iPad. Then, carefully and gently, she leaned over and tickled Katie's cheek with the end of the power cord. Katie twitched and swiped at the offending object. Carmen waited a second and then repeated her actions. Again Katie flinched, but didn't awaken. This time Carmen's brow furrowed. Seriously, what would it take? She tried once more, and stuck the end of the power cord into the shell of Katie's left ear.

Katie snorted and jerked upright in her seat. Her green eyes flashed in Carmen's direction.

"What is that?"

Carmen laughed at the miffed look on Katie's face and lifted the offending object. "It's just a power cord."

"Cute." Katie stretched and yawned before she raised her seat to an upright position.

From her tone, Carmen assumed Katie was far from amused. "Well, I did it for the good of the other passengers."

"How do you figure that?"

Carmen tried to keep the smile from her lips. "There were so many complaints that the steward threatened to put a parachute on you and toss you out over the barren land. Honestly, Katchoo, you sounded like a dental drill left on high speed."

"I did not." Katie laughed. "You know I have allergies. Traveling always sets them off."

Carmen took pity on Katie's affliction and relented. She called her friend Katchoo on occasion specifically because of the allergies. She only did so in private and sparingly at that. It was one thing to gently tease, but quite another to embarrass. Katie couldn't help that she had allergies.

"I know. Sorry for picking on you."

"No, you're not."

Carmen smiled. "No, I'm not. I guess I didn't want to be the only one awake. I'm just too excited to sleep. I've never been to Germany, much less Oktoberfest!" She wasn't about to tell Katie about her previous aberrant reaction to a total stranger.

"Okay." Katie returned her smile. "I can understand that. Apology accepted."

"And thanks too, by the way."

"For what?"

From anyone else, Carmen would suspect they were fishing for gratitude. Katie wasn't that way. Carmen knew her look of confusion was sincere. "For the first class trip to Munich for one. I can barely afford my Starbucks habit."

Katie chuckled. "That's not true. You have a really nice house in Auraria. Most police officers couldn't live in that neighborhood on such modest salaries."

"That's only because my great-great grandparents bought the property when they came over from Spain in the 1860s. Because of them, I don't have a mortgage."

"It doesn't hurt that your neighborhood is close to Country Club," Katie pointed out. "The location does great things for property values."

Country Club was an historic neighborhood in Denver. Few people could afford to live in the affluent neighborhood that encompassed an elite golf club. Centuries old elms also dotted the properties there.

"Hmm," Carmen agreed.

"And that it's what…about a half hour from the Denver airport?"

Carmen snorted. "That depends on traffic. Still, it is nice and quiet. Definitely worth the drive. I have a few acres in the burbs with really great neighbors. Hey, back to the coffee thing. I'm worried about caffeine headaches. What if I can't get any coffee?"

"You know it's really interesting how you relate everything back to coffee. I bet your blood is sixty percent caffeine. Despite that, I don't think you have to worry about withdrawal," Katie advised, patting her long blonde frosted hair into place. Her red fingernails flashed in the cabin's artificial light. "The German people make very strong coffee. You'll be fine. You know you drink too much of that stuff, Carmen. You should consider cutting back. Have you ever thought of drinking herbal tea instead?"

"Thank you, Adelle Davis. I thought you were a psychiatrist, not a nutritionist."

"Retired psychiatrist," Katie corrected. "I'm impressed. Did you know that Adelle Davis is the most famous nutritionist from the early to mid-twentieth century?"

"You don't say."

"You didn't answer my question," Katie pressed.

"Coffee keeps me sharp."

Carmen spotted the steward heading down the cabin at just that moment. She turned away from Katie to stop the young man before he could get away.

"Excuse me, could I get a cup of coffee, black?" In a teasing overly-exaggerated English accent, Carmen added, "My friend would like a cup of Earl Grey, shaken not stirred."

Katie leaned over the console between them and smacked Carmen on the shoulder. "Actually, I'd prefer chamomile if you have it. I find it very relaxing."

The steward happily agreed to bring their drinks and set off down the aisle. Carmen stopped teasing her friend and settled back against her seat. Her thoughts swirled around in her head as she pictured their upcoming trip. Carmen had so many ideas for the next two weeks that she doubted they could fit everything into the itinerary.

"Hey, Carmen. Where'd you go?"

"Huh? Oh, I'm just thinking. I'm really looking forward to the festival, but I feel like we've already missed some opportunities on this trip. I mean we've had two layovers and what have we got to show for it? Sure, the first one was at JFK and that's in the States so who cares, but Paris! Two and a half hours at Charles De Gaulle and we couldn't even look around."

Katie leaned over to pat Carmen on the knee. "I know, but it's okay. We'll make another trip to Paris sometime. Right now, let's just focus on the festival."

"I'm focusing on beer at straight up noon," Carmen confided. "I read that tapping the keg starts things off. I think it's very civilized to have beer for most of the day."

"You would." Katie chuckled. "I'm more interested in getting to the hotel so I can have a long soak. My muscles are aching, but you have managed to impress me twice in as many minutes. How is it that you know so much about the festival?"

"Well, you didn't think I'd go all the way to Germany without Googling Oktoberfest, did you? I also watched Dracula Untold last night. I want to be ready in case any vampires attack."

"Vamp…!" Katie laughed until she bent over double. When her laughter began to taper off, she took one look at Carmen's face and broke up all over again.

"What? I want to be ready for anything."

Katie managed to catch her breath. "I don't think you need worry about becoming a vampire bride. Vampires don't really exist."

"Says you."

The steward brought their drinks and Carmen asked how long it would be until a dinner time snack. She couldn't help her expression of misery when her stomach rumbled in protest.

"You just ate something three hours ago," Katie pointed out.

Carmen shrugged and turned back to the steward. "I have a high metabolism. I'm starving now. Could I get a snack?"

"Of course. I'll bring you something right away. Anything for you, ma'am?"

Katie shook her head and the steward headed off again. He returned promptly with two very large chocolate chip cookies. They were still warm. Carmen prepared to take a huge bite when she noticed Katie watching her.

"Uh, do you want one?"

"No, you enjoy. I don't want to spoil my appetite. How can you stay so skinny and eat like a goat? Honestly, you eat twice as much as I do and I'm one chicken wing away from liposuction."

Carmen chose not to answer. Instead she devoured the cookies, relieved that Katie wasn't interested. She really wanted both cookies. From there, discussion turned to the festival. Both looked forward to seeing the costumes and parades. Carmen also wanted to check out the surrounding forests and streams. Katie's interests lay largely on seeing the penthouse suite of the Atrium Hotel. The hotel wasn't far from the Bavarian Theresienwiese festival grounds so they had agreed to walk the short distance.

After awhile, a snack arrived. Carmen tucked eagerly in. Her only complaint about the food was that she couldn't get more. Carmen finished her portion and the food Katie left on her tray table as well before declaring herself satisfied. Her timing proved perfect. Just as a steward collected their refuse, Carmen heard the PA activate.

"Ladies and gentlemen, we will be starting our descent into the Franz Josef Strauss airport soon. Stewards are coming by to collect any remaining cups and trays. We ask that you please turn off any electronic devices at this time and as always, we thank you for flying Lufthansa."

Katie practically squealed with delight. "I've already reserved a rental so we can see the rest of Munich after the festival. It's a BMW four series convertible. We'll go to the hotel first and get checked in. We're staying in the penthouse suite, as you know. It's quite chic. Then we can see about a nice nap before we start looking around. Oh, you'll love their gardens…"

"Whoa, slow your roll, Lightning McQueen."

"McClarin."

"We still have to get our bags and go through Customs. Do you have your passport ready?"

Soon, Carmen noticed the slight rumble of the plane decelerating. Then their altitude started to drop. Carmen's excitement ramped up another notch as the ground drew closer, and she leaned over Katie to see the German countryside. She thought she had never seen anything so incredible. Heavy forests appeared untouched. The waters of a river below glistened in the gentle sunlight. Houses looked neat and orderly, laid out in perfect patterns as seen from above. Before she knew it, the plane bumped against the ground as the landing gear touched down on the runway.

The PA system activated again. "Ladies and gentlemen, welcome to Munich. Local time is 7:36 a.m."

Chapter Three

The weather for the first day of Oktoberfest couldn't possibly be more beautiful. The sun shone overhead and light fluffy clouds dotted the sky. Carmen enjoyed the slight chill in the air, but figured the temps would warm up soon. She didn't really know what to expect for Germany in late September, but she didn't mind a little cool after Denver's heat.

Carmen wasn't surprised to see how crowded the streets were. Traffic congested routes of travel in every direction.

"I'm glad we decided to walk," she admitted, dipping her hand into a paper bag to scoop up more goodies.

"You're going to make yourself sick. You really shouldn't eat an entire bag of jellybeans by the handful."

"I'm on vacation," Carmen pointed out. "Fair warning that I intend to eat and drink anything I want for the duration of our stay. Say, how much farther is it to the fairgrounds?"

Katie pointed into the distance. "Do you see that statue over there?"

The statue in question resembled a woman holding something aloft in her left hand. A massive bronze lion resided at the figure's right side, and the crowds seemed to funnel in that direction.

"Yeah?"

"That is the Bavaria Statue. It leads to the Theresienwiese grounds."

"And all these people are going there? That's disappointing. I thought getting there ahead of schedule would mean we'd find a good spot." Carmen heaved a dramatic sigh. "I guess I'll have to settle for being first at the beer gardens."

"You do know that the beer gardens won't officially open until the mayor taps the keg," Katie pointed out.

"Sure, but I also know that I'll be the first one there."

Despite her words, Carmen accompanied Katie to the grounds adjacent to the statue. A parade of people in traditional garb made their way through the area. Woman wore multicolored gowns complete with aprons and large bows. Pigtails and braids prevailed in a variety of twists. Carmen knew from her research that locals called the dresses *dirndls*. The positioning of the bow along the waistline denoted whether women were single, widowed or in a relationship. Men wore shorts, leather jackets with suspenders, shorts, tall socks and little pointy hats complete with feathers. The mayor also sported the *Lederhosen* and led the way in a horse-drawn carriage. Cameras flashed, people shouted and those in the carriages waved as music filled the air.

"Who are those guys?" She asked in Katie's ear.

"Those are restaurateurs and brewery people, and of course, the mayor."

Carmen nodded like she understood completely. It didn't really matter. She loved the pomp and ceremony.

The women slowly made their way from the stands into the festival hall where Carmen craned her neck in an attempt to see the front. A large podium held several dignitaries. A band already played traditional polka and oompah music as a gorgeous and graying slightly older woman played the accordion. Carmen felt mesmerized watching her. She didn't understand how someone could move both hands in different ways simultaneously. The woman played a keyboard like section on one side of the instrument while moving the sides of the accordion in and out. On the other, she tapped various buttons to adjust the harmonics. It seemed impossible.

Finally, Carmen dragged her eyes away from the very talented lady. She loved seeing all the smiling, happy people and the costumes as many of the attending tourists and locals also wore the traditional garb.

There were people crowded everywhere. To her delight, the throng of bystanders actually pushed Katie and Carmen closer to the podium. Reporters stood on the dais along with several dignitaries, and one of the men held a large beer stein. Another man, who Carmen assumed was the mayor, grasped a large wooden hammer in one hand and a tap in the other. According to long-standing tradition, the mayor would attempt to tap the keg in as few blows as possible. Carmen knew the current record stood at two good whacks. The mayor swung the hammer. One. He swung again and Carmen held her breath. Two. Good-natured ribbing broke out on the podium, but Carmen couldn't follow along since the dignitaries spoke German. Apparently, the current mayor required more effort.

He drew back his arm and swung again. The tap went in and a cheer burst forth from the spectators. A female reporter shoved a microphone in front of the mayor's face and he shouted, "*O'zapft is!*"

"It's tapped," Katie translated.

Carmen had to lean close to her friend's shouted words to be heard over the noise of the crowd. She opened her mouth to comment when a thunderous noise cut her off and made her jump. Twelve gunshots sounded from outside the hall.

"Now, the festival is open. Come on, Carmen, let's go have some fun."

"Let's go have some beer. I know I sound like I have a one-track mind, but I just want to sample what German beer tastes like. After that, I promise we'll ride some of the rides and play the carnival games. Well, maybe after I have some lunch."

"Fine. Just don't throw up on me when we ride the roller coaster."

"No promises."

Carmen and Katie spent the day packing in as much fun as possible. Carmen ate more than she should, and although she would never admit it to Katie, by dusk she felt almost sick. Still, watching the kids running around shouting and people having so much fun was exactly what she needed. Just when she decided her feet would fall off from walking so much, Katie came up with a great suggestion.

"Do you mind if we call it a day? We can come back tomorrow."

"Sure," Carmen agreed. "I'm ready to take an eight-hour nap, but can we hail a cab? I don't think I can walk all the way back."

"Bless you," Katie said. "That's a great idea."

A sudden terrified scream silenced everyone standing nearby. Only the music from the rides continued unabated. Carmen and Katie were standing near the festival entrance, and from where they stood, the scream came from the opposite direction.

"What's over there?" Carmen asked.

"Uh," Katie hesitated for a moment. "The Bavaria Park, I think. It's quite wooded."

"Come on."

Carmen took off at a run, heading for the exit. She saw Katie follow from the corner of her eye. To Carmen's disappointment, only a few other people chose to accompany her. Most of the crowd simply turned back to the festival. Before they could reach the entrance, a man stumbled in. Carmen reached him in only a few running strides. Her first impression was that someone had tried to mug the young man, but she couldn't imagine such a high-pitched scream coming from him.

He appeared to be in his late twenties, and he stopped and bent over at the waist. He was disheveled, clothes ripped and blood stained on his hands and face. He wore a suit and black loafers, and a blue tie knotted at his throat. To Carmen, his clothing seemed out of place, symbolizing a by-gone era. The tie in particular caught her attention. Blue, streaked with red. The red of blood.

He fell to his knees as Carmen reached him. She grasped his narrow shoulders and helped ease him into a sitting position.

"What happened? Are you okay?"

He didn't answer. Instead, the man, who was more of a boy, grasped his hair with both hands and rocked back and forth. Carmen thought he was crying.

"Hey, hey, look at me." She grasped his wrists and pulled gently. Finally, the young man with tear-streaked blue eyes met her gaze. Carmen spoke to him in a soft voice, trying not to spook him even more than he apparently already was. "What's your name?"

"Brian. Brian Whitmore."

To her relief, he spoke perfect English without the slightest hint of an accent. Carmen noticed a few strangers crowding around, but she ignored them for the moment. It looked to her like a crime had occurred. She focused on gathering critical information as quickly as possible before shock set in with the victim. "It's okay. You're safe now. I'm a police officer from the States. My name is Carmen. Can you tell me what happened?"

"We came for Oktoberfest."

"Right," Carmen said, attempting to foster a connection. "We came for that too. What happened after that?"

Katie squatted beside them, near but not so close as to interfere. Probably assessing his mental condition, Carmen decided.

"Jess…my girlfriend…and I decided to check out the park." He tipped his head in the direction of Bavaria Park. "We just wanted to be alone for a minute. Someone…some *thing*… came out of the trees. It came right for us."

The hairs on the back of Carmen's neck stood up. She didn't believe anyone could fake the fear she saw on Brian's face. His hands shook. He blinked his eyes constantly and kept licking his lips while casting nervous glances toward the woods.

"It grabbed Jessica and something wet hit my face. I thought it was moisture from the rain last night, but it was red." Brian's words trailed off and he began rocking again.

"Brian, where's Jessica? Where is she, Brian?"

Carmen recognized the sound of people running toward them wearing heavy boots. She realized that the local police were on the scene. She stood up to see four German state policemen arriving. They didn't have far to travel, as the State Police Headquarters resided at the head of the festival entrance.

An older man with a heavy dark mustache seemed the obvious leader of the group. She spotted the name tag on his left breast and Carmen addressed him directly. "Officer Reiter, this is Brian Whitmore. He said that he and his girlfriend were just attacked in Bavaria Park."

The tall, lanky officer stiffened his back. His black mustache seemed to droop. "And who exactly are you?"

It took Carmen a second to decipher his accent. "I'm Carmen Bravo. I'm a police officer from Denver, Colorado."

"Then you clearly have no jurisdiction here. I will thank you to stay out of local police matters. This man has clearly been involved in a crime. We will take him into custody and question him at our convenience."

"But what about his girlfriend?" Katie asked from her spot kneeling on the ground beside Brian. "He said she was attacked. Aren't you going to look for her?"

"Americans are all the same, interfering in matters that do not concern you." Officer Reiter turned to his companions. He spoke in German for a moment and then two of the other men set off in the direction of the park. "They will begin a search for her now. Satisfied?"

Carmen blinked in disbelief. "But you don't even know what she looks like."

"I cannot imagine there will be many *Frauleins* lying in a pool of blood within these woods."

Brian groaned and Carmen fought the urge to slug the state policeman. "Nice, your bedside manner could use some work. He's the victim!"

"We will determine that."

Reiter nodded at the remaining officer who immediately closed in on Brian. The officer grabbed Brian by the collar and hauled him to his feet. He handcuffed Brian behind his back and Carmen finally caught a glimpse of the other state police officer's name tag. Krum.

"I didn't do anything," Brian protested. "We just wanted some privacy. We were making out by the picnic bench when we were attacked. You have to find Jessica!"

Reiter scoffed. "We intend to, Mister Whitmore. Pray we find her alive."

"You don't understand! It wasn't a man who came after us. It was a werewolf. I think it killed her."

Carmen couldn't believe her ears. Brian couldn't possibly be serious. There wasn't even a full moon. Was there? She shook her head to clear the cobwebs. What was she thinking? Werewolves only existed in myth.

"Are you confessing to her murder?" Officer Reiter asked. "You should know that an insanity plea will not help you here. You are not in America."

"It was a werewolf," Brian insisted. He stumbled forward a step as the other officer pressed into him. "I would never hurt her."

Officer Reiter seemed to notice the interested bystanders for the first time. "Go back to the festival. There is nothing further to see here." He turned back to his partner. "Arrest him for suspicion of murder. We will organize a comprehensive search, and when we find your friend forensics will no doubt prove who the real assailant is."

Reiter gave one sharp nod and Officer Krum hauled Brian toward the station house. Carmen wanted to protest. She wanted to insist that the officers launch a full-scale search for the missing woman immediately. Time was of the essence in such cases, but caution stopped her. Here in a foreign country, Carmen had no authority whatsoever. The situation could turn very bad for her very quickly if she interfered with a police investigation. The last thing she needed was an arrest on her record. Then again, she didn't have to be involved in an official capacity. Just like that, Carmen made her decision. Still, she couldn't allow the local constabulary to lead this man off like a proverbial lamb to the slaughter. She had one last piece of advice. Carmen shouted to Brian across the distance.

"Don't say anything to them without a lawyer."

Brian attempted to turn toward her, but the state officers yanked him around and kept him moving. Silently, Carmen and Katie watched them force the unfortunate young man toward their headquarters.

"Please, don't mind Officer Reiter."

Carmen turned toward the male voice to find a stranger watching the scene. An older man with salt and pepper hair and a slight slump stood only a few feet away. His accent wasn't as hard to decipher as Reiter's so at least she could understand him. The man wore a simple pullover shirt, jeans and sneakers, but had the unmistakable air of law enforcement common worldwide. He offered Carmen and Katie a smile as he moved a few paces closer.

"And you are?" Carmen asked.

"*Kommissar* Aaron Bauer." The man dipped his head in a quick and casual bow. "At your service."

Carmen scowled a little in confusion and jumped slightly when Katie squeaked. What was a *Kommissar* and why was Katie so excited? Katie answered Carmen's question by stepping forward to meet the stranger.

"You're an inspector, uh, detective."

Bauer shrugged slightly. "In your terms, yes. Here, an inspector is a civil service position."

"Oh," Katie said. "I'm sorry if I offended you."

"Not to worry." Bauer waived the apology away.

Carmen had enough of the niceties. She wanted to know what the police intended to do about the missing woman. She was also more than a little concerned about Brian.

"You said something about Reiter."

Bauer focused his gaze on Carmen. "Despite all appearances, Officer Reiter is very dedicated. He will find the missing woman. He simply tends to become…bristly when tourists interfere in police matters."

"I'm not just a tourist," Carmen pointed out.

"Yes, I heard. I can promise you that he will not charge Mister Whitmore without proof of a crime. I can also promise that I will assist in locating his young *Fraulein*."

Bauer nodded at them again and then walked away. Rather than head toward the abduction site, Bauer strode off toward the festival. To Carmen, he didn't seem very interested in carrying out his pledge. No one seemed overly concerned about a missing and possibly injured woman.

Carmen stood quietly with her hands on her hips, assessing the scene before her and wondering why no one wanted to act. Well, even if they didn't, she did. Carmen swiveled around to eye the entrance to the park. A few tourists wandered back and forth across the area, but no one left.

"You aren't going to let this go. Are you?"

"Nope," Carmen answered sharply. "I certainly am not."

Chapter Four

"Carmen, this has got to be the most lame-brained idea you've ever had."

Katie whispered the harsh words somewhere from the darkness behind her, but Carmen heard clearly. She didn't bother to respond. Instead, Carmen crouched lower and shielded the flashlight with her opposite hand. A tree root seemed to pop up from nowhere. It snagged the tip of Carmen's stiff and newly purchased hiking boot. She stumbled before catching her balance and making quite a bit of racket. Dappled moonlight cut a sketchy pattern through the forest. The shadowy light didn't help with searching the attack site or ensuring that they weren't spotted by anyone who might actually design to investigate. Other than Carmen and Katie, of course.

Carmen wasn't accustomed to sneaking around in the woods on a manhunt. Her elements were city streets of concrete and stone. Tree branches swayed in the moonlight, chasing bizarre images of light and dark across her eyes. The constantly changing light seriously messed with any night vision she could have developed.

"Carmen, stop!"

At least Katie tried to keep her voice low. Carmen didn't want to listen, but she wasn't in charge here. Resigned to the inevitable, she dropped to one knee. At the same time, she pivoted to face her friend. Katie scooted up to her and joined Carmen on the ground. Instead of kneeling, Katie sat down.

"What's wrong?" Carmen asked, concerned her friend might have injured herself in the dark and unfamiliar forest.

Katie shook her head. Her expression spoke volumes of frustration. "What are we doing here? If we get caught, we could join Brian in jail. That is not an experience I want to add to my resume."

"Are you kidding me? You heard that officer. As far as they're concerned, Brian is the bad guy. They aren't even looking for Jessica."

"Carmen, you saw them come over here. A whole squad of officers looked for Jennifer."

"Jessica," Carmen corrected automatically. "Yeah, I saw them. They looked for all of thirty minutes. I didn't see anyone come back with her. Did you?"

A twig snapped in the underbrush, somewhere near yet far enough away to obscure the exact direction of the sound. Carmen froze and searched all around with her eyes. By instinct, she smashed her palm over the flashlight lens at the same time that she switched it off. Heavy footsteps moved in their direction, splintering brush and swishing through fallen leaves. Carmen tensed, half expecting police officers. The thought of jail in a foreign country, and thereby losing her job with Air One, slithered through her brain. She shook away the offending possibility when she heard a small sound from Katie. The noise seemed a cross between a giggle and a grunt.

Carmen's eyes widened like an owl as she realized the implication.

No, she shouted in her mind. Carmen darted toward Katie and clapped a hand over her mouth and nose. She grabbed Katie around the shoulders and held onto her friend tightly. In return, Katie put her own hand over Carmen's as she fought the urge to sneeze. She failed.

Katie sneezed right into Carmen's hand, and Carmen grimaced in disgust. To her, the muffled noise sounded like a shotgun blast going off. Seconds later, crashing steps faded into the darkness as whoever it was ran and Carmen released her grip. She lunged to her feet while simultaneously wiping her spit-covered palm off on her jeans.

Eww!

Carmen left Katie to catch her breath while she pursued the presence. She figured Katie would be safe enough and Carmen couldn't take the chance that allergies might give her away. Brian had to be wrong about a werewolf, but what about a kidnapper? Carmen cursed herself for not knowing more about Brian and Jessica. Did one of them have money?

Were there any political motivations for taking the woman? At least, Carmen assumed someone took Jessica since no one had seen her since the attack. She could imagine all sorts of motivations for the assault. What she couldn't believe was that Brian believed their assailant a werewolf. He was hysterical, probably. Witnesses weren't always reliable.

Her thoughts had her so distracted that she tripped over something in the darkness and went down hard on her hands and one knee. She bit off a grunt as one hand connected with a sharp rock. The skin part and she hissed in pain. Carmen shook her hand and then pushed back to her feet. She stood in the shadows, attempting to peer into the trees.

What was she doing? Carmen finally realized this was dumb. She had no idea who it was she pursued. Maybe it was just some random person out for a midnight walk.

The festival had closed for the night, but lights from the city cast an uneven glow around them. Carmen clearly heard the sounds of traffic. Bavaria Park served as a bit of countryside smack dab in the middle of the city. There could be all kinds of reasons for someone to be here.

Sure, Carmen thought sarcastically. Someone decided to take a midnight walk in the woods without any sort of hand light. Then they ran when Katie sneezed.

It didn't really matter now. Carmen couldn't chase anyone through these dense woods without seeing them. She wasn't a Great Dane. Annoyed and frustrated, Carmen snorted and turned to head back to Katie.

A trick of the light. The play of the wind. At just that moment, tree branches parted. A silhouette in the full moonlight stood out starkly against the night. Carmen blinked. She shook her head, but the image didn't fade. As clear as any nightmare, she saw it. The beast stood tall, taller than any man Carmen had ever seen. Shaggy hair covered its body entirely, though she couldn't define any clear details in the questionable lighting. The legs caught her eye. Strong, obviously powerful, and shaped like that of a dog. Or a wolf. The creature turned its head and she gawked in disbelief. A long snout, the fangs sharp and deadly. Clouds drifted away from the full moon and for one unbelievable instant, Carmen saw it.

A werewolf.

****

"Carmen, you can't possibly be serious. Do you really expect me to believe you saw a werewolf?"

Carmen paced back and forth across the living area of the penthouse suite. Her feet still hurt, but she couldn't sit still. Thoughts zipped through her mind with the speed of a roller coaster, not dissimilar to the one she and Katie had ridden earlier in the day. She just couldn't figure why someone would impersonate something so fantastical. And why abduct a young woman along the way?

"Earth to Carmen," Katie teased.

"I'm telling you, that's what I saw. Or at least I think it was. I only spotted him for a second through the trees."

"Next thing you know, you'll be telling me that we need to take a ride in the Mystery Machine. Don't for one second think I'm going to let you go back out there either. I couldn't stand to see you incarcerated for interfering in a police investigation. How do you think your captain would react to that?"

"I don't plan to interfere. Believe me, Katie. I don't need to wind up a permanent guest in a foreign country. Not that way, at least. I've worked too hard for too many years just to throw it all away." When Katie continued to eye her with an air of disbelief, Carmen tried again. "Really, maybe I can notice some kind of pattern if I happen to spot the suspect. Give Reiter some information to help break the case. I'll just… observe."

"It's not a gorilla in the Congo, Carmen," Katie shouted, eyes flashing. "You're talking about a werewolf."

"It's not a real werewolf, Katie," Carmen groused. "It's not a witch or a ghost either and it's not any more real than a vampire. It's just some creep we need to find before he hurts that girl. She could already be injured. Brian had blood on him, remember?"

"You're assuming that this…thing even has her. What if she's just lost in the woods?"

"Mm, that's a good point." Carmen considered the possibility for a second before she rejected it. "No, I don't think so. Those woods aren't that big and the police didn't find anything. We didn't find anything either for that matter."

Katie looked crestfallen. Her eyes dropped away and she walked over to settle on the sofa. "That's my fault. I sneezed."

"What? No. I mean yeah, you sneezed but it's not your fault. I should never have put you in that situation. What was I thinking playing Nancy Drew in the middle of the woods?"

"In a foreign country and in the middle of the night?" Katie added.

"Yeah."

"Look, Carmen. I have an idea. Research."

Carmen scoffed. "Your favorite pastime."

Even as she spoke, Katie marched across the space and disappeared into her bedroom. She reemerged seconds later with her laptop. Carmen had to admit that Katie was a master at computer research. She could find information Carmen couldn't hope to even after a week and a blueprint of how to reach her destination. While she waited, Katie fired up the machine and logged onto the hotel's complimentary Wi-Fi. After a few seconds, Carmen got bored standing there watching her friend punch the keys.

She wandered over to lean against the window sill and stared out into the night, watching the city lights and wondering. Carmen had so many questions and no way to find the answers. Frustration made her want to squeeze the sill until the wood splintered under her grasp. A triumphant whoop made her start and spin toward Katie.

"You find something?"

"Well, I hacked into the local police inter-agency site as well as the computer transcripts of their dispatch unit. Get this. The night before the festival began, German police forces focused almost exclusively on security around the Theresienwiese. Those not directly involved with securing the grounds had other concerns."

"Sure." Carmen shrugged one shoulder. "Traffic flow patterns to prevent as much congestion as possible. Coordinating medical personnel for emergencies inside the festival, and a hundred other things. What's so unusual about that?"

"Well, that means law enforcement channeled their resources into one area."

Carmen snapped her fingers. "Leaving our furry friend free to… what? And why take Jessica?"

"I'm not sure, but Carmen…"

Katie's voice trailed off and she lowered her head. Carmen couldn't figure out why her normally so self-assured friend seemed embarrassed. She moved over to stand close to Katie.

"What's going on, Katie?"

Katie smacked a fist against her thigh. "Why don't we leave this to the local police? I'm sure they're more than capable, and I came here to enjoy Oktoberfest. Not follow you around through the woods looking for a werewolf." Almost as an afterthought, Katie muttered, "I can't believe I even voiced a sentence with that word in it."

Guilt crashed down, bowing Carmen's shoulders. She couldn't stand seeing Katie looking so deflated. She spent a small fortune for this trip and Carmen felt like an ingrate. How could she be so insensitive?

"You're right. I'm so sorry, Katie. It's really none of our business. From now on, I promise to enjoy Germany just like we planned. Deal?"

That first night, Carmen found it hard to sleep. She watched one in the morning come and go on the illuminated numbers of the digital clock by her bedside. Some time, that seemed like hours, later Carmen finally nodded off. Images of a shaggy man with an animal countenance dominated. He stood upright in the woods, so close she could smell the rot from his panting breath. When he turned to look at her, his eyes glowed blue in the moonlight. Gore dripped from his deadly fangs and razor-sharp claws. When his gaze pinned on her, Carmen couldn't move. Fear left her frozen, her feet mired in ice. Her heart thumped against her ribs, threatening to break a bone and puncture a lung. She tasted terror and scented blood on the wind.

Then something else caught her eye. The dream Carmen turned her head and lost sight of the nightmare in fur. Somehow, sunshine broke through the moonlit night. Things like that made perfect sense to her in a dream, especially when Carmen saw someone else that made her heart pound. This time, she spotted bluer than blue eyes. A smile quirked from lips possessing a perfect Cupid's bow.

The woman raised an eyebrow at Carmen in either challenge or invitation. Carmen couldn't determine which. Before she could approach, the woman with the jaunty red beret turned and disappeared into the forest.

Carmen strolled around the grounds munching on the bag of popcorn. Calliope music played loudly from nearby. A boy of about ten ran by and bumped her elbow and she lost a few kernels, but shoved the rest of the buttery treat into her mouth. She still felt somewhat wiped out from lack of sleep, but the carbs helped. Beer next, she promised herself. The sugar in the brew would brush away the rest of the cobwebs.

The day had dawned partly sunny and chilly. Carmen wore a blue and white striped sweater, jeans and her new ankle high brown hiking boots. She tried to focus on the delectable scent of fried carnival foods, happy laughter, rides and the music. She really did. When thoughts of the missing woman came to mind, she resolutely pushed them away. When thoughts of the stranger from the plane intruded, she focused on them as a pleasant distraction. Katie had the gleam of fun in her eyes and Carmen couldn't in good conscience take that away from her. In fact, Carmen noted, Katie hadn't sneezed more than four or five times today.

Yet, for Carmen, the magic of the setting seemed to have vanished. The cop inside of her could hardly be repressed simply because she was on vacation. She sighed deeply and shoved more popcorn into her mouth. The press of the crowd thickened, forcing Carmen to pay attention. A couple headed directly toward her. They made eye contact, but refused to move over to allow Carmen passage. Carmen stopped walking and simply stood there. At the last minute, the woman with the old-fashioned beehive hairdo and the blue *dirndl* rolled her eyes and stepped over to allow Carmen about a foot of room.

Carmen almost ran smack into *Kommissar* Bauer.

She halted once again, in disbelief this time. Katie grunted, but from the sound she wasn't very happy. As for the detective, Carmen would have sworn he wanted to turn and run.

"*Kommissar*," Carmen said. "I didn't expect to find you here. In fact, I expected you to be trying to solve yesterday's mystery."

Katie planted an elbow in her side.

Bauer frowned, his eyebrows almost meeting above his nose, and Carmen easily picked up on his anger across the short distance. Ire practically rolled off him in a wave. At that moment, she noticed his attire seemed considerably more formal than the day before. Bauer wore creased black trousers, a white shirt with a brown paisley tie and a tan trench coat that made him look like Colombo.

"For your edification, madam, there are other crimes happening in Munich besides the disappearance of one young woman."

A growl rose in Carmen's throat. She swallowed it to say, "Meaning you don't really care."

"On the contrary, I care very much, but I am only one man. I assure you, the *Polizei* have things under control. If you don't mind, I am off to investigate another incident."

"Like what?"

"Carmen! You promised."

"It's just a question." She glanced at Katie and then back to the detective. "You were saying?"

Bauer's expression tightened. Then, he actually answered her. "If you must know, I'm off to investigate a jewelry store theft. It occurred last evening. Another theft occurred in one of the rooms at the Hotel Gio. May I go now? Thank you very much!"

Bauer attempted to step off, but Carmen blocked his way. Something, a link, had just hit her like a ton of bricks.

"One more question and then I'll leave you alone. What time did the break-ins happen?"

"Sometime around seven last evening. They occurred only a few streets over from here."

"And you don't find that a little bit of a coincidence? That girl got snatched only half an hour later."

Bauer raised his hands in disbelief. He looked at Carmen and said, "Crime happens at all hours in Munich. That doesn't mean anything is connected. Now, I'm going to tell you one final time. Enjoy Oktoberfest, explore the castles or take a tour somewhere. I don't care what you do, but stay out of police business."

Katie elbowed Carmen again, more gently this time. "Way to make friends and influence people."

Chapter Five

Carmen stood in the center of the hotel suite. She had pulled her long hair back into a tight bun, held in place by several pins. Dark jeans, a long-sleeved dark shirt and hiking boots prepared her for what she had in mind. She faced Katie, who sat staring at her from the sofa. Katie's narrowed eyes regarded Carmen with a fair amount of disappointment and anger. Carmen knew time was running out to find Jessica and she simply couldn't keep the promise she should never have made.

"Why can't you just stop? You promised me you'd leave this alone."

Carmen snarled, a direct symphonic counterpoint to her frustration. Of course, Reiter and his cohorts were competent enough to handle things. Too bad it didn't seem like anyone took Jessica's disappearance seriously. After speaking to Bauer, Carmen asked Katie to hack into local files to see what they'd discovered. Nothing pretty much covered it. Jessica had not been located. Due to the lack of evidence such as a body, law enforcement released Brian. She had no idea where Brian went after his release, apparently something else no one cared about since there wasn't any computer information.

"You don't have to go with me."

"Ah ah, no way," Katie countered, the heat of annoyance in her tone. "I'm not happy with you for pursuing this, but you're not leaving me out."

Carmen shook her head. "I'm confused. I thought that was exactly what you were saying."

"Then you weren't listening. Look, I'm pissed. I wanted to take a vacation from all this cloak and dagger, but you just won't cooperate. All that aside, I'm still your friend. If you're going to *try* and get yourself killed, the least I can do is provide backup."

"I thought you didn't believe in werewolves." Carmen could only focus on the fact that Katie actually wanted to assist. Relief that she wasn't alone in this made her almost dizzy.

"I don't, but there's nothing to keep the bad guys from killing you just as dead as any mythological beast."

Katie's voice rose on the last word and Carmen realized her friend was still pretty angry. Guilt gnawed at her, but she pushed it away. A life depended on her, she just knew it. The odds of finding a kidnapping victim alive dropped significantly after twenty-four hours. That timeline fast approached.

"How? Katchoo, you're so stuffed up from allergies you can hardly breathe." Carmen's palm itched as she remembered Katie sneezing into it.

"I'm not about to follow you back into the woods. I'll hack into local police calls and provide you with computer support, just like I did last night. Come on, Carmen. You can barely remember your own password. If you're right, and this girl's abduction is related to another crime, although I don't see how, I'm your best chance at finding the connection."

Carmen wasn't about to argue. She needed the help. Still, she knew better than to make it sound like she was happy about it. As long as Katie thought Carmen didn't want her involved, she would try that much harder to prove herself. Carmen could use her own knowledge of human behavior on the very talented psychiatrist.

"Fine," she muttered. "As for your remark, I don't believe Jessica is directly involved in any crime. I think it's more likely she saw something she shouldn't have."

"Like what? And if that's true, why not take Brian too?"

Carmen shrugged. She thought of multiple reasons. "The suspect could only grab one? He thought Jessica was easier to control? Maybe she saw something Brian didn't. How should I know? We don't have enough information to answer that yet."

"Well, at least we agree on one thing. You need me."

Katie punctuated her comment with a sneeze that left Carmen's ears ringing. She blinked and yanked a tissue from the box on the coffee table. Carmen offered it to Katie while waiting for her hearing to recover.

"I'm heading back to the park to see what I can find in daylight. You keep digging. If I'm right, you'll find more crimes in the immediate area over the last few days."

Carmen explained how Oktoberfest was the perfect cover for a string of felonies. The park itself was nothing more than the perfect place to hide out long enough to change from a costume into street clothes. After that, the suspect could easily slip away into the festival crowd.

"It doesn't matter if they did," Carmen added. "No one commits a crime without leaving behind some kind of evidence. I'm going to find it."

Carmen didn't wait for a response. She spun on her heel and swept toward the hotel suite's door. She grabbed her jacket from the back of the sofa on her way, mind already on her upcoming forest search.

"Don't forget your flashlight," Katie suggested. "You only have a few hours to sunset. You might want to call a cab, too. It'll get you to the park faster."

Carmen closed the door on the last of Katie's advice. She already carried the flashlight in a jacket pocket, but she had no intention of calling a taxi. The walk would give her time to think. Carmen's detective skills were a little rusty. She spent all her work time in a helicopter these days and left the gumshoe work to those on the ground. Still, rusty didn't mean she couldn't get back in sync.

When her feet hit the main lobby, she abruptly changed her mind. There really wasn't any point in returning to the woods. The police had combed the area already. Between them and Carmen's own crashing through the trees, she doubted any viable evidence remained. Instead, she figured it was high time she spoke directly to the source. Surely Brian Whitmore was a little calmer by now. She just needed to discover the hotel where he stayed.

She reached for the cell phone at her side. Carmen stopped with her hand on the black leather case. Katie couldn't really help in this situation. She'd have to hack into every local hotel and that would take time. Carmen also had to consider roaming charges from her carrier for making such a call. She could have paid her carrier a small fee for roaming services, but Katie sprang the trip on her at the last minute and Carmen hadn't thought about it.

She decided to directly ask someone who might know. She'd make it back to the hotel faster this way and surprise Katie. Maybe they could take that BMW Katie rented and have a nice dinner somewhere. With a smirk and a determined stride, she headed for the Theresienwiese festival grounds after all. It didn't take long to traverse the few blocks to police headquarters. Luck seemed to be on her side today. Officer Reiter almost ran into her exiting the station just as Carmen approached the front door. He glanced up and quickly stopped, the surprise in his expression obvious before he quickly masked it.

"*Fraulein* Bravo. I must say I did not expect to be seeing you again. Before you say anything, I must inform you that I may not give details in an ongoing investigation."

Carmen smiled in what she hoped was a friendly manner. "That's okay. I wasn't going to ask about that anyway."

"Oh? Then why are you here?"

"I heard you released Mister Whitmore."

Reiter nodded, a slight crease forming between his eyes. "True. We had no evidence for which to hold him."

"Would you happen to know where he's staying in Munich? One American to another, I'd just like to check on him. See how he's doing?"

Carmen could all but hear the thoughts whirring through Reiter's head as he considered her request. She knew she'd surprised him yet again and no doubt, he didn't believe her excuse. He apparently just couldn't figure out her angle. Long seconds passed. At any moment, Carmen expected him to say he couldn't help her. She kept her gaze pinned to his and waited patiently.

Finally, Reiter shrugged in a nonchalant way. "I can't see any reason to withhold this information from you. I believe he is staying at the Hotel Gio."

Without another word, Reiter brushed by Carmen and continued on with his business. She yanked her phone from the case without hesitation and pulled up a map of the area. Making phone calls was one thing, but using her data quite another. In seconds she determined that the Gio wasn't far from the festival grounds. Carmen looked at the crowd enjoying Oktoberfest not far away and shook her head. She regretted not spending more time here, but she and Katie could always come back tomorrow. For now, on to more pressing matters.

Before she could take a step to cross the street, Carmen's phone rang. She automatically answered the call and put it on speaker. Her ear usually accidentally cut the call off if she used the device as intended. Caller ID informed her of who was on the other end. With her resources, apparently Katie wasn't concerned about roaming charges.

"Hello."

"Carmen, it's me." A sneeze followed before Katie quickly continued. She sounded more congested than she had before. "I found something. Remember when Detective Bauer said a theft occurred at the Hotel Gio? Well, what he didn't say was it happened an hour before the jewelry store robbery. And get this. The victim *swears* the thief was a werewolf."

"Are you kidding me? How could he not tell us that?" She ignored the snort Katie offered in return. "A werewolf would make quite a scene. Even a fake one. Did any of the other guests corroborate the witness?"

"No. Somehow, the creature simply vanished from the ninth floor."

"Sure, and I can fly without my helicopter. Want to hear something else a little unbelievable? Brian Whitmore just happens to be staying at the same hotel. That can't be a coincidence. I'm on my way over to talk to him now."

"I thought you were going to the woods."

"Change of plans," Carmen said. "I'll let you know what I find out. Oh, and Katie? You might be getting a cold. Try hot tea with honey."

The darkening sky signaled night was fast approaching. Carmen glanced once overhead before striking out for the hotel. She caught a cab on the far eastern side of the festival grounds, turning the ten minute walk into a three minute drive. The hum of excitement in her veins told her she was onto something and she didn't want to waste any more time than necessary.

Inside the lobby, Carmen discovered marble flooring and a high, wide and ornate staircase. A heavy crystal chandelier took up an obscene amount of space far overhead. The design of the hotel interior gave open and airy ambiance to the structure. She headed for the concierge desk off to one side. Adrenaline buoyed her steps and she all but bounced on the balls of her feet. She could feel that she was close to an answer. She just needed to convince someone to give up a guest's room number to a perfect stranger. Carmen reached for the badge in her front pocket. She always carried it with her, no matter what. Even though the badge originated from another country, she counted on the hotel staff not to notice that minor detail.

A familiar voice raised in laughter stopped her with her hand in her pocket. Carmen turned around facing the hotel bar and spied the person she wanted to see. She blinked in disbelief. Brian looked very different from the last time she saw him. Gone was the devastated, clean-cut boyish businessman. Instead, Carmen discovered a debonair millionaire playboy type.

Brian stood speaking to an inviting young woman showing way too much skin an in incomprehensible purple mini dress. He held a martini glass in one hand, looking down his nose with a smarmy grin on his lips. He wore a blue and white striped polo, creased dark jeans and perfect white sneakers and had draped a deep navy cashmere sweater around his shoulders, the arms tied to prevent it from falling. Carmen watched as he leaned down to whisper something into the brunette's ear that caused her to laugh.

Okay, so maybe he wasn't as heartbroken as he had pretended. Carmen still had questions. At that moment, the concierge swept past her with a white piece of paper flapping in his left hand. He didn't hesitate to interrupt an obviously intimate conversation. Carmen had to give him credit.

"I apologize for the interruption, *Herr* Dietrich. You have an urgent message."

Instinct urged Carmen to dart up against the staircase railing. She watched Brian, Dietrich, whoever, take the message without question. He also slipped a folded bill into the attendant's hand. It took only a second for him to read the note.

Carmen watched Brian's countenance shift instantly. Something dark and dangerous took possession of his expression. The young woman evidently sensed the change as well. She took two rapid steps back before spinning on her heel, impressive considering the three-inch spikes, and took off into the bar. Brian never spared her a glance. He said something to the concierge and then strode toward the exit. She hadn't heard the words, but the unexpected German accent came across clearly.

Carmen followed him and she worried he might see her, but Brian never turned back. He stood at the curb, pacing back and forth in a tight circle. Seconds later, a valet pulled up in a silver luxury car. Brian hopped in and peeled away from the curb, leaving black tire marks on the street. Carmen hailed one of the cabs waiting in front of the hotel lobby and followed him. She couldn't believe it when they arrived back where it all began, Bavaria Park.

Chapter Six

Carmen crouched in the brush. Night had fallen with a vengeance. Though a full moon rode the cloudless sky, only intermittent light filtered through the trees. She had followed Brian by sound and what little she could make out in the shadows. She couldn't risk turning on the flashlight, though the weight of it in her pocket gave her comfort. If nothing else, she could use it as a weapon.

Brian had struck off confidently through the woods. He carried his own flashlight and didn't show any concern about someone seeing him as he followed the same direction Carmen had previously traversed. Not far into the trees, Brian stopped. He seemed to be waiting for someone.

Dry leaves crunched under footsteps not far away. A twig snapped loudly in the darkness and Carmen held her breath. An eerie undulating howl shattered the night. It seemed very close, like she could reach out and touch the one who voiced it. Goosebumps erupted along both arms and the back of Carmen's neck. She held her breath as a shiver tingled down her spine, superstitiously convinced the creature could hear the air in her lungs.

The beast lumbered past her hiding spot, less than two feet away and headed right for Brian. Carmen almost jumped to her feet to warn the man, but intuition made her wait.

"It is about time," Brian complained in a suave German accent. "I do not have all night for this. What do you have?"

He held out his hand as the werewolf, Carmen still couldn't believe her eyes, passed a heavy white bag to him. The weight of the sack caused the muscles in Brian's forearms to bulge. The monster made no verbal reply.

"I will take this back to base," Brian said. "Meet me there as soon as you can discretely do so. Make sure no one sees you."

The werewolf nodded its head toward Brian and a gaping mouth filled with wickedly sharp teeth loomed over him. The beast stood half a foot taller than the man. For a moment, Carmen thought it intended to bite his face off. It actually dipped its head and stepped away. When the creature vanished into the woods, Carmen finally released her breath.

What the hell was going on?

Carmen followed Brian back to his Audi. He opened the trunk to deposit the bag, giving Carmen scant seconds to figure out how she could follow him now. With so few people on the streets here, Brian would surely spot her hailing a cab. Carmen spotted several cars lined up against the curb. Even as she considered it, she rejected the idea of boosting a car. She lingered at the edge of the trees, wracking her brain, but couldn't come up with a solution.

Come on, think!

An older woman walked by from a pharmacy across the street. The woman sported short curly gray hair covered by a wide brimmed hat. A hunch on her back caused a limp Carmen found difficult to ignore. She carried a brown paper sack by the handle, the bottom of which brushed against drooping pantyhose.

Carmen estimated her destination to be an ancient blue Beetle parked a small distance down the street. Quickly, she calculated how much money she had in her pockets. With any luck, the motorist would accommodate Carmen with a ride if she offered her enough American cash.

A sound from behind caught her attention, a heavy footstep followed by a low growl. Still in a crouch, Carmen turned to face her worst nightmare. The werewolf towered over her, staring down into terrified eyes. Hot, fetid breath panted into her face and her mouth went dry. Belatedly, Carmen tried to move into a defensive position. Her right fist shot out, aiming for the massive gaping maw. She wasn't fast enough and the beast had a longer reach. A huge, hairy and densely muscled arm struck her above the left temple.

****

Carmen groaned and tried to open her eyes. She couldn't. Multicolored lights flashed in a kaleidoscope behind closed lids. Along with unimaginable colors came agony. Carmen could swear someone pounded out an enthusiastic drumbeat inside her cranium. Nausea roiled in her gut, but she fought the urge to vomit. She clenched her jaw and forced her eyes open. The left eye refused to accommodate with more than a tiny crack. Pain radiated from her left temple and something damp crusted her eyelashes shut. She held herself still otherwise, desperate to not communicate her wakeful state to anyone watching.

An old kerosene lamp swung from a nail pounded into a corner support. To Carmen, it seemed the only source of light. The dank, musty room carried the unmistakable and universal feel of an unfinished, dirt basement. Spiders seemed to have taken over most of the unoccupied space. She strained to pick up sounds of another person and heard a whimper. The whine didn't remind her of anything animal. Rather, it sounded like a girl.

Carmen's vision swam dizzily. It was so hard to focus. She knew that sound should mean something to her, but she couldn't think. She took a deep breath, swallowing her nausea, and tried to sit up. That was when she realized her hands were bound behind her back. She lay on her side in the dirt with her knees bent toward her chest.

Memory came rushing back and Carmen gasped. She was in serious trouble and no one knew her location. She lay on her right side and didn't feel the press of her cell phone digging into her hip. No flashlight either. Okay, they took those. Now what?

She had to get her hands free and she couldn't do so with them tied behind her. Carmen closed her eye briefly, grateful she had always been flexible. She slid her arms down until her hands slipped under her butt. Her jacket prevented her from moving any further, and she strained until her shoulders felt like they were being ripped from the sockets. Despite the pain, she wallowed in the dirt, attempting to wiggle her arms down just a little more. No matter what she did, nothing worked. Carmen swallowed her shriek of frustration. Everything she did made the pounding in her head worse.

Finally, she lay panting in the dirt. If she could just rest for a minute, she could figure this out. She must have lost consciousness. A furtive sound drew her reluctantly to wakefulness. Carmen couldn't see much out of her battered eye, but she thought someone hovered in the shadows.

"Who's there?" She barely recognized her own harsh voice and coughed, trying to relieve the dryness in her throat.

"Shh," someone whispered. Carmen couldn't determine whether it was a man or woman. The glint of a knife flashed in the flickering lamp light.

The person moved around behind her. Carmen expected the pain of a blade slipped between her ribs. Instead the person chuckled quietly at her predicament and the voice sounded familiar. Definitely a woman. She heard the knife's edge sawing against rope fibers at the backs of her thighs. Blessed relief in her shoulders caused her to sigh when her hands parted. She attempted to rise, but a small, warm hand pressed down against her shoulder.

"They are near. You must be quiet," her savior whispered.

A very sweet French accent caressed Carmen's ears. "Who are you?" she asked again, her voice stronger this time.

The woman didn't answer. Instead, she drew one hand down Carmen's arm in a long, slow caress, and she was gone by the time Carmen managed to lever herself into a sitting position. She still felt woozy. It looked like there were two kerosene lamps. The sight coalesced into one as her vision cleared. She could still barely see, but the pitiful noises she'd heard before continued. She had a pretty good idea who it was. This could only be one person.

Carmen staggered toward a dark corner at the far end of the basement. The room wasn't small and she estimated it took up the entire underneath of the house. Thick, heavy shelving lined the walls, casting more shadows and making it difficult for Carmen to see. She supported her shaky legs by holding onto the shelves as she made her way to the back. A large iron cage greeted her when she negotiated the final line of shelves. The cage held a single occupant.

"Jessica."

Tears glinted on the young woman's cheeks, leaving tracks through the dirt in their wake. Mussed blonde hair tumbled over her unkempt, ragged blouse. Fear burned from her eyes. Her hands clenched white around the bars of the cage door. A crusted over wound graced her right cheek. Carmen surmised the cut was the source of the blood on Brian's clothes after the attack.

"What are you going to do to me?" Jessica asked, her voice trembling.

Carmen shook her head and immediately regretted it. She swallowed hard. "It's okay. I'm here to help."

She knelt in the dirt and placed her hand over one of Jessica's. Jessica pulled away, clearly far from reassured. "My name is Carmen Bravo. I'm a police officer from the States."

Jessica only moved farther away, but that was fine. Carmen needed to see what she could do with the door. She discovered a rusty looking lock. It needed a key, but she hoped the old thing might give way with a good yank. It looked old enough.

No dice.

"You don't look so good," Jessica said quietly.

Understatement, if Carmen looked anything like she felt. "Did you see a key anywhere?"

"The guy who locked me in had it."

Of course. "Did you know Brian was involved in, well, whatever this is?"

Jessica looked confused. She shook her head and chewed on the corner of her lip. "Who?"

The shriek of chair legs sliding across a wooden floor made Carmen freeze. Chances were good that the goons upstairs would eventually return to check on them. She could use that. Carmen scooted back to her previous position on the basement floor. She lay down with her right cheek against the dirt and shifted her hands behind her to fool anyone into thinking she remained bound. With only seconds to spare, boot steps thumped down the cobweb-filled wooden stairs. She didn't hesitate to keep her eyes open. Loose hair from her previously severe bun covered part of her face. The eye anyone could see wasn't open very much anyway and she needed every advantage.

Luck was on her side. Only one man had deigned to investigate the hostages' status. Tall and lanky, the man sported at least a three-day growth of beard and an Adam's apple that bobbed when he swallowed. He kicked Carmen's foot as he passed, but kept moving. Probably checking to see if she was still unconscious, Carmen figured. The man continued to the back of the room.

"Please, let me go," Jessica implored. "I won't tell anyone about you."

The stranger didn't respond. He thumped back in Carmen's direction. He didn't even bother adjusting to go around her. The thug simply stepped over Carmen's feet to continue on course. Carmen took full advantage.

She swept her foot up and caught him behind the knees. The man tumbled to the ground, tangling Carmen's legs with his weight. A bony elbow struck her over the damaged eye and sparks burst through her head. Carmen reeled, but forced her way through the pain. That wasn't about to stop her. This was their only chance to escape. It wouldn't come again.

Carmen sat up as quickly as possible, aiming her fist for the prominent bulge in his throat. She connected, but only from the side. The man gagged in response, but lunged to his feet. Carmen had grabbed hold of his collar and he pulled her up with him. She took advantage of the momentum to drive her knee into his crotch. She quickly followed up with an elbow strike to the nose. She put all her weight behind the blow. The man's head snapped back as blood exploded upward from his nostrils. He folded like a house of cards and didn't move again.

Carmen crouched, poised for another attack from above, but it didn't come. Hadn't the woman who released her said *they* were nearby? How many was *they*? Time slowly crawled as she waited. No one else came. Finally, she patted down the gorilla and found the key in his shirt pocket. He didn't have a wallet on him, but she didn't care who he was. Carmen took a moment to truss him up with the leftover rope from her own bindings. Then she sprinted to the back of the basement.

"I have the key," she announced in a harsh whisper. "Let's get you out of here."

Jessica sobbed once and scooted closer to the door. She flung her arms around Carmen's neck as soon as it opened. "Thank you so much. I thought no one would find me."

"Don't thank me yet. We still have to get out of here. That woman said there were others. Stay behind me and stay quiet." Carmen patted Jessica on the back, once, awkwardly. Then she stepped away.

"What woman?"

Carmen wondered the exact same thing. Who was their benefactor? Why hadn't she stayed around to help them if she felt compelled to intervene enough to cut Carmen loose? Perhaps she was involved with the shenanigans, but drew the line at hostages. If so, she had taken a huge risk. Carmen decided to simply be grateful for small favors. She could worry about details later, presuming they survived long enough to ask questions.

The stairs proved sturdier than Carmen expected. She hugged the side of the staircase, her back against the wall for both concealment and support. By rote, Carmen pressed her right forearm against her waistband. She really missed her sidearm. Especially with a traumatized victim practically glued to her side. Too bad thug number one hadn't carried a weapon she could use.

Carmen focused on what they would find on the far side of the basement door. They reached the last few stairs and she motioned for Jessica to stay put. As slow as maple syrup running uphill, she peered around the door jam. With a limited view and one eye swollen almost shut, Carmen couldn't see anyone. Nor could she hear anything out of place. By increments, she inched into a battered kitchen.

Faded wallpaper hung in strips, more shadow than substance. Darkness ruled even in the main house. Water dripped from the faucet, sounding like a gong in Carmen's damaged brain. The stench of mildew wasn't as strong up here, but still permeated the air. More kerosene lamps rested on counters and a battered kitchen table.

No electricity, Carmen determined. She decided these people had discovered an old abandoned property to use for their hideout. Such likelihood didn't bode well for her and Jessica. Chances were, the property was isolated and far from any immediate assistance. She wished the woman who cut her free had stayed around to give them a ride out of here.

She closed her eyes and leaned back against the old sheetrock. Carmen pressed both palms flat, reaching for some hidden core of reserves. Things just kept getting harder. After a final bracing breath, she opened her eyes. They had to do this.

Another quick look into the room assured her that, at the moment, they were alone. That could change.

"Stay here," Carmen whispered.

She slipped into the kitchen on tiptoe. A cursory search revealed nothing she could use to defend herself. Carmen opened the door to a small corner pantry and stared in shock. It was all here. Piles of gems and glittering jewelry no one had bothered to sort. Stacks of cash spread out over a shelf. Beside it all, she spotted a pile of animal fur. What in the…? She couldn't resist. Carmen touched the soft material and detected harder rubber beneath the first layer. Curious now, she dug into the pelt and pulled out a hideous mask.

The Wolfman, I presume.

She *knew* this hoax wasn't real! Something more important caught her eye. Carmen's flashlight and her cell phone case. She grabbed the last and yanked her phone free. Roaming charges be damned. In the dim light it took a second to focus, but she wasn't surprised by the lack of phone signal. Carmen didn't have time to wallow. She took a step back, still scanning the pantry when she noticed a red and white tote tossed casually to the floor. She grabbed it and headed back to Jessica. At the same time, she slipped the flashlight into her pocket. She might be able to use it as a weapon if someone got too close.

"This yours?"

"Yes," Jessica hissed. She grabbed the bag and slipped it over her head before sliding an arm through the strap. "Can we get out of here?"

Carmen answered with a sharp nod. She grabbed Jessica's hand without thinking and tugged her toward the back door. At least, Carmen assumed the door at the rear of the kitchen led outside. She'd be awfully confounded if it didn't. A quick sprint across the room and Carmen grabbed the rusted old handle. The wooden door had warped in the frame. She yanked twice before it budged. The third pull succeeded and the door let go of the frame with a screech.

Cool night air caressed her face with the promise of freedom. The moon overhead lit their way off the back of a sagging rear porch in desperate need of a coat of paint. Even in the dark, Carmen could see holes here and there where the wood had rotted and given way.

The overgrown yard backed up to a cornfield. A pole held a sodium light that illuminated the immediate area. The circle of light quickly gave way to darkness. Carmen couldn't hear any traffic noise or see signs of any other structures. There were several rusted out battered cars littering the yard. Pickups and old sedans perched in various shades of dilapidation. Some tipped precariously, missing tires and entire axles. One car stood out from all the others and appeared in much better shape. It sat parked near a broken-down old tow truck, almost obscured by the giant hulk. Only the moonlight had rendered it visible.

Carmen flashed back to seeing an ancient blue Beetle. It had resided at the curb adjacent to the Bavaria Park. An older woman with gray hair and a slight hunch had been headed for that car. How in the world did it wind up here?

Excitement raced through her veins. She couldn't explain the incongruity, but at the moment it didn't matter. It was a ride. Carmen sobbed in a relief she had only experienced once before. That had been a combat zone in Kandahar. This situation gave her a remarkably similar sensation as hope flooded her and jacked up her heart rate.

Headlights sweeping around a bend cut short her elation. She estimated the car at less than a quarter mile away. Considering the isolation of their surroundings, she could guess the driver's destination.

"Time to go."

Carmen and Jessica raced across the yard directly toward the blue Volkswagen. The doors opened easily, but their escape proved elusive. There weren't any keys in the ignition. Carmen thumped the steering wheel in exasperation. Now what?

Beside her, Jessica pulled a phone from her purse. The screen lit up and Jessica stared down at it.

"Do you have a signal?" Carmen asked, mentally crossing her fingers.

Jessica nodded. "One bar, but I have no idea who to call. I'm on vacation."

"I do."

Carmen whipped out her cell, picturing grains of sand dropping through an hourglass. Lights from the oncoming car drew steadily closer.

"Get down," she whispered, listening to the phone ring.

"Hello?"

Tears pricked her eyes at the wonderful sound of Katie's voice. "Katchoo, it's me. I'm in trouble."

"What's going on?" Katie sounded all business, artfully taking charge like she did in tense situations. That personality trait made her a great psychiatrist.

"I found Jessica. Someone...hit me. I don't know where we are."

Tires crunched on gravel as the car approached and swung off the road.

"I'm on it. Is your GPS active?"

Carmen could hear computer keys tapping. "Yes. Hurry, Katie. Things are about to get sketchy. Katie...thanks for always being there. No matter what, you're the best."

"Don't you do that," Katie said sternly. "You're not allowed to give up on me. I've gotten used to you pulling my pigtails and I'm going to find you."

"I'm counting on it."

Carmen thumbed off her phone and scooted down as much as she could given her height. A spring in the ripped seat poked into her rear and she almost put her foot through a hole in the floorboard. For her part, Jessica dove into the tiny floorboard space in front of the passenger seat. Her knees almost touched her chin. Carmen swallowed against her envy of Jessica's smaller size.

The other car pulled right up to the house and Carmen heard two doors slam. She peered over the edge of the passenger door. Two men stood directly under the pole light. Her mouth dropped open slightly as she identified them as Brian Dietrich and *Kommissar* Bauer.

"Do you recognize that guy?"

Jessica inched up and looked toward the house. "Yeah, the young guy attacked me in the park."

"He said he was your boyfriend and that you were both attacked. He said you were making out in the park."

"Ha, he wished."

Carmen snorted softly, pleased with Jessica's spirit. This story had started to come together. Earlier tonight, she witnessed Brian meeting up with the "werewolf" to hand off their take from the robberies. She'd be willing to be a month's salary that Jessica had happened upon them during one such drop. The reason Brian knew Jessica's name when Carmen first saw him was that he'd gone through her bag. He had her blood on his clothes because he was the attacker. No doubt thug number one that she'd tied up in the basement had played the part of the werewolf. He was definitely tall enough for it.

Disappointment in Bauer's involvement left a bitter taste in her mouth, but it made sense. Having a detective involved would help deflect resources away from their operation. What she still couldn't fathom was why they came up with a werewolf scheme in the first place. Raised voices pulled her out of own head.

"I told you to be careful," Bauer shouted. "Now we have not one, but two hostages. You are aware that one of them is an American police officer?"

"Of course I am, but what was Heinrich supposed to do? He found her skulking around in the park."

"Following you," Bauer snarled. "So, what do you suggest we do with them?"

Brian smiled, but Carmen thought it more of a predatory grimace. Her blood ran cold. "We eliminate them."

"You sound like a bad spy movie," Bauer snarled.

"Do you have a better idea? They have seen my face. People might ignore the girl if she squeals, but not that police officer. If we release them, it will only be a matter of time before officials connect us all together."

Bauer shoved a hand under the flap of his overcoat. He removed a large black pistol and pointed it directly at Brian. "Perhaps I should simply shoot you. You are the only one they have seen."

"Don't be stupid. We can still be tied together." He didn't even flinch.

Carmen had to hand it to Brian for guts. Carmen tensed, waiting for the ensuing gunshot. It never came. Several tense moments passed before Bauer reluctantly put the gun away. Brian clapped Bauer on the shoulder like nothing ever happened and the two disappeared into the house.

"We've got to get out of here. When they find their buddy on the floor, they'll be back and we won't stand a chance." Carmen kicked open her door.

To her credit, Jessica didn't argue or ask what Carmen had in mind. She simply ran, hot on Carmen's heels toward Bauer's car. Carmen fervently hoped the detective had left the keys inside or this would be a very short escape plan. They barely reached the mid-point of the yard when someone shouted inside the house. Carmen grabbed a handful of Jessica's sweater at the shoulder and hauled her off course.

"No time. Head for the field."

Carmen sprinted for one of the burned-out cars. She dove behind it just as she heard the door open. Jessica lagged a few steps behind her and it was enough to give them away.

"Over there," Brian shouted.

Running feet headed in their direction. Given the lack of choices, Carmen did the only thing she could. She gave up hiding and dashed toward the corn, weaving behind every possible obstacle. A round hit the turf by her foot as she ran, spitting dirt into the air. Another pinged off the hood of a decrepit Opel missing half its roof. Two more shots followed Carmen and Jessica into the cornfield, missing by so close a margin that Carmen heard the displaced air.

"Hold onto my shirt," Carmen advised. "We can't afford to get separated in this."

Jessica latched onto the tail of her sweater. "How long until your friend sends help?"

"I don't know. I'm not sure how far outside the city we are. We just have to keep moving."

It seemed like forever. Carmen led Jessica in a semi circle around the farmhouse. At first, things seemed to go great. Eventually, Bauer, Brian and the newly conscious Heinrich decided to split up. Carmen crouched on one knee and listened to them move out. One went far right, one far left and one directly up the middle. Eventually, they would move into an interlace pattern and sweep the women up in their net. They had maneuvered the women back toward the edge of the corn closest to the farmhouse. From their position about twenty feet from the last row, Carmen could see the pole holding up the streetlight.

Carmen slid an arm over Jessica's shoulder and pulled the young woman against her side. Both were down on their knees in the dirt, straw poking into their legs and stalks pressing against their faces. She could feel the shivers moving through Jessica's body. As heavy footsteps approached, the whimpers started. Carmen put a hand over the scared young woman's mouth. Although battered and bruised, Carmen refused to just give in. If the men located them, she'd fight until the last second. She slipped her free hand into a jacket pocket and wrapped her fingers around the flashlight. She hadn't utilized it sooner because the light would give away their position.

Gunfire boomed, seemingly from directly over her shoulder, sending Carmen's heart into her throat. A man grunted and she heard someone off to the side hit the ground. She and Jessica exchanged frowns, completely confused by this latest development.

"Dietrich, where are you? Heinrich?"

Carmen recognized Bauer asking the questions. A voice she didn't know responded, but Brian only managed a groan. Someone shot Brian, but she didn't think his partners had anything to do with it. The woman! She was still here.

Several shots fired in quick succession. Carmen could only guess the shooter fired in a wide spread. The same footsteps that had chased them into the cornfield headed back for the house. The sounds passed by uncomfortably close. It sounded like someone dragged a body. She figured his partners pulled Brian out of the field. Carmen wanted to know, but it wasn't worth their lives to take a look. These heartless criminals wouldn't hesitate to murder them on sight. The woman who had freed her hadn't seen fit to intervene unless absolutely necessary. Carmen wasn't quite sure what met the stranger's criteria for stepping in.

Bauer and Heinrich reached the edge of the field. Both of them held one of Brian's arms. They lugged him along without much regard for any injuries. For some strange reason, Carmen noted a profound sense of relief that Brian seemed fully conscious. He groaned and helped to push himself along with one foot. They made a beeline for Bauer's car.

"Get him inside," Bauer ordered Heinrich.

"*Wo gehst du hin?*"

"To get the merchandise, you idiot." Bauer left Heinrich standing there as he sprinted toward the house. Apparently, he wasn't leaving without their haul.

Four police units suddenly peeled around the curve, approaching the farmhouse at speed. Blue lights flashed and sirens wailed. Carmen almost laughed aloud when Bauer froze in place. Heinrich dropped Brian's arm and ran into the farmhouse, bumping his partner in crime as he passed. Bauer watched him, but didn't bother to follow. Instead, he shook his head and dropped his handgun into the dirt.

Carmen let out the first easy breath she'd taken all night. She and Jessica slowly limped out of the field and into the conical of light cast over the yard. In addition to all of the wonderfully reassuring uniforms, one detail stood out.

The beat-up Volkswagen Beetle was gone.

Chapter Seven

"I still don't get the wolf man thing."

Carmen listened with half an ear. Eight days after the rescue by Officer Reiter and his men, Carmen still had a headache. She found a night in the Munich hospital an enlightening experience. Apparently, all hospitals smelled alike, but care differed wildly. No one checked on her again once admitted, save Katie of course. And Reiter, though Carmen didn't really count him since he only wanted a statement.

An elbow bumped her side.

"You're not listening."

"Sorry, just trying to concentrate. Airports aren't as much fun when you're headed home."

Katie gave Carmen a worried look, but didn't respond. The security line moved grudgingly, pulling them inexorably forward. Carmen slipped off her shoes and dropped them into a tote. Next, she removed her watch, earrings and anything else airport security could possibly focus on. She made sure the ceramic beer stein for Raphael remained securely wrapped. Everything went into her carry on, which she left unzipped before dropping it onto the conveyor belt.

"Why'd you do all that?"

"Katie, I'm a tall woman with dark hair and eyes. I also have an olive complexion. If anyone's going to get pulled out of line for a pat down, I'm your gal."

A sniff greeted this declaration. At first, Carmen thought Katie would sneeze. When she didn't, Carmen decided she just didn't agree.

"That's stereotyping, you know. I'm sure you're wrong."

A large, matronly woman approached them and waved a security wand in Carmen's face. Gray and black hair pulled back into a bun so severe, the woman's face stretched backward with it. The hairdo matched the dour lines around the agent's down-turned mouth. Carmen could see this woman cast in the movie role of a gulag guard.

"You, come with me."

Carmen clamped her jaw and raised an eyebrow at her friend. A flush rose to Katie's cheeks and she quickly looked away. As Carmen followed the airport agent off to the side, she wondered why people did that. Even her best friend acted like she didn't know Carmen when something unusual or potentially embarrassing occurred in an airport.

"What happened to your face?" the agent asked as she ran the scanner up and down Carmen's body.

Carmen caught herself before she touched her eye. She managed to keep both hands out to her sides in a non-threatening manner. "You should see the other guy."

Frown lines deepened. "That is not amusing. I asked you a question."

Man, Carmen wanted to go home.

"I'm an American police officer. I was helping local law enforcement on a case." Okay, that was a bit of a stretch. "Someone whacked me over the head and abducted me. I spent the night in the hospital and then another three days following a psychiatrist around Oktoberfest. Oh, and the guy who kidnapped me was dressed as a werewolf." She didn't bother mentioning the last few days touring the German countryside in Katie's rented BMW. It didn't seem relevant.

Absolute silence followed her last statement. Long, tense moments later, the security agent answered. "Humph. That is unlikely. Please proceed. You are holding up the line."

What line? Carmen looked around pointedly. She was the only one being humiliated at the moment. She decided not to point that out and enjoy a complimentary strip search for her trouble. Instead, she pressed her lips together and marched to the end of the conveyor. Katie stood with her back to Carmen and seemed rather tense. She turned and offered Carmen her bag. Carmen noticed the shine in Katie's eye that had nothing to do with her cold and how she chewed on her lips. Holding back a laugh, no doubt.

"What did I tell you?"

"Well, you can't really blame her. You look like Wile E. Coyote after an encounter with the Road Runner."

Carmen shoved her feet into her shoes with a little more force than strictly necessary. "Terrific, that's what every girl wants to hear."

"The black eye is most impressive. It covers half your face, but at least your eyes are open now. Mostly, anyway."

"Yeah, that's great. Raph is never going to let me live it down. What gate do we need?"

Carmen waited while Katie scanned her ticket rather than do it herself. The less she had to focus on tiny print at the moment, the better. She happily followed Katie away from the security checkpoint.

"Just tell him you were in a bar fight," Katie suggested as they walked. "By the way, you never answered me. Why the werewolf costume? I never got that."

"We've been over this. Bauer and the others thought it less likely someone would report being robbed by the Wolfman. I was more surprised that Reiter wasn't in on it."

Katie shook her head, her blonde hair sweeping against her shoulders. "Actually, he seemed rather angry when I called to report that you needed help."

"Probably mad at me for interfering again."

"Maybe, but he got there really fast from all accounts and I think there was more to it. I believe he was offended to discover a fellow policeman involved. If you ask my professional opinion, Reiter is a good man who happens to lack social skills. Just be glad you weren't far outside the city."

Carmen's thoughts drifted as Katie spoke. She couldn't refrain from inspecting the faces of her fellow travelers, especially the female ones. A flash of red and a tinkling laugh caught her attention. Her heart sped up tempo as she zoned in on the person in question. Disappointment quickly followed. She began to think back on those final moments at the farmhouse.

She and Jessica had emerged from the cornfield into a sea of uniforms. Carmen had searched the mob for one particular shape, but never spotted signs of a woman who could have cut her free in the basement. She had not imagined that. Not only had a woman released her, but someone shot Brian in the cornfield and rescued her a second time. That someone had sounded very familiar. More to the point, the beat-up blue Volkswagen Beetle vanished just before the cavalry arrived.

At least Jessica got off easy, except for the everlasting trauma, Carmen allowed. Jessica suffered a single cut and some mild malnutrition and dehydration. The hospital released her before Carmen. Small mercies, Carmen thought. If she hadn't acted and Jessica died, Carmen couldn't have lived with herself.

"You're doing it again."

"Hmm, sorry I wasn't listening."

"I noticed."

They reached a packed boarding gate. People sat on the floor as every seat was occupied. A couple stood up and walked away just as they arrived. Carmen gratefully slumped into one of the chairs. She immediately dropped her carry on between her feet and leaned back to close her eyes.

"You feeling okay?"

"Just a slight headache. The doctor said it'll probably last a few weeks."

"Maybe you shouldn't go back to work right away."

"Right," Carmen scoffed. "My boss will love that."

Katie didn't respond so Carmen took the opportunity to relax. She intended to sleep all the way home. Thank God for lie flat seats. She also looked forward to the relative seclusion of first class over coach, especially on such a long international flight. Even with her eyes closed, she could sense the bodies bustling all around her. Occasionally, someone brushed against her as they passed nearby. Comments from a myriad of conversations floated on the air along with various perfumes and body odors. If anything, the waiting area seemed even more packed than before. Carmen had no idea how so many people would manage to cram onto one plane.

Beside her, Katie sniffled on occasion. Carmen could hear the slight rasp of the tissue as she swiped at her runny nose. For some strange reason, Carmen found the sound comforting. Life went on despite any trauma. Things returned to normal. Soon she'd be home and in her own bed.

The skin on the back of her neck suddenly prickled. Carmen's eyes snapped open so quickly, she felt a twinge in her left temple. Without being too obvious, she attempted to determine who was watching her. She knew they were. She could feel the weight of a stare.

A group of six stood not far away. Four men and two women spoke quietly and showed not the slightest interest in her. One of the men, in his twenties Carmen guessed, knelt down to retie his shoe. On the other side of him a woman stood in profile wearing a red knit beret. Carmen noted the slender, albeit muscular, frame. Blonde hair obscured the side of her face, hiding her features. The stranger suddenly turned her head and met Carmen's gaze head on. Armageddon blue eyes held her immobile. The air stilled in Carmen's lungs.

The woman smiled and slowly winked.

Carmen flinched in surprise. It was the same woman with the amazing laugh Carmen had seen on the flight into Munich.

The young man finished tying his shoe and stood, blocking her view. Carmen shot to her feet, craning her head to see over and around the passenger.

"Where are you going?" Katie asked, sounding merely curious.

The group of travelers collected their bags and left the boarding area. There wasn't any sign of the mysterious woman. She seemed to have vanished into thin air. Then again, perhaps Carmen had merely experienced a hallucination brought on by wishful thinking and a mild concussion.

PART TWO

Millions of spiritual creatures walk the Earth Unseen,
Both when we wake, and when we sleep.

John Milton~ *Paradise Lost*

Chapter Eight

Carmen froze in place with one hand raised. Shouts from the other room communicated a blend of excitement, joy, surprise and even some mingled disappointment. She smiled and shoved a loaded tortilla chip into her mouth. Over the talk from the living room, she heard the television. Laughter and multiple conversations carried over into the kitchen. Carmen wasn't really into football, so she trolled the food dishes lining the counter tops instead.

"Carmen, get in here," Katie shouted. "You're missing the game."

"Let me know when someone scores," Carmen invited back.

While the Super Bowl was the biggest game of the year, Carmen wasn't really into it. She accompanied her best friend Katie out of an effort to socialize. Mutual friends Shawn and Rebecca Hartley hosted the get together every year and Carmen wouldn't have missed it. This year, they kept the gathering small. Only Shawn, Rebecca, Katie, Carmen and one other person attended. Carmen had never met Sally Freeman before, but she seemed nice. She paused in the process of scooping guacamole, sour cream and salsa onto another chip as the stranger in question walked into the room.

"Hi. I need a refill," Sally explained unnecessarily, waving an empty beer bottle. She tossed it into the recycle bin as she headed for the cooler. "Can I get you anything while I'm here?"

Carmen almost choked on the chip. From the way Sally's light brown eyes traveled from the top of her head to the tips of Carmen's ankle high Gucci boots, Carmen thought she meant something else. The heat of attraction had smacked her in the gut the moment Shawn introduced

Carmen to her long-time friend and coworker. Something about those laughing eyes, light brown shoulder length hair and the dimple in Sally's chin had drawn her in. Of course, Carmen spent most of the afternoon snacking in the kitchen and avoiding being too close to Sally. The last thing she needed were complications in her life.

From the way Sally watched her like a shark eying chum, Carmen figured she felt differently about the situation. It also sounded like Sally had something in mind to offer besides another drink. Carmen reached for the plastic bottle of Diet Pepsi to wash down the errant food caught in her throat. She coughed a couple more times before she could wheeze out a response.

"Thanks, I'm good."

"Are you okay? I'd hate to have to do the Heimlich on you." Sally stepped closer, almost into Carmen's personal space. Carmen could feel Sally's breath ghosting onto her forearm. "Then again, it would give me an excuse to get a little closer."

Carmen coughed again before she pulled herself together. "I appreciate the offer. I think. I will get another soda, now that you mention it."

Sally tilted her head slightly. "You do know this is a football party? Isn't the tradition to drink beer and stuff down as much pizza as one human being can possibly hold?"

"That's the rumor. The pizza I can definitely go for. You probably don't know this about me, but I'm a bit of a bottomless pit. The beer, however, is off the table at least for the night. I'm on call."

"Ah, that's right. Becca told me that you're a police officer?"

"Helicopter pilot for the Denver Police Department, actually." Carmen relaxed into the conversation now that they'd stumbled onto a comfortable topic. "And yes, I'm a police officer too. What do you do for a living?"

"I work with Shawn at Lockheed. I'm a software engineer."

"Wow, you must be a genius. That sounds like fascinating work."

Carmen couldn't imagine being the person behind the design of her favorite mode of travel. She loved flying her Bell GXP 407 helicopter. She didn't know if Lockheed constructed helicopters, but the principle had to be the same. Or at least close to it. She looked on Sally with fresh eyes. Not only was the thirty-something woman incredibly easy on the eyes, she had the brains to go with it. Her toned physique hinted at a regular workout routine, which meant she took care of herself to boot. From all outward appearances, Sally Freeman was the whole package.

Even as she thought that, Carmen mentally flashed back to the mystery woman in Munich who wore the cute red knit beret. She believed the woman had saved her life and to this day, her heart fluttered every time she thought of her. The fake werewolf on the scene had put a definite damper on her feelings about that time and Carmen struggled to push the memories away. Being knocked over the head and taken hostage certainly took the magic out of that episode.

"No, not really," Sally responded. "I just like numbers. It's actually interesting from that standpoint, but it can't compare to how your work day typically goes. Is it scary to be a police officer in Denver?"

"I had my moments when I was a beat officer. Things can get a little hairy with street gangs sometimes. It's not like that now. Flying over the city is…majestic." Carmen couldn't deny the wistful tone in her voice. "I love seeing the mountains, especially when they're covered in snow. Flying makes me feel like I'm completely free."

"Sounds magical. Maybe you could give me a ride sometime."

Sally inched closer and brazenly rested her hand on Carmen's forearm. From this distance, Carmen could see the gold flecks in her brown eyes. Time seemed to slow. Carmen watched as Sally's tongue darted out to moisten her lower lip. Heat bloomed in her stomach and traveled up her throat. Her cheeks heated as a blush flushed her skin. Despite the pull of desire, Sally came on a little too strong for Carmen.

"I also heard that it's your birthday. Anything special planned?"

Again, there was that soft flirty tone that left nothing to the imagination. Carmen swallowed hard. "Not quite yet. It's not for a few weeks. The eighteenth."

"And that will make you?"

"Thirty-five. Why, seeing if I fit your type?" Carmen surprised herself by the comment. It sounded suggestive even to her. Typically, she was fairly shy about approaching women. Then again, Sally made it easy. Carmen enjoyed the teasing and decided to go with the flow. What was the worst that could happen?

"Oh, I already know you're my type. In the interests of full disclosure, I'm thirty-six. I know we just met," Sally said, softly segueing to another topic, "but would you consider having coffee with me? Tomorrow night?"

"Y…yes," Carmen stammered. "I think I'd like that."

Just then, Carmen's cell phone rang. She held up a finger indicating for Sally to hold on a moment.

"Bravo," she said briefly, before listening to the caller for a moment. "Yes, ma'am. I understand. I can be there in about a half hour."

"You're leaving so soon," Sally asked as soon as Carmen ended the call, her disappointment clear.

Carmen shrugged. "Sorry, duty calls, but I meant what I said. I'd love to have coffee with you. Let me give you my number. Call me with the details for tomorrow and I'll be there."

As soon as they exchanged information, Carmen headed into the living room. She regretted having to make her excuses, but she hadn't any choice.

Katie sat on the sofa with her back to Carmen. Shawn and Becca sat on either side of her. Everyone seemed riveted on the game, but Carmen knew better. She could tell by the tension in Katie's shoulders that she'd heard the cell phone ring. Katie scooted to the edge of the cushion and held up a hand for Carmen to wait. Her eyes stayed riveted to the television screen. Carmen glanced over to see some guy in a football uniform lob the ball into the air. It came back down on the far side of the field and some other guy dropped it. Carmen didn't know who they were, nor did she really care. She only came for the company. Still, groans all around told her the favored team hadn't performed well. Katie grunted in disappointment and turned to face her.

"Called in for work?"

"Not sure." Carmen shook her head. "That was Captain Graham."

"From headquarters on Cherokee?"

"Yeah, weird." Carmen shrugged. She worked directly from the maintenance hangar at Denver International Airport, where she reported to her watch commander, Sergeant Kaminski. Being called down to the HMFIC, or head mother blanker in charge as they used to say in the Air Force, wasn't such a great thing. "I have no idea what she wants."

"You're probably in trouble again."

Carmen pulled back in feigned shocked, though her gesture was all in fun. "You say that like I'm always in trouble."

Katie raised an eyebrow, but didn't belabor the point. "Let me know what she says."

Shawn and Becca stood up to say goodbye, unlike Katie who had already returned to the game. Shawn, slight of frame and hard of muscle, gave Carmen a hug that threatened to shatter bone. Becca wasn't quite as physical. She boasted a larger frame than her wife, and her hugs were like coming home. Carmen always rested content and comforted in Becca's gentle embrace. After saying goodbye to her friends and receiving a last smoldering look from Sally, Carmen headed for the door. She could hardly wait for coffee tomorrow night.

A light glower rested between Carmen's brows all the way to downtown Denver. Stepping into police headquarters on Cherokee Street wasn't a normal part of her work day. She had never visited this structure. It seemed like any other office building, despite the extra security. The environment at Denver International differed wildly from this unaccustomed experience. Her direct supervisor promoted a relaxed atmosphere. Law enforcement personnel suffered enough stress on the job. Carmen knew Kaminski attempted not to add to the burden. Too bad she couldn't say the same for this place. Political ambiance fairly radiated from the structure's edifice. She chalked her discomfort up to the sensation of having been called to the principal's office.

Carmen offered a smile to the bored looking officer at the security checkpoint. His expression never altered and his gaze slid away as though he didn't see her. Carmen watched him closely as she waited in the short line. Others moved forward, dropped their belongings into a bin and moved through the metal detector. In many ways, this was like moving through TSA at the airport terminal. While she waited, Carmen noticed that the officer's expression never changed. Murray, according to his name tag, seemed too young to appear so jaded. Twenties, from her guess, uncombed dark hair and light beard stubble. By his rumpled trousers and scuffed black boots, he didn't take much pride in the job. She tried not to think about what that meant for his prospects.

Not her business, Carmen thought. Instead, she moved up and started through the process. Weapon cleared, magazine ejected and belongings in the bin, Carmen then walked through the metal detector. Once on the other side, Murray shoved the bin toward her.

"I'm here to see Captain Graham," Carmen said as she gathered her things. Murray only grunted, sparking her indignation. "Do you think you could point the way to her office?"

One dark eyebrow rose in response to her comment. After a brief pause, he replied with an economy of words. "Second floor. Last office on the left."

He turned away to his duties without bothering to point out the elevators. Fortunately, she spotted those by watching others milling about in the lobby. She wasn't familiar with the layout of this place at all. Carmen made it a point not to be around the political side of the job. In that way lay madness. Of course, she had met Captain Graham before. Police functions such as the annual ball mandated the rare occurrence, but visiting the woman in her private office was another matter.

She swallowed her discomfort and adopted a casual demeanor. Carmen hadn't the foggiest idea why Graham called her in, but she wouldn't find out by standing around.

Minutes later, she strolled down the long hallway. This wasn't a police station in the usual sense. Arrests and bookings didn't occur here. This building housed the police department's administrative center. In addition to Police Commissioner Berman's office, one could find financial as well as victim services. Carmen couldn't possibly name all of the entities housed here, nor did she really want to. Even walking through the hallways gave her the creeps. Captain Marsha Graham had a hand in many of those operations. As Carmen recalled, Graham stood pretty high on the food chain. Third tier down from the commissioner to be precise.

Carmen swallowed hard as she passed the doorway denoting Internal Affairs. The captain's door stood open at the far end of the corridor. Heavy blinds that covered a floor to ceiling window were up, flooding the room with wintry sunlight. Carmen identified three voices in muted conversation before she stepped around the entryway, one male and two female. She recognized Graham's voice, but not the others. Nerves gave way to curiosity.

Her first glimpse told her three things. Carmen didn't know these other people. They were not regular police and she had never encountered them on the job. Finally, the cut of their clothes and bearing screamed "Feds."

Carmen rapped the door twice with her knuckles. A tall lean man with dark hair and matching eyes looked over at her. Like Murray from downstairs, his expression told her nothing. Carmen noted the precisely combed hair, clean shave and expensive pinstripes that screamed money. He was tall, too. Carmen figured he beat her height by a few inches.

His companion stood in direct counterpoint. The top of the woman's red head barely reached his chin. Even in three-inch heels, she resembled a child playing dress up in comparison to the man. She wore her hair in a bob style cut. The elegant skirt suit probably cost more than Carmen's yearly electric bill. Carmen wondered if these two deliberately channeled Mulder and Scully. She sized the two up quickly before she turned to her superior officer.

Captain Graham flashed Carmen a brilliant smile. Her white teeth stood out against smooth café au lait skin tones. Graham wore an elegant navy-blue skirt suit rather than a uniform, and rose from her seat, waving for Carmen to enter.

"Come in, Officer Bravo. Close the door."

Carmen did as she was told before she moved closer to the captain's desk. "You wanted to see me, ma'am?"

"Yes, sorry for calling you in on your day off. I'd like you to meet a few people."

The apology seemed more practiced than sincere. Not surprising considering Graham's position, yet still somehow disappointing. Carmen shrugged it off as unimportant. These two visitors proved far more interesting than any perceived slight.

"Tactical Flight Officer Carmen Bravo, this is Ellen White and her partner, Phil Carter." Captain Graham indicated each in turn as Carmen dutifully shook hands. "They're from the U.S. Marshals Service."

"Marshals? I've never actually met a marshal before. Are you here for a fugitive search?" Carmen knew Denver boasted a local field office.

The Scully look-alike, White, smiled and shook her head. Carter chuckled and answered.

"No, we're actually here for quite another more pleasant reason."

"Really? What's that?"

Graham captured Carmen's attention with a deep inhale. "Why don't we sit down? This is going to take a minute."

"Whatever it is, I didn't do it." Carmen held up both hands in mock surrender.

Her comment garnered a few chuckles and managed to lower the tension in the room. Marshal White responded to Carmen's remark.

"Actually, you did. That's why we need to speak with you."

Everyone took a seat around a small area set up for such purposes. Carmen chose a hard wingback chair while Graham occupied a similar seat to her left. White and Carter settled on a small sofa. A circular glass table occupied the space between them. Carmen kept her mouth closed, erring on the side of caution. She presumed these two would quickly make their point. Again, White spoke for both of them.

"In the interest of cutting to the chase, your adventure in Germany has recently come to our attention."

Carmen tensed. And things had been going so well. She certainly hadn't expected this. "You mean the whole man-in-a-werewolf costume? That was months ago, and I don't see what that has to do with the Marshals Service."

"It's okay, Bravo," Graham reassured her. "You're not in any trouble."

Carmen remained skeptical. She doubted these two would show up for kicks. "I don't see how I could be. Germany is a little outside United States jurisdiction and I didn't do anything wrong."

Carter cleared his throat and scooted closer to the sofa edge. "Uh, that's not quite true."

"Which part?"

Carmen definitely experienced the beginning flutters of serious concern. U.S. Marshals enjoyed more arrest and enforcement powers than any other policing body. She should have listened to Katie while in Germany and kept her nose out of things that didn't concern her.

"Well, both actually." Carter seemed to warm to his subject, hands moving animatedly as he spoke. "We actually have four field offices abroad. The Service works with Interpol to apprehend foreign fugitives. This gives us limited authority overseas and we often hear of other activities. As for you, your actions weren't *illegal*, but you did interfere with German officials."

Marshal White raised a hand and Carter quickly quieted. It wasn't hard for Carmen to discern the chain of command.

"However," White interjected, "that isn't our concern. My partner mentioned we have a number of foreign field offices. They are in Jamaica, Mexico, Columbia and the Dominican Republic. That last office is where you came to our attention. The men you assisted in apprehending were part of an international jewel theft and smuggling ring. Interpol has tried for the last two years to shut down their preposterous schemes. You managed it within days while on vacation in a foreign country with no resources."

"I got into trouble for that."

White nodded. "Only because you hadn't any authority. You still did the right thing despite the circumstances. We want to give you that authority."

Carmen thought reality had taken a jump from Captain Graham's second story window. Nothing made sense. She walked in expecting an official reprimand, not a pat on the back.

"How? I'm a helicopter pilot. I left the patrol beat years ago."

"Don't be modest," White grated, her eyes flashing. "Never downplay your gifts."

Carter took over, reciting Carmen's history. "Honorable discharge from the Air Force with the rank of major. Twenty-seven aerial missions flying helicopters in Kandahar and the Middle East. Awarded the Bronze Star for bravery. Top of your class at the police academy."

"You know an awful lot about me." Carmen's eyes narrowed. "Why do I get the feeling you have an ulterior motive?"

Carter ignored the question, smiling a little smugly. "We know more than that. Mother's name is Maria Bravo, age sixty-seven. She's a florist, I believe. You're the older of two girls. Sister is Della. Four years younger. You have a maternal aunt named Sophia. Father's name is Giorgio."

Carmen's temper rose. Heat suffused her face and her grip tightened on the chair arms until her knuckles whitened. Before she could accuse Carter of overstepping, White intervened.

"Enough, Phil. Apologies, Officer Bravo. It's not our intent to freak you out. You must understand that our job is to thoroughly vet potential new recruits."

There was that sensation of heading down the rabbit hole again. "Excuse me? Quit beating around the bush. What do you want?"

"Why, to offer you a job of course."

White's tone had a way of making Carmen feel thick, but she couldn't hide her surprise. Carmen flinched and blinked. "You want me as a recruit for the Marshals Service? How would that even work? I'm almost thirty-five years old. Isn't that a little old for a recruit, not to mention some pretty extensive training? Do you have any idea where I'd end up? I have so many questions I wouldn't know how to list them all."

"I know it's a lot to take in," White allowed.

"You're damn right."

"Let me begin by saying that we have recruits older than you. Age isn't a primary concern. You already exceed requirements for becoming a federal agent, to include a bachelor's degree and extensive law enforcement experience. In addition to that, you've shown clear thinking under pressure and you're loyal and dedicated."

"So is your average cocker spaniel," Carmen pointed out.

White ignored her sarcasm. She passed over a plain white business card that held only a phone number. "Consider our offer. If you decide to accept, we can be reached here. If you decide to pass, toss the card and you won't hear from us again."

The marshals stood as one. They crossed halfway to the closed door before Carmen could gather her stunned faculties.

"One question."

The two turned back and waited.

"Where would I go for training?"

White exchanged a brief glance with her partner. "The Federal Law Enforcement Training Center in Glynco, Georgia. Training lasts for eighteen weeks."

"FLETC, isn't that where the Border Patrol trains?"

"Yes, as well as ICE and many others. Is that all?"

Carmen nodded and the marshals left without another word. After a brief silence, Carmen turned to Captain Graham.

"You were awfully quiet, ma'am. What do you think?"

Graham took a deep breath, just as she had before the discussion started. Carmen had already deduced it was her way of gathering her thoughts. Graham's dark gaze lingered on the industrial gray carpet between her feet.

"I think you need to seriously consider your options." Graham finally looked at her directly. "When the Marshals Service approached me, I took the liberty of reading your file. You've always been a bit of a maverick, Carmen. You get results, but usually on your own terms. That quality makes you a great chopper pilot, but not necessarily a good police officer."

"What are you saying?"

"Only that this is an amazing opportunity and I believe you'd be great. This job would give you much more latitude. You could do a lot of good on a larger scale."

Tears pricked Carmen's eyes and she blinked away the sensation. "I'd have to give up everything I've worked for and start over. What are the odds I'd be stationed at the Denver field office? Everything would change."

"I know it's a lot to take in, but nothing stays the same forever." Graham gently rested a hand on Carmen's forearm. "Why don't you take some time and think things through? Take a week."

Carmen's chuckle held little humor. "I just had time off in Germany, remember? That's how we ended up here today."

"That was four months ago. Honestly, I've never met an officer before who hated taking time off as much as you." Graham stood abruptly, her patience clearly at an end. "Go, that's an order. I'm sure Kaminski can find another pilot to fly your shift. I don't want to see you back at work for at least a week."

Carmen could see fine lines from age as well as exhaustion on Graham's face. A few strands of gray shot through her dark hair, hinting at her age. She knew she should take a clue and leave, but Carmen could never shut her brain off. Thoughts of taking seven days had her doing mental calculations.

"Actually, that would turn into ten off. After my duty shift, I'm off for three and on again another three."

Carmen's teeth snapped shut when Graham shook her head. A glare of aggravation drew the dark brows down and Carmen quickly stood. "Sorry, Captain. I'll get out of your hair. Uh, one thing. Should I call the sarge or…?"

"I'll take care of it."

Graham turned to her desk and Carmen scooted out. She pulled the door closed and let out a breath when she heard it latch. Automatically, her eyes tracked to a nearby wall clock. The meeting lasted less than twenty minutes, but so much had changed. Carmen had no idea what to do. She needed to speak with Katie. She also needed to run all this by her neighbors. In truth, they were more family than neighbors. Joy and Ryan lived next door to the Bravo house since before Carmen's birth. She always knew she could count on them for sound advice, even if she didn't want to hear it.

Chapter Nine

Speaking with Katie hadn't done much to alleviate Carmen's anxiety. She still had more questions than answers. Indecision weighed heavily on her heart. She thought speaking to Joy and Ryan might provide more insight, but at the moment she craved silence. Carmen retrieved a glass of white wine from the fridge.

She padded through the house in stocking feet. Dressed casually in faded jeans and a button-down flannel shirt, she opted for the deck to sit and think. High cathedral ceilings with heavy wooden oak beams gave the home a cozy feel. The caramel colored hardwoods added to her comfort as she walked through the large kitchen and through the formal dining room. Carmen slid aside a French door and stepped onto a covered composite deck. The only things out here were a few chairs, a massive fire pit and the view.

Her home boasted two stories along with a completed basement. The basement served to elevate the first level to proper viewing height. From here on the deck, Carmen looked out upon a magnificent scene. Ice-capped mountains rose in the backdrop, grand, regal, and imposing. Birds flew overhead in a blue sky of scattered, fluffy clouds. The many trees in her area served to provide a sense of solitude and sanctuary. She took a deep breath of crisp, late winter air. Although the calendar proclaimed it February, the weather promised early spring.

With the sun on her face, Carmen settled onto a cushioned lawn chair. She used a remote to ignite the outdoor fire pit. As flames danced away the chill, she attempted to focus. Despite the monumental decision before her, she couldn't order her thoughts. The whole situation seemed surreal. She raised her glass to sip the wine as the phone rang at the exact same moment and she jumped a little. Carmen wiped a crystal drop from her chin and pulled the cell from her shirt pocket.

In typical fashion, Joy Sullivan launched into a full-blown discussion as soon as Carmen answered.

"Hi, we were on the phone with Matthew and Lindsey when you called. Ryan and I are heading out in the morning. I don't know if we'll be here for your birthday. It depends on what the weather does. Are you there?"

Carmen snorted a quiet laugh. She could picture Joy's animated features, blue eyes sparkling and a smile no one could resist. Even in her seventies, Joy's energy level put Carmen to shame.

"Yes, I'm here. How long are you guys going to be gone?"

"We're planning on ten days in Arizona. Ryan wants to stop overnight halfway coming and going. That'll make it two days each way, but it's better than a fifteen-and-a-half-hour drive."

"True. So, with driving time, you'll be gone two weeks?"

A quick pause ensued before Joy responded. "Almost. It'll end up being right at ten or twelve days. Ryan, get the clothes out of the dryer. So, did you need something?"

Carmen realized Joy had limited time so she got directly to the point. Her friends already knew about the Germany incident so it didn't take long. In minutes, Joy put her phone on speaker so her husband could join in. Carmen trusted these two implicitly. They were from a higher social status, but never gave any indication they felt superior, and they treated her like a daughter. Birthdays and major, as well as minor, holidays were shared across both households. Because of their close association, Carmen held nothing back. When she finished, Ryan was first to speak in grandfatherly tones.

"Would you need to decide right away or could you wait until we get back?"

"I don't think I'd have to make a decision anytime soon. They gave me a card and said to call when I make up my mind."

"Well, you know we don't want you to go anywhere. That said, it sounds pretty interesting. Hey, you can get me out of trouble if I shoot one of Hosey's cows."

Farmer Hosey maintained a hundred acres adjacent to their properties. His livestock escaped on a regular basis since he was too old and infirm to maintain the fence line. Hosey's son and daughter apparently had little interest in helping him out.

"You wouldn't do that. Just call the Sheriff's Department next time."

Carmen heard the impatience in Joy's voice as she redirected the conversation. "I imagine the job comes with a significant pay raise. You'd have to travel a lot, too. Who would take care of the house? I hope you aren't thinking about selling."

"Truthfully, I hadn't considered anything at all. I guess if I got stationed somewhere else, Della could live here."

"Uh uh," Joy stated firmly. "You are not letting that *woman* live in your house. You know she'd sell anything of value she finds."

Ryan added his thoughts. "She wouldn't keep the place up either. I know she's your sister and we shouldn't say anything."

"Yes, we should," Joy disagreed. "We love you, Carmen, but Della Bravo has taken advantage of your good nature enough. Whatever you decide, we'll support you. But you are not setting her up next door to us. Got it?"

"Yes, ma'am."

Carmen couldn't find it in her to defend her sister, no matter how much she knew she should. Joy and Ryan knew Della as well as they knew Carmen. They had witnessed her use and manipulate Carmen over and over.

"Now," Joy continued, "we've got to get busy. We're heading out before daylight tomorrow."

"Why don't you just fly? That would save you four days of travel time. You could probably go straight from Denver to Yuma without a layover."

Joy humphed. "You know I only fly first class and it's too short notice. We'd never get a seat. Besides, Ryan wants to drive the new truck."

"What about Minion? You're not taking her with you, are you?"

"No, we're going to board her this time. You know we usually like to take her, but the weather could turn anytime. She gets a little wound up sometimes. Ryan says it's distracting." Minion was a two-year-old, sixty-pound lab mix Ryan and Joy had adopted from the shelter.

"Are you leaving her with Charlie?" Carmen knew the woman in question. Ryan and Joy trusted her anytime they couldn't take the dog along. "Leave my number with her in case you need me to take anything over there."

Discussion shifted to trips people had lined up. Carmen mentioned Katie's upcoming visit to a ski lodge in Switzerland. In a way, she felt a little deserted in her hour of need.

"I like Katchoo. She has a good heart. You should marry that girl."

Carmen smiled at Joy's use of the nickname. "She's not gay, remember? And you know that we're just really good friends."

Soon after, Joy rang off. Carmen had no more answers than she did before the call. She hadn't time to dwell on the disappointing turn of events as the phone rang again almost immediately.

"Speak of the devil. Joy and I were just talking about you."

"All good things, I hope. Listen Carmen, I just had a great idea."

"Oh no, Katie. No good conversation with you ever started with those words."

"Now here me out," Katie insisted. "I want you to come on the trip with me."

"To a family reunion in Switzerland? Your family's liable to think we're a couple if we do that."

"Who cares? Europeans are very progressive. They wouldn't care a whit even if it were true."

Carmen wasn't the least bit surprised by the invitation. This was just like her compulsive friend. For half a second, Carmen considered saying yes. Reason finally intervened.

"I'd love to, Katie, but I can't. I have a coffee date with Sally tomorrow night. Plus, it's a little short notice to buy a plane ticket. Joy couldn't even get reservations for her and Ryan to fly to Yuma."

"Sally, that girl from Shawn and Becca's party? That's great honey, and I want all the juicy details later. Rest assured your date won't interfere with our plans. I've chartered a plane for the day after tomorrow. We'll fly out of Denver at dawn. All you need are your passport and ski clothes. You have to come. How many more chances will we have to take these spontaneous trips once you leave?"

Listening to Katie chatter made Carmen feel better than she had since leaving headquarters. Katie had a way of relieving stress with just her good intent and a few well-chosen words.

"It's a job, Katie. I'm not moving to the moon."

"Well, if you leave it might as well be the moon. You'll be working all the time. The best thing about the lodge is that my cousin owns it. You won't even have to pay for a room."

"Of course he does," Carmen mumbled. "Did you say you chartered a plane? Who does that?"

"What's the point of having money if you don't spend it? You have the time off and you need to get away to clear your head. What better place than a chateau in the Bernese Alps? You can almost feel the fresh powder under your feet."

As well as the trees I'll crash into, Carmen thought.

"Does this cousin know that you've invited a guest?"

"Lucien won't mind. Besides, I believe the lodge is a little rundown. He recently purchased the property and it needs some fixing up. Lucien will jump at the chance to entertain a potential investor. It's one of the reasons he wanted the family reunion there. I understand he's also invited a few old friends to check things over."

"I'm not an investor," Carmen pointed out.

"Don't tell him that. It'll be fun. What do you say?"

Carmen hesitated. She really couldn't think of a good argument to refuse. She enjoyed skiing and Katie had a point. Carmen worked so much she couldn't remember the last time she had fun in the snow. She'd just have to remember to call and request a few additional days off.

"Where are we going?"

"Yes! It's a small place in Lohner, Switzerland. If you look on a map, it's a little south of Adelboden. Oh, Carmen, you're going to have so much fun. You won't regret this."

"That's what you said last time."

Carmen stood on the tarmac of the small airfield in Zurich. The Swiss winter day had her shivering into her parka. Carmen had her gloved hands stuffed as far inside the pockets as she could and her feet were like blocks of ice. Despite the frigid twenty-degree temperature, the view alone made the fourteen-hour trip worthwhile.

Snow covered everything save for the airport tarmac. Even the evergreens carried a heavy dusting of the powder. She and Katie had deplaned from a roll up stairway set up on the airstrip. They stood around shivering while they awaited a shuttle to whisk them to the terminal. Carmen wished they'd stayed in the plane until it arrived.

"What do you think?" Katie whirled around once in excitement. "Isn't it beautiful?"

"It looks like a Christmas card," Carmen said, scrunching down so her collar blocked the frigid wind. "I'm actually glad I came, but I have one question."

"What?"

"Why aren't you sneezing? Your allergies always act up when we travel, but I haven't heard a sniffle out of you for the last twenty minutes."

Katie shrugged. "I guess the cold prevents me from having an allergic reaction to airborne pollens. Maybe I'll move here so I don't have to deal with all that anymore."

"If you do that, we really will never see each other again. I'm not turning into an ice cube on a regular basis just to visit." Carmen laughed when Katie stuck her bottom lip out and pouted. A black shuttle heading their way caught her attention and she forgot about their teasing banter. "Ah, I believe this is our ride."

The shuttle headed directly toward them. About thirty feet away, the vehicle abruptly heeled to the right and pulled up with the nose near the aircraft's aft section. Fortunately, the driver kept the speed down so as not to frighten the two women. A few seconds later, a woman emerged from the driver's door. Two men exited the rear of the shuttle and headed directly toward the plane.

"They're grabbing our luggage," Katie volunteered.

Carmen nodded, but her eyes stayed on the female driver who stalked in their direction. Straight dark hair reflected what little sunlight existed. Dark eyes, brown skin and high cheekbones proudly pronounced this woman's heritage. Combined with her short stature, aquiline nose and almond shaped eyes and Carmen guessed her to be Native American. A bouncy step hinted at good physical condition.

"Hi," the woman said with a wide smile. She held Carmen's gaze and offered a hand. "I'm Malia Bearcat. Welcome to the Alps." Carmen shook her hand before Malia turned and offered the same courtesy to Katie.

Carmen was content to watch the scene unfold. Katie began asking questions while Carmen took a second to check Malia out. She was surprised to find herself drawn to this stranger. Carmen had to admit, she hadn't enjoyed this feeling while having coffee with Sally the night before. If anything, her date with Sally turned out to be a bit of a letdown. All that saucy chemistry in the kitchen had sizzled into nothing. She tuned back into the discussion when Malia flicked a glance her way.

"Excuse me? Sorry, I missed that."

"You'll have to forgive her, Malia," Katie said. "Her brain is frozen."

Malia laughed. "I understand completely. I reacted the same way the first few years I lived here. I was just saying that as soon as the guys grab your gear, we'll head back inside. I believe Mister Caisson has arranged a car for you."

"You believe? Don't you know for sure?" Carmen asked. She wasn't concerned, merely curious. They could always rent a car should the need arise.

"Not my department. In fact, I'm not even the usual shuttle driver. I'm just helping out since Jerry had to take a lunch break. My ride is over there."

Malia nodded back toward the terminal building. Carmen followed her gaze and spotted a red and white helicopter with a red cross painted on the side.

"You're a pilot." Suddenly, Carmen was extremely interested in this woman. "So am I. I fly for the Denver Police Department."

Malia's smile grew even larger and she moved closer to Carmen. "You're a rotor jockey? I fly for Whitetracks. Some of the pilots work as medics. Others fly customers around to different lodges in the area. As you can see, mine is a medical chopper. What do you fly?"

Carmen and Malia launched into an animated discussion of their favorite pastime. As they spoke, Carmen found the distance between them shrinking. Soon, she could feel the heat from Malia's breath. She lost track of time as she found herself drawn into the dark gaze. Malia surprised her by deftly changing the subject.

"So, where are you headed?"

Carmen glanced at Katie, but her friend proved no help. Katie had walked away to supervise the ground crew loading their bags. "My friend there invited me to her cousin's lodge for a few days of skiing. It's in some place called Lohner? Does that sound right?"

Malia gave a sharp nod. "Yep, that tracks. I heard Lucien, Mister Caisson that is, bought a rundown chateau somewhere. I just didn't realize he chose that place, much less had it up and running. Bad karma, if you ask me."

"Why is that?"

"You don't know?" At her blank look, Malia shrugged once again. "Rumor has it that Tribulation Peak Lodge is what's left of an old buried village. About five years ago, one of the largest avalanches in area history buried a resort. I guess some people lost their lives, but the bodies were never found. From what I've heard, no one has ever discovered signs of any of the buildings either."

"Tribulation Peak? That sounds ominous. Surely something would have turned up once spring arrived." Carmen couldn't imagine an entire village vanishing without a trace.

"I'm just telling you what I've heard. Anyway, now that I know where you're headed, maybe I'll drop in for a visit while you're here. I wouldn't mind getting to know you better. If you're interested, that is."

A gust of wind blew Carmen's long hair into her face. She used the distraction of tucking it back under her beanie to buy time. "I actually really like the sound of that, but I don't know."

Carmen held her breath as Malia looked confused. The pensive expression made her even more attractive.

"Let me guess. You're seeing someone."

"No, not really. I mean we only had one date. That was just last night and it was only coffee."

Malia's expression cleared. "Good, then you're available. And don't worry, I'm not proposing marriage. You'll be leaving in a few days and I won't. Why not enjoy a little fun while you're here?"

Carmen couldn't argue with her logic. Nor did she have a chance as

Katie chose that moment to crash the party.

"Are you two finished? I'm freezing my buns off and we still have a three-hour drive to Lohner."

Carmen turned to Malia. "How far is Lohner from Adelboden?"

"Not far by helicopter. It's about an hour by car. Your friend is right though. You should head out if you want to make it to the lodge by dark. The weather forecast shows a system moving in tonight. No telling how much snow we'll get out of it. Believe me, you don't want to get caught out in a snowstorm in a car."

"In that case, we better get moving," Carmen agreed. "I look forward to seeing you again if you have time."

"Count on it. Save me a warm brandy."

Everyone loaded into the shuttle and Malia gave them a quick ride back to the terminal. Much to Carmen's disappointment, she vanished fairly quickly after that. The promised car already waited in front of the Zurich airport, but it took another twenty minutes before they were ready. Katie didn't have much to say after they climbed into the rear of a squarish black SUV. Carmen wondered if her friend was a little jealous of Malia's attention. She decided not to pursue the topic since she found that unlikely since Katie wasn't that way. Carmen leaned her head back against the cushions and closed her eyes. Her body finally relaxed in the heat of the car, luring her into a doze.

Thoughts drifted, tenuous, nebulous, and intangible. Exhaustion from an extended flight, the cold and now the sudden warmth made it difficult to keep her eyes open. Carmen considered the mystery of a possible avalanche-buried town. Fascinating! Tourists would flock to such a site. Tales of ghosts walking the area would burst into existence. Combined with the picturesque setting of the mountains and Lucien's venue, it sounded like a sure fire hit. Good thing for him. From what Katie told Carmen, her cousin desperately required a cash infusion. Bad investments had apparently siphoned off the bulk of his resources.

Carmen could do without the potential fallout of family reunion drama. Spending her free time on the slopes could alleviate that possibility. As the trip droned on, Carmen drifted again. Contentment lured her into a heavier sleep. Her head bobbed forward, bumping the glass window, and she briefly glanced at the passing countryside. She closed her eyes again, determined to rest while she could.

Suddenly, a gust of wind hit the side of the SUV. Carmen heard displaced air strike the window she leaned against. Carmen snapped awake. Wide-eyed, she scanned the area around the car. "What was that?"

The Humvee-type vehicle swayed sharply from the abrupt increase in pressure before the driver could compensate. Katie's fingers dug into Carmen's arm in her fright.

"The storm front has moved into the area sooner than expected." It took a moment for Carmen to adjust to the driver's heavy accent. "Do not worry. We shall arrive within the half hour."

Karl, Carmen remembered. His name was Karl. She felt as though sluggishly grasping for straws by attempting to remember his name. What did it matter? Except that it did. In times of stress, even the most mundane detail served to center her.

The updated arrival information surprised Carmen more than the weather. A quick glance at her watch confirmed Karl's assessment. She must really have slept hard. Sunlight that existed earlier had vanished into a slate gray sky heavy with the threat of snow. She could smell it in the air. Carmen sensed the oppressive weight of the impending blow in her skin.

Snow and bits of debris rushed across the roadway. Now and then, the wind attempted to push the car into a ravine. Carmen had initially thought the heavy vehicle safe for these conditions. Now she wasn't so sure. Despite the driver's words of comfort, Carmen noted his white-knuckled grip upon the wheel.

Darkness fell at an alarming pace. Not surprising given the season, but disconcerting given the conditions. The two lane blacktop ahead serpentined its way forward seemingly into infinity. Snow that had fallen so gently a short time ago surged across the road like flour dusted from a sifter. The overcast sky had grown thicker, with false twilight giving over to the real thing. Malia's words of warning echoed in Carmen's memory as a shiver traveled the length of her spine.

Her morbid imagination treated her to the picture of the car blown off the road from the severity of the storm. Images of frozen bodies trapped under a heavy snowdrift took weight and seconds stretched into hours in her mind as she pictured freezing to death in a ton of manmade steel. Her only hope at that point lay in Malia discovering the gelid corpses after the spring thaw.

Carmen closed her eyes and gave herself a mental shake. They weren't dead. This blow merely heralded an impending snowstorm. She repeated the mantra to herself, desperately essaying to ignore imagined portraits and real-life rumors of a long forgotten and buried town. The car tires stuttered suddenly, releasing their grasp to throw the car into a sideways swerve that thrust her stomach into her throat. In seconds, Karl managed to right the conveyance. Only then did Carmen realize she had clasped Katie's hand in a circulation-prohibiting grip.

"Sorry." Her lack of control embarrassed Carmen. At least in this darkness, Katie couldn't see her blush of shame. She eased up on her hold.

"No problem." Katie tightened her own grip even more.

Unaccountably, Carmen was reassured. There was something to the phrase about misery loving company. She gulped and briefly closed her eyes, silently praying for an end to the harrowing journey. Karl abruptly slowed the SUV and turned sharply to the left. Initially, Carmen thought he had given up driving and decided to wait out the storm on the side of the road.

Her heart ricocheted off her ribs at the thought, but Karl kept moving. After a moment, Carmen realized he had turned onto a narrow lane where trees pressed in closely on both sides, cutting down the worst of the wind. The car rose over a hilly crest and a structure emerged through the haze, dim lights glowing at the windows. While dark and foreboding, the prospect of arriving unscathed hit Carmen so intensely like a miracle that she bowed her head in relief. The structure might look like something out of a nightmare, but its existence promised sanctuary.

"We're here," she muttered before Karl had the opportunity.

Moments after her pronouncement, the SUV swerved onto an all but entirely snow-shrouded clearing and pulled directly in front of the lodge. Karl didn't bother to shut off the engine. Instead, he advised the passengers to offload their belongings as quickly as possible. Carmen was in full agreement. Almost before the vehicle stopped, she flung open the door. She sank up to her ankles in fresh powder, but pushed through the obstruction to the back. Snow hailed from the sky in a white, swirling barrage. Just as she reached the back end, the hatch popped open and slid upward. Carmen began to fling baggage onto the once pristine surface without consideration of the contents. Wind whipped the heavy flurries into her face, peppering her with particles that stung like needles. She could barely discern clear details a few feet in front of her.

Her first sight of the lodge failed to inspire confidence. Combined with the shriek of wind and blankets of snow, the resort loomed darkly in the close backdrop. Carmen could just make out lights behind window coverings on the lower floor. The upper part of the structure remained shrouded in Stygian portent. The building seemed in poor repair, like a haunted mansion from a horror movie. Even from her snow-obscured perspective, the chateau seemed to be missing a few pieces. On a second floor, one dark shutter dangled menacingly from a single upper hinge. The bottom hinge had apparently fallen away in a time long past. The forlorn shutter pitched to and fro in the near gale force winds, banging repeated against the resort's wooden exterior. Smoke curled from one of four fireplace chimneys, lending Carmen strength enough to swallow her trepidation.

Fear left her mouth dry, but she didn't care if Michael Myers owned this lodge. All she desired was to get inside out of the weather. In seconds, the intrepid Katie McClarin joined her. Carmen mostly noted her presence by the heat from her body. In this swirling dervish of blustering snow, body heat radiated like a furnace. Carmen always believed Katie a bit pampered, soft and somehow weaker. Her best friend proved how flawed her assessment. Katie tossed luggage like a lumberjack, without hesitation. Carmen had known Katie for years, but this performance showed her a new facet and a fresh insight. Never would she underestimate Katie again.

Gratitude for Katie's fortitude made Carmen's heart swell. Moments later, Karl and a few young men from inside the lodge joined them. The porters grappled with luggage, mostly Katie's. With bags tucked under each arm and both hands loaded, the porters led the way into the lit chateau. Carmen noted how her footsteps pressed deeply into the falling snow. She surged onto the short staircase leading upward, and a concentrated burst of air caused Carmen to stagger sideways. Her ribs impacted a powder-covered stair railing, saving her from a pitch onto the turf. Carmen sucked in a lungful of air and struggled upright. Her thoughts centered on a raging fire and a hot drink. Almost reflexively, she grabbed Katie's forearm as the shorter woman slipped in the snow.

"I have you." The wind snatched away Carmen's words.

A heavy oaken door opened and porters crossed the threshold. Carmen focused on the sight of artificial light and imagined heat. Seconds later, she crossed that imaginary plane to succor and salvation, Katie in tow. The door slammed, either from the storm or from some unknown benefactor. All Carmen knew was that they had endured to evade certain death. Heat bloomed on her cheeks as they escaped the raging storm.

Carmen almost sobbed in relief.

"Welcome."

An unfamiliar male voice punctuated the truth that she really had survived. When Katie sagged against her, she knew she wasn't alone in her reaction. Carmen pulled herself together. She drew in a steadying breath, sniffled against the cold and straightened to face their host. Although Carmen hadn't noticed previously, they stood inside an ornate and formal entryway. Black and white marble lay under their feet. A highly polished wooden staircase lay at the center. Steps rose up to a second level where the landing split into two directions. A heavy, golden chandelier hung suspended overhead. Weak electric lights encircled the exterior, resembling an artifact straight from the Titanic. Standing only four steps above her stood a man who reminded Carmen of Count Dracula.

This man generated a whole new appreciation of fear. He was almost gaunt, his white hair reflecting artificial lights, with pale flesh and he wore period garments. Light reflected from his deep purple cape, tan breeches and knee-high brown boots. Carmen could have sworn she witnessed a diamond pinky ring glint from the stranger's left hand as it reflected in the chandelier's glow. At that moment, she truly didn't care if he possessed horns. A little fear didn't matter. It was good for the circulation. Right?

"Lucien," Katie breathed, shocking Carmen into reality. "Thank God we made it."

Carmen echoed the sentiment, yet she remained silent. Apprehension and frozen limbs robbed her of her voice. The recent ordeal rendered her very nearly incapable of speech and in that instant she could only look around as though dazed. Carmen remained content to observe as Lucien descended the remaining few steps to join them. He gathered Katie into his arms for a brief embrace. Despite the disjointed sensation, his gesture seemed forced. Disingenuous. He air-kissed each side of Katie's cheek. Carmen realized that in her relief, Katie didn't seem to notice. She fell into his embrace and tears shimmered in her eyes.

Carmen loudly cleared her throat, deliberately breaking into the moment. "I'm sorry to interrupt. I'm worried about Karl. The storm is pretty bad."

Lucien stepped away from Katie. He grasped her hands as he withdrew and took an inordinate amount of time as he gazed into her eyes. For a moment, Carmen entertained the idea that he deliberately ignored her. Then he turned to address her directly. His Prussian blue eyes stood out in counterpoint, leaving her mesmerized by the unusual color.

"I assure you that Karl is well. Even as we speak, he pulls into the heated garage. Karl will dwell in a cabin I have established specifically for this happenstance. I have already had a fire laid for him. Fear not."

If it weren't for his absolute sincerity and her exhaustion, Carmen might have found it within her to argue. Instead, stiffness flooded from her muscles like air from a punctured tire. "Glad to hear it. I'm Carmen Bravo and I hate to be rude, but I feel like I've been pulled backward through a turbine engine. Is there any way to get a coffee? And maybe a bathroom?"

"Of course. Please forgive my lack of foresight." Lucien released Katie's hands to approach Carmen. When only a few paces away, he stopped and stared directly into her eyes. "I regret your experience. Unfortunately, the squalls in these mountains oft times descend abruptly. My people will see your bags to your rooms. In the meantime, please, I invite you to enjoy the fire I have stoked for your comfort. I am relieved to see you all safe. The weather service did not predict a blizzard to develop from such an innocuous front."

Katie exclaimed in surprise at the word blizzard, but Carmen stopped listening. She turned back toward floor to ceiling windows. Heavy draperies covered them in order to repel the cold. Carmen couldn't resist drawing one panel aside to peer into the tumultuous night. The monochromatic world outside caused a chill to climb up her spine and chafe her neck. Swirling snow struck the glass panes with a roar that resembled a ravening beast. Darkness competed for dominance with the tempest. Carmen had once heard a phrase describing winter as a season of death. Never until now had she experienced the truth of that statement in her bones. She allowed the drapery to fall back into place, standing stationary to consider the implications.

She jumped when something brushed her shoulder. Her heart leapt into her throat as she spun around.

"Katie! You scared ten years off me."

"Sorry. I called your name twice, but you seemed captivated."

Carmen swallowed hard and shrugged, speechless for a moment. A brief memory of the limo tires shuddering to grip the road flashed. Newly acquired reality crashed down to meld with the hard truth of human frailty. Without question, Carmen knew all would have died had they crashed.

"I've never seen anything like it before. The blizzard is impressive."

Katie flashed a smile holding little amusement. "That's one word for it. Come on, Lucien has hot drinks and a snack waiting for us by that gorgeous fire."

Lucien gestured with his left hand to punctuate Katie's statement. Only then did Carmen glance over to note a massive blaze in an obscenely huge stone fireplace. The flames roared from a stately gathering room not thirty paces away. Natural pale granite lined a hearth twice the size of any she'd ever seen as the heat radiated into the foyer. Without another word, Carmen drifted as though hypnotized toward the flames. She sank onto the hearth and stared into the inferno, lost in the fiery dance and folded her hands together on her thigh. Carmen slumped slightly, exhaustion, relief and finally blessed warmth permeating her being. The flames threw a golden glow across the floor and the furniture, chasing away shadows from the room and from inside Carmen's heart.

Katie joined her seconds later. "Are you okay?" she asked after a moment.

"I'm good." Carmen swallowed hard to clear a dry throat. "I've never experienced anything like that storm. Now I understand all the stories I've heard of people freezing to death."

A hand rested over hers in a reassuring grip. Katie tightened her hold before responding. "I thought the snow was so pretty while we were at the airport. Now, I'm just glad we're out of it. There is a positive side to this though. Once the storm blows itself out, the skiing will be amazing."

Carmen smiled and closed her eyes briefly. "Trust you to find the positive side of things. What you haven't considered is that this blizzard will likely leave us snowed in for days."

"Then this will be your chance to get away from it all. You *are* here to forget about things for a while."

A small commotion near the sitting room entrance drew Carmen's attention. Servers pushed silver trolleys loaded with snacks, small plates and steaming pots surrounded by small cups. Carmen smelled strong coffee and bitter tea. Her mouth salivated and her stomach rumbled. In moments, food and drinks covered a nearby round table. The servers lost no time in heading toward the door. They shared several sharp words with Lucien before exiting.

Lucien's expression quickly cleared when he saw Carmen observing. "Uh, the help is leaving now. They will not return until after the storm has cleared."

"In other words, it'll be three days before they come back," Katie murmured in an aside to Carmen. "We'll probably starve to death by then. Do the words Donner Party mean anything to you? I say we eat Lucien first."

Chapter Ten

As her bones thawed, Carmen became aware of other occupants in the room. Aside from herself and Katie, six others resided on various period furnishings. Five men and one woman wore expressions ranging from sympathy to irritation to boredom. The female stranger affected the latter. Striking in visage, the woman couldn't bother to look her way. Twenty-something, brunette, brown eyes and high cheekbones hinted at an aristocratic heritage. She wore an expensive cut red pantsuit complete with a matching North Face parka. The arctic jacket boasted a fur-lined collar. Sling back heels, of all things, completed her ensemble. Sepia brown eyes floated lazily around the room, assessing and bypassing furnishings of a by-gone era and people alike. In counterpoint to her air of superiority, the woman perched on the arm of a French Louis style winged-back Bergere chair. A dichotomy existed between the woman and the man who occupied the seat beside her.

Where the woman's aquiline features hinted at European heritage, the man clearly hailed from somewhere in the Middle East. He seemed small in comparison to his wife. At least Carmen thought the younger woman his wife, judging by the matching rings. The man offered Carmen a smile before raising a hand to smooth thinning brown hair. He seemed at least twenty years the woman's senior. While he offered compassion in his smile, his style of clothing matched his wife in opulence.

Another man cleared his throat, drawing Carmen's attention. Average in stature, with lank blonde hair and round glasses, this man stood leaning one hip against the wall. The very top of his head glinted in the muted light, testament to premature balding.

"Welcome to the frozen tundra. My name is Charles Wrighton III. I'm sure you've heard of me." The Englishman offered a clipped bow and raised a blonde eyebrow, as though inviting Carmen to gush some meaningless praise. "No? Author of *Love's Boundless Glory*?"

"I'm sorry. It doesn't sound familiar."

"My dear woman, I am a world-renowned romance novelist. Surely, you've heard of *Naked Flame*?"

Again, Carmen could only offer a baffled shrug. Wrighton seemed to deflate in his brown three-piece suit and heavy tweed coat. He clamped a Sherlock Holmes type pipe into the corner of his mouth. To Carmen, Wrighton lacked only a monocle to go with the pompous attitude. After a second, his expression brightened suddenly.

"No matter. I'm sure the frigidity of the environment has temporarily affected your sense of recall. Allow me to make introductions. This lady and her esteemed spouse are Sahari and Tiffany Nazem. Mister Nazem is a quite industrious oil baron, if I'm not mistaken."

The woman, Tiffany, failed to respond to the introduction. Doe soft eyes had drifted to and focused upon the fireplace conflagration. Sahari scowled at Wrighton's descriptor, but offered Carmen a polite nod.

Wrighton moved on without pause, waving a hand toward another man to his left. This person's hair was so blonde that it competed with the paleness of the swirling snow outside. Lean, pale of face and light of eye, this stranger sat center in a lime-colored settee that resided at an angle from Carmen.

"This gentleman is Pymer Skullen. He is a local man. I'm not sure if he intends to invest in Lucien's enterprise, but that does seem to be the reason for our presence, yes?"

Pymer didn't react to Wrighton's boorish remarks. Instead, he scooted to the settee edge, hands gently clasped between denim covered thighs. Pymer wore a cozy looking cable knit sweater, but no coat. Of everyone present, he seemed least affected by the cold.

"Don't mind Charles," Pymer said with a crooked smile. "He means well, I suppose. In fact, I live over the next hill in Adelboden. Lucien and I have been friends since primary school. I am here to enjoy the skiing and this lovely reunion, though I fear that will not take place now. Surely no one save the eight of us will be present once this storm blocks the roads. That said, I am pleased you arrived safely."

The compassion in his earnest expression eased the dread in Carmen's body. She relaxed slightly. "Thank you. Things got a little dicey there toward the end. I'm Carmen, by the way, Carmen Bravo. This is my friend, Doctor Katie McClarin."

"Hi," Katie said simply.

"Of course. You're Lucien's cousin. He speaks highly of you. Are you a medical doctor?"

Katie shook her head. "I'm a psychiatrist."

Pymer smiled politely and completed the introductions by indicating the remaining men in the room. Kofi Gowan stood by the tea service, pouring a steaming cup. Dark of hair and skin, his complexion matched almost perfectly with his black trousers, loafers and heavy coat. He did offer a brief smile, but deigned not respond as Pymer explained Kofi's profession as a diamond exporter from South Africa. The final member of their group appeared sullen and withdrawn. Nose somewhat elevated, the man with close-cropped red hair and freckles joined Kofi at the snack table.

He loaded a small plate with bite-sized morsels before brushing an errant crumb from the lapel of an immaculate and clearly newly purchased blue puffer coat. Apparently, as an investment banker from Modesto, California, Mike Doyle saw no need to interject a comment or even acknowledgment.

Carmen thought someone in his late thirties or early forties might develop some manners. Apparently not. Of those present, only Pymer, Kofi, Sahari and Wrighton showed any friendliness. Of those, one kind of creeped her out. Wrighton stared at Katie as though casting her as lead for an upcoming romance novel.

"Quite an eclectic group," Carmen observed. "I assume almost everyone is here for the investment opportunity?"

"Almost everyone," Pymer insisted. "As I said, I am here for the food, the party, and the skiing."

"As long as the yeti doesn't eat us first, that is."

All eyes turned to Wrighton. His tone carried amusement, but Carmen noted the seriousness of his expression. Almost immediately, he seemed embarrassed. A flush climbed his throat and took up residence on his cheeks. Wrighton's jaw tightened as he clamped down on the pipe.

Kofi the diamond exporter turned away from the food, showing true interest for the first time. His dark gaze assessed Wrighton intently. When he spoke, Carmen noticed that his accent sounded more refined than that of the Englishman.

"Come now, you don't truly believe in such tales. They are nothing but childish nonsense."

"My good man, perhaps you weren't paying attention. I am a novelist. It behooves one of my profession to remain open to all manner of possibilities."

"Excuse me." Katie broke into the discussion from beside Carmen. "It's said that after Alexander the Great conquered his kingdom, the next thing he wanted was to see a yeti. Tales of such creatures predate 300 B.C."

Carmen wasn't surprised by Katie's knowledge. Her friend was a veritable treasure trove of unusual trivia. That Katie actually defended the hypothesis of yeti did catch her off guard.

"You believe in yeti?" Carmen couldn't resist asking. In the last hour, Katie had managed to surprise her twice. "I've known you for years, yet sometimes I don't feel like I know you at all."

Katie patted Carmen's knee and offered a sad looking smile. "How well does one person truly know another?"

"Here, here!" Wrighton's voice was loud enough to make the recalcitrant Mike Doyle jump slightly. "Stories of Sasquatch, Yeti, and Bigfoot have circulated for centuries. I believe they are in fact related to Neanderthal, which any scientist worth their salt will say most surely existed."

Kofi scoffed, a harsh sound deep in his throat. "Then why has no proof ever been found? A bone or a single strand of DNA? You might as well believe in aliens."

Carmen remembered her college anthropology classes. The same discussion, almost verbatim, had once taken place then. At the time, such musings struck her as absurd. In this setting, with the howling wind causing the lodge to creak and groan, with snow piling up by the foot, she reluctantly revised her narrow opinion.

"Neanderthals were cannibals." Carmen spoke softly, not so much arguing in favor as pointing out possibilities. "They didn't bury bodies. They ate them. As for aliens, I'm quite certain life exists somewhere else. I'm not convinced an alien has ever visited Earth, but considering the size of the galaxy, I think it's pretty arrogant to believe we're alone."

The conversation ended abruptly after Carmen's pronouncement. Either she had left them speechless or everyone suddenly felt as wrung out as she did. People, including Katie, wandered toward the food and beverages. Carmen kept her seat, but gratefully accepted the steaming cup of black coffee Katie brought back for her.

A short time later, Lucien returned. He entered the sitting room with a sway of his cape and a twinkle in his pale eyes. "Your rooms are ready. If you will all please follow me."

Carmen wanted to stay by the fire. For a brief moment, she considered offering to wait until Lucien escorted the others to their accommodations. One look at Katie's raised eyebrow changed her mind. Katie had a way of challenging her with only a simple gesture.

Carmen rolled her eyes and placed the empty cup on the stone hearth. She stood and sighed in an overly dramatic fashion. She snagged a sandwich on the way out of the room. "I am never visiting you if you move here. I can't feel my toes and intuition tells me those rooms will be as cold as a meat locker."

"Oh, Carmen. Where's your sense of adventure?"

"I left it at the airport."

Carmen shivered. She kept her eyes closed, attempting to force Morpheus to return. She burrowed deeper into the heavy, albeit musty-scented, covers, tucking her face under despite the smell. Her body had generated warmth that she enjoyed briefly. Moments later, she decided she couldn't breathe. Carmen snorted in disgust and finally gave up. She flung the covers aside and bounded out of the bed. Goosebumps erupted as she dove toward her heavy winter clothing. Fortunately, she had possessed the foresight to lay out her intended outfit across a chair the night before.

A quick glance told her the blaze in the ancient and soot-covered fireplace had gone out long ago. Cold ashes and the lack of scarlet embers explained the chill in the room. Cracked mortar and time-worn stone struck her as somewhat forlorn without the cheery flames.

Shivering so hard she thought her bones might shatter, Carmen didn't bother to sit as she stuffed herself into a thick sweater, jeans and a blue and white down parka. A sigh of relief escaped her after cramming her feet into socks and heavy brown boots. Blessed warmth permeated her muscles and she closed her eyes to revel in the sensation. A thump at the door interrupted the moment.

"Yes, who is it?"

"It's Katie. Open the door."

The scent of strong coffee assaulted her nose as soon as she opened the door. Katie balanced a loaded silver tray between both hands. The tray held a large ceramic pot that oozed steam into the air along with a covered plate and two empty mugs. Carmen had no idea what secrets lay under the lidded plate, her attention focused on only one thing. Another source of heat that she could consume. Katie eluded Carmen's grasp for a mug as she struck out across the room for a small table that inhabited a cobweb-riddled corner.

Carmen followed without delay, snatching a ceramic mug from the tray before Katie could set it down. Wordless for the moment, Katie filled her mug. Carmen cradled the heat between her palms before she took a large sip that burned all the way down her throat and exploded in her belly. The ice lodged there slowly began to melt.

"My hero. It seems Cousin Lucien hasn't gotten around to servicing the central heat yet. I'm freezing my girls and my toes off." She stamped her feet for emphasis. A pointed look toward the cobwebs preceded her next observation. "I guess he hasn't hired a cleaning crew for this place yet either."

Katie smiled and lifted the covering from a huge pile of pastries. Carmen snatched up something slathered in gooey chocolate. She inhaled half of it in a single bite. A large dollop of Bavarian cream trailed down her chin before she interrupted the flow. Katie filled her own mug as Carmen quickly sucked the cream from her thumb.

"He did have the heat serviced, actually." Katie slid into a chair on one side of the table. "It went down in the storm last night. Pymer's out there trying to repair it now. Apparently, he's some kind of mechanical genius. Phone service is out too, but Lucien says he has a satellite phone for emergencies. Apparently all the resorts in the Alps carry one. As for the cleaning crew, I don't think they're the only ones who haven't been contacted."

"What do you mean?" Carmen didn't like the sound of that.

"I found out this morning that Lucien hasn't invited anyone else. There is no family reunion. This was all a ruse to draw people he specifically expected to invest in the lunacy of this lodge." Katie sounded put out, but refrained from a derogatory remark about her cousin. Instead, she sniffed against the cold and sipped at her coffee.

"Devious. I wonder what else he hasn't told us." Carmen finished her pastry and reached for another. She studied it briefly. "If Pymer is working on the heat, I guess at least the snow has stopped. That's something."

"Yes, but it's like we feared. The roads are closed and there's no telling when the plows can get through, if they come at all. This place is rather off the beaten track and Lucien says we got more than a foot of snow overnight. From the way he's acting, that's some kind of record."

"Crap. We could be here until spring." Carmen was already cold. She could imagine herself freezing to the hearth trying to suck as much heat as possible from a meager wood fire.

Katie smiled again, discarding her gloomy expression from earlier. She raised her half empty cup in mock salute. "Let's just hope Pymer can get the heat going. On a more interesting note, we had a break-in last night."

Carmen choked on her coffee and wiped her mouth with the back of her hand. "What? Someone broke into the lodge? How's that even possible? No one could have survived that blizzard for long and we're in the middle of nowhere. Did they steal anything?"

"That's just it. Mister Wrighton swears it was a yeti and the thing was only after food."

"Not that again." Carmen rolled her eyes.

"Last night you seemed to think they were real enough."

"In theory," Carmen stressed. "Now tell me about this break-in."

An elegant one-shouldered shrug attended Katie's explanation. "Wrighton went in search of a cup of tea this morning before anyone else stirred. He discovered the kitchen door almost torn from its hinges. Lucien entered a few moments later to prepare breakfast. He corroborated the story saying that the door hung open and snow covered the floor, blown in by the storm no doubt. Both of them swear to having seen huge, man-shaped footprints. The fridge was still open and a thawed pork roast appeared to be the only casualty."

Carmen snorted in disbelief. "Just because they found large footsteps doesn't mean it was a yeti. Anyone could have wandered inside."

"You don't understand. The footprints weren't made by a pair of boots. They were bare footprints."

"No way. A person out running around barefoot would have frostbite in nothing flat. I don't buy it. Maybe it was a bear."

"A bear that knows how to open doors?"

"Why not? Animals are a lot cleverer than people give them credit for, but you do have a point. I think Wrighton could have staged the whole thing before Lucien showed up. More fodder for his next book and whatnot."

"Maybe. At any rate, I don't believe a yeti wandered in out of the cold right after we finished discussing them. Wrighton probably exaggerated the whole thing. He does seem to enjoy the sound of his own voice."

"He's a writer," Carmen pointed out. "Even if it's only romance, his job is to have an active imagination. Could be he helps fuel that imagination by embellishment."

"What's wrong with romance?"

"No plot. Hey, have you heard anything about Karl? Is he okay?"

"Lucien said he's fine. Apparently he and his wife stay at a cabin on the property. I guess Lucien likes keeping him around in case he needs to go anywhere."

"Can't drive himself, huh?" Carmen held up a hand, interrupting the conversation as she listened intently. Air rushed into the room from a mysterious source. "Hey, do you hear that? I think the heat's on."

"Wonderful! Now that we won't freeze to death, can I interest you in checking out the area? Hey, how do you feel about some sledding this weekend?"

Carmen arched an eyebrow and shrugged. "Why not? We can bring an orthopedic surgeon with us when we go."

After a long and gloriously hot shower, Carmen braced herself to face the day. She thumped down the steps in insulated hiking boots and spotted people occupying the main gathering room. A perpetual fire roared in the same oversized hearth as the previous night, lending a cheery ambiance to the space. Wrighton dealt cards onto a table that appeared made of oak. It occupied the space directly in front of where he sat in a wingback chair. No doubt he'd confiscated the piece from somewhere else for his own personal use.

Pymer stood a few paces from Wrighton near one of the floor to ceiling windows. He wiped his hands on a grimy cloth as the two spoke. Wrighton seemed to do most of the talking, going on about one of his literary creations. A third person occupied the room and Carmen smiled when she spotted Katie. Katie had beaten her downstairs, looking quite refreshed as she occupied her customary place upon the hearth.

Despite the frigid temperatures Denver reached in winter, this place was far more extreme. Carmen decided that Katie experienced the cold as intensely as she did, hence her perch only a few feet from the blaze.

Katie nodded in greeting to Carmen. She smoothed a loose strand of hair behind her ear and spoke to Pymer. "Thank you for fixing the heat. We're lucky you were here."

Pymer flapped his rag in the air and his cheeks flushed. "It is no concern. I enjoy using my hands. I should have the ski lifts operational by early afternoon as well."

"That's great news." Carmen entered the room and headed for a seat beside Katie. She noticed the pink in Pymer's cheeks and thought it sweet how he seemed so shy. "I was worried the lift wouldn't function after that blizzard."

The room seemed much warmer than the previous night. Combined with the good news, Carmen couldn't help but feel that things were looking up. Then again, she hadn't just entered the lodge in near white out conditions.

Someone had thrown open the curtains and sunlight streamed into the room. A glance outside showed a pristine blanket of white. Fresh powder glinted in the bright new day, standing out sharply where it rested on the bows of evergreens. The sun reflected off the white drifts, causing the snow to wink merrily in the bright new day. From her vantage point, the trees seemed still, meaning that even the wind rested calm.

"As I was saying," Wrighton's gaze stayed on the cards he flipped one by one onto the table. "My first novel, *Love's Fierce Heart*, made the New York Times best seller list within the first week of its publication." Flip went another card. "Of course, I wasn't surprised in the least. I still consider it my best work, if I may be so bold."

Carmen swallowed hard. The arrogance shown last night was apparently not a fluke. She wondered how long Katie wanted to sit and listen to this. Maybe she would find that breakneck sledding she'd mentioned earlier more preferable. Like right now.

In mid-flip, Wrighton pinned Carmen with a beady-eyed gaze. "Would you ladies care for a game of cards? It's really too cold outside for anything else. Additionally, I could regale you with the plot of my latest novel while we play."

Katie fidgeted beside Carmen. Her expression appeared tight. "Um, you mean like poker or something?"

Wrighton had the nerve to bat his eyelashes in what he obviously considered a coquettish manner. It reminded Carmen of a sleepy snake, especially when paired with his smarmy grin.

"In truth, I thought something more along the lines of *strip* poker. It would help to fuel my...creative juices."

The mental image set Carmen's teeth on edge and sent a shudder of disgust through her midsection. That was enough. She stood abruptly, hauling Katie up by the bicep beside her.

"No thanks. I prefer mystery to horror."

Pymer's blue eyes widened. He spun away from Wrighton and slapped the greasy rag over his mouth. Great guffaws of laughter made his shoulders and wavy blond hair shake. He bent over slightly, bracing himself with a hand upon the window sill.

Katie looked at Carmen in shock, eyes twinkling in mirth.

Wrighton wasn't nearly so amused. His face flushed and the veins in his neck stood out so sharply Carmen feared they might rupture. The remaining cards in Wrighton's fist never stood a chance. He crushed them in a single squeeze.

"What she means to say is that we have plans to check out the proposed ski areas. Lucien has the snowmobile waiting for us."

Carmen grunted and zipped her parka up to her throat. "Sure, Katie. That's what I meant. Let's get out of here."

The Lynx snowmobile rested at the base of the lodge's main steps. Someone had thoughtfully started the machine so it could warm up in advance. A helmet and ski goggles hung from each handlebar. Carmen tugged her gloves up tighter and slid onto the seat. She heard Katie snickering behind her, but kept her gaze firmly fixed upon the helmets. After selecting the red one for her own use, Carmen passed the yellow helmet off to Katie.

"Carmen, that was rude." Katie still chuckled, but didn't hesitate to cram the helmet onto her frosted blonde hair.

"When we get back, I'd like to take a look at the back door. Maybe I can figure out what, or who, really broke in last night. I bet it was a person."

The mirth in Katie's eyes died and her lips tightened. Even under the helmet, the concern in her gaze transmitted clearly. "What is going on with you? It's not like you to let someone get under your skin so easily. Although, I will admit Wrighton deserved it."

Carmen twisted the throttle with her right hand. The roaring sound of the engine unaccountably helped to settle the anger burning through her blood. She allowed the noise to die away while gathering her thoughts.

"He just made me so angry. I didn't come all this way to listen to some wanna be perv. Strip poker! Really? Is that the best he could do?" Carmen looked into Katie's eyes again. That wasn't quite the truth. Guilt forced her to reconsider the reason for prevaricating. Katie deserved the truth, but Carmen wasn't sure she even knew what bothered her. "I know, I know…I overreacted. I deal with leches like Wrighton every day."

"Then what is it?" Katie slid onto the seat behind her and rested her hands upon Carmen's hips.

"I don't know, really." Carmen reached inside herself, trying hard to put the feeling of dread into words. "Everyone here is so strange. Cousin

Lucien dresses and acts like Count Dracula. Then there are the rest of them. Wrighton is the most outspoken, but I'm not sure he's the worst of the lot. Don't tell me you haven't noticed it. There's just something off about this place. I feel it, like something dark and malignant just waiting to spring out and rip us apart." Carmen stopped talking and slid the helmet over her dark head.

"Wow. That's not melodramatic at all. And not like you either, Carmen."

"I know." Carmen nodded and looked over the snow scape, trying to decide where to go first. "It's probably nothing. Let's go find a good place to sled."

Chapter Eleven

Carmen and Katie rode the snowmobile all over Lucien's proposed winter wonderland. They couldn't possibly traverse the entire five hundred odd acres in a single winter-shortened day, but that was fine with Carmen. She enjoyed the snow, watching white rabbits dart through the undisturbed terrain as they bolted from the sound of the snowmobile. Once, Katie pointed out a small red fox and a deer-like creature with thick, ridged horns. Carmen thought it was an ibex, but she wasn't completely versed in Swiss animals. All of this peace, as well as the animals she saw, would vanish once humankind arrived.

Lucien had already marked ski runs, varying with numerous double diamond signs down to a few bunny slopes. He planned for two lifts to carry customers everywhere. Assuming he received the backing needed, this place could be a gold mine. That sad truth made Carmen all the more grateful to be here now before the press of humanity intruded on this sanctuary.

She stopped the Lynx atop a large piste adjacent to a marker depicting a blue square, high enough to look down upon the chateau and the surrounding clearing from the intended intermediate run. She wondered if Lucien planned to give the runs cutsey names such as Devil's Backbone or Glory Hole. She chuckled slightly, considering that he might take suggestions at this early stage.

From here, she could imagine the resort fully restored to its former glory. Carmen could envision areas where food and beverage carts would fit in. Faint snowmobile tracks led from a cabin to the rear of the resort. Several other cabins lay nestled in a loose cluster. From this distance she couldn't determined the exact number and Carmen wasn't sure if Lucien planned to rent those out during the ski season. Pristine snow-capped mountains, blue skies, evergreens and fresh powder rendered her speechless. It really was a living postcard. The beauty before her caused a lump to grow in her throat.

"Wait until all the runs are active." Katie leaned over Carmen's right shoulder and called out to be heard through their helmets. "Lucien plans forty-five runs and two lifts."

Carmen only nodded, thinking how much work needed to be done. It took more than marked ski slopes and a few lifts for a successful resort. Perhaps Cousin Lucien had developers interested in building shops and restaurants nearby. A darker patch of ground on the far side of the lodge caught her eye. From this height she could see far into the winter-denuded trees behind the cabins. The area stood out from the stark white setting.

"What's that?" Carmen pitched her voice to carry over the engine noise as she pointed toward an elevated area. The patch in question rested awkwardly amongst the evergreens. While covered in snow, darker borders near the base outlined an obviously artificial structure.

"Where? I don't see anything. Come on, Carmen, let's head in. My butt's freezing to the seat."

A shiver traveled over Carmen, encouraging her to agree. They had ridden for hours and the sun had passed its zenith. Her fingers and toes felt like lumps of ice. She could use a late lunch anyway and the strange terrain would be there later. A quick nod and Carmen slapped her visor down into place. The thought of a minor mystery reminded Carmen of the recent break-in Katie had mentioned. She turned the Lynx toward the lodge and gunned the engine. The intense cold had her body craving calories. Rather than her standard black coffee, Carmen wanted hot chocolate with tiny marshmallows. Either that or a warm brandy.

After parking in front of the steps, Carmen shucked her helmet as fast as she could. Katie still beat her up the stairs, eschewing to wait for her. Carmen grinned at her friend's haste, but took time to shut down the machine and neatly suspend the helmets from the handlebars. She stomped the snow from her feet before following Katie inside.

Heat, both artificial and fire-generated, hit Carmen like a wall. After spending hours outdoors, the warmth embraced her like an all over body caress. Carmen loved snow sports, but there was nothing like a thawing fire and a hot drink after. From the sparkle in Katie's eyes, her friend felt the same way. A heavenly aroma filled the air, a combination of smoke from the fire and cooking food wafting somewhere inside the lodge.

Three other people already occupied the great room, partially answering Carmen's question as to why she hadn't seen another person enjoying the snow. She had spotted Pymer working at one point, but no one having fun. Tiffany occupied her husband's chair from the night before. Now, she dressed in a posh pink and white ski outfit, complete with a striped beanie and puffer coat. She looked bored. Her husband, Sahari, stood in the corner speaking in low tones with Mike Doyle. While Carmen surveyed the room, Katie ignored them all and headed for her favorite seat perched on the fireplace hearth.

Her friend had a bounce in her step that Carmen hadn't seen in quite some time. Years, in fact. Carmen wondered if Katie had truly enjoyed life since Jack died. No, that couldn't be right. Katie laughed and teased all the time. Still, Carmen realized that the light had never quite reached her eyes like this since the tragic night her husband died. If playing in the snow, and the lack of allergies here made Katie so happy, Carmen figured that made the whole trip worth anything.

"What?" Katie scooped the beanie off her head. She watched Carmen with a questioning gaze. "Is something wrong?"

"No, not at all. I'm just glad you're having a good time. Who's up for a hot drink?"

"Definitely me. Are you headed for the kitchen to check the scene of the crime like you flatfoots like to say?" Katie yanked off her gloves and dropped them beside her along with the beanie.

Tiffany ignored their conversation, as usual, her gaze fixed on the scenery outside the large window. Sahari and Mike continued to speak in low tones near the far corner of the room. They stood as far as possible from anyone else while still being in the same space. On occasion, they glanced toward Carmen before turning their backs to her in a pointed way. Carmen hadn't a clue what they whispered about, but that nagging sense of something wrong made her scalp prickle.

"Carmen?" Katie stared at her in concern.

"Sorry. I guess I'm just tired. As for your question, yes. I'm headed to the kitchen. How does hot chocolate sound?"

"Like heaven. See if you can find something to eat while you're in there."

Carmen nodded and headed off to where she thought the kitchen lay. Basically, she planned to follow her nose. She heard Katie ask Tiffany about skiing, but passed out of range before the standoffish woman replied. If she bothered. Carmen thought Tiffany seemed depressed. Probably bored with her husband's apparent interest in only conducting business and ignoring her. Maybe Katie could interest Tiffany in playing in the snow. Making friends might bring Tiffany out of her shell.

The aroma of mouth-watering food lured Carmen to the kitchen like a fish to bait. Her stomach rumbled, reminding her that she hadn't eaten anything filling in almost a full day. The finger sandwiches last night and a few donuts this morning didn't really count as food.

Carmen discovered quite the scene when she walked into the room, easily the largest kitchen she'd ever seen outside of a restaurant. The usual commercial grade double sink, huge refrigerator, cabinets and dishwasher lined the wall to her left. In the center of the room stood a wooden-topped prep area almost as long as the room. Currently, so much colorful food and containers covered the butcher's block that Carmen couldn't identify anything specifically. Pots and pans dangled above the island from a bronze-colored ceiling pot rack.

None of these things surprised Carmen more than the cook. A strange woman stood in front of a double door gas range with at least ten burners on top. The heavy-set woman wore a once-white apron. Wisps of graying black hair stood out from sweat-soaked temples as she juggled with various boiling pots, stirring this and glancing into that.

Two other occupants looked up from the wooden table in the corner and smiled at her. Carmen smiled back, happy to see Karl seeming quite healthy. She absently noted this was the first table she had seen that wasn't circular.

"Good afternoon." Lucien's greeting seemed sincere. He had dressed like a mere mortal today in jeans, heavy boots and a cable knit sweater. "May I offer you some tea?"

Carmen glanced toward the cook who hadn't bothered to turn

around at her entrance. "Actually, I was hoping for some hot chocolate and maybe some lunch. Karl, it's good to see you safe."

Karl had dressed in bulky work clothes and a warm coat with a fur collar. He blushed at her attention and nodded. "I must apologize for last evening. It was not my intent to frighten everyone."

"Hardly your fault. Actually, I doubt anyone else would have had the skill it took to get us here in one piece. Without you, we'd be sitting in a ditch, so thank you."

Karl seemed even more embarrassed by her gratitude. He glanced at the woman behind the stove and waved toward her in an obvious attempt to deflect the conversation. "This is my wife, Anna."

"We could not function without her." Lucien added the comment with a less than sincere tone. He bustled over to gather a ceramic pot, mugs and other items. "I shall prepare your cocoa."

Carmen raised an eyebrow at the thinly veiled sarcasm. She definitely sensed tension beneath the surface, but shrugged her impression away as unimportant. People living closely together always harbored secret grievances. For now, Carmen wanted to know more about the cook, and consequently, the food.

The woman, Anna, turned to regard Carmen for the first time since she walked in. Instead of plump cheeks with a merry expression, this woman offered a scowl. Face flushed and moist from the cooking fires, Ana gave off an impatient vibe that made Carmen regret her search for sustenance. Anna used a wooden spoon to indicate Carmen's damp boots.

"You are dripping water everywhere." Her accent wasn't as heavy as that of her husband. "I have prepared a tray of *Walliser Fleischplatte*, just there." Again with the spoon, she pointed out a dish on the corner of the larger butcher's block. "That should satisfy everyone for a few minutes. Lunch will be served in twenty minutes precisely."

Carmen noticed a heavy platter loaded with a variety of rolled meats and various cheeses. She thought she saw olives and other items as well. Since she needed to wait for the drinks, Carmen drifted over to stand by their host. She decided to stay safely away from the cranky cook.

"I must apologize for Anna." Lucien kept his voice low as he prepared the drink. "She has not been herself of late. Perhaps the cold is, as you say, getting to her."

Carmen appreciated the sentiment. At least he seemed willing to keep the peace. An important trait for a resort owner, to be sure. Since this was a business, Carmen realized she had probably stepped out of line. "I shouldn't have come in here uninvited. I suppose guests really aren't allowed in these areas."

"Nonsense, we hardly have the staff on hand to assist at the moment and the lodge isn't active as yet. I wish everyone to explore any areas they desire. How else would they know what their investment is worth?"

Guilt forced Carmen to express the truth. "Uh, about that. I'm not an investor. I'm just a police officer from Denver. Katie invited me because we're friends."

"There are other ways to invest than financially. You have many friends, I presume. Word of mouth advertising is priceless. It is how we will attract guests to the resort." Lucien added a few small plates on the tray along with the pot and mugs.

"I appreciate the sentiment. Uh, while you're finishing up there, would you mind if I check out where the break-in occurred?"

Lucien indicated the back door with a wave, but kept up his preparations. He didn't seem concerned about a possible burglar, instead taking everything in stride.

A brief check showed a heavy, solid oak door. The latch was splintered, but hastily repaired with a scrap of wood. Someone had moved the lock onto the makeshift patch. No person broke in here. Any intruder would require a battering ram. Maybe a bear was heavy enough to do this kind of damage.

"Katie said there were tracks in the blown in snow, human-like. Could it be a bear instead?"

Lucien shrugged in an offhand manner. "There are many brown bears in these woods, but I'm unsure one could operate a *kylanläggning*."

From the context, Carmen figured that he meant the refrigerator. "I don't know. I've seen animals do some pretty amazing things. I find it more interesting that no one heard anything. That door coming apart should have sounded like thunder. It would take a lot of force to break it open."

"This structure is quite large and none of the accommodations are near the kitchens, for obvious reasons. With the ferocity of the wind from the storm as well, I can understand how no one would hear." Lucien chuckled as he finished his preparations, grasped the silver tray and turned to face her. "Of course, Mister Wrighton believes a yeti responsible for the incident."

"There's no such thing."

"Exactly as you say." Lucien nodded toward the platter of food. "Since Anna is serving lunch in the dining hall, perhaps we should bring these things to the parlor. I will carry the cocoa if you bring along the *Fleischplatte*. Karl, I shall return momentarily so that we may finish our, uh, business."

Lucien chivalrously followed Carmen back to the parlor, both bearing nourishment for the others. Eyes lit up as they entered and settled the trays onto the same larger table near the center of the room. In seconds, the others joined them, no longer shy about helping themselves.

"Lunch will be served soon in the main dining hall." Lucien took a step back as the guests crowded him out. "You will find it directly down the corridor to my left."

Carmen grabbed a couple of small plates, passing one to Katie. She took advantage of her proximity to the snacks to load up. "I need to explore this place. It's so big and I'd like to know exactly what we, or rather you, are investing in."

"Isn't that what we've already been doing, exploring?" Katie darted forward to grab a meat roll.

"Yes, but only outside. I'd like to check out the inside of the lodge, too."

"Feel free to explore as much as you'd like," Lucien invited. "No areas are off limits."

Mike backed away from the table with a heaping mound of food. "Is there a bar in this place? I could use a drink to warm me up from the inside out."

"Of course," Lucien said. "You will find it located in the dining hall. Now, if will excuse me. I will see you all at lunch."

Mike quickly suggested everyone adjourn to the dining room to get comfortable and Carmen didn't see any reason to argue. Without another word Mike, Kofi and Sahari scooped up the food and drink trays in their free hands, somewhat eager to lead the way.

Carmen followed the crowd, as curious as everyone else. Shock had her mouth hanging open when they arrived. She figured this space could seat around a hundred at a time. For the moment, various small wooden tables and chairs were shoved against a wall. A single long table took center stage, clearly intended for this more intimate gathering. Bench style seats lined both sides with straight backed chairs at the head and foot. The bar Mike inquired about took up a great portion of the wall opposite the stacked furniture. Multi-colored bottles of every shape and size adorned shelves behind the pale wood, heavily shellacked bar.

While Mike wasted no time in dropping his load at the table to stride off behind the bar, Carmen preferred to inspect the room. Their host seemed to have started his renovations here. The first thing she noticed was that there wasn't a cobweb in sight. Everything gleamed new from the polished hardwood floors to the heavy beams overhead. A large brightly lit chandelier hung from the center of the ceiling with numerous smaller canned lights scattered throughout. Floor vents along the walls poured heat, making this space feel cozy and welcoming despite its size. A bank of double paned windows offered an uninterrupted view of the grounds surrounding the lodge.

The tantalizing aroma of food drifted into this room from the nearby kitchen, making her mouth water. Carmen spotted a set of double doors situated between the stacked piles of furniture and deduced they led to an alternate kitchen entrance.

"Wow." Carmen decided immediately that she loved this space. With this as an example, she couldn't wait to see the rest of the resort once Lucien completed the rework.

"You can say that again."

Katie sounded as awestruck as Carmen was. Their eyes met and they shared a pleased smile. Carmen glanced around to see if the others appeared as awestruck.

Tiffany appeared bored, as usual, quietly pouring a hot beverage and adding a few morsels to her plate from one of the side benches. She barely glanced around. The men laughed as they went through Lucien's liquor selection and mixed drinks.

"Huh, guess we're the only ones impressed. Why don't we have a seat?" Carmen joined Tiffany at the table, still speaking to Katie.

"Remind me not to overeat. Karl's wife, Anna, is working up quite a spread and I don't want to spoil my appetite."

Katie snorted as she sat beside Carmen on the opposite side of the table from Tiffany. "Who, you? I've seen you eat more than a man twice your size. I'm glad Karl's okay. I wondered if he used snowshoes to walk up here from a cabin."

Carmen shook her head and swallowed. "I don't think so. I saw snowmobile tracks leading to the lodge when we were up on the ridge. Plus, he had to bring his wife over since she's apparently the cook."

"Well, at least one of the cooks." Katie blew on her drink before sipping. "There will be quite a staff once things are up and running. I hear the skeleton crew should return tomorrow and then we won't need to fend for ourselves as much."

"Speaking of missing people, I wonder where Mister Wrighton has gotten off to. He's typically under foot, from my perspective," a new voice interjected.

Carmen glanced up from her plate in surprise. She had never heard Tiffany speak before. The slightly bored tone lingered, but Tiffany possessed a light, well-modulated voice.

Kofi interrupted by dropping into the seat at the end of the table to Carmen's right without hesitation. Ice clinked in his amber colored drink and Carmen smelled whiskey.

"He's taking a nap," Kofi said.

"It's the middle of the day." Carmen hoped she sounded curious rather than nosey. "I'm surprised he isn't exploring the grounds. You know, doing research or something."

Kofi shrugged. "In truth, Wrighton left the lodge on skis shortly after your departure this morning. He accompanied Pymer to the lifts to enjoy some of the more sedate runs, or so he said. I believe Pymer is still working. He seems quite driven to assist his friend in making the lodge functional."

Carmen enjoyed Kofi's easy manner and his smooth South African accent, but his explanation made no sense. Pymer had told them the lifts weren't yet operational. His goal today was to get at least one of them working. She had seen him at one point, but not Wrighton. She and Katie had explored a great deal of the property, but Wrighton wasn't on any of the slopes. Then again, she hadn't seen Kofi outside either, but the snow on his jacket when Carmen saw him in the parlor belied that fact. Perhaps another slope existed somewhere behind the lodge in an area she and Katie hadn't explored.

Katie distracted her from her thoughts. "Did you notice we all call each other by our first names except for Wrighton?"

Kofi smiled, a quick flash of stark white teeth. "The man is somewhat insufferable."

The double kitchen doors suddenly parted and Anna strode into room bearing a loaded silver tray in each hand. She carried them high, near either side of her head, quite impressing Carmen with her show of balance and strength. Lucien followed close behind her, also bearing food dishes. A rich, creamy cheese fondue, a staple in Switzerland, took center place along with chunks of hearty bread and long handled forks. Bowls of thin barley soup with carrots, leeks and onions led things off on a lighter note.

Pymer made an appearance soon after the soup arrived, scooting in beside Tiffany and Sahari before shucking a greasy pair of leather work gloves. Carmen noted a sheepish expression as he scanned the other occupants before tucking into the soup. His red-tipped ears and ruddy cheeks lent credence to him working half a day in the cold. Carmen caught the quick eye contact between him and Kofi before Pymer concentrated on his meal.

Beautiful smooth potato pancakes with bacon, sausage rolled in Swiss chard leaves and a plate of bratwurst arrived, taking all of Carmen's focus from her companions. Anna might be a cranky cook, but Carmen considered her a wizard in the kitchen. By the time dessert arrived, Carmen thought she might actually burst. She couldn't identify the treat from its appearance, but Katie saved her the trouble.

"Oh, panna cotta!" Katie's eyes sparkled as she announced the custard-like mold drizzled with a brownish substance.

While a little skeptical, Carmen certainly wasn't hesitant to try something new. She took a tentative bite and her eyes widened in delight as the flavors of coffee and caramel exploded over her taste buds. She forgot about her full stomach as she quickly devoured her portion.

"Absolutely wonderful." Mike sat back in his chair, rubbing his stomach and sipping his drink. "Lucien, if this is what you can manage with a single staff member, I can't wait to see this place in full operation."

"I agree," Katie said, raising her mug in salute. "Well done, cousin. You can count on me to contribute."

Lucien smiled. "Thank you both. And you shall have your wish, Mister Doyle. Karl has heard that some of the porters and wait staff shall return later today and that the roads should be cleared by tomorrow. Even with only seven guests, the lodge will soon become quite active."

"I, for one, am relieved." Tiffany sounded slightly irritated. "The conditions so far are deplorable. No offense intended, Lucien, but I expect a more comfortable atmosphere from a supposedly high-end resort."

Sahari patted his wife's hand before withdrawing completely when she pulled away. "Now, now my dear. He can hardly control the weather. You must forgive my wife, Lucien. I am afraid that she is accustomed to a more pampered experience."

"No apologies necessary." Lucien waved the sentiment aside. "I assure you, madam, eventually there will be more than enough personnel on site, even during inclement conditions to keep all guests at Tribulation Peak satisfied."

From her expression, Carmen didn't think Tiffany believed him. Obliged to change the subject and ease what fast approached an awkward situation, Carmen changed the subject. "Say, Lucien, I just noticed that Wrighton didn't make lunch. Have you heard from him?"

"He is fine, I'm sure. Very likely resting from his adventures. I shall ensure he eats something once he awakens. As a matter of fact, Karl and Anna will depart after they clear lunch, but I expect a great deal of leftovers. Anna is unaccustomed to cooking for so few. Please, feel free to help yourselves in the kitchen if you grow hungry before dinner."

Lucien informed them that dinner would be at eight. That seemed a little late to Carmen, but she was more interested in a hot shower and a nap at this point. The others agreed that resting sounded good. The group began to break up when Carmen heard a familiar low throb and sensed a rumbling approach all the way to her bones. The pressure built on her eardrums as she identified the sound.

"That's a helicopter."

Chapter Twelve

Up and out of the room, Carmen sensed the others close on her heels. She stopped short at the huge windows looking out onto the front of the grounds. Without a coat, she didn't intend to stand in the wind generated from rotor wash. Carmen grinned when she spotted a red and white helicopter with a cross on the side. Malia, it had to be.

The other guests crowded around Carmen as they watched the helicopter drop toward the snow a respectable distance from the structure. Snow whipped from the ground, creating a fog around the chopper as evergreen boughs leaned away from the disturbance. The skids on the helicopter touched down gently without a discernible bump. Seconds later the engine cycled down and the rotors slowed to a stop. Carmen watched as the pilot removed a headset and helmet. Then the rear cargo door opened and six people stepped into the fresh powder. Men and women bundled in hats, parkas, gloves and scarves trudged toward the lodge.

The two women in the group appeared completely different from one another. One stood tall and lean like a bean pole. The other looked shorter and much more curvaceous. Carmen noticed a few wisps of shiny blonde hair drifted in the breeze, having escaped from her red knit beanie hat with a pompom on top. For a moment, Carmen couldn't take her eyes from the women. She wasn't interested in the other four, after all, they were men. Then Malia hopped out of the pilot's seat on the right side of the helicopter. She reached back inside, retrieving a black duffle bag before heading toward the lodge. Carmen forgot about the cold. A goofy grin took possession of her, despite her determination not to show her delight at the unexpected appearance.

Carmen hurried out the door to the edge of the steps. She crossed her arms for warmth while she waited for Malia to walk toward her. The six strangers flowed around the snowmobile parked in front of the steps and then around Carmen like a tide but she hardly noticed them. Absently, she caught the sweet, spicy scent of the smaller stranger's perfume. Then Malia bounced up the steps and caught Carmen in a welcoming one-armed hug. To her own surprise, Carmen returned the gesture briefly before taking half a step back.

"Hi there." The sparkle of pleasure in Malia's eyes matched her smile. "You're going to freeze if you stand out here without a coat."

Heat rushed to Carmen's cheeks. "Yeah, I guess I am acting a little silly. I didn't expect to see you so soon. Not that I'm unhappy about that. What are you doing here?"

"Why, I'm bringing some of Lucien's people to work of course. I don't usually act as a taxi, but they needed a ride and I couldn't think of a reason to say no. In fact, when I found out they wanted to come here, I realized this is my chance to get that hot drink with a hot woman."

Carmen laughed. "Well, you're certainly bold, I'll give you that."

"Too bold?"

"Not at all. I find it refreshing." Really, Carmen found Malia's interest flattering. She enjoyed having someone interested in her who made no bones about it.

"Good, now why don't we head inside?" Malia brazenly slipped her free arm around Carmen's waist. "The helicopter has climate control, but it never gets warm enough during the winter."

Carmen allowed herself to be directed inside. "I know what you mean. Denver gets pretty cold at times too. You just missed lunch, by the way. Are you hungry?"

"Depends on what you have in mind."

Carmen shook her head, a little overwhelmed by Malia's directness. Rather than answer, she led Malia inside. The whole dynamic inside the resort changed with the arrival of the new group. Where before tedium seemed to weigh on the guests, now excitement permeated the atmosphere. Lucien slapped some of the men on the back, welcoming them to work. Everyone engaged in smattered conversations in both

German and English. Even Tiffany smiled for the first time since Carmen met her. Lucien took the opportunity to address all of those present.

"I am pleased to have all of you here. However, the time has come for a few words of warning. As you all know, we had quite the storm last evening. Due to the amount of snow received, we are at an enhanced avalanche risk. Some of you may have heard the stories about a village near here buried in such an event a few years past. While I do not foresee anyone here placing themselves in such danger, I do recommend that anyone attempting the slopes wear a personal beacon. Pymer has informed me that the southern facing lift is now operational so that you may enjoy yourselves."

"I cannot wait to try them, Lucien," Kofi said. "And I promise to wear my beacon, but I must ask when you intend to inform us of this investment opportunity. I fully intend to enjoy your hospitality, but I remain quite aware that we are all here for a purpose."

"Ah, but you have beaten me to the proverbial punch." Lucien sounded pleased by the development, no doubt having waited for just such a happenstance. "After dinner tonight, we shall discuss my proposal. I will have everything waiting in the drawing room. For those of you who have not located this particular room as yet, I shall give you directions later. In the meantime, please enjoy yourselves."

Carmen sensed the impromptu meeting breaking up and stopped Lucien before he could make a getaway. "Speaking of the village, where was it exactly?"

"Well, you are standing inside part of it," Lucien answered. "The lodge was the only structure not completely buried. The village itself was actually quite small and located near where the cabins are situated now, but if you choose to examine this area I must encourage caution. It is quite unstable."

"Hey, maybe we should have a scavenger hunt." Mike looked around to see who would take him up on the idea. "I bet there's all kinds of stuff still buried inside those buildings."

"No thanks," Carmen said. "I've had quite enough adventure in the last few months, but I wouldn't mind checking out the area. Just out of curiosity." She thought Lucien's directions sounded very near where she'd spotted the strange topography earlier.

"For those of you not in the mood to further explore the grounds, there is a large sun room on the rear side of the lodge," Lucien said. "Simply pass through the dining hall and through the glass doors. You will find an indoor, heated pool as well as a hot tub and several seating areas to appreciate the view."

Sahari perked up, interested in something besides business. "Now you speak our language. Tiffany, would you care to join me?"

"God, yes. I can't wait to finally get warm."

Carmen thought the hot tub sounded great, but she decided now wasn't the time to interrupt the couple and she had other plans at the moment. She didn't know what Malia had in mind, but figured it involved a great deal of privacy. A few minutes later, chatter tapered off as Lucien led his employees away.

"I'm so glad to see some actual employees," Tiffany said. "Now, perhaps, we shall see how this resort will truly function. I hope some of them are ready to serve drinks while we're in the hot tub."

Mike nodded, still smiling. "That does sound nice, but why are they here? They'll just be snowed in, too."

"Not to worry." Malia spoke up without hesitation, clearly not intimidated to be around a group of strangers. "They wouldn't be here if they didn't have a way home. This is Switzerland so we're used to clearing roads quickly. These people are merely the advanced guard, so to speak. The roads will be cleared sometime later today and the rest of Lucien's people, at least the ones he has on staff at the moment, should be here early tomorrow."

Malia's pleasant confidence bolstered the original group. She explained that the people she brought in the helicopter would occupy the various cabins overnight. Everything would soon return to normal. With the new infusion of positive energy, many of Lucien's guests suddenly gave in to urges to explore the slopes rather than sleep. One by one, they drifted away to their own activities until only Carmen, Katie and Malia remained standing in the foyer.

"Are you staying overnight too, Malia?" Katie asked the question foremost in Carmen's mind.

Malia hefted her duffle and nodded. "That's my plan. Dispatch can reach me on the radio. No cell reception up here you know."

"That presumes you're near the radio to hear them call," Carmen pointed out.

"Oh, I never leave anything to chance." Malia pulled a small satellite phone out of her jumpsuit pocket, waving it back and forth before tucking it away. "I'm looking forward to time with a beautiful woman, but I'm always ready to go."

"In more ways than one," Katie mumbled. She cleared her throat lightly, definitely looking uncomfortable. "Uh, right. Well, I think I'll check out the lift Pymer has working. Maybe there's a nice intermediate slope beside it. See you guys later?"

Guilt at ditching Katie caused Carmen to hesitate. She wanted to spend time with Malia, but wasn't happy leaving Katie to risk her safety on the untried slopes alone. "Are you sure?"

"I'm fine. Go ahead, Carmen. This is your vacation, too. Besides, I'm a big girl. It'll be nice having some me time."

After Katie left, Malia turned to Carmen. "So, do you have some place where I can change?"

Carmen led the way upstairs. By habit, she had left the door to her room open. With so few people present, the lodge gave off the energy of a house rather than a resort. She supposed that would change now that Lucien's people had arrived.

"Here we go. My humble and very temporary home away from home."

Carmen closed the door to give them some privacy. She watched Malia's gaze scan the room. Dark eyes swept from the cold fireplace all the way around to the unmade queen bed. Carmen suddenly felt self-conscious about the state of her room. She retrieved a pillow from the floor before placing it on the bed. She hadn't expected company. Would Malia notice the cobwebs in the corner?

"Cozy. Early Swiss Goth meets House of Frankenstein. Seriously, does Lucien think customers will pay good money for this?"

"It's not so bad. In fact, it's quite comfortable when the fire's going and I'm sure the place will be much better when he finishes the remodel."

"Hmm, maybe." Malia looked skeptical. "I can definitely see why he's looking for investors, but it's not important right now."

Malia dropped her bag onto the bed and unzipped her blue flight suit all the way to her crotch. She kicked off her boots before shucking out of the garment without any hint of modesty. Carmen spotted a white t-shirt under the suit and spun around with her back to Malia before she saw anything too revealing. She didn't consider herself to be a prude, but she barely knew this woman. It seemed a little soon to see her in her underwear.

"Hey, want to grab a drink on the patio?"

"Patio?" Carmen didn't realize the resort had one. "I still haven't completely explored the inside of the lodge. I'm afraid that Katie and I spent most of the day outside riding around on a snowmobile."

"That sounds fun. Maybe we can do that later. I saw the patio from the air when I flew over. I know it's cold, but I could swear I saw a gas fire pit. We can check it out together." Malia's voice took on a low, teasing quality. "You can look now."

Carmen turned around to find Malia standing much closer than expected. From inches away, Carmen could see flecks of yellow in the soft brown gaze. A small scar split the arch of Maria's left brow. Warm breath ghosted across her cheeks. Carmen anticipated the kiss.

Her eyes drifted closed as Malia leaned in slowly, giving Carmen time to pull away if she wanted. The gentle consideration allowed Carmen to drop her guard and go with the moment. Malia's lips whispered against hers, a bare brush that invited rather than claimed. Carmen surged into the kiss, sliding one arm around Malia's waist and cupping her cheek in her left hand. She stroked Malia's cheek with her fingertips and drank the kisses, tasting and learning Malia's mouth.

Once the initial flare faded, Carmen quickly realized something wasn't right. She didn't feel the way she had expected. Malia's kiss was fine, but Carmen's heart wasn't in it. Slowly, she ended the lingual caress. Then she withdrew and forced a smile for Malia.

Voice husky with regret, Carmen said, "Are you ready to find the fire pit? Maybe the others will still be in the pool." She felt disconcerted by her reaction and hoped to redirect where things were headed before they spiraled out of control.

"Uh, sure. And the hot drink. Don't forget the drink."

Malia sounded confused, but went along with Carmen. They grabbed heavy jackets and headed through the lodge to find the outside patio.

As it happened, they needed to walk through the sun room Lucien had mentioned. Mike Doyle, Sahari and Tiffany were there. Mike sat on the stairs in the heated pool wearing a pair of blue shorts, his legs floating in the shallow end and a drink in his hand. Sahari and Tiffany occupied the hot tub and kept shooting Mike dirty looks.

"Hey, there they are." Mike spoke to them as Carmen and Malia strode through on their way outside. "Come on in, I already warmed it up for you."

Eww. Carmen shuddered and noticed how bloodshot his eyes were. His drink sloshed over the rim of his glass and into the water. "Wonder how many of those he's already had, or if he has any friends with class." Carmen kept her voice low as they walked by without responding. She briefly thought about Wrighton, whom she still hadn't seen since the morning.

"Probably started before I even got here."

"He was drinking at lunch earlier. That's okay, I guess. Maybe he intends to get everything he can out of this trip before he decides to invest."

As they stepped onto the patio, Carmen spotted the two women who arrived with Malia. She couldn't discern any features since they were bundled up for the weather out here. The concrete patio could easily host a large contingent and the ceiling tied in directly to the roof of the lodge, ensuring protection from bad weather. Individual green cast aluminum tables with a lattice weave design dotted the space with four matching chairs around each.

Carmen spotted the large round fire pit near the center of the space. The pit was constructed from pale natural stone with a small, hard bench and a smattering of contoured rattan chairs surrounding the feature. She was delighted to see blue and yellow flames already dancing.

"This is nice." Malia looked over toward the employees. "Excuse me, can we get a couple of drinks over here?"

Carmen quickly eschewed the bench for one of the chairs. She didn't want to encourage something further with Malia by choosing the two-seat bench. The shorter blonde employee went back inside, but the other woman headed their way.

Malia occupied a chair next to her and Carmen was relieved she didn't seem to notice anything amiss. She was probably making too much out of the seating arrangements considering the concrete bench didn't look comfortable and didn't even have a back rest.

"Hello, you're very brave to willingly come out here in the cold." The employee pulled her scarf down so they could see her face and offered them a smile. "I am Eva. What may I bring you?"

Eva had an open face with a friendly smile and twinkling eyes. Strands of bright red hair escaped her blue skull cap and Eva absently brushed them away. Carmen liked her instantly.

"I'll have a coffee. Black, please."

Malia surprised her by ordering the same. Carmen had expected her to ask for a hot alcoholic beverage of some sort.

As soon as they were alone, Malia cut to the chase. "So, what's wrong? You've been acting strange since I kissed you."

"Actually, I think I kissed you."

"Don't split hairs. Did I upset you somehow?" Malia sounded curious rather than angry.

Carmen sighed and shook her head. "You didn't do anything I didn't want you to do."

"But?"

"Oh, I don't know what my problem is. I wanted you to kiss me, but when you did, I'm sorry. I just can't explain it."

Malia smiled a little, but Carmen saw the sadness in her expression. "There wasn't any magic?"

"Sounds ridiculous, I know."

They drifted into a strained silence and Carmen focused on the view from the back of the lodge. From the corner of her eye, she noticed Malia doing the same. It was quite the view. Mountains stretched toward the sky, almost obscured from view by the blend of coniferous trees. Spruce, pine, fir and larch trees blended together, creating a wind break while offering concealment and habitats for wildlife. Carmen closed her eyes briefly and listened to the world.

She could hear the gentle breeze swaying the trees and Malia's soft respirations. The rare bird called, adding to the sense of peace. If not for the dreadful cold, Carmen could live here.

Approaching footsteps announced Eva's return. Carmen looked up and returned the woman's perpetual smile. Eva placed oversized coffee mugs between Carmen and Malia on a small patio table. She made her escape as soon as she ensured they wanted nothing more.

The first sip warmed Carmen down to her stomach and caffeine exploded through her system. Coffee always heated her almost instantly. In this case, she was happy for that.

Malia broke the silence between them. "So, you never filled me in on that date you mentioned."

The unexpected topic change had Carmen grasping. She finally remembered having coffee with Sally and briefly telling Malia about it at the airport. "There's not much to say. Her name is Sally and I met her at a friend's Super Bowl party. She was cute and nice and she came on a little strong, kind of like you. I thought, why not go out with her and see what happens?"

"So, what did happen?" Malia sipped her coffee, but kept her eyes riveted on Carmen. The glow cast by the fire pit danced in her gaze.

Carmen considered brushing the matter aside, but finally decided it didn't matter. She'd never see Malia again and gave in to the urge to confide in her. From their brief association, she got the feeling that Malia didn't judge, which made it easier to share.

"Nothing, unfortunately. There just wasn't any chemistry."

"Is that what you're looking for, chemistry?"

Carmen hesitated, attempting to answer in a way that would convey the deep down truth of things. "I'm looking for the way my dad looked at my mom. Like no other woman existed in the world. I want that rush and I want it to last. I want to feel like my partner is the only person in the universe for me."

"Have you ever felt that way?" Malia asked the question softly, encouraging Carmen to open up.

"Once. I looked into a pair of storm blue eyes and thought I could fall forever." Carmen chuckled and shrugged, attempting to lighten the suddenly somber mood. "The woman was a complete stranger on an airplane, but if I could feel that way about her maybe there's hope for me."

Malia smiled. "You're a romantic, Carmen Bravo."

"Maybe, but I want forever. Not just casual sex."

"I assume you're trying to get a point across. You know, Carmen, there's nothing wrong with having a little fun. It doesn't have to mean anything."

Carmen adopted a teasing tone in an attempt to avoid hurting Malia's feelings. "It does for me. Don't get me wrong, I definitely feel some of that famous chemistry with you, but it can't last. I thought I could just let go for once and enjoy myself but apparently, I'm not built that way. I'm sorry if I've disappointed you."

"Hey don't worry about it." Malia waved her words away as she set her coffee cup on the small table. "My ego is healthy enough to get over a little disappointment. I still think we could have some fun together, even if it isn't by getting naked. What do you say we ditch the resort and find some trouble to get into?"

Carmen smiled, happy to go along and that Malia still wanted to pursue a relationship, if though a platonic one. "I think I have just the thing. How do you feel about exploring a deep, dark, mysterious place in the woods?"

"Oh...sounds spooky. What are we waiting for?"

Chapter Thirteen

The snowmobile sliced through the snow, eating up the distance between the lodge and the area Carmen believed held a buried structure. Strong arms hugged her waist from behind while Malia warmed her back by leaning against her. The distance wasn't truly far from the resort, but the route carried them past the sundry cabins and into the woods.

Ski tracks, as well as a myriad of foot prints, informed her that others were here recently. She understood the lure of a mystery, but hoped the previous visitors had already left. She wanted the solitude to inform her own impressions of the lost village without distraction. She had seen Katie slipping along one of the slopes looking quite content in her solitude. That left Kofi, Pymer and Wrighton off on their own. Carmen and Malia wouldn't have a lot of time left to explore either. A quick glance at the sun told Carmen only an hour or so of daylight remained.

Carmen stopped the Lynx several yards away from their destination. She shut off the engine and pushed up her visor, but stayed seated as she checked out the immediate area. The tracks she saw led right up to an impressive rise in the snow and seemed to vanish underneath. Other impressions led around the side of the formation. From this proximity, she could tell this was definitely a buried structure. The snow lay across at an odd angle, indicating that much of the edifice had collapsed. A heavy sensation hung over the region as though something waited. Goosebumps broke out on her arms under the sweater, but Carmen believed they had nothing to do with the cold. A strange odor floated in the air, slight but definitely present. She tasted it in the back of her throat rather than truly smelling it.

"Something wrong?"

Carmen hadn't noticed that Malia now stood beside her, her helmet already removed. Rather than hop off, she took her time removing her own helmet before standing and placing it on the seat. "No, not really."

"Come on, let's explore." Malia led the way toward the old building, supposedly one of the many that once dotted the landscape. "I can see why this caught your imagination. How cool would it be if we found something that belonged to someone who lived here?"

"Like bones? You forget this was a village. That means people probably died here."

Malia squatted on her knees where the tracks disappeared in front and leaned over to peer underneath. "That's depressing."

Carmen dropped down beside Malia. Despite her words, she was excited to see what they could find. The child inside said there could be something amazing, like buried treasure. Darkness greeted her immediately and it took a moment for her vision to adjust. She saw a surprisingly open space ahead. Debris had blocked the sides, but there was plenty of room to squeeze inside. She lay down on her belly and squirmed into the opening.

"Hey, where are you going? There could be an animal in there."

"It's an abandoned old house. What's the worst that can happen?"

Carmen stood up as soon as she had clearance. Without the illumination from the setting sun and with the entire structure covered in snow, shadows prevailed. Only the ambient light reflecting off the snow from the opening they used eased the shadows. Fortunately, Carmen had prepared for this. She pulled a small flashlight from her jacket pocket and switched it on.

Splintered wood from fragmented walls, broken furniture and personal items greeted her. A few photos had fallen to the ground, the glass smashed. Snow littered the moldy and ripped carpeting while wallpaper hung in strips along the walls. Not even cobwebs lived here. A gaping hole in the ceiling allowed a view of the snowy canopy overhead where it had packed in tight and created a tentative blockade. Foot prints led off further into the former dwelling.

"Holy cow," Malia breathed the words, a touch of awe in her voice. "This is incredible. How many of these things do you think are still standing?"

"I don't know. The avalanche supposedly happened about five years ago. Maybe the rest already collapsed. Rotted wood would disintegrate back into the earth. They might never be found. Let's check it out."

The dank, humid smell Carmen noticed outside was stronger in here. She thought it stank like an animal's den. Maybe Malia was right, but Carmen didn't believe it was anything dangerous. If so, it would already have attacked. Maybe rabbits or birds moved in once the humans left.

Scraps of torn fabric and a discarded metal fork lay on the floor between the former living area and the kitchen. Icicles hung from a stainless steel water faucet. Malia scooted ahead of her, no longer timid now that they were inside. She pulled open a cabinet door.

Carmen spotted glassware. "What are the odds the dishes are still intact?"

"I guess as long as this part of the house still stands, things would be okay. I've heard that areas with plumbing are more reinforced. The owners probably dug out of the snow and left everything behind. Insurance would cover the loss." Malia removed one of the glasses and studied it closely. "I don't even see dust. Guess the snow and the cabinet door kept the elements out."

Voices startled them both and Malia dropped the glass. It shattered impressively when it hit the frozen floor. The sound was like a bomb going off in the preternaturally silent house. Carmen gasped in surprise at the unexpected noise. The voices below stopped immediately, but she wasn't concerned. Whoever it was were likely guests of the lodge and had been surprised by the demolished glass, too.

The voices had come from a door at the far side of the kitchen. It stood ajar and Carmen guessed it led to a basement or root cellar of some sort. She headed for the door.

"Want to see if they found something else?"

"Do you think that's a good idea? We don't even know who it is."

Carmen glanced over her shoulder. "I doubt it's an axe murderer. Let's go find out who it is."

Malia groaned, but scooted close. She rested a hand on Carmen's shoulder and followed as close as she could without stepping on Carmen's feet.

"Scaredy cat," Carmen teased. "It has to be Kofi, Pymer or Wrighton."

"How do you know?"

"Because we've seen everyone else. Except Karl and his wife of course. I doubt they'd be stumbling around out here."

Carmen shoved the basement door open further and peered into the darkness. A light glowed dimly below. Suddenly, she flashed to another basement in another structure in Germany from only a few months ago. She had awakened from a bash on the head, tied and helpless while waiting for a werewolf to show up and eat her. Carmen swallowed hard at the memory and realized the odor she had detected was stronger in here. Now she could identify the smell and realized Malia had a point. There was something dead in the basement.

She swallowed and called down into the darkness. "It's okay. We just dropped a glass."

No one responded. Carmen suddenly had a bad feeling, but she didn't want to look foolish after teasing Malia. Mentally grasping her courage, Carmen stepped forward. She rested a hand on the old railing. Splinters snagged her glove. The handrail creaked ominously. Carmen removed her hand when she registered the condition of the wood. With Malia on her heels, she headed down.

Carmen could see better down here. Part of the cinder block wall had blown out, presenting a frequently traveled path leading upward into the woods. Fading sunlight revealed numerous tracks, both human and animal. Old crates lay smashed and littered throughout the space. The remains of a rusted-out motorcycle rested near a wall, covered in cobwebs, dirt and snow. Finally, cobwebs. Silly as it was, the signs of previous life bolstered Carmen's confidence.

"Well, whoever it was, they're gone now." Malia moved around her and walked over to the opening. A light breeze ruffled her hair.

"True. I wonder what they were up to." Carmen hesitated to admit the relief she experienced. For some reason, she had sensed a threat. The sensation didn't completely fade, but she felt a little better knowing they were now alone.

"Oh my God, gross. What is that?"

"What?"

Carmen's heart pounded as she tried to identify the danger. The she saw it. Old, dried blood stained the snowy path leading outside, not in droplets but in a swath. Human prints trampled the stain, but Carmen's eyes tracked the trail to a torn pelt lying discarded in a darkened corner.

"Looks like a fox. Wait, I see more bodies and some bones. Rabbits, maybe? Whatever this place used to be, something's using it as a den. Guess that accounts for the stink."

Malia ambled toward the corner, but stopped after only a few paces. "It could be worse. The remains are frozen, but I think some of these kills are fresh. Hey, look at this!"

Carmen couldn't believe it. This had to be a hoax. She blinked, but the impression remained. The largest footprint she had ever seen. Individual toes, all six of them, left a clear impression. Obviously made while the blood was fresh, the print stood clearly outlined.

She cleared her throat and met Malia's gaze. "Do you believe in yeti?"

Malia shook her head and pointed behind a crate. "No, but I do believe in hoaxes. You there, come on out."

Carmen walked over beside Malia to see who she had spotted. She saw a brown thermal insulated hiking boot and the cuff to a pair of tan snow pants. From the size of the boot, she guessed the lurker was male. Malia took a step toward the person, but Carmen caught her arm, holding her back.

"Wait. Something isn't right. Stay here."

In the fading light, Carmen noticed some droplets that were darker than mere shadow. The fact that person hadn't reacted at all to their voices hinted at disaster. Carmen's mouth went dry as she inched toward the crate. Before she looked over the edge, instinct told her what she would find.

Open eyes stared into oblivion, a look of perpetual surprise on the man's frozen face. Four parallel gashes opened his throat, almost severing the head. Blood had sprayed out in an arc over the floor and had drenched the upper portion of a pale green parka, making it look two-toned. Nausea burned in her stomach and Carmen turned her head away, clenching her eyes and jaw shut as she fought not to throw up.

"Is he...?"

Carmen put up a hand, gesturing for Malia to stay there. She didn't need to see this. After a second, Carmen regained control of her own visceral reactions. She took a shaky breath before looking at Malia while studiously attempting to ignore the carnage. Carmen nodded.

"He's dead. It's Wrighton." From the looks of him, he had been here several hours. "You need to get on the sat phone and call dispatch."

Malia's eyes widened. "I can't. I forgot it in my jumpsuit."

"Crap. Well, it's fine. We should head back anyway. It's getting dark. We'll call it in from the lodge."

A sudden deep throated roar filled the air so close by that Carmen's hair stood on end. Fear stuttered through her heart and her eyes sought the opening into the woods. At any moment, she expected a bear to come lumbering through the hole. That was one encounter she could forego.

"Why don't we head out the same way we came in?"

Malia already sprinted up the steps toward the kitchen. "Good idea."

Carmen wasted no time in following. They scooted through the destroyed house and slid back out through the opening on their bellies. Since Malia had jumped into the front of the seat, Carmen grabbed her helmet and dropped behind her. She struggled with the headgear as Malia gunned the snowmobile and tore off into the woods.

An object glinted through the trees off to Carmen's right. They weren't far from the demolished old house, but her heart rate had dropped enough for her to notice her surroundings once again. Someone moved over there and she remembered the voices in the basement. Although she hadn't heard them clearly enough to identify the speakers, she felt certain it was Kofi and Pymer. Finding Wrighton dead had made her forget all about them as connections clicked in her mind.

"Stop," she called out over Malia's shoulder.

Malia instantly slowed and came to a gradual halt. The engine still chattered and Carmen asked her to shut it down. Quiet reigned now. Carmen slid off the Lynx and moved around where Malia could see her clearly. She gestured for silence and removed her helmet, her eyes pinned in the direction where she saw the movement.

Snow here in the woods wasn't as deep as in the cleared areas, the trees lending a broken canopy overhead. That allowed her to walk without the need for skis or snowshoes though she still sank halfway up her boots.

"I saw something." Carmen whispered to keep anyone nearby from overhearing.

"What is it?"

Carmen shook her head. "Let's find out."

"Do you remember the dead guy?" Malia sounded outraged though she managed to keep her voice low. "I'd rather not join him. It's going to be dark soon and we won't stand a chance if we run into someone carrying a gun."

"I have a flashlight." Carmen realized she hadn't addressed Malia's primary concern.

"Carmen, no. We are going to the lodge and reporting the murder. That is a crime scene and *that* is the priority." Malia's tone indicated she wouldn't back down.

After a tense moment, Carmen relented. "You're right. Sometimes I get carried away."

Reluctantly, she donned the helmet and slipped her visor down before she climbed back on behind Malia. She wasn't happy to let go of this, but the level of danger here urged caution. They weren't armed and twilight fast approached. The snowmobile's single headlight illustrated the lateness of the hour by cutting sharply through the shadows.

Kofi and Pymer weren't going anywhere. It would be stupid to force a confrontation without preparing. Carmen intended to do that by following them around until she discovered why they killed Wrighton and exactly what they were up to.

Carmen remembered the four slashes across Wrighton's throat and the roar that came from the woods. Again, she thought of the yeti possibility. She quickly disregarded that explanation. Yeti didn't exist. Humans had killed Wrighton for mundane, typical human reasons.

Carmen sat on the bed in her room drying her hair. The hot shower had warmed her through, but her thoughts remained troubled. As agreed, she and Malia had called in Wrighton's death, but now Carmen was on her own. Malia's superiors had recalled her to transport the Swiss investigators as well as a medical examiner. They probably wouldn't return until sometime tomorrow. Carmen knew they couldn't scrutinize the scene in the dark. The basement remained deeply shadowed even in full daylight. The forensics team needed to bring lights and other equipment to perform a thorough job. Even after that, Carmen knew Malia would leave. She had to transfer them and the body back to Zurich. Of course Lucien had to be informed of the incident, but Carmen had asked him to keep it to himself. They couldn't afford to tip off the killers until they had no choice.

Carmen glanced at the clock on her bedside table. The dinner hour fast approached. She wasn't hungry, but wanted to see if Pymer and Kofi made an appearance. She wondered if they would act guilty in any way. She headed downstairs to the dining room, surprised to find she was last to arrive. Kofi barely glanced at her. Pymer offered a smile and then turned to engage Lucien in conversation.

Just like any other day.

The whole idea made her blood boil. She didn't understand how anyone could casually take another life.

Katie paused with a forkful of something lifted halfway to her mouth. "Hey, Carmen. Not like you to be late for a meal. You okay?"

"Sure. Fine. Guess I'm tired. It's been a long day."

"Where's Malia? I thought you two would be getting to know each other better." Katie refrained from wiggling her eyebrows, but Carmen definitely heard a tone.

Normally, she would take such a comment from her friend in good humor. With her current state of mind and her emotions in turmoil, it just made her snappish. Carmen swallowed her ire and settled into her usual seat.

"She got called back."

Katie seemed to take the explanation at face value. After shoveling the food into her mouth, she set aside the fork and passed a food platter to Carmen. By rote, Carmen placed food on her plate and forced herself to eat. She took no pleasure in what was usually a sensual experience for her. Carmen wasn't even sure what she ingested. Eva and a few male serving staff wandered in and out of the room, bringing full dishes and carrying away the empties. Eva ensured drinks remained full.

Carmen ignored them all, her focus remaining on her primary suspects. She tried not to stare and give away her interest so she occasionally spoke with Katie, but her heart wasn't in it.

"Hey, has anyone seen Wrighton lately?" Mike asked the question and looked curiously around the table for a response. "I haven't seen that guy since this morning. I have to admit that I don't really care for his attitude, but I'm starting to get a little worried."

Pymer cleared his throat and swallowed. "I saw him up on the southern slope about an hour ago. He said he'd take dinner in his room later. He wanted to get in a few more runs. I'm sure he's up in his room now showering off the cold."

Carmen's blood froze. Her eyes narrowed, but she clenched her jaw to keep from calling him out. From the head of the table, Lucien met her gaze. His eyes were wider than normal, but he did a great job not reacting. They both knew Pymer's explanation for a lie. The fact that he did so just confirmed what Carmen already surmised. Smattered conversations engaged around the table, but Carmen couldn't eat another bite. She sipped a hot brandy, attempting to act natural.

Eventually, the meal wound down and the staff cleared away the dishes. Lucien invited everyone to join him in the drawing room, reminding them about the upcoming investment discussion. As the other guests followed their host, Carmen lingered. She waited until everyone left and then hurried back up the stairs.

Now was her chance. With everyone occupied, she intended to go through Kofi and Pymer's rooms. If she found something incriminating, it would make any risk acceptable.

Because this was not a hotel and Lucien had such a small guest list both worked in Carmen's favor. No one had keys to their rooms. That would come later with more renovations. She slipped into Kofi's room, two doors down from her own and on the opposite side of the hall. Carmen eased the door closed and looked around in disbelief. The place was an absolute disaster.

Despite his always pristine appearance, apparently Kofi didn't apply that standard to his surroundings. Clothes hung over every available surface. The covers on the bed hung over the edge, trailing onto the floor. Carmen picked her way across to the bureau and yanked open the top drawer. A coffee cup sat on top of the dresser and she noticed congealed milk in the bottom.

Carmen grimaced in distaste and quickly went through Kofi's

things. She searched the dresser, the closet and even looked under the bed. She found his suitcases at the bottom of the closet empty. Nothing. She believed it possible that Kofi watched too many spy movies and had hidden something inside a vent, but she didn't have time to locate a screwdriver to check.

Aware of time slipping away, Carmen left Kofi's room and hoofed it to the far end of the hall. Pymer had the last chamber on the right. Carmen grabbed the handle, but it wouldn't turn. Panic raced through her until she realized the old mechanism was merely stuck. She tightened her grip and put her shoulder to the door to force it open. With the door so hard to open, Carmen couldn't push it completely shut. She couldn't take a chance on getting trapped in here.

Unlike Kofi, everything sat perfectly ordered. Carmen doubted a speck of dust existed in the room and she didn't find a single cobweb. Wow, she needed him to clean *her* room.

Carmen focused on why she was there and headed for the dresser. It rested along the wall to the left of the door. Carmen was aware of that particular point since she wouldn't be visible to anyone in the hall if the door happened to swing open slightly. To her, time slipped away like sand through an hour glass. Adrenaline spiked her heart rate as she went through the drawers. She had to be more careful here. Kofi was a slob and probably wouldn't notice that someone had gone through his things. Not so with Pymer. The need for caution slowed her down to an uncomfortable pace.

Three of the six drawers remained for her to search when the door suddenly opened and a woman stalked in. Carmen froze, her eyes opened wide and a hand still inside Pymer's underwear drawer. Gazes locked and she identified the cobalt blue eyes immediately. Perfect china-doll skin tones, full lips and the blonde pixie style haircut sparked her memory and made it hard for Carmen to draw breath.

She could have kicked herself. The woman had arrived on the helicopter with Malia. Carmen saw her, noticed her above all the others. Even distracted by Malia, Carmen had instinctively recognized this smaller woman, but she was too distracted to pay attention. The sensation of being ambushed rendered her speechless.

Unlike Carmen, the woman seemed annoyed rather than surprised. A line creased her forehead between her eyes, but she took time to partially close the door before confronting Carmen.

"Why are you following me?"

Carmen blinked. She certainly hadn't anticipated that response. "I was here first. If anything, you're following me. I remember you from the plane and again in Germany. You're the one who cut me free in the basement."

"Humph, I had hoped the concussion would make you forgetful."

"Not funny. Who are you? Or should I ask Lucien?"

"You will do no such thing."

Carmen also remembered that incredible French accent. She could never forget this woman after the adventures with the so-called werewolf. Carmen had dreamt about her several times. "I'm waiting."

"I am Faye Joubert, special agent for Interpol. I am here to apprehend an individual named Kofi Gowan. Now it's my turn. Why do you continually show up on my investigations?"

Carmen didn't know how to respond. This all just seemed so crazy. It also didn't explain why Faye was in Pymer's room if she was here for Kofi. "Believe me, I have no idea. Fate?"

"I find that unlikely." Faye crossed her arms, looking determined not to move until she had answers. "You clearly know that something here is amiss. Just like in Germany, you involve yourself in matters that do not concern you. Why are you searching this room?"

Carmen debated for about two seconds before spilling the beans. Without Malia here, Carmen had no backup and she felt a little exposed. Faye had saved her life in Germany and Carmen trusted her without reservation, especially since she now knew her for an Interpol agent. She told Faye everything that had happened since she and Katie arrived. She even informed her of finding Wrighton's body and her suspicions concerning the two men. Carmen went on to say that Malia would likely return in the morning with a whole swarm of forensic experts and a coroner. Throughout the lengthy explanation, Faye's expression remained the same.

"I think they even imitated a yeti's roar at the house. Probably trying to scare us off so they could come back and clean up the evidence. It was already getting dark though, so they might not be able to do that until daylight."

Faye finally unfolded her arms and her gloomy expression eased. "Then we haven't much time. How do you feel about night skiing? I need to examine the scene before others arrive and destroy any evidence. Don't forget to bring a headlamp."

"You want me to go with you?" Carmen shook her head as she realized the inanity of the question. "Of course you do. How else would you find the house? Sorry."

Faye smiled for the first time and Carmen gasped at the strength of her reaction. It was like someone had kicked her in the stomach and removed all the air from the room at the same time. She found this woman stunning.

"Even if I knew where to find this structure, I would ask you to go along. I don't intend to go without reinforcements and you're a very good detective in your own right. I saw that in Germany."

"Uh, thanks?" Carmen deduced she'd been complimented and insulted in one statement. Faye called her a good detective, but insinuated she just didn't want to go in without support.

Faye sashayed confidently to the door and stopped with her hand on the knob. "Who do you think recommended you for the Marshals Service?"

Something from the werewolf incident still caught in Carmen's memory. Something that left a bad taste in her mouth. She couldn't keep the outrage from her tone. "You also left me on my own to save Jessica. Those guys had guns and we were hurt."

"I kept an eye on things from the rooftop of the barn. I had a sniper rifle. You handled the situation quite well without my assistance."

"Thanks loads. I still feel like you hung me out to dry."

"Well, no reason to believe that now. I have my sidearm if we run into difficulties."

That was good news. Carmen latched onto the information like a lifeline. "I don't suppose you have a spare?"

Again, Faye smiled. It seemed like a satisfied expression this time. Clearly, she knew she had Carmen. "Get dressed and meet me at the tree line behind the rear patio in one half hour. Tell no one, not even your friend. If someone asks, you are merely going for a ski."

"You act like this is my first time on an investigation." Carmen wished she didn't find the French accent so sexy.

Twenty-nine minutes later, Carmen waited in the cold. She wore all black. Gloves, snowsuit, beanie and neck gaiter. Even her skis and boots were black. Moving through the trees, she figured she'd look like a shadow. She would stand out like a sore thumb if forced to stand on an open slope. Carmen had thought to pack a small knapsack, which she appropriated from the supplies Lucien provided his guests. It didn't hold a lot, but hopefully they wouldn't require much. Her small headlamp cast a pinprick of light, hardly illuminating a few feet in front of her. Her hair lay in a single plaited braid down her back, held in place at the end with a thick rubber band. In these types of situations, she found it best to tie down the thick, unruly mass lest it interfere with her vision at a crucial moment.

Just when she thought Faye had left without her, Carmen heard the swish of an approaching skier. She noticed Faye managed to pull off classy even while wearing a bulky white ski suit. She stood out only because of the lit headlamp. Like Carmen, Faye also wore black gloves and boots, but her skis were blue. Carmen's mouth went dry and she tried to concentrate on their task.

She offered Faye a slight nod and then set off through the woods, traveling cross-country style on her skis. Carmen followed the snowmobile tracks from earlier, but it took much longer to reach the buried structure than before. Both stayed quiet, abstaining from conversation to focus on their breathing. The moon had already climbed midway in the sky before they arrived.

Carmen immediately headed for the rear of the dilapidated old house where the breached wall existed. She had no desire to crawl on her belly through the smaller hole again. This would be quicker than traipsing through the house and down the basement stairs.

She stopped where the snow slanted under the house. She unclipped her boots from the bindings just as Faye pushed up next to her. After both ditched the skis and poles outside, Carmen led the way to Wrighton's body. Her fastened boots made it feel like she was walking in double casts.

"Here." Carmen point at the bloody snow that trailed inside. "I'm pretty sure this is animal blood, but you can see something was using this as a den. Wrighton's inside behind a crate."

Carmen took the time to point out the "yeti" footprint. She made sure Faye knew Carmen believed it was a hoax. She reiterated to Faye the almost convincing roar that startled her and Malia enough to head back to the lodge.

"I just can't figure out why they would fake a print here except to make people think a make-believe creature killed Wrighton."

Faye pulled a small flashlight from a deep pocket and squatted to examine the print. She took her time, silent as she inspected every aspect of the impression. "I can't think of any reason for them to do this. I heard something about there being more prints inside the lodge. You think these people orchestrated that scene as well?"

"Yes, they had to have." Carmen nodded though Faye wasn't looking at her. "Someone broke through the back door and took food out of the refrigerator. Or so I'm told. No animal could break through that heave door from outside. It makes sense that it was Kofi and Pymer since there's another print here. Maybe they did that at the lodge in case they needed a distraction later."

"Hmm, in my experience, murderers are not so forward thinking. Why are you so certain these men are guilty?"

Faye moved over to examine Wrighton's body while Carmen considered her answer. Again, Faye took her time. She refrained from touching anything, but she seemed very thorough. At one point, she leaned close enough to smell Wrighton, but Carmen realized she was inspecting the throat wound.

"Because we, Malia and I, heard voices when we arrived. They were the only ones unaccounted for. Mike Doyle was drunk in the pool, Sahari and Tiffany Nazem were in the hot tub. My friend Katie was on the slopes, we saw her. Since Lucien was still at the lodge, that leaves only Pymer Skullen and Kofi Gowan." Carmen wouldn't normally use people's full names, but thought Faye would appreciate the attention to detail. For some reason, it was very important to have Faye's approval. "In *my* experience, criminals have the IQ of a chair. They probably had no idea someone would accidentally follow them here and put things together. Although that roar they let loose was pretty convincing."

"You do that a lot. Accidentally follow trouble, I mean."

"Cute. Are you finished? I'd like to follow their tracks and see where they went while we're out here. Maybe we can figure out what they're up to."

"One question before we go. How do you know there is no yeti?"

Carmen thought Faye was teasing until she noticed her serious expression. "For the same reason I know werewolves don't exist. Now please, we're wasting time. Lucien's presentation is probably over by now and I don't want to be surprised by those two. Who knows if they'll wait for daylight?"

She didn't give Faye the chance to argue. Carmen left the creepy, dank cellar and snapped back into her skis. They set off as soon as Faye was ready and followed more ski tracks off into the woods. These veered sharply toward the mountains. The woods thinned as they traveled. Eventually, they left the trees and struck out over a clear, white plain of compacted snow. The full moon rode the sky overhead, illuminating the ground and making the headlamps unnecessary. Occasionally, clouds drifted over its face and cast strangely moving shadows over the ground. Both women left their lights on in case something unexpected happened. As before, neither spoke.

More than a little self-conscious, Carmen couldn't think of anything witty to say that wouldn't sound inane. She had realized within minutes of meeting Faye in the lodge why her dates with two attractive women hadn't worked out. How could they when Faye still occupied her thoughts and dreams? It didn't make sense. Carmen had no relationship of any kind with this woman, but she found her fascinating. They also had a vague and tenuous connection.

While in Germany, Faye had saved her life countless times. Carmen knew she had dressed as the old woman who provided her with the blue Beetle. Then she stood guard over both Carmen and Jessica while they hid in the cornfield. Of course, she hadn't known that at the time. Still, Faye's appearance as a small, feminine, and dainty woman contrasted with her obvious abilities as a law enforcement agent and left Carmen in awe. There were just so many layers to unravel. Then there was the way one look from those incredible blue eyes made Carmen's heart pound.

That was chemistry.

Carmen guessed less than a half hour had passed before she noticed a change in the terrain. Trees grew close again and the ground rose steadily upward, leading to the foot of a smaller peak. Inky blackness at its base hinted at an opening that grew in size as they approached.

"Is that a cave?" Carmen panted as she spoke for the first time since leaving the murder scene.

Faye dug in with her poles as she slid along the snow. "I'm fairly certain it is a decommissioned mine."

"There are mines in Switzerland?"

"Mining once played a small role in the Swiss economy, but no more. Iron, silver, gold, even diamonds came out of the ground in very insignificant amounts. Eventually, the Swiss government closed the last of the mines in the early 1960s."

Carmen was impressed. "You sound like an encyclopedia."

The remnants of a steel and wood track were barely visible as the women stopped near the mine entrance. Carmen noticed the base of an old pull rod standing just above the snow level. In this light she couldn't see a great deal of detail, but figured the mechanism was rusted through and the rod had snapped long ago.

"I do my homework. Someone has cleared the entrance recently. Look there and you can see indications of digging."

Carmen agreed. The signs were obvious that someone had put a great deal of effort into this project. A mound of snow at the mouth of the mine showed where some enterprising individuals had moved it out of the way.

"Uh, suddenly I'm not so sure about this." Carmen's instincts told her it wasn't a good idea to explore this mine at night without anyone aware of their location.

Faye shucked her poles and skis. She unfastened her snow boots and allowed the front to hang open in order to allow more movement. "Why? Are you frightened of the yeti?"

Carmen didn't mind the gentle teasing. In fact, she quite liked Faye's casual interaction that made it seem like they had just grown closer. Pleasure warmed her cheeks and she busied herself removing her own gear. Carmen stashed her skis and poles with Faye's against the snow mound on the side facing the mine, but decided to keep the backpack. She followed the smaller woman's example and unhinged the front of her boots to allow her ankles to flex.

"I'm just not sure Kofi and Pymer were out here mining. I don't see any equipment and I doubt Kofi brought it over from South Africa in his suitcase. On the other hand, Pymer is a local. Maybe he moved something in without Lucien noticing."

Faye walked over to the mine entrance. She reached out to touch the face of the mountain adjacent to the opening. "No. Mining is a loud activity. Dynamite is often necessary for blasting through the rock. Someone would have noticed."

"You said the Swiss used to mine diamonds. South Africa is a leading diamond exporter. Kofi is from South Africa and Wrighton mentioned that he's in the trade."

"All right, but why this place? This mine is not active and I see no reason to meet here in order to smuggle diamonds. Smuggling of such small items is easily accomplished in a much more comfortable setting. Say in a drawing room while sipping a glass of wine. No, there is something we are not seeing."

Carmen tried to fathom the reasons for coming way out here in the middle of nowhere. She didn't like going into a dark hole in the ground, but some things were more important. Finding out why a man died fit into that category. In the end her sense of honor won out. "Well, they came out here for a reason. We got dressed up and came all this way. I say we check it out."

The wind picked up unexpectedly, making Carmen's parka flap about her shoulders. She grabbed at her beanie to keep it from flying away.

"Does it feel colder to you?"

"Maybe, or we could just be feeling the exposure. We have been outside for quite some time."

Carmen shivered and stuffed her hands into her jacket pocket. She swore she saw snow flurries as she followed Faye into the mine.

Chapter Fourteen

"Okay. Color me confused."

Carmen stared down the darkened tunnel into the throat of the mine. Her headlamp illuminated a limited field of vision, but she was pretty sure there wasn't much here anyway. Chunks of splintered wood from overhead support beams littered the floor in scattered clumps for as far as she could see. Scattered snow had blown in and iced over in places. Carmen clearly saw the uneven dirt floor along with the remains of a track. A large, square metal box sat near the limit of her light. She squinted and thought it was the remains of a mining cart. Behind that, the mine curved away out of sight into the mountain. Debris had rained down over the years, forming mounds that obscured much of the tunnel.

Somehow, she had expected to walk into the mine and discover positive proof of nefarious activity. This was anticlimactic. Her nose felt frozen and her cheeks stung from exposure. Carmen sniffled and pulled a tissue from the inside of her left glove. After all this time freezing their buns off, there wasn't anything to find.

Carmen blew her nose, trying not to make a production of it in front of Faye. "This was a huge waste of time."

She stood there watching as Faye wandered farther into the darkness. Carmen was perfectly content to wait where she stood. She still had no idea why Wrighton was dead, but believed they wouldn't find the answers here. With frustration riding high, she was ready to come right out and confront Kofi and Pymer. At least she would have the element of surprise.

Faye walked right past the mine cart and followed the tunnel around to the left. A separate corridor led off to the right. Carmen didn't know how far either tunnel went, but she didn't believe separating inside a mine shaft was a good idea. When Faye crossed out of sight, Carmen finally chased after her.

"We should stay together. I don't know much about mines, but I've heard they can be dangerous."

Her voice echoed through the space, hinting at a long open shaft ahead. When Faye didn't respond, Carmen hurried forward until she rounded the corner. She spotted Faye standing about ten feet away. Her posture seemed off somehow. Carmen realized that Faye stood ramrod still, staring at the ground. The light was even worse in this curved section and she couldn't see what Faye looked at. A horrible thought occurred to her and Carmen raced over to join her.

Carmen put a hand on Faye's shoulder and peered through the shadows to find out what had her so fixated. She expected another body. Instead a spider shaped machine lay against the rock wall. One of the arms had snapped off and lay discarded a few inches away from the main body. Carmen stooped down and reached out to roll the object over. A large camera was attached to the machine's underside.

"Is this what I think it is?"

Faye knelt beside her, close enough for Carmen to feel her body heat. "It is a drone. From the size and the carbon propellers, I'd guess it is commercial grade. Not a cheap toy."

"About how much do you think this thing costs?"

"Somewhere in the twenty thousand dollar range? That's a guess of course, but this drone is capable of carrying a substantial weight."

"What on Earth?" Carmen looked up and realized this section of tunnel held more than a disabled drone. "Hey, there's some other stuff back here."

Carmen and Faye discovered a heavy metal chest about the size of a freezer. A shiny new padlock held it tightly closed. Four more drones sat in the dirt, lined up neatly against the wall. Carmen remembered the almost pathological neatness of Pymer's room and thought this was his doing.

"I think I have an idea what your friends are up to." Faye's voice was low, her tone merely conversational. She didn't sound upset, just preoccupied. "Mines contain shafts that creep underground like veins in the body. In many cases, they can go on for miles. For years, cartels in Mexico constructed super tunnels to run drugs into the United States. At the time, the tunnels were fit with lights, motorized cars and even climate control units. It's my job to know these things. Interpol is very active in efforts to prevent smuggling."

Everything clicked into place for Carmen. "This isn't about diamonds at all. It's a drug smuggling operation. I bet that chest is loaded with some very expensive product. But no one could cook up drugs out here. There isn't any power and there isn't any at the old house either."

"No," Faye agreed. "But the house can be used as a meeting point. Snowmobiles bring in a sample of the product for inspection. The drugs are stored here where no one would stumble across them and drones are used to move them along in the chain."

"It's creative. Have a light aircraft or helicopter standing by in flight range, drop the product and fly out without anyone the wiser. This is a massive operation. There's no way two people could pull this off." Carmen sat on the chest, thinking for a minute. "All right, go with me here. The house is far enough into the woods that no one would notice people coming and going. Pymer lives nearby, but he stayed at the lodge because of the blizzard. That's why we didn't find anything in his room."

Faye picked up on the theory. "This Kofi must be a buyer. He flew to Switzerland to meet with Pymer to sample the product and make arrangements for transport."

"Exactly. Wrighton seemed like a nosey sort of guy. He probably followed those two to the house and saw something he shouldn't have. He was a loose end."

Faye nodded. "They returned to move the body, but you turned up before they could."

"Okay, we have the who, the what and the why. All we need are the details."

"That and any actual proof," Faye pointed out. "This is all circumstantial evidence and best guess."

"Then I suggest we contact the authorities and get a team out here with a warrant to open this chest. We can't break in because anything we find won't be admissible."

"You are thinking like an American police officer."

"Sure." Carmen figured that seemed self evident. "I'm trying to do things the right way so it'll stand up in court."

"I am an Interpol agent. Different rules apply when investigating international drug smuggling operations, especially when a murder has occurred. There is also a time factor involved. By the time any detectives arrive, this entire operation could be shut down."

Carmen had to admit that Faye had a point. A thought occurred to her and she clenched her eyes shut. "Oh no, no, no."

"What's the matter?"

"They know we found the body." Carmen looked at Faye.

"What are you talking about?"

"Malia and I heard someone talking in the basement. It surprised her and she dropped a glass. After that, I walked over to the basement and yelled down that things were fine." Carmen shook her head. "I can't believe I was so stupid. I told Lucien not to say anything, but those guys already knew."

Faye wasted no time. "Then we need to go. If you're right about who is responsible for this, and I believe that you are, the body will be gone by morning. This will be the next stop and everything will disappear. If they find us here, we'll be the next victims."

"Hey, wait a minute. I thought you said you were armed?"

"I am, but drugs and guns go hand in hand. Also, I have a 9mm. Smugglers typically use automatic weapons. How long do you think we shall last?"

"It would be like bringing a knife to a gun fight." Carmen stood and headed for the front of the mine. She had the feeling they had dallied too long already. "Time to go. They could be on their way already."

Carmen believed everything Faye said as absolute truth. Unfortunately, she disagreed on the order of events. Yes, a dead body presented a problem for smugglers, but drug sales figured into the millions. In their place, she'd take care of the product before she worried about a dead guy who wasn't going anywhere. Carmen and Malia were loose ends that the men already knew about and she didn't want to add Faye to that list. She also knew that she didn't have any real proof of their involvement. It would be her word against theirs that they killed

Wrighton. Something they had no need to worry about if all witnesses disappeared.

Before she worried about bringing them to justice, she and Faye needed to survive the night. Carmen could best ensure their survival by getting back to the lodge and being surrounded by other people.

Carmen and Faye had cleared the exit and dashed toward their skis as fast as possible in the bulky ski boots. They stood between the mine and the tall pile of snow. Carmen leaned over to snap her boots shut when bright lights swept across the ground from a short distance away. She grabbed Faye by the sleeve of her suit and yanked her down.

Faye started to complain, but Carmen slapped a gloved hand over her open mouth. "We just ran out of time," she whispered harshly. She switched off her headlamp and urged Faye to do the same.

"We take care of the writer next. Let's dump him in the woods for the animals." The swish of skis coming to a stop punctuated Pymer's remarks.

"It is too cold for animals."

Carmen experienced no pleasure in being right about the identity of the smugglers. They would come around the embankment of snow any moment and immediately spot the women cowering in the open. Faye pulled out a pistol and Carmen experienced only a small measure of relief. The weapon wasn't much, but it was better than nothing.

"Then the elements will dispose of him for us." Pymer spoke casually, clearly unconcerned with killing a man.

"You check on the merchandise. Make sure it is undisturbed. Fly the drones to the landing site. The pilot will be there at exactly midnight. We must be prompt as she will not wait."

"And what are you going to do while I am doing all the work?"

Now Pymer sounded irritated. Carmen could only hope for an argument between the two that would provide a distraction for her and Faye to slip into the trees.

"I need to change my bandage. My arm is still bleeding." Kofi's normally placid accent held a touch of anger. "I never expected a weakling like Wrighton to fight back so hard."

Pymer snickered. "Yes, he stuck you pretty good with your own knife before you killed him. Perhaps you need stitches."

Snow crunched under foot as Pymer strode toward the mine. He had just rounded the pile of snow. Carmen saw his foot as he stepped forward. She leaned a little too far back trying to remain hidden and bumped into a set of skis. They toppled and slapped into the snow. The situation spiraled quickly out of control from there. Things seemed to happen all at once.

Kofi and Pymer rushed them from both sides of the embankment. Faye turned to face Kofi who rushed her with a large hunting knife. She raised her sidearm and fired once. The round caught him high in the right shoulder and blood sprayed out onto the snow. Carmen watched Kofi pitch backward. He lost his grip on the knife. It sailed into the air before dropping away into the night. Carmen had already turned to face Pymer before Kofi hit the ground.

Rather than rush her, Pymer fumbled to pull a black machine pistol from where he had slung it on his back. When Faye spun around to bring her weapon to bear, Pymer dodged behind the snow bank. For a long tense moment, the world seemed to freeze. Carmen held her breath. A thunderous bellow from the nearby tree line reverberated through the night, stealing her attention from the man intent on murder.

Carmen's heart raced in fear along with heavy, lumbering steps that rushed toward them. Growls punctuated by snuffling grunts steamrolled directly for them before Carmen's brain finally engaged. Even as she grabbed Faye by the back of the jacket and hauled her toward the mine, Pymer fired off a burst of shots.

The horrible sounds of an animal attack continued and Carmen couldn't help but glance back over her shoulder as she ran. Something from hell raced out of the woods. It resembled a polar bear, but stood upright. Moonlight gleamed off of the red eyes as it roared again. The ground shook from the impact of the beast's paws pounding the snow. Pymer continued to fire until the Uzi's bolt locked to the rear.

Either he was a terrible shot or the creature never registered the impact of the weapon's fire. Carmen focused on running when the beast reached pouncing range from Pymer. Clambering along in the hard ski boots wasn't easy, but the instinct for survival spurred the women on. Carmen and Faye sprinted into the mine. Carmen briefly considered the tactical error of being trapped, but the mine provided the only sanctuary available. Just as they crossed the threshold, Pymer screamed. The sound of his terror was nothing compared to the sound of the creature smashing into his body.

Carmen heard the sob that escaped her own throat. She smelled the sweat-induced fear generated by Faye's body and the cordite in the air from all the bullets fired. Everything seemed brighter, sharper. Even her eyesight. She didn't need the headlamp to race down the mine shaft as adrenaline surged through her. The daypack bounced against her back in keeping with her footfalls, but she barely noticed it.

About twenty feet into the tunnel, the ground began to shake. Carmen stumbled to the side and released her handhold on Faye's parka. Carmen's shoulder hit the rock wall and she struggled to keep her footing. Another roar echoed down the mine and the shaking increased.

Whumph!

The sound was like someone had dropped a sack of corn from fifty feet in the air and it hit the snow. The ground shook harder than before. A deep, low rumbling began from somewhere far away and then Carmen heard a loud *crack*.

"Avalanche, run!" Faye shouted the words and scrambled for the back of the mine.

Carmen's long legs allowed her to easily pass Faye as they ran for cover. Instinctively, she knew they had to reach the turn at the back of the mine to have any hope. She slid into the darkness and around the corner before slowing to look back at Faye. Faye was only a few steps behind when a wind slab tore into the mine entrance and burst down the narrow corridor. The force of the gust picked her up and slammed her into the end of the tunnel.

Outside, Carmen heard tree branches snapping and a sound like a hurricane. Debris poured into the mine, carried on the shrieking winds and raining down like hail. Carmen struggled to get to where Faye lay unmoving on the ground, but the tempest pushed her back. Carmen dropped to her knees and lunged forward enough to grab Faye by the wrist. She hauled backward with her remaining strength and yanked the smaller woman toward safety. Carmen's gloved hand slipped and she tightened her grip.

The rumbling sound grew a million times louder now and possessed a new quality. It resembled the sound of an onrushing train. Carmen risked a glance toward the mine entrance and her mouth dropped open. A wall of snow rushed toward the mine at speeds far greater than she could guess. The slide came from an angle rather than straight on, but proved no less frightening. She kept pulling, sobbing in her desperation. Faye's upper body slid toward her and out of the main shaft. When the snow hit the mine, the impact shook Carmen like a rag doll in a giant's fist.

The force of the impact tossed her into the air and she attempted to curl into a ball. Her head struck the corner of something hard, unyielding and metallic. The world disappeared.

Chapter Fifteen

Carmen's head throbbed. The inside of her mouth was as dry and gritty as sandpaper. Why did she have a hangover? Carmen didn't remember drinking last night. No, that wasn't right. Memory slowly returned along with awareness of an intense cold like the inside of a freezer. Her whole body felt encased in ice and her feet throbbed. Carmen lay on her side, but something bulky dug into her stomach there. She groaned as the gears started turning again and she remembered the avalanche. Something soft and wet covered her face, blocking her vision. Carmen moved the hair away from her eyes, but still couldn't see anything. She needed to touch her eyes to make sure they were actually open. Tomblike darkness persisted. The avalanche must have completely blocked any light from entering the mouth of the tunnel.

Carmen groaned and forced herself up. The small backpack she still wore slipped back into place though the right strap had slid halfway down her arm. She didn't quite have the strength to stand yet, but sitting seemed just as good. She'd lost her headlamp in the concussive force of the snow slide. Carmen adjusted the straps on the pack.

"Faye." The word came out husky. Barely above a harsh whisper. Carmen cleared her throat and tried again. "Faye!"

When Faye failed to respond, Carmen struggled to her knees and began sweeping the area around her with both hands. She encountered the corner of the heavy chest and mentally oriented herself. Systematically, she searched along the container's edge and around behind the side deepest into the shaft. Debris littered the floor of the tunnel. Tree limbs and twigs mixed with metallic pieces of the destroyed drones. With the thick ski gloves on, she couldn't distinguish between wreckage and the headlamp. Propped on one hand and her knees, she removed a glove with her teeth.

Eventually, Carmen brushed against the soft nylon headband. Carmen grasped the headlamp, but the nausea that burned in her stomach forced her to sit down. She squeezed the button on the light and flinched at the unaccustomed brightness. Several long, heaving breaths later, she managed to wrestle the queasiness under control. Carmen donned the lamp and put her glove back on before she tried to stand. It took a few tries. By using the chest as a brace, she managed to climb to her feet.

"Oh my God," she muttered.

Snow and debris stripped from the coniferous trees had blown through the main tunnel, down the shaft and even around the corners. The bulk of the influx lay near the entrance to the mine and about twenty feet farther in, blocking the mouth of the mine completely. From there, the height of the snow tapered off quickly to a layer only a few inches thick. That thin coating leveled off to the normal dirt floor only a few feet past the curve of the shaft, though debris from mangled trees carried farther along.

Carmen stumbled toward Faye on wobbly legs. She dropped down beside the unconscious woman, dusting snow from her body and away from her face. Faye appeared almost blue in the weak light, but she was breathing. Carmen brushed the pale bangs away from her face and caressed her cheek. The kinetic energy from the avalanche had thrown Faye forcefully into the wall and Carmen hesitated to roll her over.

"Faye, come on now. You have to wake up."

Faye tensed and moaned. Her face clenched in obvious pain.

"Ow."

Carmen laughed, easing the tension in her chest. "You have a talent for understatement. Can you move?"

Faye drew up one knee as prepared to stand. She suddenly froze and shrieked in pain.

"Don't move." Fear and concern zipped through Carmen. She placed a hand on Faye's back to hold her in place. "What hurts? Is it your back or your neck? You shouldn't move or you could cause more damage."

Faye growled. "*Fils de pute*! It's my arm. I think it's broken."

"Let me help you."

Carmen brushed twigs and snow from Faye's body and helped her into a sitting position. Faye's right arm looked strange, a little twisted. Faye hugged the arm to her chest, grimacing in pain as Carmen removed her day pack.

"Turn on your headlamp. We need the light to take care of you."

"Don't tell me you have a hospital triage in your bag," Faye teased, though the pain clearly resonated through.

"We're in trouble here. No telling how long we'll be stuck in this tunnel and that arm could be an issue."

Carmen knew she sounded harsh. She didn't mean to. She was worried. Faye could suffer shock even from a minor injury with this cold. Carmen didn't have a lot in the tiny pack, but what she did have might prove vital to their survival. A small camper's first aid kit provided them with a sling and a blister pack of painkillers. Carmen freed the tablets and handed them across to Faye along with a small plastic bottle of water. She had to break the seal on the water first.

"Be glad we weren't outside. Those poor men."

"Poor Kofi," Carmen corrected. "Pretty sure that thing killed Pymer, but I know Kofi was still alive."

"Maybe he reached the tree line before the avalanche struck."

Carmen pictured the speed needed to outrun the snow slide. "Not unless he had a rocket stuffed up his butt."

Faye chuckled at the gallows humor and swallowed the painkillers. Carmen helped her with the sling after that. She moved gently, but still heard Faye hiss in pain. She finished the minor triage by tying a knot in the sling at the back of Faye's neck.

"You look as though you could use some first aid yourself." Faye reached up to touch a cut on Carmen's chin before trailing her fingertips lightly across her temple. "You have a lump here on your head and several small cuts on your face and neck. It looks like the gash on your temple has already stopped bleeding."

"Other than setting a new record for the Shriek and Flee event, I'm fine. It's nothing major. At least it's cold enough that I shouldn't have to worry about any infection."

Faye grimaced slightly, but let it go. "Now what? I don't suppose you brought a satellite phone in that tiny pack."

Carmen shook her head. "No such luck. Malia had the sat phone and since there isn't any cell service, I haven't carried my phone since the first day. I did, however, remember to wear my avalanche beacon." She concluded the statement by pulling out and activating the small Black Diamond beacon she carried on a string around her neck.

"That's wonderful, *Cherie*. I brought mine as well. There is only one slight issue I can foresee. These things have a maximum range of fifty meters. We are well and truly beyond that distance from the lodge. Also, I did not advise anyone of our intention to ski."

"Neither did I. Everyone was at Lucien's meeting, but you're forgetting something." Carmen panted slightly as she laid their supplies out on the mine floor. "You're forgetting my friend, the spunky Katie McClarin. Knowing her, she's already out looking for me. Okay, we have a couple of protein bars, a bag of nuts, and a few bottles of water. We need to ration those. I also have a packet of waterproof matches, a small pack of tissues, and a flint fire starter, but I'm not sure those will do us any good. Oh, and I have this."

She held up a tiny reflective square approximately three by three inches and about an eighth of an inch thick.

Faye looked at her blankly. "And that is?"

"It's a thermal blanket." Carmen shook the thin material out until it covered about five by seven feet. "People use them for camping or emergency bags. It's made of Mylar. Haven't you ever camped?"

Faye sniffed at the idea. "I do not sleep on the ground."

"I can see that about you. You seem a little too sophisticated for that. Would you go if you could sleep in a cabin?"

She stood and helped Faye shift over where she could lean against the wall. Faye cooperated by leaning forward so Carmen could drape the Mylar blanket around her shoulders. The conversation seemed a little inane, but Carmen thought it better not to become overwhelmed by their current situation. Speaking of everyday things could mitigate their concerns.

"I'm not sure that could be considered camping."

She had a point. "I guess not, but you could still make a fire and have s'mores. Why don't you try to rest and I'll check out how bad the blockage is? Maybe we can dig our way out."

Faye raised her eyebrows, but refrained from comment. She leaned her head back against the dirt wall and closed her eyes.

Despite her attempts to sound composed, Carmen was afraid. She wanted to present an optimistic outlook for Faye, but common sense told her their odds against a way out of the mine. Still, hope burned bright. Soft snow couldn't be too hard to dig through.

Carmen walked all round the obstruction. The center of the tunnel contained the highest level of snow. The mound dropped off steeply on the sides, but she still couldn't reach the front of the mine. She tried climbing the recently dislodged snow, but sank up to her ankles on the first step and deeper with every subsequent stride. In a last ditch effort, Carmen attempted to squeeze between the lower edges of the snow and the walls of the tunnel. She got close enough to reach out and touch the mine entrance before she learned the awful truth.

The force of the avalanche had compacted snow against the front of the mine. Attempting to dig through it would be like trying to shovel through cement. The loose powder Carmen saw inside the shaft was merely what had blasted through before the bulwark of the snow slide struck. Her day pack didn't hold the tools to excavate through this.

Carmen put her hands on her hips and closed her eyes. She lowered her head as she considered their options. They were limited. She turned and retreated back to Faye, her mind still on ways to escape.

"I see from your expression that our situation has not improved." Faye lifted one side of the blanket, inviting Carmen into the warmth.

Carmen sat beside her and pulled the blanket as close around them as possible. Faye had generated some body heat under the blanket that Carmen thought felt like heaven. "We can't dig ourselves out, but we'll be fine. Katie will find us. We just need to stay warm and not give up."

"It is important to have hope," Faye agreed, "but we must also be realistic. We are buried in a mine and no one knows our location. Even if your friend suspects trouble and begins a search, it will take hours to dig us free. Or days. And that is *if* they locate us or even think to track the beacons. What is more, that is not even the worst problem. All of this snow has lowered the temperature even further inside this mine. Without a fire, we will freeze to death before we are rescued."

Carmen opened her eyes and looked down at Faye. "Are you always so positive?"

"Hmm, there are several small twigs and branches that were blown in here. I also saw many places where the mine's overhead beams have splintered and fallen apart."

"There you go," Carmen said. "The branches and stuff from outside might be too wet, but those beams are old. Even if they're damp, they should catch fire. I can use some of those Kleenex as kindling. We'll have a fire going in no time."

She scooted out from under the blanket to begin scavenging for anything that would burn. It took time. She collected sticks of every size from the width of her finger to as big around as her wrist. Carmen reserved a few chunks of wood beams to use as the main fuel source and eventually she had enough to construct a small fire. Since she didn't have any rocks for a fire ring, she just piled the kindling and tinder into a gob about six feet from where Faye rested. Carmen stuffed tissue papers under some of the smaller kindling. Tiny twigs and the smallest bits from the old wooden beams seemed dry enough to catch.

Farther down their shaft, Carmen found an area that had partially collapsed sometime in the distant past. Splintered timbers lay in a heap, pointing accusing fingers at the dirt ceiling. Overhead, ancient beams had broken apart in the recent barrage. They hung precariously, threatening to drop at any second. The detritus on the floor provided a bit more of fuel to haul back to their makeshift campsite. She was concerned by the lack of material. Most of the beams were too long and heavy to be of use. Carmen worked quickly, afraid the remains above her would drop at any second.

Her hands already shook from the cold before she removed her gloves and she could barely hold the waterproof matches. Her violent shaking caused the first one she struck to go out. In frustration, Carmen tossed the useless bit of wood onto the pile.

"Stay with it. You'll get it."

She looked up to see that Faye knelt beside her. "When did you get here?"

Faye chuckled. "Try again."

Carmen nodded and struck a match. She placed it close to a tissue and held her breath when the paper flared. The flame went out, but a reddish color still outlined the edges. Faye leaned close, her face almost against the logs. She blew softly and the embers flared. Carmen watched intently as Faye patiently coaxed the fire to life. Long minutes passed before a small, but healthy, fire burned. Carmen loaded a few of the larger pieces on. Having a fire inside a closed off mine wasn't a good idea, but desperate times called for desperate measures. Without the fire, they would die faster.

"That won't last." Carmen hoped Faye couldn't hear her teeth chattering. "I need to find some more wood. We need something bigger that will burn longer, I think."

Faye shook her head, adamant in denial. "Come under the blanket first. You are too cold. Once you warm up a little you can look for firewood."

Neither of them admitted that any fuel for a fire would prove extremely scarce. Instead, Carmen braced her back against the tunnel wall and waited as Faye tucked up against her side. Carmen put her arm around Faye and pulled the reflective blanket around them. Both women pulled their knees up to generate as much warmth as possible in the little cocoon. She hugged Faye close and shivered as she waited for her body to warm. Carmen rested her forehead on her knees.

"You should turn off your headlamp so we can conserve battery power. I'll keep mine on for now."

Faye nodded at the suggestion and switched off her beam. She snuggled against Carmen and they settled down to wait.

As her muscles unwound, Carmen considered the events that brought them here. A shiver went through her that had nothing to do with the temperatures. Her whole body ached and her head pounded. Carmen's feet were so cold they hurt. The snow boots weren't much on insulation.

"What do you think that thing was?" Carmen kept her voice low, almost superstitiously afraid her question would draw the creature.

"A Himalayan bear?"

Faye didn't sound certain. For good reason, Carmen thought. "I don't think so. We're nowhere near the Himalayas. Does Switzerland have any white bears?"

She felt Faye shake her head against her shoulder. "I'm afraid that is a little outside my expertise. I've always focused on criminals and their habits. I usually know what they are going to do before they do. If it's not a dog or a cat, I have no idea."

"That's funny. I figured you knew just about everything."

"Sorry to disappoint."

Conversation died down. Carmen relaxed as heat from the fire warmed the space. A cold breeze whispered down her neck from time to time, but this was a definite improvement. She didn't realize she had almost dozed off until Faye suddenly tensed against her side.

"Carmen, watch the smoke."

"Hmm?" Carmen opened her eyes to see smoke from the campfire trailing away down the curved portion of the shaft, the opposite direction from the mine entrance. "It looks like there's an opening down there. At least we won't die from suffocation."

"Do you think it could be large enough for us to get out?"

Carmen considered the lack of light down the passage and the way the smoke drifted. "I doubt it. Anything large enough for us to squeeze through would probably send a breeze toward us instead of sucking the smoke away. Also, I know it's night, but the moon is full. With light reflecting off the snow, we'd be able to see something."

"I believe it is still worth investigating."

Carmen found it difficult to argue Faye's firm tones. If she wasn't so tired, Carmen might have insisted on it herself. She took a deep breath and summoned the strength to move. "All right. I'll check it out. You stay here. I don't want you injuring your arm more than you already have."

Reluctantly, she crawled out of the warm spot. She followed the trailing vapors as they drifted toward the end of the shaft where Carmen had noticed the collapse. The smoke particles thinned past the point of visibility the farther she walked from the fire. This had to be the source of any break. Carmen glanced at the hazard overhead. If it was going to fall, she figured, it already would have.

"I'm taking my life in my hands, crawling through a dark dank mine, looking for a crack. Just to make sure that we really are getting fresh air. Makes total sense. Who am I kidding? I'd try to dig through the wall with my bare hands if she asked me to. Not that she needs to know that. She's bossy enough."

A gust of air blew over Carmen's face and she stopped muttering. She clambered carefully over the heap of old wood, twisted branches and scattered snow. The mess seemed to grow worse until it unexpectedly cleared less than a foot from the rear wall. The wind blew steadily back here. The fresh air she inhaled highlighted the damp, moldy smell in the mine. At first, Carmen couldn't find the opening. She leaned over, propping her hands against her knees and squinted into the feeble light cast by her headlamp.

"There'll be no living with her now."

After a heavy sigh, Carmen dropped to her knees and crawled forward. A jagged opening about the width of a snowboard provided her a clear view of the Bernese Alps. Black rocks poked up like teeth, offering to rip through her skin like a shark if she attempted to navigate the opening. Carmen leaned her head against the side of the breach, regret flooding her veins. She'd need to wiggle out on her belly and the hole didn't provide a lot of room. It resembled a squeeze in a cave.

She could climb out. Faye couldn't. Not with a broken arm. Carmen turned around and headed back toward the fire. She paused to add their last piece of wood to the fire and then scootched in under the blanket with Faye.

"Well, what did you find?"

"It's just a fissure. Enough to let the smoke out. Try to rest. I'm sure we'll be saved soon."

Carmen let out the breath she'd been holding when Faye didn't argue. She wasn't sure she could keep the tears at bay if she had. There was no way she was going to leave this woman to freeze alone in the dark. Carmen tightened her grip around Faye's shoulders, taking comfort from the scent of her skin.

"Why do you always smell so good?"

Faye chuckled. "You're delusional, *mon amie*."

"Can I tell you something?" Carmen wanted to admit how she seemed drawn to this woman. She wanted to confess that she hadn't thought of another woman seriously since seeing Faye on a plane. She didn't understand why her emotions seemed so jumbled around her. It was all ridiculous, but if Carmen had to die here, she had to say something.

Even if she couldn't completely admit the depth of her emotions.

"No deathbed confessions. We will survive this."

"Now you're an optimist? No, it's nothing like that. I just wanted to say that you have the most amazing eyes I've ever seen. Are you wearing contacts?" Carmen chickened out. She just couldn't take the chance that Faye didn't return her interest.

"No contacts. This is my true eye color. My turn. There is a reason I watched you at the cornfield in Germany and failed to act."

"Really?" Carmen definitely considered this more interesting than an emotional admission.

"Your courage left me breathless. I was astonished by your capabilities even without resources or weapons. Most of all, the kindness for the woman you protected, a complete stranger, captivated me. I knew if ever I met you, you could quite possibly steal my heart. I couldn't allow that to happen. Instead, I lay on that barn, watching through my scope, keeping silent watch."

"You did more than that. You saved my life when you shot Brian. Even then, you showed an incredible amount of compassion by only wounding him. You could have killed him."

Faye looked up at Carmen, her expression gentle. She was so close that Carmen could see her eyes dilated by the darkness.

"I missed."

Carmen laughed much harder than the comment warranted. The fear and tension eased as she hugged Faye closer. Faye told her that Carmen might steal her heart. She hadn't said that she truly cared, but the possibility made Carmen feel warm all the way through. She rested her cheek on silky soft hair as Faye snuggled into the crook of her neck. While Carmen realized this closeness stemmed from a need to survive, her heart wanted to believe it meant so much more. She had no right to push her desires so she stayed quiet. This was enough. It had to be. If they survived this ordeal, Carmen would return to Denver and never see Faye again.

She wanted to weep at the unfairness of life's timing. In this hour of uncertainty, she finally admitted the truth. Desire had struck on an airplane four months ago when she looked into Faye's eyes for the first time. She hadn't known her name, barely knew her still, yet couldn't deny the truth. Now it made sense why she couldn't pursue relationships with Sally or Malia. Her heart had embraced possibilities even if her head lagged behind. Carmen didn't know if what existed between them could turn to something more and she found it unlikely that she would ever find out.

She snuggled closer and pulled the blanket tighter around them. Carmen tucked in the edges to close off any drafts and closed her eyes. She allowed Faye's gentle respirations to lull her into a light doze. Absently, she noticed the fire burn lower.

Time passed. The rhythmic pulses of the avalanche beacon lulled her toward sleep. The drifting campfire smoke imparted a sense of cozy comfort and hominess that drew her in. Carmen tried to keep her eyes open. She needed to find more wood or they would surely die. At the same time, she knew there wasn't any more fuel to locate. Her head dipped as she nodded off and she jerked awake. A few minutes later it happened again so she leaned her head back against the mine's wall. Quickly after, she fell into a deep slumber where she dreamt she lay naked inside an enormous freezer.

Images flashed, disjointed and sporadic, like clips in a film cut together out of order. Carmen refused to meet a suddenly too bright light and clenched her eyes shut. The cold in her bones lured her back toward oblivion, but a sliver of tender heat beckoned.

"Carmen, it's me, Katie. We've got you. Wake up, honey."

Something hard rested under her back. At first, Carmen thought it was the mine wall until she realized she lay flat. Stiff cloth brushed her chin and tucked around her shoulders. Carmen missed the poignant emptiness of a forgone embrace. She tried to speak. Her mouth was too dry, but she persevered. Carmen had to know.

"Faye?" she managed. A delay in the answer scared Carmen enough to crack one eye open. The other stayed pasted shut. Weak light on the horizon hinted at coming day, but allowed her to see Katie's face. "Is she okay?"

"She's alive, Carmen. Rest now."

Carmen closed her eyes, secure in the knowledge they were safe. She experienced the jostling sensation of being loaded onto a helicopter. Heard the rotors spin overhead and the engine engage. They lifted slowly into the air and Carmen turned her head as she sought the gentle sunlight. She opened her eyes fully to appreciate the sight of rising above the Burmese Alps. Then she blinked in disbelief.

A mammoth sized creature strolled along the top of the nearest ridge. The thing seemed more ape-like than bear-like. Covered in grayish white fur, the being's arms appeared overly long. Its fingertips reached its knees. The beast didn't react in any way to the helicopter.

Carmen closed her eyes. She was hallucinating.

Chapter Sixteen

The smell of flowers awakened her. The perfumed scent approached the overwhelming, lending the sensation of lying in a botanical garden. Underlying the sweet scents, Carmen identified an unfortunately familiar stench. Hospitals all stank of antiseptic with a hint of urine. She opened her eyes to an unbelievable sight. Blooms of every hue adorned shelves, ledges and any flat surface, causing a lump of emotion to rise in her throat. Tears pricked the corners of her eyes, yet Carmen had awakened alone. Unaccountable, she felt abandoned.

At least she was finally, mercifully, warm. She reached up and discovered a good-sized bandage on her left temple.

The door opened smoothly silent and Katie tiptoed into the room. Carmen drank in the sight of her friend, moving only her eyes. To see Katie here meant everything, at the same time explaining how Carmen survived the mine. Katie carried a Burger King sack. Only she would bother to track down American fast food, Carmen's favorite, in a foreign country.

Katie rounded the foot of the bed before glancing at Carmen. She blinked when their eyes met and a huge grin took possession of her face. After dropping the bag onto the hospital table she rushed to Carmen's side.

"You're awake. I was so scared." Katie threw herself over Carmen in an awkward hug.

Carmen held onto Katie firmly. The hug helped heal the fear and vulnerability Carmen suffered after the avalanche. Tears finally escaped and ran down her cheeks. Her emotions rested on a razor's edge. Not surprising given the recent ordeal and she knew Katie wouldn't judge her for any lack of control.

"Don't you ever do that to me again." Katie's voice held a husky quality. She pulled away and pinned Carmen's eyes, her gaze fierce. "How do you feel?"

"Stiff. My fingers and toes don't want to move. How is Faye?"

Katie's eyebrows rose as she settled into the bedside chair. "The woman who was with you? To be honest, Carmen, I don't think she's doing so great, but they won't tell me much since I don't even know her. From what I understand, her arm is broken in two places. She has light frostbite on the fingers of that hand and she had pretty severe hypothermia. So did you, but not as bad."

Carmen swallowed with difficulty. The petite woman with the larger than life personality had come to mean so much in such a short amount of time. "I'd like to see her."

"Not right now. You need to rest and get your strength back." Katie swiveled the hospital table into place. "I thought Burger King would help you with that."

"My hero. I'm starving."

Faye would recover. Hospital staff would do everything to ensure that. All Carmen needed to do was show a little faith. That didn't mean Carmen wouldn't hobble down the hall with her IV pole to find her at the first opportunity. As she pulled out a Double Whopper with cheese and a large order of fries, Carmen asked, "What room is she in?"

"Uh uh. Eat."

Katie's concern generated a smile Carmen attempted to hide by pressing her lips together. She dumped tiny packets of catsup on the tray before flattening the bag and laying the food out on top of it. She moaned at the taste of flame broiled goodness.

"How did you find us?" Carmen mumbled around the food.

"Therein lies a tale."

Katie told Carmen of searching for her after Lucien's presentation. No one had seen her and Katie found the door to her room open. She wasn't concerned at first, but did notice Carmen's skis missing. A short time later, Katie saw Pymer and Kofi leave the lodge heading for the slopes.

"I thought it funny that everyone suddenly wanted to ski at night, but hey, who am I to judge?"

Carmen tore open a couple of catsup packets with her teeth, waiting patiently for her to continue.

"Oh, here. I brought you a Coke." Katie pulled a can out of her purse and placed it beside the food. "Anyway, about an hour later, the phone at the lodge rang. Malia wanted to let you know that she was delayed coming back because she had to wait for some equipment."

Katie went on to say that during the course of the conversation, Malia grew concerned. When she learned about the men skiing off into the night, Malia broke down and told Katie everything. She included Carmen's suspicions of the two killing Wrighton. It wasn't much of a stretch to figure Carmen went off investigating without backup.

"Knowing your penchant for trouble, I told Lucien. We organized a search party and Lucien was smart enough to bring the lodge's sat phone with us, just in case. Mike, Karl and Sahari volunteered immediately. Even Tiffany insisted on helping out. We found the house right where Malia said it was. Since I already knew there was a dead guy inside, everyone stayed out of the basement except Lucien.

I almost lost it when he came back out without you. There were a lot of tracks right outside and I had no idea where to go from there. Someone, I think it was Tiffany, suggested trying to follow them. You know, there's more to that woman than I could have guessed."

Carmen swallowed four fries liberally drenched in catsup. "Is Malia here at the hospital or did she have to fly back to the resort?"

"She was here, but she had to get the forensics team out to collect Wrighton." Katie shook her head in wonder. "Malia was a godsend, Carmen. If it wasn't for her, I think you and Faye would be dead. She was supposed to wait here until the authorities had everything together to check out the murder site, but she refused. Malia organized her own team of searchers to help, and trust me, we needed them. She even thought to bring generators and work lights."

Malia and eight strong men with whom she worked had crowded into the helicopter. Katie told of trailing ski tracks toward the mountains. She described the search party's terror when the avalanche struck, throwing everyone off their feet. A few people wanted to turn back, but Katie refused. In the end, Lucien convinced the naysayers to push on.

"After the avalanche, I switched my beacon from transmit to receive. There wasn't anything for the longest time, but I finally picked up a signal." Katie smiled, but the expression seemed a little sad. "You always get into trouble, but you always seem ready for it. As long as that beacon of yours transmitted, I wasn't about to give up."

Carmen fumbled with the lone remaining fry. "I knew you'd come. I told Faye that you would find me."

"Who is this woman, Carmen? I've never seen her before."

"Finish your story and then I'll tell you."

Katie's mouth twisted and she gave Carmen an irritated look, but relented. "Fine. Let me continue by saying that you got lucky."

The avalanche struck the mine a glancing blow from an oblique angle. The snow slide blocked the mouth of the mine, but not to the extent searchers couldn't approach. At first, Katie almost panicked, believing Carmen was buried under tons of snow. Lucien informed them of the mine and gave everyone the heart to keep going.

"We'd brought folding shovels and poles with us and we got to work. I called Malia on Lucien's sat phone about an hour later and told her where to find us. Those extra diggers and the lights made the difference. When we found you…at first, I thought you were dead. You were both so cold and you actually had ice crystals on your hair and eyelashes." Katie cleared her throat. Her eyes flashed and she repeated, "Don't you ever do that again!"

"I promise." Carmen held up three fingers on her right hand in a mock Girl Scout salute. "From now on, I'm carrying an axe in my pack. More firewood would have made the difference."

"Not funny." Katie socked her lightly on the thigh. "Now tell me about this Faye person."

Carmen hesitated. "Did you find Kofi or Pymer?"

"No. Now that you mention it, I didn't think about them again after I started looking for you. What has Faye got to do with those two?"

"Faye is an Interpol agent."

"What?"

Carmen smiled at the anticipated reaction, but quickly turned serious. More alert with a full stomach, she quickly organized recent events in her head. The newfound strength allowed her to open up to Katie with the whole story.

"Faye Joubert is her name. She arrived at the resort when Malia brought Lucien's employees to work. Do you remember the two women who came in that day?"

"I remember Eva, but I never even spoke to the other one. She was just kind of there, you know? Lurking in the background."

"Hiding in plain sight and gathering intel. She tracked Kofi to the lodge on an international warrant."

"I still don't understand," Katie admitted. "How did you end up together in that mine?"

Embarrassment made Carmen's cheeks flush. She looked down and picked at the cotton blanket. "She caught me searching their rooms."

"Carmen, what were you thinking? What if those guys walked in on you instead of her? You said they killed Wrighton. I doubt they'd mind dropping one more body!"

"It's okay. I'm okay. Please keep your voice down." Carmen expected a nurse to burst into the room to look into the commotion, but the door stayed closed. "I knew they were at the meeting so I had some time. And before you say anything, Faye and I had already met. Well, sort of. She's the same woman I saw on the plane ride over to Germany. The same one who saved my life when I was tied up in that basement."

Katie leaned back in the chair and digested that information for a moment. "That's quite a coincidence."

"You know, it really is odd that I keep running into her. Maybe I'm always in the wrong place at the wrong time."

"Carmen, no one has that much bad luck. Something else is going on here."

Katie's eyes hinted at concern mixed with a measure of excitement. Carmen figured she regretted missing out on the action. Katie enjoyed a good mystery almost as much as her. No, Carmen decided. Katie only liked working on them from behind the scenes. She definitely didn't appreciate the dangerous side of the equation.

Carmen was just imagining Katie as a dogged detective when she ruined the moment. Katie turned her face into her elbow and let loose with a thunderous sneeze. She waited a moment and then sneezed again.

"Blasted allergies." Katie sniffled. "The second I get back to civilization."

"I'm sorry about that. In a way, I feel responsible. It's my fault you're here instead of at the resort."

"Forget all that. What happened next?"

Carmen offered her usual one-shouldered shrug. "Same as yours. We followed tracks to the mine. We found out they were using the mine to hide smuggled drugs. Then they showed up and tried to take us out."

"No!"

Carmen described how Faye shot Kofi right before something, probably a weird bear, attacked the men. After that the avalanche hit and trapped Carmen and Faye in the mine.

"That's pretty much it. You know the rest." Carmen saw no reason to tell Katie about the yeti hallucination.

"Well, we didn't find any bodies. They're probably still buried under all that snow. That must have been some bear, though."

"What do you mean?"

Katie's brow furrowed. "I didn't think anything of it until now, but when we reached the site something was off. It was hard to tell with only our headlamps, but it seemed like someone had already started digging before we got there."

A chill shot through Carmen, sending ice through her veins. She remembered the wound on Kofi's arm and Pymer's scream as the beast charged. The smell of blood must have drawn the creature. After dispatching the men, it likely tracked Carmen and Faye's scent to the mine. Hunting for more meat. Carmen shuddered.

"It did a nice job, too. About a quarter of the area in front of the entrance seemed clear. I just thought the snow slide was ragged. Hey, are you okay? You look a little pale."

"Fine." Carmen knew her voice sounded weak. "Just tired, I guess."

Katie took that as her cue and stood up. She draped her purse over her shoulder. "Right, sorry. I should let you rest. How about I come back in the morning and bring you a decent breakfast?"

"Sounds good. Speaking of coming back, where are you staying? You aren't driving back and forth from Lucien's?"

Katie halted with her hand on the door pull. "I rented a hotel room here in Zurich. I'm not going back until you're released."

"My dear Katie, nothing on God's earth could induce me to return to the lodge."

"I get that." Katie chuckled. "Hey, what happened to the drugs you found?"

"Still in the mine. I expect the investigators will retrieve them when they go out for Kofi and Pymer."

"Yeah, probably," Katie agreed, but shook her head. "Of course that won't happen until the authorities talk with you. Faye's still unconscious and no one else knew about those two until you told me."

"You're right. I hadn't considered that." Just the thought of running through her story again left Carmen exhausted. All she wanted now was to sleep, preferably in her own bed. "Katie, can we get our flight moved up? I'm ready to go home."

"Sure. I'll take care of it. Get some rest, Carmen. You'll be home before you know it."

Carmen stared at the hospital ceiling. She heaved a sigh expressing deep and abiding boredom. She absently twirled her long hair where it lay fanned out on the sheets. The Swiss hospital had insisted on keeping her a second full day, just to be safe. Carmen had finished her sentence last night and now only waited for parole. Katie promised it would come by the end of the work day. A medical facility in the States would have kicked her out the moment she opened her eyes. At least the entire ordeal was almost over.

Police detectives had taken her statement the day before and Katie had already arranged their flight home. Late tomorrow she would be back in the United States.

When Katie gave her the news, she also let it slip that Lucien was over the moon with the latest turn of events. Swiss media had jumped all over the story of Wrighton's murder and the drug smuggling. He felt certain of the resort's lucrative future since reporters mentioned Tribulation Peak by name. Carmen found his reaction a little disturbing. Lucien seemed to easily forget that a third of his guests perished and another spent days in the hospital. He also failed to express any disbelief at his good friend's criminal involvement and subsequent demise.

Malia had also visited to say goodbye. Her hospital contacts had given her Faye's room number, which she happily passed on to Carmen. Malia filled her in on the forensics investigation before imparting her own rather alarming bit of information. Police located the chest inside the mine exactly where Carmen said. Unfortunately, they found it empty. The drugs were gone. Carmen speculated that some of the other "guests" were involved. Or maybe all of them. The whole idea sounded like the plot of an Alfred Hitchcock movie.

Carmen sighed again and decided she needed some physical activity. The IV came out last night so she threw the covers off without hesitation and headed for the closet. Thank goodness for Katie, who had brought her a change of clothes in anticipation of her release. After dressing, Carmen slipped furtively down the hall. She didn't know how the staff would feel about one patient sneaking into another's room.

She needn't have worried. No one even glanced at her sideways. Carmen attributed the lack of reaction to her wearing street clothes instead of a gown with a slit down the back. A good thing too. Finding Faye's room wasn't easy. She located it on the opposite side of the hospital floor at the far end of a side corridor. She pushed the door open and stuck her head in to make sure she had the right place. Her heart lightened when she saw Faye awake and staring at the television. A narrow tube ran from an IV and was taped to the crook of her left elbow. A cast encased her right arm from just above the elbow to halfway down her hand.

Faye spotted Carmen immediately. She smiled and used the remote to click off the TV. "You're okay."

Carmen heard the clear relief in her voice. She sat on the edge of the bed when Faye scooted over for her. "I am. They're letting me out later today. How are you feeling?"

Spreading warmth invaded her stomach when Faye took her hand. The clasp was gentle, allowing for the cast. Carmen was grateful the closeness between them hadn't evaporated with their rescue. Carmen reached out with her free hand to stroke the bangs away from Faye's amazing eyes.

"Much better. I still feel a little cold, but that may have something to do with this." Faye nodded toward the IV. "They promised to remove it in a few hours."

Carmen swallowed the lump in her throat. "That's really good news. You had me worried. I finally snuck out of my room to come see you."

"You'll have to change back into your gown when you go back so that no one notices you escaped."

"It was worth it."

Carmen shifted closer and took Faye into her arms. There was so much she wanted to say. She longed to admit the depth of her emotions and ask if Faye could ever feel the same. Carmen wanted to promise anything in exchange for the slightest mutual interest. Instead, she kept silent and took what comfort she could. Faye was practically married to her work with Interpol. Carmen would never expect her to give that up. Faye would return to France and Carmen to Denver.

Sometimes life was so unfair. Carmen resolved to put on a brave face. She intended to make this easy for Faye by keeping her feelings to herself. Decision made, she released Faye and shifted a few inches away.

"After I get out of here I can bring you something to eat. If you want."

"Why?" Faye sounded genuinely confused.

"Because hospital food is gross, and it's tradition to bring the patient something tasty."

"I see. I appreciate the gesture, truly, but it isn't necessary. I actually like hospital food."

"There's something seriously wrong with you. Maybe they should run more tests."

Both laughed, easing any lingering awkwardness. They spoke about their individual experiences during the hospital stay before Faye redirected the topic.

"The Swiss police stopped in this morning. Have they spoken to you?"

Carmen nodded. "Yeah, I gave my statement yesterday. Did they tell you the drugs are gone? Someone got there first."

"Yes, I heard. It's just as I feared. This was a much larger operation than two men alone could handle."

"True. I guess I just hoped to put an end to this particular enterprise."

"Carmen, attempting to stop drug runners is like trying to end terrorism. When one falls, there is always another waiting to take their place."

"I know. Let's talk about something more positive. When are you heading home?"

"Hopefully in the next few days. As an international law enforcement agent, I am allowed any open seat on a flight. I don't usually take advantage of the privilege, but I think this time I will make an exception."

"Good idea. I imagine you'll have some time off until that arm heals."

Faye nodded and scratched at her upper arm above the cast. "I am not looking forward to desk duty. What of you? Have you decided about the Marshals job?"

"Not yet, but I'm not in a rush. Maybe I could call you? You know, to weigh the pros and cons?" Carmen didn't know why she said that. Apparently, she just couldn't leave things alone.

"Ah, that reminds me." Faye indicated a scrap of paper on the hospital table a few steps away. As Carmen retrieved it Faye said, "I've written out my numbers in France. I would very much like to hear from you sometime."

Carmen took the paper and glanced at the international numbers before stuffing it into her jeans pocket. She found a pen and tore a cardboard corner off a tissue box to return the favor. Carmen handed over her cell number and was ready to say something clever when the door opened.

A middle-aged woman wearing a white nurse's uniform walked in. She carried a food tray and stopped when she spotted Carmen. Impatience or annoyance ghosted across her features and quickly vanished.

"Visitor's hours aren't until four. I must ask you to leave."

Carmen and Faye exchanged a glance. They could hardly argue. Carmen wasn't supposed to be out of her room.

"Guess I should get back."

Faye offered a mischievous grin. "Wouldn't want to be arrested for breaking hospital rules."

"I'll call you when I get home," Carmen promised.

"You'd better."

Carmen stood and surprised them both by kissing Faye on the cheek.

Chapter Seventeen

As soon as they touched down at Denver International, Katie offered Carmen a ride home. Absently, Carmen switched her cell phone from airplane mode. Multiple dings greeted her, informing her of five missed calls.

"I appreciate it, but I think I'll grab a cab. That way you can head home without dropping me off first. I'm sure you're as exhausted as I am."

"I don't know," Katie disagreed. "After almost freezing to death, I'm sure you have me beat."

"I do feel like one giant bruise and all that travel time hasn't helped me any."

Carmen had another reason for refusing Katie's offer. She wanted to call Faye and talk privately. She should delay that until she got home, and she quashed the impulse to act like a school girl with a crush.

"Take a hot bath when you get home. I know I will."

Carmen promised to do exactly that. She also planned to sleep for at least twenty-four hours afterward. After giving Katie a hug, Carmen retrieved her luggage and then headed out of the airport. Taxis lined the curb, waiting for fares. The sky was an ominous shade of gunmetal gray and snowflakes drifted toward the ground. The air temperature seemed warmer than Switzerland, but other than that, Carmen could believe she never left.

She jumped into a cab and directed the driver toward her house. Then Carmen dialed Faye's number and listened to it ring. When the voicemail picked up, Carmen left a message and hung up. Disappointed, she did some mental calculations and determined it was the middle of the night in Switzerland. She tucked her phone back into the holster, determined to call again in a few hours.

"How long were you gone?" the cab driver asked.

"What's that?"

"How long were you gone? I assume you just flew in from somewhere."

"Oh right. Yeah, I was gone about nine days. Ten if you count today, but I've been flying for almost twenty hours."

"Then you probably don't know, but you're lucky you made it. There's a big winter storm moving in. I heard a few minutes ago that it's coming in from Arizona."

"Honestly, will this ever end?" Carmen pressed her fingertips to her eyelids. Would summer never come again? "Arizona, you say?"

"Yeah, apparently it came up from Mexico. You got lucky because there'll probably be flight delays later. Should be just a one-day storm though."

Carmen grunted noncommittally and glanced down at the falling snow. The snowfall rate did look to have increased since she walked out of the airport. Fortunately, the bad weather kept the traffic lighter than usual.

The door closed to Carmen's house and the silence embraced her. It seemed like weeks that she'd been in Switzerland rather than the ten days it truly was. The heater kicked on and she pushed her shoes off with her toes before heading into the kitchen. As usual when away, Raphael had kept an eye on things. Her mail lay neatly stacked on the countertop, but she had no interest in junk mail right now. Instead, she leaned against the cabinet for a moment. She still felt a little overwhelmed from the whirlwind events of the last few days. Carmen remembered the missed calls on her phone, but decided she needed a long soak in the tub first.

She left the mail where it sat and walked through the house into the master suite. A little pampering seemed in order, all things considered. She dropped her clothes to the bedroom floor and slipped on a silky, knee-length robe. Carmen turned on the taps and added lavender scented bath salts. Steam drifted into the air as the water rose.

Carmen had just placed one foot into the hot water when her cell phone rang. She glanced at the phone where she'd placed it on the vanity. Carmen considered ignoring it, but finally pulled her foot out and stepped onto the mat before she reached for the phone. A quick glance at the Caller ID made her heart race. The readout said Matthew Sullivan. Ryan and Joy's son. Carmen remembered seeing a few missed calls from him when she checked her phone at the airport. She hadn't thought anything of it at the time, but a third call didn't bode well. Matthew rarely contacted her.

Carmen accepted the call as she reached for her robe. "Matthew, is everything okay?" She heard a shaky breath on the other end before she recognized Matthew's wife.

"Carmen, this is Lindsey. Something awful has happened. We got a call from State Police in Trinidad a few hours ago."

"Trinidad, Colorado? What did they want?" Carmen held her breath, dread a heavy weight in her chest. She experienced a horrible sense of foreboding. In her fright, she couldn't remember when Joy and Ryan were supposed to head home from their trip.

Lindsey's voice cracked when she answered. Carmen heard tears in her voice. "Matthew's parents were caught in a late season storm on their way home. I'm sorry to tell you this, but there was an accident."

Carmen held the phone to her ear with her shoulder as she dashed toward the dresser. Exhaustion forgotten, she reached for fresh underwear. "Trinidad's only three hours from here. I can leave in about twenty minutes."

"Carmen, no."

"Ten minutes," she bargained, ignoring what she instinctively knew. "What hospital are they in?"

"Carmen, listen." Lindsey's gentle tone stopped her more effectively than a shout. "You can't. The accident was bad. Really bad. They're gone, honey."

A sob escaped her as Carmen went to sit on the edge of the bed. She missed and slid to the floor. Carmen leaned over her knees, her hair creating a curtain between her and the rest of the house. For a moment, she couldn't think. Reality took on a dreamlike quality. Carmen heard Lindsey crying softly through the connection and the nightmare worsened.

"Is Matthew okay?" Carmen managed. Tears tracked down her face and dripped from her chin.

Lindsey cleared her throat. "He's handling it. You know Matthew, but I think it really just hasn't hit him yet. He's too focused on trying to get them home."

"Is there anything I can do to help? Please, Lindsey. I need to do something."

"There is one thing, actually. We need you to pick Minion up from the boarder."

"Oh, God. I didn't even think about her. Of course, I'll call Charlie after we hang up." Carmen focused on trying to contribute to their need rather than her own grief.

"That's great. It'll be one less thing for Matthew to worry about. We're getting ready to leave here soon. Once we do what we can in Trinidad, we'll be there to get Minion."

"Please don't rush," Carmen said. "The snow is picking up here, too. I'm happy to take care of her until you can drive up. I have a key so, with your permission, I'll go next door and get her things."

"You don't have to ask, Carmen. We appreciate it. You can't know how much this means."

With the details out of the way, something else occurred to Carmen. She felt a little uncomfortable asking, but she had to know. "Uh, I hate to ask so soon, but do you know where services will be? I'd really like to be there for you, and for them."

"Honestly, we haven't had time to even think about it, but I'm sure they'll be held in Denver. Most of Matthew's family still lives there. Listen, Carmen, I really have to go now."

"Right, call me if you need anything."

Carmen pulled her car into the garage. The last few weeks had been tough with the double funeral, helping Matthew to organize his parents' house, and returning to work. Sergeant Kaminski had approved a few extra days off after her neighbor's accident, but he wasn't happy about it.

Now, after another full day flying over Denver, Carmen craved a nice glass of wine in front of the fireplace and a long conversation with Faye. They talked for a few hours almost every night. It seemed to Carmen that they never ran out of anything to say. It wasn't a true romantic relationship because Carmen couldn't find the courage to confide her true emotions to Faye. Carmen had never truly confided her heart to anyone. She had a wall up inside that she didn't know if anyone could ever tear down. Still, it had to be enough. For now, it *was* enough.

She had just walked into the kitchen through the attached garage door when Matthew called. Carmen dropped her keys onto the counter top and answered the phone. She hadn't heard from him since finishing up with the house last week.

"Hello, Matthew. How are you guys doing?"

"It's been tough," he admitted in a soft baritone. "That's part of why I'm calling. I wanted to let you know the will's been probated."

Carmen knew there was no actual "reading of the will." That was Hollywood. In reality, the will of a deceased was probated in court until an executor was approved. Generally, the executor was named in the will itself so that part was more a formality than anything unless a problem cropped up.

"Did everything turn out all right? I can't imagine there were any surprises since you're their only heir."

"No, everything went as expected. I did want to let you know that there was a clause that might shock you a little. Mom and Dad left you a small stipend."

Matthew sounded casual and Carmen thought it likely he knew about the clause in advance. Their family tended to discuss everything to avoid any drama. The thoughtful gesture that was so like her friends caused her to choke up again. She never expected or wanted anything from them other than their affection.

"That was sweet of them, Matthew, but it's not necessary."

Matthew snickered like he was in on a big secret. "Don't argue with me, Carmen. Just accept that they wanted this for you. It's not like we didn't discuss it when Mom and Dad first drew up the will."

"So you've known about this all along?"

"Of course, I just hoped we'd never have to use it. Anyway, the thing is, I need to get with you to sign some documents."

That seemed unusual. Carmen estimated a small personal check should take care of any monetary gift. "What are you talking about? How large a *stipend* are we talking about?"

"Nothing major," Matthew assured her, merriment in his tone. "Since Lindsey and I live here, they left you the house."

"What?"

She was certain she misheard. Homes in this neighborhood were prohibitively expensive. Carmen didn't need both her home and theirs as well, but found the gesture so typically magnanimous of the Sullivans.

"I appreciate it, Matthew, really. But I can't accept. That's too much. You should take the house and sell it. Put it in a college fund for when you have kids."

"Sorry, Carmen, it's a done deal." She could almost see him shaking his head. "This is what they wanted. You have to honor it."

When he started pulling out the honor card, Carmen knew she hadn't any choice. He could be pretty determined, especially when it came to matters of integrity. His whole family was like that and it was one of the things she loved most about them. Carmen liked to think she learned her sense of fairness from Joy and Ryan Sullivan.

"I'm speechless, Matthew. I guess I'll just say thank you. That's very considerate."

"Yes, they were that. I have to be honest though. That's not the end of the clause. You have to take the house as well as two million dollars from their estate."

Chapter Eighteen

Carmen stared at the view encompassing the Air One helicopter with the Rocky Mountains in the distance. She never tired of this sight behind the maintenance hangar at Denver International Airport. She stood just inside the door, memorizing the sight of the helipad with the sun edging down toward the snowy peaks. A light breeze lifted the bangs of her newly shortened hair and whispered down the nape of her neck. She wished she'd cut her hair years ago, never imagining the fullness of sensation without the protection of the thick mane.

"You all right?"

Carmen turned to Raphael Lopez and passed her flight helmet off to him. "I'm good. I didn't think this day would ever come, but I have this sense of peace I haven't had for a long time. I know I'm making the right decision."

Raph scratched at his newly grown chin whiskers. He had always reported to duty clean shaven for the years she'd partnered with him and this took some getting used to. He seemed so proud of the thin hairs, constantly touching them. Like no one ever had whiskers before him. Carmen thought it was cute. She tilted her head slightly and realized it wasn't just the new goatee. He seemed different since she'd returned from Switzerland, more relaxed and comfortable in his own skin.

"You could always stay."

Carmen grinned at his deliberate attempt to tease her. "No, it's time. So much has happened in the last year that I need some space. I need to spend time somewhere that there isn't any stress and I'm afraid police work does not fit that description."

He scratched his chin again and Carmen wondered if facial hair itched.

"Good thing you didn't take the Marshals job. You'd have hated that, but I'm never going to forgive you for sticking me with Simpson. Kaminski just told me that Jerry's my new partner."

"What's wrong with Simpson? He's a good officer."

Raph snorted. "He stinks like fish. When he isn't smoking a cigar, he's chewing on one. It's gross."

"Sorry." Carmen didn't really mean it, but it seemed like the thing to say. She glanced at her watch. "I guess I should get my stuff before shift change comes in. Thanks again for looking after the house for me. I'm not sure how long I'll be gone."

"No problem, buddy. Just make sure you call me before you head home. I'll need time to clean up from all the parties I intend to have there." Raph chuckled at his own joke. "Still not sure you need to go all the way to Ireland to find yourself or whatever."

Carmen shrugged. "I've always wanted to visit there. Now I can finally afford it."

Raph adopted a speculative expression. "There wouldn't be a woman involved, would there?"

"Maybe."

Faye had agreed to meet her a few weeks after Carmen had time to settle in at a Bed and Breakfast in Dublin. Carmen hadn't seen her since leaving Switzerland two months ago. Their respective jobs and all of the upheaval of the last few months kept that from happening. Carmen worried that things would be awkward once they saw each other again, but she couldn't help be excited.

"Hey, I just thought of something." Raph smiled with a definite hint of mischief. "You'll get a chance to say bye to Stanley. I hear he's back on duty at the gate."

The bushy-browed older curmudgeon never failed to give Carmen a hard time when she left work. For the last two weeks no one had seen him. Carmen had hoped to never encounter him again.

"Terrific, that's just what I need. One final encounter with Mister Sunshine."

Raph laughed and hugged Carmen. He extracted another promise for her to call as soon as she landed in Ireland before she made her escape.

Carmen loaded a cardboard file box with the possessions from her locker into the back of the Subaru. One final loving glance at the Bell helicopter and she drove toward the exit. From ten yards away, she spotted Stanley's balding pate shining in the guard shack. She didn't even mind the attitude she knew Stanley would show. This was the end of a chapter and everything from here on out would be fresh and new. The possibilities were endless and even this man couldn't ruin her day.

She halted beside the minuscule window and held up her ID. "Stanley." She greeted him the same way she had for years.

To Carmen's surprise, Stanley offered a broad smile, showing a fine set of very white dentures. "Officer Bravo, so good to see you this fine day."

Despite her resolve to remain unflappable at his aversion, this turnaround caught her unprepared. He'd treated her like a particularly annoying insect in his shorts for the last two years and now he made it clear how happy her departure made him. She had to ask.

"So now you're happy because I'm leaving? Please tell me, Stanley. What did I ever do to you?"

The familiar scowl drew his bushy eyebrows together. "Excuse me?"

"It's clear you never liked me. I'd just like to know why." She made sure not to interject any acrimony into the question. She sincerely wanted to know and wouldn't find out by upsetting him.

"Oh." Stanley's cheeks reddened, surprising Carmen further. "I can understand why you'd think that. The truth is that I had gallstones. I've been in pain a long time, but the insurance company wouldn't approve me getting them out until a few weeks ago. Now, I'm as good as new."

He beamed at her again. Carmen took a second to work through what he said and then she laughed in surprise. "I guess that's what I get for assuming the world revolves around me. I'm so sorry, Stanley. I had no idea."

"Don't worry about it. It's only normal you'd think my attitude meant I didn't like you. I'm the one who's sorry and I'm also very sorry to see you go. You're one of the good ones, Officer Bravo."

Happy that her sunglasses concealed the tears welling in her eyes,

Carmen offered Stanley a smile and a wave. Then she drove away from Denver International Airport's Gate Five for the last time.

PART THREE

Never put your faith in a Prince.
When you require a miracle, trust in a Witch.

Catherynne M. Valente~ *In the Night Garden*

Chapter Nineteen

Carmen pushed open the cabin door and stepped out into the fresh, crisp morning air. The dappled sunshine of early summer filtered through the trees to gently warm her face. Her worn and scuffed hiking boots sounded softly on the wooden porch as she moved to lean against the railing. She closed her eyes and inhaled the calming scent of damp earth and growing things and listened to the gentle breeze singing softly through the forest and the multitude of birdsong. When she opened her eyes, the peace of the wooded sanctuary soothed the ache in her heart.

For a moment, Carmen contemplated how she landed here in Pennsylvania's Poconos area. She had enjoyed Ireland. It was gorgeous, but eventually it became an empty experience. The brogue spoken by the locals proved difficult to interpret, lending her an isolated sensation. The food didn't agree with her and the beauty of the countryside quickly paled as she missed the more familiar surroundings of home. Then there was Faye.

Ah yes, Faye. The incredible woman Carmen believed was her soul mate. For a time. Now Carmen knew the truth. Such sentiments were the product of poets and children. Love didn't truly exist. People merely learned to delude themselves and compromise to avoid solitude. The certainty of her belief left Carmen feeling hollow. An indefinable ache throbbed inside her that she couldn't understand.

A red-breasted robin alighted on the railing a few feet away, drawing Carmen's focus from unpleasant thoughts. She kept very still. The small bird peered at her for a moment. Apparently not considering her a threat, the robin offered her a soft trilling aria.

"Well, good morning to you too." Carmen spoke softly to prevent frightening the creature. "Should I put up a feeder so you can visit for breakfast?"

The bird cocked its head this way and that. After briefly eying Carmen, it flitted lazily away into the forest. Left alone again, she acknowledged solitude existed here too. This isolation was different though. Here, the quiet conveyed healing, warmth, and comfort. No sirens from emergency vehicles disturbed the air. Not another structure existed to break the view.

Carmen pushed away from the rail and struck off away from the cabin. She followed a well-worn game trail into the woods on a now familiar trek. Each morning for the last two months, she walked this path. High grass swayed and brushed against her knees. She stepped over the occasional fallen branch or around a tangle of thorns. A teasing breeze lifted her bangs and caressed the nape of her bare neck.

The trail sloped slowly away from the cabin. Fresh deer and rabbit tracks crisscrossed, leading Carmen ever deeper into the woods. Soon, she heard the sound of rushing water. An energetic stream hove into view, glimpsed through the undergrowth and massive tree trunks. White foam collected over the top of the water, swirling and bubbling over hidden obstacles. A recent rain storm contributed to the water level as well as the intensity of the flow.

Carmen's path meandered loosely adjacent to the torrent. As she rounded a curve, a series of larger stones and then proper boulders littered the trail. The rock marked the rise of earth that led almost immediately to an escarpment. Carmen's pace increased as she neared her objective. She stepped from the loamy trail onto a large stone, then she climbed up onto a boulder the size of a Buick. The sight from here took her breath away, as it had since the first moment she spied the scene.

A three-tiered waterfall flowed across the face of the rock wall. Water pounded into the stream-fed pool below. The pool formed an almost perfect circle, with the exception of a channel on the far side that allowed the current to continue on its way.

Carmen had spotted a plethora of animal tracks here since arriving. Clearly, the pond served as a popular watering hole. She settled down with her elbows propped on her knees near the edge of the boulder to watch the spray of water. Along the base of the falls, a darker area hinted at an opening behind the cascade. Carmen's imagination pictured a grotto filled with hidden treasure. In reality, she thought it more likely a small, waterlogged crevasse housing tiny fish.

The snap of dry twigs shattered her reverie. Seconds later, another person intruded on Carmen's secret lagoon for the first time since her arrival, outside of the weekly supply runs into the nearby village of Wolf Hollow. Apparently not so secret, though one glance at the interloper intimated that this woman belonged here in this natural setting more than Carmen.

Slight in stature with shoulder-length curly raven hair, the stranger exuded a peaceful presence that silently broadcast across the short distance. When the sun broke through the trees, Carmen saw streaks of fire in the dark locks. Finely sculpted pale features boasted a slightly pointed and cleft chin that added to the image of a child of the woods. A tender smile accentuated high cheek bones. The woman dressed sensibly in a red-checked flannel shirt covered by a denim jacket, jeans and ankle high hiking boots. She carried a wicker basket with the handle draped over her left forearm. More surprising than her unexpected appearance was the animal that followed closely on her heels.

A good-sized black cat wound through the hiker's legs when she stopped in front of the falls. A blaze of white on the cat's chest broke up the monochromatic vision. Together, the pair cut quite the image. They seemed to belong here, an integral element of the forest. Carmen stayed quiet, feeling intrusive though she was actually here first.

Suddenly, the woman turned her head and looked at Carmen as though she had known she was there all along. The smile grew wider, embracing Carmen in a friendly, welcoming expression. Cat-shaped eyes boasting a smoke green color captured her in their gaze. The shade held a timeless quality Carmen found riveting.

"It is quite an impressive sight, isn't it? Cricket insists on coming here every day, no matter the weather. I see you enjoy it also."

Carmen had already lost track of the conversation. "Cricket?"

The stranger glanced at her furry companion before closing the distance between them. Cricket followed cat-quick before rushing ahead. To Carmen's surprise the animal didn't balk at the sight of a stranger.

Instead, it stopped a few feet away before settling onto its backside and watching Carmen with an appraising stare. The woman easily scaled the other side of the boulder on which Carmen resided and halted beside her little friend.

Carmen stood reflexively. She curbed the impulse to shake hands and instead offered a smile of her own. "I'm sorry. if I'm trespassing. I haven't been here very long and I'm afraid I'm not sure of the property boundaries. I'm Carmen Bravo, by the way."

"Grace Wickford, and it's a pleasure. This is my lovely girl, Cricket." Her voice was even, pleasant and unhurried. "There are no boundaries here. You're welcome to come and go as you please."

"Okay. Let me try again. Do you own this land?"

Grace shook her head, causing her curls to bounce slightly. "This is all actually part of the State Game Lands. Except for the property directly adjacent to your cabin of course."

"Of course."

Grace had a calming presence, but her way of anticipating Carmen's concerns left her feeling a little off balance. She wasn't flirty, just friendly. Grace had an open expression with a hint of impishness in her green eyes. Carmen searched for a safe topic as she tried to gather her composure.

"So, what do you have there?"

Grace lifted the wicker basket hosting a colorful menagerie of yellows, greens, black, and dark blues. "The black mushrooms are chanterelles. Quite a delicacy and much harder to locate than their yellow cousins. Green herbs, blackberries and dandelions. The dandelions make great wine. Or tea if you prefer."

"Isn't it dangerous to pick mushrooms? You could poison yourself."

Grace only offered an enigmatic expression. She bit her lower lip as though containing a smile. Then she laughed a wonderfully intoxicating sound. Up until now, Cricket had sat perfectly motionless watching Carmen. When Grace laughed, the elegant cat's mouth dropped open slightly. Her eyes squinted half closed and Carmen saw a flash of her little pink tongue. She was staggered by the certainty of witnessing a cat laugh.

"Only if you don't know what you're doing," Grace said. "The stems give everything away. Chanterelles have a hollow stem. The poisonous type have a solid stem, but I have the feeling you aren't here to discuss mushrooms."

"Oh, you mean why I'm here in Pennsylvania?" Carmen had a hard time keeping up.

She nodded. "I'm simply curious why you would choose to buy a cabin in the middle of the Poconos. Most of the locals have spent their entire lives here."

"How do you know that I bought it?"

Grace cocked her head in a manner similar to the robin on the porch rail earlier. She showed no annoyance at Carmen's evasion of the question. "Wolf Hollow is a very small community. Gossip travels quickly, even if one prefers to avoid it."

"Fair enough. Let's just say that a lot has happened in the past year. I am, or *was*, a police officer. I needed somewhere to help me feel grounded again."

"This is a good choice. Nature always helps me feel centered, but Pennsylvania wasn't your first choice."

Carmen found herself agreeing, though she briefly wondered how Grace knew that. "No, I traveled to Ireland first. Stayed there for a few months actually."

"But it didn't work." Grace frowned, her voice reflective and the words stated as fact. "You came here seeking solace."

Carmen had no idea how to respond. From anyone else, she would resent the impertinence and wouldn't hesitate to let them know. Instead, she felt compelled to justify herself to a complete stranger. Grace's presence seemed hypnotic, inclining Carmen to reveal things she normally wouldn't. Fortunately, she didn't have to.

Cricket looked away from Carmen and toward her owner. She blinked once and issued a very clear, "Meow."

Grace chuckled affectionately. "Yes, of course dear. We're going just now. I'm sorry, Miss Bravo, but Cricket is ready for her breakfast."

"You understand her?"

"She makes herself quite clear."

Carmen didn't know much about cats. Despite that, she believed Grace capable of communicating with any animal, feline or otherwise.

She couldn't express exactly why she had that sense, but Carmen had no doubts. Perhaps it was the magical atmosphere of this setting. Perhaps Carmen merely needed something to believe in at this point in her life. Still, her stubborn nature insisted that she argue the point.

"She's a cat. Can't she just catch a chipmunk, or a mouse or something?"

Grace's eyes widened. "Oh no, not my girl. Cricket prefers warm meals on a proper plate. She has a very refined palate. It's fresh salmon and greens this morning."

Cricket chose that moment to rise up into a crouch. She launched herself into the air and wrapped herself around Grace's shoulders like a stole. From a few feet away, Carmen heard the loud purring buzz of feline contentment. Grace didn't even flinch when the animal jumped. When her owner offered her an affectionate look, Cricket returned the favor by rubbing her forehead against Grace's chin. Then Cricket pinned Carmen with an eerily intelligent gaze. Carmen tensed, almost expecting the animal to speak.

Grace broke the tension. "Maybe we'll bump into each other again. As I said, we come here daily."

"You're welcome to come up to the cabin for coffee anytime." Carmen didn't know why she issued the impetuous invitation, but she couldn't stop now. "I usually brew a pot when I get back from my morning walk. You can bring Cricket if you want. Just follow the game trail. It leads right to the cabin."

"I would enjoy that very much. Perhaps tomorrow?"

A warm feeling rushed through Carmen and she nodded. She hated feeling at a loss for words, but couldn't think of anything witty or charming. In a way, Carmen thought she must be feeling desperate for a friend up here in the middle of nowhere. She hoped that wasn't too obvious. "Uh, wait. Where do you live?"

"Up on the mountain." Grace waved at a general direction back the way she had come.

Grace rested her free hand on Cricket and turned away, departing through the trees. Carmen watched them fade into the woods. Once they vanished out of sight, Carmen took her first full breath since meeting the pair. Her head cleared and she felt like she'd just surfaced from a dream.

"What the hell just happened?"

As she drove into the small borough of Wolf Hollow, Carmen noticed two signs. The first was always there, announcing her entrance into town and proclaiming the population at five thousand inhabitants. Carmen had no idea when it was updated last, but didn't believe the size of the population had changed much since its installment in any case. The second sign was new. It proclaimed the Twenty-first Annual Beerfest. Smaller lettering under the colorful announcement stated the celebration would be held this weekend at the city park. Not that there were many other places nearby at which such an event would ensue.

Carmen followed the rural highway that cut through the area. She could traverse the entire length of the town in less than three minutes. Along that strip were two gas stations and a strip-mall with a laundry mat, a Mexican restaurant and a few struggling shops. The town had a Sonic as well as the small park adjacent to the dollar store here as well. Farther along, on the way out of town, was a Walmart Supercenter. Carmen believed the Walmart existed merely because Wolf Hollow was the county seat.

Despite the appearance as a near ghost town, Wolf Hollow boasted more than met the eye. Carmen turned left at the corner with the Sonic and headed toward the true heart of town. Aptly named Main Street, the thoroughfare led to the center of town where the bustle of country living actually took place. She arrived at the square when her tires struck archaic cobblestones. A lone courthouse and post office took center stage. Businesses ranging from a pharmacy and hair salons to a mom and pop diner and antique stores surrounded the central structures.

She bypassed the dentistry, library and feed store as she made a right and headed to the end of the block. Only a few older citizens crossed the streets without bothering with any crosswalk. Not that any existed. Carmen hadn't any trouble finding a parking spot as she pulled into the lot at the end of the street. This early in the afternoon only a few vehicles occupied the spaces between time-worn paint. Both of those were old battered pickups with bashed in rear bumpers and more than a few side dents. Straws of hay stuck out defiantly from one of the tailgates. Carmen glanced up to ensure the open sign showed on the front of the edifice.

Laurel's Diner, much like the rest of the town, was much more than its faded brown façade insinuated. A coffee and pastry shop in the morning, the establishment morphed into a restaurant and the local watering hole by noon. The owner, Laurel Hawthorne, claimed she supported Wolf Hollow's revenue stream all by herself. Carmen could believe it.

She slammed the car door and headed inside without bothering to lock the Subaru. No one locked vehicles here. It wasn't neighborly and with the crime rate so low, it wasn't necessary. Also, the small police station resided inside the courthouse right across the street.

A bell over the door signaled her entrance. Carmen's eyes took a moment to adjust to the gloom as she entered from a sunshine filled day. High pub tables with equally tall chairs were smattered throughout the space. A few shorter tables lined the walls for folk whose climbing days were gone. Two older farmer type men occupied the farthest corner. After a quick glance, Carmen focused on her objective. A husky woman with a cheerful red apron puttered behind the bar. As usual, Laurel's shoulder length highlighted hair looked perfectly coiffed. She stopped humming as Carmen walked in and slid onto a bar stool.

"Good afternoon, Carmen. In for your weekly supply run?"

"Yes, but you know I have to fortify myself here before I brave Walmart. I swear that place is busier than any grocery store in Denver."

Laurel paused in wiping the bar with a damp white cloth. "What do you expect when it's the only place to shop for at least thirty miles? You should go early, before people get the young ones up and dressed. Your usual?"

"Please. I can't believe I've been here long enough to have a 'usual.'"

A thick ceramic mug plopped down on the counter. Carmen inhaled the sweet scent of a caramel mocha. It took more than thirty seconds to make a coffee drink and she eyed Laurel with good-natured suspicion. "How did you know to make this? Did you put a tracker on my car when I wasn't looking?"

Laurel chuckled and her plump cheeks turned rosy. She nodded toward the windows that lined the front of the diner. "Saw you pull in."

Carmen took a sip of the scalding hot beverage. She had more than one purpose for her visit here. Laurel wasn't really a friend, just one of the few people Carmen actually knew in town. She quickly formulated how to word her questions without sounding nosy. Carmen decided to start with the innocuous.

"I saw a sign saying there's going to be a beer festival this weekend."

Laurel huffed and went back to wiping the already polished bar. "Blasted thing takes place every year. Don't get me wrong, I do enjoy the festival. Lots of booths, food, and music. They even have a goat race, if you can believe it. The kids love it and it gives everyone a chance to get out and socialize."

"So, what's the problem?"

Laurel's eyebrows rose as she redirected her attention to Carmen. "Oh, there's no problem with the festival. It's that darned planning committee. They've been in here every morning for the last three days, taking up my whole diner with their bickering. Bad for business. Still, I guess they need to hold their meetings somewhere and it is only for a week so I should probably keep my complaining to myself. Never mind all that. What have you been getting into since last week? Are you tired of the leisure life and looking for a job yet?"

"No such luck." Carmen found it amusing how Laurel always tried to rope her into hiring on at the diner. "Something interesting did happen this morning though."

"Really? What?"

Carmen hesitated before she blurted out, "You don't happen to know someone by the name of Grace Wickford, do you?" Carmen took a larger than necessary gulp of coffee to hide her sudden case of nerves and ended up scalding the back of her throat. She tried to muffle her reflexive cough.

"The witch." Laurel stopped cleaning and leaned against the bar on her elbows. She seemed fully vested in the conversation, her expression keen and pinned on Carmen to gauge her reaction.

"Witch?"

"Well, not really. People just call her that because she's a little eccentric. They don't mean anything by it. Grace is super nice and everyone simply adores her. She comes in for lunch on the odd occasion. How did you meet her?"

Carmen fiddled with the half empty mug. "I went out for a walk in the woods this morning and I just sort of ran into her. She had a cat with her."

"Cricket." Laurel's head bobbed once. "Something odd about that creature. It follows Grace around like a dog. One day, I actually saw it sit outside the Post Office and wait for her to come back out. As far as running into her in the woods, I can't say I'm surprised. Grace works for the Forestry Department. She's some kind of zoologist or something."

"Now that does surprise me," Carmen admitted. "She was collecting all sorts of herbs and mushrooms. I figured her for the holistic type."

"People can surprise you. That cat though, there's something strange about that one. Never did understand cats. Give me a good old obedient dog any day."

At that moment, the bell announced the arrival of a young couple. The pair headed for a pub table and Laurel stalked away with a couple of menus.

"I like cats," Carmen mumbled to herself.

Left to her own devices, she slowly finished the coffee. She considered what she had learned and decided that a zoologist would definitely spend a lot of time in nature. After all, their area of study centered around animals. A quick glance at her watch told Carmen she'd lingered longer than expected. It was time to get moving.

She had a visitor due in the morning and wanted to pick up some nice flavored coffee. Did Grace take cream and sugar? Carmen would buy some just in case. If Grace didn't use the cream, maybe Cricket would enjoy it.

Carmen had only driven a few miles outside of town when her phone rang. A smile curved her lips when she saw the Caller ID. Carmen answered the call by pressing a button on her steering wheel to engage the hands-free setting.

"Katie, how are you?"

"Missing you like crazy," Katie answered, launching right to the point in her usual friendly manner.

"I miss you too. I can hardly believe it's been four months."

"Four *long* months without seeing you even once. That's actually why I'm calling. Carmen, how long are you going to be roughing it? You can't honestly tell me you're enjoying the backwoods after living in the city for so long."

This was one of the reasons Carmen had avoided talking with Katie. She knew she had a point, but Carmen didn't want to have to justify her motives. That being said, Carmen loved Katie too much not to answer honestly.

"It's peaceful here and I just needed some time alone. I should have told you that before instead of evading the issue. I'm sorry, Katie."

"Yes, you should have just said that. I am a psychiatrist, you know. After Faye dumped you in Ireland, of course you'd need some time to get your head together."

Carmen huffed at Katie's description of what happened. "She didn't dump me. We spent two very nice weeks together before she had to go back to work."

"Right, she got what she wanted from you and then totally ghosted you. I mean, did she call you even once after she left?"

"No, she never even answered the phone when I tried to call her."

"Or bothered to return a message," Katie added.

Katie's peeved reaction to Faye's behavior warmed Carmen's heart. It was nice to have someone defend her and she wondered why she'd avoided confiding in her best friend. The combination of loyalty and meeting a new potential friend in Grace that morning went a long way toward healing Carmen's self-esteem. Carmen cleared her throat against the emotion that threatened.

"So, besides bolstering my confidence, was there another reason you called or did you just want to chat?"

Katie chuckled. "You know me so well. Actually, I wondered if you'd like to have dinner Thursday night."

"What? You're in Wolf's Hollow?"

"Darling, I love you with all my heart, but there is no way I'd be caught dead in such a dreadfully unsophisticated place. No, I'm in Allentown for one of those CME things."

"Continuing medical education? I thought you were retired?"

"Yes, but I still like to keep my credentials up to date. You're only an hour away, right? Say you'll come have dinner with me. I haven't seen you in so long."

Katie's voice had taken on a pleading quality. Normally, Carmen would tease her mercilessly for it, but in this case decided to be more understanding.

"I'd love to see you. Text me the details and I promise to be there."

The conversation segued to them catching up on details of their lives. Before she knew it, Carmen turned off the main road onto the gravel lane that led to her cabin. Gooseneck Road, as it was so colloquially known, continued past Carmen's home and meandered farther up the mountain. She had never explored the entire lane and wondered briefly if it neared Grace's residence.

"Listen, Katie. I've got to let you go. I just turned onto my road and I don't have very good cell reception up here. I'm going to lose you any second."

"I understand. I'll text you the information in a few minutes and you better be there, Carmen. No excuses."

"I promise. You don't have to worry about that anymore. I'm retired too now, remember, so I don't have to worry about work interfering. Love you, Katchoo."

"You too, kiddo. See you Thursday."

Chapter Twenty

Carmen rose at dawn, too excited at the prospect of a visitor to sleep any longer. No one else had set foot in the cabin since she purchased it and Carmen looked forward to showing it off. It didn't hurt that the visitor in question happened to be a beautiful woman with mysterious eyes who emanated peace and compassion. What Laurel told her about Grace merely made Carmen more curious. As fascinating as she found Grace, Carmen had to admit that she was equally intrigued by her magnificent black cat. The pair of them presented an image Carmen could believe was magical.

Carmen tanked the idea of a walk in lieu of her preparations. After hastily pulling the covers up on the bed, Carmen passed a critical eye over the cabin. It seemed presentable enough, but she quickly discovered a stray sock under the small dining table in the kitchen.

She threw open the living room window and only then did she realize how briskly the wind blew. She just as quickly closed it again. The weather had changed overnight from sunny and clear to overcast with the threat of a storm as iron gray clouds filled the sky. The wind blew strongly enough to bend the tree tops and Carmen noted a definite chill in the air.

Disappointment loomed, making her feel somewhat deflated. Early summer meant unpredictable weather fronts and thunderstorms and the day seemed to brace for exactly that. Grace probably wouldn't come. Worse, Carmen hadn't bothered to ask for a phone number so she couldn't even call to confirm.

Carmen drew her fingertips through her hair, finger-combing the short locks into place. She heaved a sigh and headed for the bedroom. She wouldn't go back to sleep now, so she decided to dress for the day and make coffee anyway. She dressed casually in gray lounge pants to match her mood and an oversized navy blue Denver Police Academy t-shirt. After that, she padded barefoot into the kitchen and leaned against the counter before reaching for the small container of specialty coffee. When she discovered the chocolate-raspberry flavor at Walmart, Carmen hadn't believed her luck. It seemed a little self-indulgent now, but even if Grace didn't come, Carmen wouldn't deprive herself of the treat.

She set the pot to brew and tuned the radio to a relaxing station that aired classical piano. Soon the heavenly aroma of chocolate and raspberries filled the entire cabin. Carmen heard the first spatter of raindrops tapping on the front windows. The coffee pot made a fine accompaniment to the sound with its burbling noises, luring her into the kitchen. Carmen had just touched the handle of her favorite ceramic mug when she heard a tap on the door.

Disbelief made her freeze. Her heart rate increased as she finally hurried through the cabin to fling open the door. Windswept and tousled, Grace stood there with a merry smile and twinkling green eyes. Cricket sat quietly at her feet, looking every bit as obedient as any canine.

"You weren't on the trail," Grace said by way of greeting. "I wasn't sure the coffee invitation still stood, but I decided to take the chance."

"Of course it does. Come in, please. Both of you."

Cricket pushed ahead and hurried inside, seeming eager to be out of the wind. Grace followed with more composure. She held the wicker basket Carmen recognized from the day before. Instead of the wild plants and berries, Carmen spotted something lumpy covered by a blue and white checkered cloth.

Carmen closed the door with some difficulty against a stronger gust. "I'm surprised you walked all this way with a storm about to hit, but I'm happy to see you."

"Are you kidding? It's glorious. I love Mother Nature in all her moods. Where do you want this?" Grace held up the basket with a flourish.

Carmen reached for the hamper, but Cricket distracted her by butting her head against Carmen's shin.

"She likes you. She's asking if you'd like to pet her."

"I would very much."

Carmen's gaze remained riveted on the cat. She'd wanted to touch the soft fur since the moment she saw her. Carmen dropped slowly to one knee before reaching out. She took her time to avoid startling Cricket. The cat met her halfway, stepping onto Carmen's bare toes and pressing into the light touch. Feeling emboldened by the response, Carmen used both hands to stroke the black fur. Cricket's coat was as soft as silk and very thick. Under all that hair, her frame was unexpectedly lean.

After a moment, Cricket turned and walked toward the beige sofa nestled against the front wall. She paused and stretched out each back leg in turn. Then she spread the dainty toes of one foot and shook loose a small leaf. Feet appropriately clean, Cricket hopped onto the sofa and settled down facing the women. Her contented purr started at the same time that she began kneading the cushion.

Throughout the entire episode, Grace stayed quiet. Carmen thought maybe her guest was worried how she would react to Cricket making herself at home.

"Wow, I'm impressed. I don't even wipe my feet before I lay on the furniture." Carmen chuckled and took the basket from Grace.

"You don't mind, do you?"

"Absolutely not. I find her fascinating and I like that she feels comfortable here. She's not like most cats I've seen. Come on in the kitchen. You're just in time."

Carmen led the way. They left Cricket to amuse herself while Carmen gathered mugs, sugar and cream. She placed everything on the table, watching surreptitiously as Grace took a seat and glanced around the room.

"It's very inviting in here. Comforting."

"Thanks." Carmen thought the same thing. Shades of beige and pale blues played off the smooth, dark logs that made up the cabin walls. A wood burning fireplace with a white brick façade in the living room further brightened the space, lending a cozy feel.

Carmen filled the mugs with coffee and carried them over. She sat across from Grace and asked, "So, what's in the basket?"

"Nature's bounty." Grace's voice held an impish quality as she flipped the checkered cloth aside. "Fresh blueberry muffins."

"Oh, yum. Are these made with the berries you picked yesterday?" Carmen jumped up and retrieved two small plates. "You didn't have to do this, but I'm not about to refuse."

"I love to bake. Anytime you need real food, I'm happy to help out."

"You say that like you already know I'm the world's worst cook."

Carmen plucked out a muffin and took a small polite bite. She followed that immediately by a much larger mouthful. Her eyes closed at the taste of the perfectly cooked bread. "This is amazing. The best blueberry muffin I've ever had."

Grace hid her smile behind her cup, but the crinkling of her eyes gave her away. A few moments later, Cricket wandered into the room. Carmen noticed that Grace took her coffee black so she decided to go with her backup plan. She slipped the saucer from under the creamer bowl and passed it over to Grace, who apparently caught on right away.

"That's very kind of you." Grace poured a measure of cream into the saucer and placed it on the floor. "Here you are, my darling. Isn't Carmen thoughtful?"

A silver necklace swung out from the top of Grace's shirt when she leaned over. She grasped it quickly and tucked it away when she sat up, but Carmen had already noted the design. A five-pointed star inside a circle. A pentagram. She gulped quietly, remembering the conversation at the diner. Carmen's thoughts were in a jumble.

She watched Cricket lap up the cream, considering if the witch rumor could be accurate. Unlike yeti and werewolves, witches actually existed. Not like Samantha Stevens, of course, who could make things happen with a twitch of her nose. Carmen believed real witches cast spells and attempted to curse people. She remained unclear if any of the spells actually worked, but that didn't keep people from trying. Still, that could be one explanation why she had felt off kilter since meeting Grace.

The cat finished the milk and looked up at her. Carmen noticed a white film on her chin before Cricket settled onto her rump and began washing. Grace had only given the cat a tiny bit of milk so it hadn't taken her long to finish the portion. Carmen wouldn't have cared if she drank more, but it was probably best not to overdo it. She didn't want to see Cricket with an upset tummy.

Carmen realized she had focused on the animal as a way to avoid her internal debate. Actually, she didn't care about the witch thing one way or the other. She received nothing but good vibes from Grace, and Carmen always considered herself a good judge of character. She still wanted to get to know more about Grace and decided to go with what little information she had already gleaned.

"I hear you're a zoologist. What's it like working for the Forest Service?"

Grace fiddled with her mug before meeting Carmen's gaze. "You've been speaking with Laurel. She's the only one who calls me a zoologist. And you just saw my medallion so I can imagine what else she told you. Why don't you ask what you really want to know?"

The teasing quality of the question gave Carmen the nerve to do exactly that. "Okay, she said you're a witch, but not really. Yet, you wear a pentagram. So, what's the deal? If we're going to be friends, I'd like to know if you're going to cast some witchy spell on me."

"Who says I haven't already?"

Carmen's eyebrows rose at the suddenly flirtatious inflection in Grace's voice. Never one to be outdone, she responded in kind. "You do know that water melts witches."

"You'd have to get to some first. Besides, you don't really believe everything you hear, do you?" Grace had the daring to punctuate her question with a wink.

Carmen stifled her smile. Pleasure surged through the pit of her stomach. What began as a friendly encounter had somehow morphed into something more. Recent experiences with women urged her to proceed with caution so she attempted to redirect the banter with reasoning.

"It's a fact. At least if you watch enough television about witches."

"Only if you believe in *The Wizard of Oz* as a source guide."

Carmen burst out laughing, caught off guard by Grace's charming manner. In seconds, both of them were laughing. Cricket took that as an invitation and leapt into Carmen's lap. As the merriment subsided, Carmen was petting the cat before she even realized it.

"I do work for the Forest Service," Grace confirmed, "but I'm a wildlife ecologist. I also happen to have a Masters in forestry and biological science. Basically, I evaluate the impact of scheduled events on park lands. I also have a degree in animal sciences so I help out with any wounded wildlife when I can."

Carmen whistled. "I can see why Laurel calls you a zoologist. That's a lot to take in."

"It is. Speaking of which, we should probably be going. I have a shift later."

"Right, sorry. I didn't even think about you needing to work."

Grace picked up the saucer from the floor before carrying it and her cup to the sink. She rinsed out both as she answered. "I wouldn't have missed this for anything. In fact, I'd like to return the favor. Would you like to do something this weekend?"

Would she? Carmen had been wrestling with a way to invite Grace somewhere. Anywhere, just as long as they could spend more time together.

"Wolf Hollow is having a beer festival this weekend. Would you like to go?"

Grace dried her hands on a dish towel. She dipped her head once. "That sounds like a lot of fun. I would love to go with you. The Beerfest is a wonderful event. I can't wait to show it to you."

Carmen and Grace worked out the details, agreeing to meet at the park entrance early Friday morning and finished by exchanging phone numbers. Grace left the majority of the muffins behind on a paper plate before collecting her basket and heading for the door, feline companion dutifully in tow.

"Would you like a lift home? I'd hate to see you late to work and soaking wet to boot."

Grace's curls bobbed as she shook her head. "It's already stopped raining and don't worry. We won't be late."

"We?"

"Cricket doesn't like to stay home alone."

"Right."

When Carmen opened the front door for her guest, she saw that Grace was right. The rain had stopped completely. The sun struggled to come out from behind the clouds, lending the day an overall watery feel. She didn't know how Grace came by her forecast insight since the woman hadn't even left the table or glanced out a window when she made her prediction. She seemed to possess an intuitive feel of nature that Carmen found enthralling.

Alone again, Carmen deflated like all of the positive energy had departed the cabin along with her guests. Both woman and cat had considerably brightened the space and relieved a loneliness Carmen didn't realize existed. She also realized that Grace never said yes or no to any of her questions. She seemed content to allow Carmen to draw her own conclusions or answer in a way that implied a certain meaning.

The certainty of that belief told Carmen she needed to interact more with other people. She had rolled into the area convinced she craved time alone to think and would quickly return to her life in Denver. Now she thought she just needed immersion in a quiet, laid back life without the stress of crime busting.

In the days that followed leading up to Thursday, Carmen did her best to accidentally bump into Grace. She continued her pre-coffee walks to the waterfall hoping to meet Grace and Cricket. It never happened and she felt somewhat let down. After yet another unsuccessful encounter on Wednesday, Carmen admitted she was hooked.

She appreciated that Grace didn't come onto her like gangbusters. She had gently flirted with Carmen, or so she thought, but Carmen wasn't really an expert on subtlety. What happened between them during coffee could be attributed to mere friendly banter. Her limited romantic ventures often left her clueless or reading into something that simply didn't exist. Whether Grace actually flirted with her or not, it was more than just that. Grace carried a quiet strength of character. Her actions were supple and unhurried, rather like her cat. She smiled a lot and had the laugh lines around her face to prove it. Around her, Carmen grew calm and peaceful inside.

She had lightly accused Grace of being a witch, but upon further reflection, realized her mistake. According to everything she'd ever read, witches cast dark spells and used people for their own nefarious purposes. Grace did not fit that description. Instead, the word Wicca came to mind. Wiccans were supposedly pure in heart. Deeply spiritual and compassionate, they held no hidden agendas and existed in harmony with nature through the five elements. The pentagram Grace wore could easily fit into that scenario. Carmen liked it. The explanation seemed logical and explained so many little things. The concept lent a whole other dimension to her budding friendship with the unusual woman.

Of course, she had no idea if any of this was true or only a fantasy created by her runaway imagination. Either way, the possibility made Grace, and Cricket by extension, even more intriguing. For the rest of the day, flights of fancy about Grace's Wiccan powers kept Carmen occupied until she remembered her dinner plans for Thursday.

Chapter Twenty-One

Loud conversations buzzed all around. Combined with the thumping music that blasted through overhead speakers and the children that ran unsupervised throughout the establishment, conversation proved impossible. Carmen sipped the craft Irish beer from a tall pilsner and studied her dinner companion. For once, she wasn't enthusiastic about her beverage. Her concern for Katie prevented that simple enjoyment. Not only did Katie look different than the last time Carmen saw her, but her behavior also seemed off.

While perfectly polished and dressed as usual, Katie sported new lines around her eyes and mouth. Her shoulders seemed tense, almost hunched as though awaiting a blow. Katie carried stress like an invisible cloud. She seemed to have aged years in only a few months. The choice of this place for a dinner setting only added to the mystery. When Katie suggested *The Red Fox*, Carmen hadn't anticipated an Irish pub. Her friend's choices typically leaned to the more posh and sophisticated set.

An older man with a heavily grayed dark beard and wearing a stained newsboy cap staggered around their table. The thick press of mostly unwashed bodies caused him to stumble. Carmen figured from the strong smell of whiskey that his balance was impaired to start, making him unstable on his feet. When he bumped into her chair before skewing off into the crowd, she'd had enough.

Carmen leaned across the slightly sticky wooden table and her half finished Reuben to close the distance. She had to shout to be heard. "Katie, are you all right?" She kept the question simple. With this din, she didn't want to add to the confusion.

"What?" Katie leaned forward, indicating that she still couldn't hear.

Carmen shook her head and stood up. She tossed a few folded bills onto the table. "Let's go."

Leaving the food and drinks behind, they stepped out onto an equally crowded sidewalk. Allentown seemed perpetually busy, causing Carmen to appreciate even more her choice of home in Wolf Hollow. Briefly, she experienced a slight shock that she had acclimated to a more sedate environment so quickly. Pushing that revelation away, Carmen focused on Katie. Something troubling had happened and she intended to find out what had Katie so disturbed.

"Let's find a quiet place to talk."

Carmen pulled out her cell phone and searched for a nearby coffee lounge. The day was moving on and she wanted to hash this out before she had to head home. If necessary, she would book a hotel room for the night and drive home in the morning. She'd be a little late for her date with Grace the next day, but she knew for certain Grace would understand. Not that Carmen wanted a plausible excuse to bow out from the Beerfest. She most definitely did not, despite the nerves that made her hands shake when she thought about the upcoming festival. Even a week ago, she couldn't have imagined looking forward to something so much. No question, she looked forward more to the company than the venue.

After locating a promising coffee shop only a few blocks away, the women set off on foot. By the time they could hail a cab, they could walk the distance. Carmen offered to drive, but Katie preferred to walk, saying that she could use the exercise. Feeling dubious that Katie could manage given how exhausted she looked, Carmen nevertheless kept silent and fell into step beside her friend.

Five minutes and two jaywalking soirees later, Carmen held open the door to the bistro. The scent of fresh brewed coffee, milk and sugar hit her like a heavenly wave. The coffee house was small, only eight tables, but it was quiet. Only two other souls occupied the seating area. Grateful for small favors, Carmen allowed Katie to order first. They took their drinks to the farthest table in the corner, away from anyone who might wander in. Although she expected Katie to start talking right away, Carmen was doomed to disappointment. Katie seemed content to merely sit staring into her cappuccino with both hands wrapped around the ceramic cup.

"Katie." Nothing. She didn't even look up. Carmen wondered if she heard her. "Katie?"

"What?" Katie flinched and met her eyes. She flushed slightly and took a sip from her drink. "Sorry. Guess I'm a little distracted."

"Come on. Tell me what's going on. This isn't like you at all. You act like you just got bad news from the doctor." A horrible thought occurred to her and Carmen blanched. "You didn't, did you?"

Katie offered a wan smile. "No, nothing quite so dramatic. I just have a lot on my mind."

"Other than the conference?"

"Conference? Oh, right. The conference."

Hand tightening around her own mug, Carmen froze in sudden contemplation. "You are attending a psychiatric conference here in town. Right?"

"Oh yeah. Sure."

For the first time in their long affiliation, Carmen wasn't sure she believed her. The idea of Katie lying was hard to fathom and Carmen discounted the possibility as absolutely ridiculous. "So, what's the matter?"

Katie scowled and suddenly seemed furious. Her eyes flashed and her jaw clenched. "You know, Carmen, why can't we just have a nice visit? Why do you always have to make something into nothing? Not enough to do out in Deliverance Village that you have to stir things up into some kind of mystery as soon as you see me?"

"Whoa! Where is this coming from? As for having a nice visit, you mean at a pub where I couldn't hear myself think, much less have a conversation? If you wanted to avoid me, why did you even call and invite me to dinner?"

All the fire went out of her and Katie slumped. She dragged her fingers through her hair in a gesture that Carmen had never seen her use before. "You're right. I'm sorry. I do owe you an explanation, but I guess I'm just a little embarrassed."

"About what? You know you can tell me anything."

Katie sighed. "The truth is that I've been involved in a long-term business deal that just went south. I believed in someone who promised a large return on my investment. Needless to say, that didn't happen."

"Let me guess. You lost it all."

"More than that." Katie chuckled without humor and shook her head. "The money is gone and so is he. Vanished without a trace. Him and his business partner."

"This just gets better and better." Anger bubbled below the surface that anyone could take advantage of Katie, but Carmen held in her ire in check. "What are their names? I still have friends in the Denver P.D. I'm sure we could track them down."

"No." Katie sounded adamant and slammed her mug a trifle forcefully onto the tabletop. "I forbid it."

It wasn't only her tone. Just the fact that Katie *forbid* Carmen to do anything caught her off guard. There was more going on here than a simple failed contract. Pulling in her proverbial hackles, Carmen tried to think how she would react if she were on the receiving end of such a problem. True that Katie had loads of money so the situation was slightly different, but Carmen thought pride might have a lot to do with her reactions.

"Okay, you don't want me looking into things. Can I assume you're just looking for moral support?" Careful wording would hopefully prevent a blowup. Carmen didn't care for the feeling of walking on eggshells.

"Precisely."

Carmen nodded. "Tell me what happened."

She sat sipping her mocha while Katie unloaded. Apparently the deal began over two years ago. In exchange for investment capital, Katie would reap the benefits from international commodities exchanges. A brokerage affiliated with the Intercontinental Exchange in Europe consisting of two men had contacted Katie to see if she'd be interested in partnering with them. Katie never questioned their motives. She, being a gifted computer guru, had checked them out. All seemed above board. Katie transferred a sizable amount of money, she refused to say how much, and things went along trippingly for a time.

"The quarterly checks stopped coming in sometime last year. Of course, I was busy traipsing all over Germany and Switzerland at the time so I didn't think anything about it."

"When did you realize something was wrong?"

"About a week ago." Katie slammed her mug against the table again. The couple a few tables over glanced toward them and then away again. "I know, it's not like I can't afford a loss, but I feel like such an idiot. Now I can't even get hold of these guys. I think I'm more angry than anything."

"You said they were with the Intercontinental Exchange in Europe? That's a very high-profile organization. Can't you just contact them and report these guys?"

"Did I say ICE? Maybe they were with the London Metal Exchange. I don't really remember."

Once again, warning bells went off in Carmen's head. Katie was far too organized to mix up the details of a business deal. ICE and the Metal Exchange dealt in very different commodities.

"Uh Katie, no offense, but exactly what were you trading in?"

"Oh you know. Gold, silver. Sometimes other things. I trusted the brokers to handle those details."

Katie looked up from her cup and Carmen saw the anger simmering below the surface. None of this made any sense. More than that, she sensed that Katie was angry with *her*. Carmen had the feeling that this entire story was bogus. She had no idea why Katie would make up such a thing. Unless she really had made a bad investment, but didn't want to share what had actually happened. Either way, she clearly didn't want Carmen to do anything but listen. Carmen could do that.

"I'm really sorry, Katie. I wish there was something I could do to help."

Katie suddenly smiled, showing a little too much teeth. "Me too, kiddo. Look, let's change the subject."

"Are you sure? You look awfully exhausted. If this is weighing on you that much, maybe you should report the problem to the International Exchange Commission."

"I said drop it, okay?"

The anger was back. Carmen had never seen Katie act like this before and she didn't like the change in her friend. That being said, she searched for other reasons to excuse the behavior. In truth, Carmen felt a little responsible. If she had been a better friend and kept in touch with Katie more regularly rather than dropping off the map, maybe she could have prevented this. Then again, Katie said she got involved with these people two years ago, long before that first fateful trip to Germany.

Regardless, Katie didn't give Carmen the chance to shoulder the responsibility for the situation. Suddenly, she downed the rest of her coffee. "I'm done. I think I'm going to head back to the hotel. The panels are going to start up early again in the morning."

After a little mental juggling, Carmen caught up. Katie was ending their time together and sending Carmen packing. This entire disastrous evening started to grate. Katie hadn't shown any true desire to talk about their lives, catch up or even socialize on any level. Carmen had the feeling Katie wanted to vent about something and it was not a bad business deal. Instead, she came up with a lame story of losing money that didn't make any sense and then shoved Carmen, figuratively, out the door.

"Sure, Katie. Whatever. Give me a call when you really want to get together."

Leaving a half full coffee cup, Carmen strode toward the door. She expected Katie to call her back, but that didn't happen. As she left the bistro, Carmen chanced a look back and saw Katie walking to the counter. With her eyes on the menu overhead, Katie clearly intended to order something else.

Katie just wanted to get rid of her, Carmen realized. Hurt and feeling a little betrayed, Carmen shook her head and set out to find her car. It was time to go home.

Warm, gentle sunshine caressed her arms and face. Grace stopped beside the triple falls, closed her eyes and tilted back her head. The sound of water crashing into the semi-circular pool enhanced the moment. Nerve endings sang as she focused on the feel of nature and took in the healing energy. When Cricket's lithe body pressed against her and the tail wrapped around her leg, Grace smiled. Everything in nature connected. She shared a sense of oneness with not only Mother Nature, but her feline companion as well. Grace finally opened her eyes to look down and meet the slightly cross-eyed golden gaze.

"Yes, it is quite a beautiful day. Not too windy. Not too warm. Too bad I can't take you with us to the festival."

"Meow."

"Because dogs will be there. You know people can't stand to go to these events without their fur children. That's not a bad thing, mind you. And yes, I'm aware that you qualify as a fur child."

Cricket let loose a plaintive cry that tugged at Grace's heart. "I'm sure she wants to see you, too. What if I promise to ask her to stop for coffee on the way home? It's better than some slobbering canine chasing you in the park. Will that work for you?"

Cricket's meow transitioned into a low disgruntled growl. She unwound herself and moved over to the edge of the water. While the cat pretended to slap at little fish and frogs, Grace knew her friend better. Cricket had agreed to the compromise, but she wasn't pleased. One last glance at the fluffy clouds and Grace turned for home.

Light feline steps trailed behind. Grace allowed Cricket to sulk quietly during the short walk home. At one point they rounded a curve that crisscrossed the game trail. A doe astride the path ceased chewing new growth and woody plants. Her fawn ceased its play and hurried to the doe, though neither bolted for cover. Grace offered a soft greeting before she led Cricket on a wide berth around the pair. The animals in the area rarely considered them a threat and Grace did her best to keep things that way.

Soon, they crested the rise onto a hilltop with no name. Grace spotted their patch of sanctuary and took a moment to enjoy the sight. Just as she always did. An angel's view looked out over the forest, shadowed by the Poconos high overhead and not far away. Smoke curled invitingly from the chimney of the small gabled house. White shutters gave color that popped against the earth-brown structure. Flower boxes lining porch railings and window boxes overflowed with a kaleidoscope of varying blooms. A visitor currently resided on one of the rails near the uppermost step.

"Good morning, Mister Robin. Here for a morning meal?"

The red-breasted bird ruffled its feathers upon spying the cat. It offered Grace a light chortling song, which she took as confirmation.

"Well, you should come inside like a proper guest."

Grace pushed open the door, but stayed in place on the porch. While Cricket rushed ahead, the bird flew to Grace's shoulder. She smiled, thinking what Carmen's reaction would be to this. Very likely, she'd attribute the bird's behavior to a magical spell. She couldn't know Grace had discovered an abandoned nest of light blue eggs a few years ago. After observing the nest for days, Grace realized the mother wouldn't return. Either something happened to her or the silly creature lacked any maternal instincts. Grace carried the eggs home in their original nest and placed them into an incubator intended for chicks. Only one of the eggs hatched.

After it did, Grace diligently nursed the baby through infancy and often carried him around in her pocket. He'd ventured off on his own as soon as the power of flight allowed, though he often returned for a hand out. Grace never bothered to name him since she didn't own him in the traditional sense.

Once across the threshold, the bird zipped off to alight on a perch reserved especially for him. Grace gave the little songbird some dried mealworms and left him to his breakfast. She paused to open a window so he could leave when ready. Finished with her hosting duties, she prepared to meet the day with some light meditation in the altar room.

Grace settled onto the floor before a wooden chest equipped with rollers. She folded her legs and lit a single light gray candle. The color of the taper called on female energy and helped her to feel centered. After only five minutes, she concluded the calming ritual. She showered and dressed to meet Carmen. Her pulse quickened thinking about the woman. Attraction of this sort was new to Grace, but she had recognized Carmen for the special woman she was as soon as they met.

In fact, she knew they had a connection, a shared fate that existed long before the encounter in the woods. That was one reason she had no need to overtly vocalize her interest in an obvious way to Carmen. Everything was already pre-ordained.

She looked up to where Cricket lay atop the bookshelf. Ready to go, Grace slipped a black leather shoulder bag over her head. It angled across her body and lay under her left arm. "Now try to behave while I'm gone, Cricket. No dead mice in my bed when I return. Get it, my love?" A quick pat on the head and she left. The robin had already departed.

The ride down the mountain and into town didn't take long. Less than ten minutes later, Grace turned down the street leading to the park entrance. She spotted Carmen already waiting. Just seeing her there, leaning casually against the split-rail perimeter fence made the sunshine seem brighter.

The lot was packed, but a battered sedan backed out from a front space just as Grace turned in. She waited a second for a much older man to move along before taking the spot.

"Wow, you have great parking karma," Carmen said as soon as Grace exited her Jeep.

Grace slammed the door without locking the doors. "Of course I do. Are you ready to have some fun?"

"Yes! I skipped breakfast and the smell of corn dogs and funnel cake are driving me crazy."

Grace laughed and linked her arm through Carmen's. She felt warm all over when Carmen tightened the grip. "We'd better get some food in you then. I wouldn't want you to swoon from intoxication after your first beer."

"I never swoon."

Somehow Grace expected her to add the words "except over you." Carmen didn't say it, but the impression lingered in the air.

Chapter Twenty-Two

Inside the grassy arena, owners and handlers stood beside their goats. Three women and two men proudly waved at the crowd. Grace recognized Judith Blake, a fifty-two-year-old florist as one of the contestants. The breeds and sizes of goat ranged from dwarf to pygmy. Some were brown, others black and white and every variation in between. Like all goats, both the males and females sported horns. People crowded the stands and filled the area around the temporary arena. It was standing room only. Grace used the mass of residents as an excuse to press her thigh against Carmen's. Her eyes stayed pinned on the happenings of the race though she held her breath. To her relief, Carmen placed a hand on her knee. Grace felt like a giddy teenager exploring the first blush of a new relationship. Neither had actually said anything to that effect, but the mutual interest seemed apparent.

Just then, the announcer spoke through the overhead public address systems.

"Okay folks get ready for the first race of the day! Our first five contestants are lined up and ready to go. Now as a reminder, local companies will be naming their latest brews from the winners of each race. From left to right, we have Daisy, a Nubian goat from Wiltshire farms. Beside her we have Jellybean, the black and white pygmy. Then Jumper, Banana and finally Casanova. I hear he's a real charmer with the ladies."

The crowd chuckled with good humor as the contestants prepared to go. A horn went off and so did the contestants. Goats scampered in the general direction of the finish line with people running alongside them. One of them, Daisy, stopped suddenly and ambled over to a cluster of flowers. Fortunately, the distance wasn't but a few hundred feet. The smallest of the creatures, a pale brown Nigora about the size of a shepherd raced across the finish line.

Shouted laughter, cheers and applause roared from the crowd.

"Whoa, we have our first winner! Green Forest Brewing will be naming their first pale ale of the season after Banana, a Nigora weighing in at eighty-five pounds. Congratulations to Judith Blake, ladies and gentlemen. Be sure to come back in ninety minutes for our next heat!"

Along with the rest of the crowd, Grace and Carmen left the stands to explore the rest of the festival. The goat handlers wandered through the crowd allowing everyone to interact with the animals. Grace wanted to see the goats up close just as much as the children, but her desire to focus on Carmen won out.

"What do you say we grab some lunch?"

Carmen nodded and bumped shoulders lightly with Grace. "Sounds good. I could go for a chili dog and a Banana Beer."

Both laughed and walked to the nearest hot dog vendor. With no line, Grace carefully watched as Carmen collected their food. Despite her growing attraction and the fun of the festival, she had a feeling something was wrong. A hint of sadness colored Carmen's aura. Grace kept her concerns quiet until they retrieved a couple of pilsners and found a seat. She sat her plate and plastic cup onto a picnic table. Grace slid onto the bench and waited for Carmen to join her.

"Cricket wants to see you. Do you think you could come by for a bit after we leave here?"

Carmen had just taken a bite of her chili dog. She nodded her head and swallowed. "Cricket does, huh?"

The melancholy residing beneath the teasing comment was clear. It hurt Grace to see Carmen in such emotional pain. "I promised her this morning before I left that I would ask."

"In that case, how could I refuse?" Carmen smiled, but the expression seemed forced.

"Carmen, is there something wrong? You just seem like something is bothering you." Grace placed a hand on Carmen's thigh. "Please tell me."

Carmen placed the dog on her plate and concentrated on wiping her hands on a napkin. The way she avoided eye contact told Grace that she needed a moment to gather her thoughts. Grace realized they hadn't known each other long, but she hoped Carmen knew she could confide in her.

"It's my friend, Katie. Something happened at dinner last night. Well, actually nothing happened, but it was just so weird."

Carmen proceeded to tell Grace a story that seemed as confusing as it did nonsensical. Katie sounded sullen and more than a little resentful. From everything Carmen said, they were great friends and nothing like this had ever happened before. Grace learned about all of the events both had experienced in the last year. A fake werewolf and a supposed yeti were the least surprising things she heard. People did all kinds of things motivated by greed and avarice. That she found more interesting was that Carmen didn't seem to see what was right in front of her. Especially as a police officer and someone who enjoyed solving a good mystery.

No longer hungry, Grace pushed her paper plate away and took a sip from the beer. "Carmen, I hate to ask this, but how well do you really know this person? I mean really. Have you not noticed that Katie was present every time something happened to you?"

"So was I. What are you saying?"

"She invited you to both places, Munich and Switzerland. Both invitations were seemingly legitimate. I just find it a little too coincidental that in each case something bizarre happened. And by your own admission, Katie was never there when you got into trouble."

Carmen frowned, her eyebrows pulling down sharply. "Are you saying Katie was responsible?"

"Not at all. I'm saying it's possible she found out more about what was going on and doesn't want to tell you. Then again, maybe she reacted as she did at dinner because she just has a lot on her mind. I think anyone would be upset given the circumstances. Give her time. She'll come to you when she's ready and everything could be just as she said."

Carmen stayed silent for a long tense moment, her eyes on her plate. "You're right. I just feel so frustrated that she's in this situation." Carmen stood abruptly and threw her plate into a nearby aluminum trashcan. Her movements were sharp, abrupt and easily conveyed her frustration. "It really is none of my business, but I can't help it. I just feel there's more going on here."

"All I can advise is to trust your instincts. They'll rarely steer you wrong."

"You're right." Carmen nodded once, sharply. "Katie was rude yesterday, but we all have our bad days."

"Of course. I'm just sorry to see you so upset."

The fire went out of Carmen's eyes and her shoulders slumped as she sighed. "Thanks. I appreciate that. It's just that so many things she said just don't add up."

"Such as?"

"The story Katie told me about losing money. She said she made a bad investment two years ago, but she couldn't tell me with whom. Then she mentioned gold and silver, as in jewelry. And why won't she tell me who these people are? It's not like I'm going to try and arrest them or something."

Grace reached up and took Carmen's hand. "This speculation is tearing you up. Why don't you try calling her when you get home and hash all this out?" Grace tried to think of a way to get Carmen's mind off her troubles, even if only for a short time. "Would you like another hot dog?"

"No, but I'll take another beer." Carmen drained her plastic cup and held it aloft. She wiggled it playfully.

A chilly breeze lifted Grace's bangs and she glanced at the sky. The sun already headed toward the horizon.

"I'd love to, but I think I'd better get home to Cricket. There's beer at home if you'd like to come with me."

Carmen pitched the cup. "Lead the way. I can't let Cricket down."

After dropping Carmen's car at her cabin, they proceeded up the mountain. Carmen quickly realized Grace's competence behind the wheel. She handled the Jeep easily and immediately, but carefully slowed to allow the occasional raccoon to dart across the road. Night woods pressed in close on both sides of the narrow blacktop. If not for the bloated moon riding the sky, Carmen could believe they traveled a roadway that tunneled through the dark, fathomless earth.

The trip didn't take long. At the apex of the hill they stopped at a four-way intersection. They waited as another vehicle closed from the driver's side. Carmen squinted at the glare of fast-approaching headlights.

"Thanks for the high beams, fella," Carmen complained softly.

"He's going too fast to stop at the intersection. I'm glad there's never a lot of traffic on this road."

Before Carmen could respond, a dark sedan shot across in front of them without slowing down. Just as it did, a large shadow crossed the road from the woods opposite where Carmen and Grace sat. From the size and shape, Carmen thought the shadow was a large dog.

"Oh God." She closed her eyes and turned her head away. Carmen knew what would happen before she heard the screech of tires and the sickening thud. When Grace's car lurched onto the shoulder, Carmen chanced looking.

The driver's seat was empty and the door ajar. Grace had reacted instantly by pulling the car over, throwing it into park and heading to the scene before Carmen even opened her eyes. As she watched, Grace raced across the road to where the animal lay. The sedan didn't bother to hang around. The rear end fishtailed before the tires grabbed the road again. Taillights disappeared in an abrupt right turn about a hundred yards away.

Carmen climbed out of the car and ran to Grace's side. "Is it dead?"

"Get a blanket out of the back of the Jeep. She's alive, but I can't tell how badly she's hurt."

A black dog the size of a shepherd lifted its head and whined. Dark eyes glanced at Carmen before the animal lay back down.

"On it."

Carmen helped Grace wrap the dog in the blanket and carry her to the back of the Jeep. Blood soaked through the blanket. Without hesitation, Carmen climbed into the cargo area and cradled the dog between her legs. In what seemed like only a few seconds, Carmen rocked back from the Jeep's sudden acceleration. The animal shivered and Carmen wrapped her arms around her to provide additional warmth. She tried to stay sitting straight up as Grace hung a sharp right turn and shot down the road. Carmen peered down the lane where the sedan had disappeared as they passed.

She didn't see anything. She held on as Grace made a right turn onto the next gravel road and then a quick left, trying not to injure the dog anymore than she already was. In minutes, Grace pulled the Jeep to a stop beside a one level house built with a crawl space and wrap-around porch. Massive timbers made up the four columns supporting the roof line over the front of the structure. While she couldn't see a lot of detail in the dark, Carmen noticed the gabled roof and the warm lights glowing from inside. Then Grace threw open the rear hatch.

"Let's get her inside quickly. I have an exam room set up in the back for when I have to care for animals from work."

Carmen didn't question the statement. She remembered Grace saying that she often helped the Forest Service with injured animals. The dog weighed every bit of seventy-five pounds and even together they had trouble wrestling her inside. Neither woman bothered closing the door as they hefted her toward the rear of the house. Focused on the injured animal, Carmen had only a flash of comfortable furnishings, green and flowering plants, and an open window. In seconds they entered a room that stood out starkly from the rest of the home. A stainless steel exam table and sink along with white wall cabinets, strong overhead lights and a medical storage cabinet made Carmen feel like they had stepped into a vet's office.

Without needing to be told, Carmen helped lift the dog onto the exam table. Once Grace pulled the blanket aside, Carmen got a good look at the dog. She did in fact look a lot like a German Shepherd, but there were notable differences. This animal had legs that seemed just a little too long. She had a broad snout, short ears, and a very long tail. She looked lean, but extremely muscular. Carmen also noticed the collar and ID tags. At least they could contact the owner.

Grace left the room, but returned quickly with a portable x-ray machine. While she wrestled the machine into place, Carmen removed the collar. The dog panted in shallow breaths, but she appeared unconscious.

"She's gorgeous. What kind of dog is she?"

"She's not a dog. She's a wolf. There are lots of them around here.

It's how the town got its name."

Carmen squeezed the collar she held. "Someone owns a wolf?"

"The owners took her in as a pup. Can you brace her so that she doesn't fall off the table? I'm going to give her something for pain before I take the x-rays."

"You know the owners?"

Grace pulled a sterile syringe from a cabinet drawer and then turned to the medicine storage chest. She answered while she worked. "Uh huh. I saw the Lukrens at the festival when we were leaving. They probably don't even know she's out. We'll call them once we get Leyla stabilized."

Together Carmen and Grace worked to help Leyla. X-rays showed no broken bones though she did have a large laceration on her right side where the car had struck her. Carmen listened with a sense of relief as Grace shared her prognosis. She said Leyla was lucky the car had slammed on the brakes enough to avoid killing her instantly. Although she wouldn't know anything definitive for a while, Grace seemed sure Leyla was more stunned than anything.

Carmen glanced down at her denim shirt. It was ruined. Blood covered her front and had already started to crust on her forearms from where she held the wolf. The cost of a shirt seemed a low price to pay to help the animal. Carmen decided it was time to call the owners. She left Grace settling the wolf and walked back toward the front of the house. Carmen pulled her cell phone from the holster and dialed the number on the collar. Over an hour had passed since they arrived at Grace's house and Carmen hoped the Lukrens would be home by now. While the phone rang, she wandered through the house. Carmen leaned against the door frame to a darkened room as a man answered the call.

"Hello?"

"Hello, is this the Lukren residence?"

"Yes, who is this please?"

"I'm sorry, you don't know me. My name is Carmen Bravo. I'm a friend of Grace Wickford's. Listen, I'm sorry to call you so late, but we have your wolf." Carmen had almost said dog.

The man's voice sounded excited. "You have Leyla? Oh, thank goodness. The neighbor was out target shooting and the sound scared her. We were so worried something might have happened. Where are you?"

"Mister Lukren, please slow down. We're at Grace's house, but Leyla was injured. She was hit by a car."

After reassuring him that the injuries seemed minor, the man finally calmed down. At first, he seemed so upset she was worried he would faint. Due to the lateness of the hour, he agreed to trust Grace's skills enough to come by the next morning. Carmen found his willingness to wait unusual until Mister Lukren said he knew of Grace's work with the Forestry Service.

"Grace knows more than any vet. If she says Leyla is okay, then that is good enough for me. We'll allow my darling girl to rest and come by in the morning. I have to go now and let Lisle know what's happening."

Once the call ended, Carmen realized she'd stood staring into the darkened room throughout. Her eyes had adjusted somewhat to the gloom. Combined with the moonshine through the window glass, she had a pretty good view of the space. An antique-looking brown chest drew the eye as a focal point. A black, cast iron kettle resembling a cauldron rested on top right in the center. Multiple colored candles surrounded the pot.

Drawn forward by the sight, Carmen trailed her fingers over the chest. Leather. Small nicks and scuffs attested to the piece's age. She looked around out of curiosity. Candles adorned many surfaces, including shelves and tables. None were lit at the moment, but other things caught Carmen's eye. A thin line stretched across one end of the room. Herbs and mystery plants hung suspended and drying there. The scent in the room from the plants and wax combined to create a natural and comforting environment. Carmen closed her eyes and inhaled deeply. She still felt on edge from all the excitement and this helped.

When she opened her eyes, sudden movement caught her attention. She looked up to find golden orbs watching from atop a weathered armoire.

"Hi, Cricket."

"Meow." The cat's response seemed far from friendly.

"Are you trying to tell me that I shouldn't be in here?" The growl issued low in the feline throat was answer enough. "Yeah, I thought so."

Carmen spun on her heel and walked out just as Grace entered from the opposite side. The pain and worry in her eyes spoke volumes. Without thinking, Carmen held out her arms in silent invitation. Grace fell into her embrace. For a long, comforting moment, Carmen simply held her. Finally, Grace sniffled, tightened her grip slightly around Carmen's shoulders, and then pulled back. The misery on her face had lightened considerably. Carmen kept her arms loosely around Grace's waist.

"Are you okay?"

Grace nodded. "Better now. Thanks for helping me with Leyla."

"Of course. I got a hold of the owner. Mister Lukren said they'd come by in the morning."

"Good. I'm glad it's the weekend. I'd like to keep an eye on her for a while."

"You're such a caring person," Carmen said softly. "Not everyone would have rushed to help her like you did."

Grace reached up to cup Carmen's face. Her thumb gently stroked her cheek. Grace spoke in equally quiet tones. "You would have."

"Yeah, I would."

The moment had turned unexpectedly intimate. Lost in Grace's dark gaze, Carmen barely registered her own response. Her emotions rode high in the aftermath of the ordeal. Carmen didn't experience the same pain as Grace, but adrenaline and endorphins had yet to dissipate. Combined with the attraction between them, it seemed so natural to close the short distance between them.

Carmen's eyes closed at the whispered touch of lips. She intended the caress to be gentle and unhurried, but those intentions didn't last. After that first light touch, all thought of consequences and hesitancy vanished. Arms slid around her neck to pull her close and Carmen lost all thought of anything but Grace. The softness of her skin, the taste of her kiss and the quiet sigh of arousal were Carmen's entire world for long, sweet moments.

A warm body at ankle height broke the spell by winding between them. Carmen pulled away when Cricket bit her lightly on the shin. Both Carmen and Grace laughed at the cat's behavior.

"Did she just bite you?"

"Not really." Carmen dropped her arms to her sides. "I barely felt anything through my jeans. Maybe she just wants some attention."

Grace bent down to scoop Cricket up into her arms. "She has been alone all day. I'm sure she's ready for a proper dinner."

"Right. It's starting to get late. I should get home."

Leaving was the last thing Carmen wanted. In fact, she couldn't think of anything more wonderful than kissing this enchantress all night long. Rather than get ahead of herself or pressure Grace in any way, Carmen took a step back. She needed the space to help cool her raging libido. She also recognized that Grace might regret anything that happened in the aftermath of a traumatic situation.

Grace took Carmen's hand. "As much as I'd like for you to stay, I think that's wise. We're going to have a long night here. I need to steep some willow bark to keep Leyla comfortable and that's going to take a while."

"Uh, I think I should tell you something before Cricket does. I saw your altar room."

Grace didn't contradict the description. "Wait until you see my garden. Why don't you come by in the morning to check on Leyla and I'll show it to you?"

"I'd like that." Again, Carmen experienced the sensation of falling under Grace's spell.

"Let me grab my keys and I'll drive you home real quick. Cricket can keep an eye on Leyla until I get back."

The image of a cat keeping watch on a wolf left Carmen speechless. She fairly floated out of Grace's house and into the car. During the short drive, Grace reached across to rest a possessive hand on Carmen's thigh. Her touch generated a goofy grin on Carmen's face that didn't fade until halfway back to her cabin.

When Grace rounded the curve to her home, Carmen's smile vanished. A very familiar car sat parked in front of her porch. From just the illumination of the headlights, Carmen recognized the BMW.

"Who is that?" Grace asked, curiosity reflected in her tone.

"Katie."

Chapter Twenty-Three

After Carmen slammed the car door, Grace backed out and left. They both decided that now wasn't the appropriate time for introductions. Leyla needed tending and this discussion with Katie seemed destined to belong and painfully drawn out. Carmen took a long, steadying breath and approached the BMW. Movement inside the sedan attested that Katie still sat inside the vehicle. Carmen had no clue how long she'd sat out here in the dark. Carmen passed by the vehicle and stepped up onto the porch. With arms folded, she turned around to wait.

Katie stepped out of her car right on cue. She walked over to stand looking up at Carmen. The nearly full moon played with the shadows across her face, concealing her emotions. For her part, Carmen knew she stood in the darkness cast by the porch cover. Good. She wasn't sure why Katie had come and didn't want to give anything away until she knew how to react.

"Hi."

Carmen nodded, but doubted Katie could see her. "Hi back."

Katie heaved an exaggerated sigh. "I came to apologize."

That was unexpected. Carmen relaxed her defensive posture. "Why don't you come inside? I'll put on some coffee."

Carmen unlocked the door and crossed the threshold, listening for Katie to follow. While she might leave the car unlocked everywhere she went, that same philosophy didn't apply to her home. Anyone out for a hike in these mountains could wander in. Suddenly nervous, Carmen scanned the inside of the cabin as she walked inside. It seemed clean enough.

Once Katie entered, Carmen closed the door. She had left several lights burning when she left for the festival since she knew she wouldn't get home until after dark. For that reason, she clearly saw Katie's surprised expression. She resembled a startled owl.

"Is that blood? Are you okay?"

Carmen reflexively glanced down and up again. "It's not mine. Grace and I helped a dog that got hit by a car." She didn't know why she didn't say wolf.

"Grace, huh? Is that who dropped you off?" Katie's voice was loaded with innuendo. She shook her head and chuckled. "Even here in the sticks you manage to find someone willing and able."

"Are you here for an actual reason? It's late and I'm tired."

Katie shrugged and adjusted the handbag on her shoulder. "I told you. I wanted to apologize."

"You're off to a great start." Carmen was tempted to cross her arms again. The only reason she didn't was that she didn't want to give Katie the satisfaction. As a psychiatrist, she would immediately see through to Carmen's insecurities. The idea of such a possibility made Carmen angry. She inhaled deeply to control her responses.

Katie's eyes drifted to the floor. Her cheeks flushed and she adjusted the purse again. A sign of her own discomfort. Seeing it made Carmen feel a little more in control.

"That's fair. I deserved that after last night. I'm sorry, Carmen. Listen, can we talk? I mean really talk. I don't think I was ready last night."

Carmen nodded. "All right. Come in the kitchen."

After coffee each morning, Carmen's habit was to set the pot for the next day. With the brew already set, she had only to switch on the machine. Soon, the scent of strong chocolate raspberry coffee filled the room. Carmen busied herself by pulling out two cups as Katie helped herself to a seat at the table. She glanced around the room briefly, a direct counterpoint to the long appreciative look Grace had given the same space only days ago.

"Charming. In a Mayberry sort of way."

Carmen turned her back on Katie to pour a couple of cups. She put one in front of Katie before taking her place. It looked like Grace wasn't the only one with a long night ahead. "Are you ready to tell me what's going on with you?"

"I already did, but I shouldn't have told you the way I did. I didn't mean to act so nasty to you."

Hands wrapped around her cup in her typical thinking posture, Carmen stared deeply into the brew. At this moment, she could really use some advice from Grace. Maybe she could read Carmen's tea leaves or something. Of course, this wasn't tea. She decided she didn't need that reading after all. Carmen already knew she was willing to forgive and allow Katie some leeway.

She interjected a teasing quality into her tone. "You drove a long way just to tell me that. You could have just called."

Katie smiled, and just like that, the tension vanished and things seemed like they always had. "Maybe I decided to see why you like this area so much. Last night, you seemed so relaxed I thought I'd give it a try. I mean, what's the worst that could happen? So, I booked a cabin not far from here for a few days."

"You hate nature. Unless it involves skiing or hot tubs with martinis on the side, that is. There's nothing like that up here. Just lots of nature. I think it's fair to warn you that you're doomed to disappointment."

"You speak the truth, but I think I'll give it a shot anyway. After everything that happened, I could use some time away from corporate deals and shady characters."

That sounded reasonable. Carmen knew how badly she had needed to get away after her friends died. She'd left Denver months ago, but she wasn't sure she was ready for company in her home. Normally, she would invite Katie to stay with her. Though Katie said she had rented a cabin, Carmen had the feeling she still expected that offer. Carmen wasn't comfortable with that idea. Life had turned suddenly complicated for her considering the budding relationship with Grace.

She also still felt somewhat at odds with Katie considering she believed her friend had shaded the truth about the financial situation. The thing that bothered her was there wasn't any reason for it. Surely, she knew Carmen would never judge any mistakes she'd made. God knew Carmen had made enough of her own.

At least Katie had made the trip to extend an olive branch. In light of that, Carmen attempted to get to the bottom of what was really happening. Not because she was being nosy, but because she truly worried for Katie and wanted to help.

"I can appreciate that. I'm glad you decided to take some time for yourself. You were so upset last night that I was really concerned." Carmen picked at the table cloth, attempting to carefully choose her words.

"You would be too if you'd just found out you were swindled." Katie tone hardened again. Her emotions seemed so volatile and she swung from friendly to furious in an instant.

Carmen remained undeterred. "Speaking of which, have you found out anything else about those guys?"

Katie's expression closed and her jaw tensed. Her eyes looked flat, like a shark. Carefully, she placed her coffee cup on the table. At least she didn't slam it down this time. "Drop it, Carmen."

"Katie, I'm sorry, but you aren't acting like yourself and the story you told me has a lot of holes in it."

"Are you calling me a liar? Maybe this is one case I want to investigate for myself. This isn't Germany and I'm not looking for a sidekick."

Something clicked. "Is that how I make you feel? Like I'm the detective and you're just there for backup?"

"You do have a tendency to try and take over. Just the hint of a mystery and you're pulling out the magnifying glass and fingerprint powder."

The comment stung, but Carmen tried to be objective. From Katie's point of view, Carmen could see why she might think that. "I never meant to make you feel small. I'll butt out, but know that I'm here if you need anything."

"Thanks. That's all I ever wanted. Now, can we talk about something else?"

Carmen got up to refill their mugs. She took a moment to let go of the hurt. "Like what?"

"Tell me about this woman you met. Grace, is it? How'd you meet?"

A smile slipped into place just thinking about Grace. Things seemed like old times as Carmen told about seeing Grace for the first time at the waterfalls. She described Grace's beauty and the calmness she projected.

"She works for the Forest Service and has this amazing cat named Cricket. Cricket's a black cat and follows Grace everywhere. Of course, I shouldn't be surprised. Every witch needs a familiar." Carmen chuckled, lost in her thoughts about the other woman.

Katie jerked slightly and sloshed coffee over the rim. She dashed the liquid from her chin with the back of her hand before leaning forward to catch Carmen's eye. "Did you say witch?"

"Well, Wicca. She's not really a witch."

"Oh no, Carmen. Not another monster. Honestly, I don't know how one person can attract so many of these creatures. And you really like this woman?"

Fury boiled in Carmen's veins. Just like that, all the newly formed closeness dissipated. Katie could tell Carmen to stay out of her business, but Carmen drew the line at her insulting Grace. Carmen's stomach burned from the combinations of beer, coffee and her anger. Her silence must have communicated her ire to Katie.

"I don't know why you're getting mad. I'm just looking out for you."

"By judging someone you've never even met."

"I'm not judging," Katie said in a condescending tone. "I'm just…"

"No. I don't want to hear it. True that I don't know everything you've been through in the last few months, but you have no right to talk about Grace that way. She is a wonderful, beautiful, caring woman. She's the kind of woman that takes care of wolves hit by cars without a second thought to her own safety."

"You said it was a dog."

Carmen ignored her. "I'll give you that she's different. Personally, I like that. She doesn't act like everyone else just so she can fit in."

"You mean like me."

The sarcasm had begun to get on Carmen's nerves. "Not everything is about you, Katie. Now, thanks for coming, but I think it's time for you to go."

"Why, so you can bed the witch?"

Carmen slammed her coffee cup down so hard that it shattered. The remaining coffee inside ran over the surface of the table and onto the floor. Carmen stood in one fluid movement. "That's enough. You need to leave, Katie. Right now."

"Fine." Katie sniffled, clearly offended. She stood up, acting extremely proper by taking a moment to wipe her fingers on a napkin. "I've never known you to be so sensitive."

"And I've never known you to be so insensitive. Thanks for the apology."

Outside on the porch, Katie turned. The expression of contriteness had reappeared. "I shouldn't have said that, Carmen. My emotions just seem to be all over the place right now. I feel really awful. Maybe we can get together again while I'm up here."

Carmen literally couldn't keep up with Katie, but she wasn't about to let her off the hook by saying it was okay. It *wasn't* okay. She had started to think Katie was bipolar and had hidden her condition all the time they'd known each other. If so and Katie was off her meds, that would explain a few things. She figured Katie owed her for acting like a jerk so she pushed things a little.

"Out of curiosity, you said you're investigating the people who stole from you. Do you think they're up here in the Poconos?" Before Katie could fly off the handle again, Carmen raised both hands. "I've no intention of getting involved. Just wondering if that's why you're really up here. Aside from getting some fresh air, I mean."

Katie hesitated for a moment. "Maybe. Maybe not. I'll have to see how things pan out. Bye, Carmen."

Katie walked sedately back to her car. Carmen watched her drive away, wondering. Her evasive answer gave Carmen more information than she realized. As a seasoned peace officer, Carmen had connected a few dots. Katie did believe those guys were in the area. Whether a victim or a willing accomplice, Katie was actively searching for them. That meant she knew more than she let on. In any case, Katie's unpredictable emotional shifts didn't bode well for an amicable outcome if she managed to locate them.

Her instincts screamed for Carmen to intercede. Instead, she stood with her hands shoved in her pockets and watched Katie leave. At this point, Carmen had changed her mind. She didn't want to get involved. She had more than enough going on in her life at the moment.

At the entrance onto Goose neck Road, Katie turned right and headed up the mountain. Carmen frowned, wondering where she was going. Grace's home lay at the top of the rise and there weren't many other cabins up there that Carmen knew of. The memory of a dark sedan fishtailing onto a narrow side road flashed through her mind. Goosebumps caused by concern and disbelief broke out on her arms.

No way. Too coincidental. Carmen shivered and went back inside.

Chapter Twenty-Four

Heart thumping in anticipation, Carmen awaited a response to her knock. When the door opened, she thought it would ricochet out of her chest. Each and every time she saw Grace, her fondness seemed to increase exponentially. Carmen almost blurted out something inane like "How are you?" Until she recognized the signs of exhaustion. The bloodshot eyes and lines of strain around Grace's mouth gave it away.

"Hi. Did you get any sleep at all?"

Grace chuckled and stepped back for Carmen to enter. "You really know how to charm the ladies."

"Yeah, I've often been told that I'm a pretty smooth operator."

"Pretty, yes. Smooth, not so much."

The remark rendered Carmen unable to process. She willingly complied when Grace unexpectedly hugged her. She closed her eyes to concentrate on the warm body and the sensation of Grace's breath on her neck. Carmen had worried about awkwardness generated by the kiss last night. Instead, she reveled in Grace's open and continued affection. She hadn't changed her mind and didn't pretend nothing had happened between them. Unlike most people in her experience, Grace seemed never to worry about presenting a front. She was exactly as she appeared to be, without any agenda but authenticity.

"Good morning," Grace said, breaking into Carmen's thoughts. "I assume you're here to check on Leyla."

Carmen released her when Grace pulled away. "Yes, but not just her. How are things?"

"Leyla's doing much better. I just fed her as a matter of fact. No fractures. Just the gash on her side and a scuffed snout. A few stitches took care of the side, but she'll be sore for a while. Come on back and I'll introduce you properly. There's someone else I'd like you to meet."

Grace took her hand and led Carmen through the house. This time, Carmen took the opportunity to glance around some. More colored candles adorned the living room and complimented the overstuffed cloth furniture. The walls were painted a pale beige and Carmen noticed the window remained open from last night. A gentle breeze fluttered the pages of a magazine resting on the mahogany coffee table.

"You sure do like candles."

"I prefer natural light in the evenings. I find them comforting."

Just as they crossed into the hallway, Carmen spotted something out of place. A wooden stand mounted over a white melamine surface took up a fair amount of space off to one side.

"You have a bird? How does that even work with a cat?"

Grace spared her an enigmatic look. "Not always and Cricket isn't like most felines. She enjoys company."

Carmen let it go and focused on the moment. The heat of Grace's hand took the spotlight. Carmen tightened her grip, gratified when Grace did the same. Despite her concerns with Katie, or perhaps because of them, this touch seemed even more exquisite. Seconds later, they passed through the clinic area and through a door at the back.

Considerably smaller than the triage area, this room wasn't what Carmen expected. Rather than a kennel area like any other vet's office, this space mirrored the balance of the home's comfortable coziness. A plush, brightly colored area rug and a few comfortable chairs invited visitors to stay. A large crate that resembled a toddler's playpen occupied a corner. Only the metal top gave away its true purpose. For the moment, the cage stood empty.

A man and woman occupied the chairs sitting center stage. Leyla rested on her haunches between the two. Her eyes closed in bliss as they stroked her head and scratched behind her ears. Leyla resembled any other canine companion except for the thick white bandage wrapped around her ribs. Carmen blinked at her first sight of the two people.

Both appeared squat and strong. She could believe them identical twins with their lumpy noses and sharp chins. If not for her having breasts and him a beard, Carmen might not easily tell them apart. Although set a little too closely together, two sets of piercing blue eyes easily conveyed happiness with the wolf's condition. From how they fawned over Leyla, Carmen assumed these were her owners.

"Oh, Argos, she's almost as good as new." Mrs. Lukren sniffled, becoming a little misty.

Argos Lukren chuckled, a high tee hee sound. "Yes, indeedy, Lisle. Almost. Almost. That's my beautiful girl," he said to the wolf.

The pair of them seemed to suddenly realize they had an audience. As one, sapphire eyes flew up to pin Carmen in place. She found only joy and acceptance in their eyes. Carmen experienced the sensation of sharing time with kindly grandparents.

"You must be Carmen," Mrs. Lukren pronounced. She surged out of the chair and waddled across the room, her movements quick and sure. The top of the gray-haired woman's head stopped even with Carmen's upper chest. "Grace told us what you did for our girl. We're in your debt."

Astonishingly comfortable with the short, but impressive, woman, Carmen shook the offered hand. "No debt owed at all, Mrs. Lukren. I'm just glad I could help."

"Now none of that. It's Lisle. And this is Argos. Leyla, come say hi to the nice lady. She helped save your life." Lisle added in an aside to Carmen, "I expect she was quite out of it when last you saw her."

Carmen almost parroted Argos's words of "Yes, indeedy." She caught herself and snapped her mouth closed. When Leyla obediently padded over, Carmen thought her mind would short circuit. The whole scene resembled a fairy tale. Here she stood with two people who very much resembled dwarfs. Owning a black wolf added to the imagery. On top of all that, each of them now stood in the home of a witch. Carmen stifled the urge to giggle, afraid she'd sound somewhat insane.

Instead, she dropped to one knee, certain Leyla wouldn't swallow her whole. This wasn't the wolf from Grimm's Fairy Tales.

"Hello there. Are you feeling better?"

Leyla responded by offering a paw.

"Would you look at that?" Lisle sounded so proud. "She wants to say thank you."

"Sure." Why not? Carmen took the huge paw into her hand.

At first everything seemed fine. Leyla acted like a dog performing a trick. She shattered the illusion when the panting stopped and she lowered her head. Brown eyes remained on Carmen's face. The ambient light gave them a brief crimson glow. Carmen flinched away and landed on her backside. A surge of adrenaline made her heart pound.

Then Leyla's tongue lolled sideways out of her mouth and she trotted back to Argos.

"Are you okay?"

Grace's hand rested on her shoulder. Both she and Lisle regarded Carmen with some concern. "Uh, yeah. Guess I'm more tired than I realized."

"Let me help you up."

Carmen stood with support from Grace's arm under her pit. Thankfully, Carmen showered just before she left the cabin. Her head swam before the room settled. Surely, she had imagined the fire in Leyla's eyes.

A curious glance flashed between the Lukrens. Carmen noted the exchange, though she felt so flummoxed that it barely registered. Somewhat less graceful than his counterpart, Argos struggled from his chair. After sparing one more lingering caress for Leyla, he shuffled over to join the women. He glanced at Carmen and the easy feeling vanished from the room.

"You're quite the miracle worker, Grace, but we should go. Uh, when can we take Leyla home?"

A pinched expression caused a crease between Grace's eyes. Carmen figured she also picked up on the change. Probably. She hadn't known her long, but Carmen didn't think Grace missed much.

"Tomorrow afternoon. I'd like to keep an eye on her for one more day. Just to be sure."

Both Argos and Lisle nodded in tandem with twin smiles. Lisle chose to answer aloud. She patted Grace firmly on the hand. "Thank you, dear. I'll bring you some of my famous *khazad*."

After bidding a sweet, albeit brief, goodbye to the wolf, the intriguing and mysterious duo zipped for the door. When they decided to depart the house, it happened fast. It seemed Carmen blinked and they were gone.

She stood staring at the closed door.

"Carmen? Something wrong?"

"Are you sure those two are human?" She looked back to gauge Grace's response.

"Funny you ask." Grace had a twinkle in her eye. "I wondered the same thing when I first met them."

As usual, Grace didn't really answer the question. Carmen let it go. "What's *khazad*?"

"A casserole with bacon, cabbage, and bread crumbs. From what I hear, it's also got lots of butter and is very filling."

Carmen stifled a shudder. "Sounds disgusting."

"Possibly. Although I do hear that it's quite hearty. If you're all right, I'm going to walk Leyla and get her settled."

Carmen turned back to the front door. For some reason, the way the Lukrens departed the house still bothered her. "Hmm, I'm good." She didn't expect the dwarfs to return. She just couldn't wrap her head around what spooked them in the first place.

While Grace took care of the wolf, Carmen left the living room and made herself at home in the kitchen. She made coffee as something to do with her hands while she attempted to suss out all the intricacies of what happened in the kennel area. While the pot brewed, she stared out the small window over the sink. She didn't really see the woods. In the end, she realized she hadn't any answers. All she knew for sure was that they bolted right after Carmen noticed Leyla's eyes shine.

She jumped slightly as arms slid around her from behind. Carmen relaxed and leaned back against Grace. A chin rested on her shoulder. "She all settled?"

"I gave her some valerian. It's good for pain and will help her rest."

Carmen turned in the gentle embrace. "You are a very impressive woman. And I can't wait to get a look at your incredible garden."

"Done. Follow me."

Carmen's eyes dropped to Grace's lips. "In a sec."

Distance closed. Time seemed to slow. Carmen's eyes began to drift shut in anticipation. A rapid fluttering startled her as the sound quickly approached. Carmen fairly leapt away from Grace. Spinning on one heel to confront the threat, Carmen assumed a defensive posture. At the same moment that she identified the creature, she heard Grace giggle.

Adrenaline had caused the fine hairs on her arms and scalp to stand. Those as well as her heart rate returned to normal slowly.

"That's why you leave the window open? For a robin?"

The bird landed on the corner perch. It offered a brief song before tucking into the filled cup. Carmen could swear she spotted dried worms of a sort. She decided she didn't really want to know and turned back to Grace.

"He likes to visit sometimes."

Coming from Grace, the explanation sounded obvious. "You know that's actually kind of interesting. A few days ago, a robin landed on my porch railing. I stood right there, but it didn't seem scared. Do you think this is the same bird?"

Grace cocked her head as she considered. "Perhaps. Like anything, birds are creatures of habit. I've been feeding this one for a while now so he might not be frightened of humans. From a general standpoint, of course. You know, robins are a symbol of good luck."

Carmen looked down as Cricket sauntered into the room from some secret place. After she took a moment to stretch and yawn, she seemed to take note of the bird. Carmen expected an instant attack, in the manner befitting a proper feline. Instead, she strolled over near the perch before leaping to the top of a bookcase. The robin fluttered in reaction before settling back down. It apparently recognized the cat as nonthreatening. For her part, Cricket took a playful swipe at the bird before lying down on top of the bookcase and closing her eyes. Seconds later, Carmen watched in disbelief as the robin hopped onto Cricket's back, shimmied down into her fur and joined his friend in slumber.

"Would you look at that?"

"I did say that Cricket likes company."

"Yeah, for breakfast. That is not normal. Next thing you'll say is that she helped you bandage the wolf."

Grace tugged her hand lightly. "Let's go see the garden."

"Are you trying to distract me?"

****

Blending into the wooded landscape and mountainous backdrop, flowering hanging vines, climbing roses and honeysuckle perfumed the air. The foliage grew all around, creating a roughly rectangular space filled with blooms of every color. Variegated greens, blues and browns mixed with bursts of yellows and cherry reds. A few trees also adorned the garden. Just like the flowers, they bloomed in shades of purple and white. Carmen listened to the whispered hum of bee wings and watched multicolored butterflies flittering and landing. Heavenly scents tickled her nose, almost blinding her to numerous furrowed herb rows.

Carmen's knees wobbled. She felt boneless as she dropped onto a wooden bench with curved iron armrests. The words she managed to utter came out in a whisper. "It's magical."

A bluebird flew out of a tree and landed on a nearby fountain. Water spewed into the air. The little thing hopped into the water and began to bathe. In a few moments, other birds joined it. Sparrows, pine siskins and cardinals among others.

Grace slipped onto the bench beside her. She leaned against Carmen's side. Somehow, they held hands though Carmen couldn't recall moving. Birdsong and rushing water combined with the sights and scents, creating an enchanting paradise on Earth. Carmen had never experienced such a feeling of total peace. Tears blurred her vision.

Feeling surrounded by calm and sanctuary, Carmen let down her guard. She described the encounter with Katie at the house the night before. Grace's grip on her hand tightened as Carmen confessed her hopes and fears. She explained the strange mood swings and Katie's determination to get to the bottom of things herself.

"You can't fix everything bad in the world, Carmen. People have to do it for themselves. All you can do is be there for her if she needs you."

Carmen sniffled. "You're right, but don't you find it interesting that she headed this way after leaving my cabin?"

"What do you mean? What's bothering you?"

"Too many little things." Carmen shook her head. She could almost see pieces of the puzzle falling into place. "The car that hit Leyla seemed out of place. A shiny new black sedan in the Poconos Mountains? Not a few hours later, Katie shows up looking for a couple of crooks. And she just happens to rent a cabin in the same area where we saw the car? Too many coincidences. My instincts are telling me that everything is connected."

"Then you should listen to them."

Carmen looked at Grace with surprise. "Most people would call me crazy. Why do you believe me?"

"For a couple of reasons. Carmen, we have instincts for a reason. They keep us alive. Yours are finely honed after years of police work. If you say these things are related, then I believe you."

Carmen released Grace's hand to slide an arm around her shoulders. It seemed natural with Grace tucked against her side. "What's the other reason?"

"You won't believe me."

"Hey now, you believed my loony theory. The least I can do is give you the benefit of the doubt."

"Okay, but don't say I didn't warn you." Grace took a steadying breath, piquing Carmen's curiosity. "I knew the moment you arrived in Wolf Hollow that something important would happen. I thought it was just this, us. Now, I believe it's more. The truth is, I knew you were coming before you arrived."

Carmen tried to think of anyone who might have talked about her before she bought the cabin. "Did the realtor mention me?"

"No. I dreamed about you. I saw your face and I knew we were meant to be. More than that, I knew you would do something important here."

Carmen swallowed. Despite the fact that the comment had a stalker kind of vibe, she didn't consider Grace a threat. "I didn't think people could dream about faces they'd never seen before."

"And yet here you are. I suppose it's my turn to sound crazy."

Carmen shifted around to look into Grace's sable eyes. "You are the sanest person I've ever known. What you said makes perfect sense."

"It does?"

"Yes, though I'll admit I didn't dream about you before we met. I do think I had a dream about Cricket though."

Grace laughed and the sound broke the too serious mood. She dug her fingers into Carmen's ribs and tickled her. Very quickly, she relented. "Shame on you for teasing me."

"I may not have dreamed about you, but you are the woman of my dreams. I knew the second we met that you had me under your spell. I'm right where I want to be."

Carmen bent low as Grace's fingers slipped around her neck. Their lips met and Carmen lost herself in the kiss. Alone together in the garden, she let go of all the nagging worries. Only Grace and this moment existed. Carmen allowed the passion to rise as never before. She pulled Grace closer, soft breasts crushed against her. She accommodated the change of position as Grace rose up to straddle her lap.

Stars exploded behind Carmen's eyes. All she wanted was Grace naked beside her.

Carmen hooked her arms under Grace's rear and stood in one fluid motion. Without losing contact with warm, supple lips, she mumbled, "Your bedroom. Where?"

"Through the kitchen. The door on the right. Hurry."

Nothing short of invading trolls could have stopped her. Carmen hustled into the house and paused just long enough for Grace to push the door shut behind them. She almost dropped her precious cargo when sharp teeth nipped the sensitive skin on her neck.

The red haze of desire made everything appear blurry. Carmen took in a lungful of air and made for the bedroom. As she crossed the threshold, the thought of a mischievous cat popped to mind. She really didn't need Grace's clover-toed companion showing up at the most inopportune moment to critique her performance. Or sticking her nose in places where it didn't belong.

Carmen kicked the bedroom door closed.

One large, upright black ear flicked back toward her skull. The moans, gasps and cries from the humans had grown progressively louder. This shout in particular almost caused Cricket to jump. Almost. After all, she had her feline dignity to consider. Lying atop the cage where the dog that was not a dog rested, Cricket had to remember that. Dignity above all. Dignity and loyalty. Grace was her person. As long as the Carmen woman was her mate, she was Cricket's person too.

Cricket licked her paw and rubbed behind the ear, pretending to wash. The humans were silent now. So was the dog that was not really a dog. Cricket wondered when the dog-thing would answer her. It was simple really. Would she help or not?

Finally, Leyla lifted soulful brown eyes to meet Cricket's golden gaze. She communicated her irritation. Leyla saw no reason to help the people. True, she liked Grace, but she didn't know the Carmen woman. Though she gave nice scratches.

Cricket reminded Leyla of the ones who hurt her. Those same people were doing bad things in the woods. Things Leyla already knew about. That was why she was out there sniffing around instead of safely at home when the steel box with wheels hit her. Those people hurt other people and animals alike. They needed something bad to happen to make them stop. Cricket knew this because both Leyla and the bird with red on its front told her. Even now they had humans tied up inside their people cages. The people cages had doors and windows clever animals could go through to help. Cricket was clever. She thought Leyla could be clever, even though she was a dog. Didn't Leyla want to hurt the bad people the way they hurt her? To Cricket, this seemed very logical.

Finally, Leyla sighed. She agreed to help the Carmen woman only if she got in trouble with the bad people.

Pleased with her communication skills, Cricket returned to her bath. She knew Carmen would get in trouble. She heard her talk with Grace in the garden before they started mashing their mouths together. Carmen talked about another girl person and mentioned the place where Leyla got hurt. For some reason, she seemed confused about who the bad people were, but Cricket knew she would soon understand. If not, Grace would, and would tell her. Grace was very smart and nice. That was why Cricket loved her.

Cricket looked forward to fighting the bad people. She hadn't bitten anyone for such a long time.

The dog that was not a dog didn't seem as happy about the whole idea. Clouds drifted away from the light in the sky and Leyla lifted her impressively long snout into the air. Jaws parted to show wicked sharp teeth. The wildness in the dog-thing created a response to the bone-white moon that made Cricket cringe. She listened to the first impressive howl, though it really was louder than strictly necessary. The second lonely cry sent Cricket off to find a quieter place to rest. Sometimes, she just didn't understand dogs.

Chapter Twenty-Five

Carmen yawned and took another large gulp of too hot coffee. If not for Grace's need to prepare to return to work, she felt sure they would both still be lying in her bed. Carmen smiled, thinking about the incredible night of loving. Afterward, they had fallen into an exhausted sleep, disturbed only by the howling of a very close wolf. Carmen couldn't really complain. It was in Leyla's genes. Really, the howls only added another layer to the surreal experiences that seemed to follow Grace around.

Already, Carmen missed her fiercely. She had always considered herself independent. Carmen didn't want to need someone so badly that she couldn't stand being away from them. All of that changed the day she met Grace. In her bones, Carmen knew they were fated, just as Grace said. That explained why she couldn't bring herself to get involved with Sally or Malia. Carmen also knew it was why things hadn't worked out with Faye. All along, her heart had waited for Grace.

Carmen chuckled at the realization. All of her hurt surrounding Faye's post-coital behavior eased. Carmen had her pride hurt when Faye disappeared without a word. Nothing more. What they shared couldn't hope to compare to what she had found here. On a lonely mountain in a quiet wilderness, Carmen found what she needed most. Though she hadn't known Grace long, Carmen had fallen in love the moment Grace emerged from the woods beside a waterfall.

The cell phone rang, interrupting her thoughts. Carmen snatched it up, expecting the caller to be Grace. She wanted to hear how things had gone with reuniting Leyla and the Lukrens. Out of habit, she glanced at the Caller ID. Her smile vanished. For a second, she considered letting the call go to voicemail. Just as quickly, Carmen answered the line. Hadn't she just decided there wasn't any reason for hard feelings?

"Good morning, Faye. Or should I say good afternoon?" France was a full six hours ahead of Pennsylvania.

"Hello, Carmen. I regret disturbing you, but we need to talk."

Carmen snorted in disbelief. "Isn't that something you should have said before you snuck out in the middle of the night?" She could have kicked herself when she heard Faye gasp. Apparently, Carmen did still harbor some resentment, but she needed to get over being petty. "Sorry, I shouldn't have said that."

"No, you have every right. I am the one who should apologize. All I can say is that I received some disturbing news that night and I had to leave quickly."

At one time the accent and apology would have melted Carmen's ire. Not anymore. While she could take the high road over the way the relationship ended, that didn't mean she wanted to listen to excuses. "And you haven't bothered to call me since. Cut the crap, Faye. What do you want?"

"Fine. Here it is. I left because Interpol received an anonymous tip. The caller implicated Kathryn McClarin as the head of the international smuggling ring I have been investigating."

"You can't be serious. Katie would never be involved in such a thing." Carmen pushed away the fact that she had known something serious was going on with her friend. She never imagined it could be this. "Let me guess. You figured that if Katie was part of this *gang*, then so was I."

"It was a possibility." Faye sounded far from repentant. "I didn't know you well. How would it look for a senior Interpol agent to be found sleeping with a member of an organized crime ring?"

"Coward. Instead of talking to me, you just took off. You let me wonder what I had done wrong, why you would just leave. Well, you win the prize. This is way worse than anything I could have imagined."

"Carmen, please. Hear me out."

"Why? Is this some lame attempt to lure me back? If so, it isn't working."

Faye cut her off before Carmen could let her know just how much the situation had changed. "No, it is so much more. I called to say that I am not in France. I am leading a team of agents working with law enforcement in the United States right now. Carmen, we followed your friend to Pennsylvania."

Carmen's blood seemed to freeze. She knew exactly what Faye meant. "You're planning to arrest her and you wanted to share the good news. Thanks for that. How can you be so callous?"

"*Mon Dieu*, will you listen? We believe Ms. McClarin and her people are hiding out near your location. This safe house, if you will, could hold all the evidence we need to finally put these criminals away."

"Exactly how do you know where I am? Been keeping tabs? And exactly what proof do you have, aside from an anonymous phone call? Surely, you're smart enough to know people can say anything. It's probably the real ring leader attempting to shift blame to an innocent woman."

"There is a paper trail." Faye spoke calmly, her tone intent enough to make Carmen really hear her. "We know for a fact she is involved directly. There were bank transfers between her and the others for many thousands of dollars. Carefully hidden mind you, but we were diligent in following the trail. Also, she was present at every city where the smuggling ring operated."

Carmen huffed. "If you mean Germany and Switzerland, I was there too."

"And Paris, Chicago and British Columbia? Were you present in these locations too, Carmen? No, you weren't. Did you think I wouldn't ensure your innocence before I phoned?"

Carmen felt sick. This couldn't be happening. "Why are you telling me this at all, Faye? You could compromise your case."

"I thought you deserved to be present when we make the arrest. I wanted to give you the chance to speak to your friend. Consider it a professional courtesy."

"I'm not a police officer anymore, remember? I retired."

"Then call it a common courtesy. I know this is hard, Carmen, but you deserved to hear it from someone who cares rather than on the nightly news. This is a chance to say goodbye to your friend, likely for quite some time."

Faye had finally crossed the line. Carmen knew Faye wouldn't jeopardize an upcoming bust in any other circumstance. The only reason she did so now was owing to their personal history. The lack of professionalism bothered her more than anything else.

"Why would you think I want to see that? I'm going to say it once more. You're way off base. Before you start deciding Katie's guilty, try considering all of the evidence. There could a perfectly logical reason for what you believe is her willing involvement."

The sound of Faye's sigh carried through the connection. "You cannot say that I didn't afford you this chance. Since you have declined, I cannot give you any further details, but the arrest will happen soon. You may regret your decision."

Carmen didn't like anyone pulling a guilt trip on her. The taunting made her ask, "How do you know I won't call Katie and tell her everything you just said?"

"Because you may no longer carry a badge, but you believe in justice. You are still a police officer at heart. Also, as much as I still care for you, I will arrest you if you interfere."

"That's nice. Call me and give me info I shouldn't have and then threaten me. Only one problem, Faye. You're Interpol. You don't have any powers of arrest. Especially in the United States."

Faye lost her patience and shouted back. "You are splitting the hairs. I will issue a Red Notice and have the Marshals Service arrest you if you inform your friend. Satisfied? I'm sorry we could not discuss this civilly, but for your own sake, stay out of my way. Goodbye, Carmen."

After she heard the click of the terminated call, Carmen sat staring at the phone. All of her concerns for Katie had risen to slap her in the face. Recent doubts gained strength and warred with Carmen's trust in her friend. Now, she couldn't even call Katie to work out their personal differences. Any contact from Carmen could be taken as obstruction. With one call, Faye had taken away all her options.

Carmen put her head down on the dining table and burst into tears.

****

Sleep refused to come. Carmen lay with Grace tucked against her side, her mind whirling with worry for Katie. Even after hours of strenuous love making, Carmen couldn't relax. She went over everything she knew, from Faye's call and Katie's inconsistent story to the location of the newly rented cabin. Carmen couldn't shake the image of the dark sedan being near that same location. Just as she'd told Grace, Carmen knew it was all connected. Frustrated that couldn't even call Katie to discuss the possibilities, Carmen wanted to break something.

A viable way around the legal issues suddenly occurred to her. Carmen couldn't risk a phone call, but no one said she couldn't take a walk through the woods. She would feel so much better if she could just check out the cabin Katie rented. It wasn't far from Grace's house, only a few roads over. Maybe half a mile through the woods as the crow flies. If Katie really was just putting distance between herself and a trying situation, then Carmen would leave quietly. Katie would never even know she was there. Carmen could call Faye back and intercede on Katie's behalf. Maybe then Faye would listen, reconsider, and search for the real criminals. The most important part of the whole operation was not getting caught until she had proof of Katie's innocence. Carmen realized she walked a legal tightrope here, but the stakes were too high not to take the risk.

Carefully, Carmen eased away from the warm body. Grace grumbled quietly and rolled over in her sleep. Carmen froze for a few seconds until she was sure Grace wouldn't awaken. Then she climbed out of bed, scooped her clothes off the floor, and tiptoed out of the room. A small thump let her know that Cricket had jumped off the bed in pursuit.

Carmen carried her clothes into the living room to dress. As she pulled on her jeans, she noticed Cricket watching from the corner of her eye. Once finished donning her shoes, Carmen met the slightly cross-eyed feline gaze. A cool breeze through the open window caressed the side of her face.

"If things go south for me, tell Grace she can find me where we saw the black car." Carmen rolled her eyes. "What am I saying? I'm treating a cat like Lassie and it's not like you can tell anyone anything, is it?"

After ensuring the door latched quietly behind her, she trotted to her car. She needed the flashlight from the driver's side door pocket. Carmen couldn't drive because she couldn't risk the engine noise waking Grace. She glanced at the moon, gauging the natural light. This jaunt would have been easier with the full moon from a few nights ago. With the waning light, things could get dicey. Shadows would be deep even with the flashlight, but she couldn't. She had to refrain from using artificial light as long as possible.

She decided to stick to the gravel roadways and blacktop. Doing so required more time, but it also minimized the chance of getting turned around in the woods.

With a flimsy and poorly conceived plan, Carmen struck off down the lane leading to the main road. She kept the flashlight in her pocket, hoping to save the batteries for later. Plus, the light would give her away to anyone within a quarter of a mile.

Carmen realized this was a total shot in the dark. A shot that could get her killed for lack of foresight or prove completely fruitless. Other country roads existed up here on the mountain where numerous rental cabins existed. Pure conjecture had her heading over to where the mystery car disappeared. Her sole idea for this jaunt hinged on walking down the road in the middle of the night hoping to see Katie's car. Or the black car. Either one would do. She didn't exactly have a lot of other options. No matter how misguided, at least now she was actually doing something.

"I'm an idiot, that's what I am." She mumbled under her breath, being completely honest since no one could hear her. Carmen didn't believe she could find Katie or an international criminal syndicate. The chance of locating them both together was even less likely. "Yeah, but I certainly won't find anyone or prove Katie didn't do this if I don't try."

The main road stood out ahead. In the darkness, it resembled a long black snake twisting away into the distance. From there, Carmen reached the next lane over pretty quickly. Once she stepped onto the gravel road, Carmen slowed her pace and hugged the shadows near the edge. Oftentimes, people renting cabins didn't turn on lights during the night. With low light and heavy woods, Carmen didn't want to miss anything.

Almost at once, she realized her biggest mistake. She had no idea how far the road went. It could go on for miles before winding around and running back down the mountain.

No, that couldn't be. Parts of the Poconos were impassible. Hence the windy mountain roads in the first place. The escarpment with her favorite waterfall resided in one such area and wasn't far from here. The residential roads up here tended to be short and bumpy. Felling a little more confident, Carmen worked her way down Ant Trail Road slowly.

An hour passed before the land suddenly ended. It just stopped at a guardrail blocking a two-hundred-foot drop. Carmen leaned over the aluminum rail and stared down into a black abyss. She had counted twelve cabins in total, but wondered if she'd spotted them all. Determined to pay extra attention, she walked all the way back to the main road without spotting anything new. No sign of the black car or Katie's Beemer.

She stood at the juncture of the two roads, unsure what to do now short of exploring all the nearby gravel roads. There wasn't time. Faye would arrest Katie soon, perhaps in only a few hours. After that it could take months to clear her name. Carmen couldn't stand the idea of Katie languishing in jail for something she didn't do. She sighed in frustration, knowing she'd have to chance waking Grace. She needed her car.

Had she truly missed an entire cabin? Feeling frustrated and backed into a corner, she spread her arms to the sides and turned in a circle. There had to be something else here. The flashlight spun out of her hand and hit the ground. The light came on and the beam shown away into the darkness. Carmen huffed and squatted to retrieve it. When she looked up, she saw that she had indeed missed the obvious.

In the dark forest and intent on finding Katie's car, she had missed another track. Trees grew together closely at an angle leading away from Ant Trail. The pines pressed so close that they grew into a canopy overhead and concealed the mostly dirt lane. Without the flashlight beam, the opening merely resembled a break in the forest. Up close, Carmen spotted tire tracks. This narrow road could barely accommodate a single car at a time. A rusty sign attached to a thin t-post leaned at an awkward angle near the edge. The sign simply stated "POC-A9." This wasn't even a true road. Just a mountain trail.

Carmen hesitated to speculate how many of those she'd passed in the darkness. More importantly, how many more cabins existed up here? This could take days.

Well, there went that great idea.

Carmen switched off the flashlight. She turned away from the dark lane feeling defeated. She had no choice but to return to Grace's house and the nice warm bed. With a little luck, she could slide back in beside Grace without disturbing her.

Angry voices stopped her after a single step. Two men shouted from somewhere up the track. It sounded like an argument, but Carmen was too far away to hear the words. Never one to miss the chance to put herself in danger, she crouched and scooted toward the voices. Carmen knew she shouldn't investigate on her own, but then again, why not? Why waste an opportunity?

Keeping the light off, she headed deeper into the dark forest. With the limited visibility, navigating proved difficult. Carmen tripped on tree roots and dry shale. The precarious footing caused her to slow her pace further. Still, she refused to utilize the light. The lateness of the hour insured practically zero cars up here and no one would mistake a flashlight for headlights. Someone would spot her in an instant.

The breeze picked up a little, blowing dust into her face. Branches swayed and swished. Dried leaves swirled and flew away, pelting her softly. On the track itself, tall grass growing between the tire ruts brushed against her shins. The minor front rolling through thrilled her. Sounds from the wind and the tops of the stately trees moving overhead masked any sounds she made.

Taking advantage, Carmen scampered closer to the tree line as she approached the voices. Before long, she edged near a large clearing. The light cast through a window shown brightly, giving her a clear look at a small hunting cabin. Unlike most of the so-called cabins of the Poconos, this was truly a log cabin with rough hewn timber. Katie wouldn't be caught dead in such a place. Again, Carmen experienced the sensation of barking up the wrong tree. Instinct made her duck when a man spoke from less than twenty paces away. He didn't sound happy.

"All I'm saying is that you should be careful talking to her like that. You don't know who you're messing with."

The voice sounded strangely familiar. Carmen crouched behind a tree trunk and peered around the side. She felt like a voyeur. Once she verified these guys didn't own the dark sedan and that Katie wasn't here, she'd leave.

The second man lowered his voice to a snarl. "Why? How's she going to know anything? She's not psychic. Are you going to tell her?" The tone changed to that of a taunting bully. "Poor little Mikey. Gotta run to mommy."

"Shut up, you moron. I won't have to say anything. She'll know and she won't hesitate to skin you alive."

From the fear in his voice, Carmen didn't believe the speaker meant that last bit figuratively. Also, regardless of the second man's mockery, he hid his own fear poorly. Carmen wondered who the "she" was and why these men were so frightened of her. In her experience, bad guys usually had a worse person to whom they answered. Mobsters had a boss. Narcotics traffickers worked for drug lords. Typically, such leaders were men. Carmen wasn't accustomed to hearing a woman referred to with such dread.

Curiosity got the better of her. Carmen inched closer until she crouched just inside the forest. The black sedan seen only once before sat between Carmen and the men. She could just see the top of one dark head. The other man was shorter and she couldn't see him at all. Carmen wanted to see their faces, but she couldn't risk moving any closer.

Movement from the far side of the window drew her attention. Carmen gasped when she recognized Sahari Nazem inside the cabin. She'd last seen him at the resort in Switzerland. Carmen couldn't fathom his presence here. It seemed so out of place that she was stunned.

"What was that?"

Carmen clamped a hand over her mouth and huddled closer to the ground. *Crap.* She held her breath, childishly hopeful that doing so would help her go unnoticed.

"You're imagining things." That was the snarky man's voice.

"Can you take the chance that I'm not?"

The taller of the two men barreled around the back of the car. When he moved near the trunk, Carmen saw his face. In the light of the waning moon, she recognized him. Shock rendered her unable to move. They made eye contact and Mike Doyle smiled. His gaze lifted to something just behind her and the smile morphed into a feral grin.

Carmen spun around at the sound of a twig snapping. A third man, short and husky with swarthy skin stood less than two feet away. He offered her a lopsided smile.

"Hi."

The casually friendly tone took Carmen by surprise. "Hi."

She realized how ridiculous her automatic response sounded and started to stand. No reason to hide now. Before she could straighten up, the stranger swung a thick tree limb toward her head. Carmen barely saw it coming.

Thwack!

Chapter Twenty-Six

Cricket sat atop the sill to the open window. Her tail swished in worry as she watched the woods for the Carmen woman. It seemed like such a long time ago since she walked into the night. Golden eyes lifted to see that the sky light had moved much farther away. Cricket decided the human was in trouble. She didn't feel happy about that, merely satisfied. She knew that would happen. Cats were very shrewd. Cricket flicked an ear in sudden annoyance. Waking Grace would make her grouchy. She didn't like it when she made Grace grouchy.

Turning on one graceful hind foot, Cricket trotted into the bedroom. She hopped onto the soft covers and sashayed right up on top of Grace's chest. Undisturbed, her Grace continued to sleep. Cricket scooted closer and stared at the pretty face. Eyes moved under the lids, but refused to open. She sat on Grace's chest, considering what to do now.

The round thing on the wall made ticking noises. Cricket knew that meant Carmen was in more trouble as time passed. She worried how Grace would feel if something happened to her mate. Finally, Cricket reached out with one paw and patted Grace's cheek. Grace frowned and turned her head a little. Good, she wasn't dead.

Cricket stood and inched her way up until she rested just under Grace's throat. She tried tapping Grace again, a little harder this time. When Grace failed to wake up, Cricket added her sweet voice to the tiny slaps.

"*Meeooww!*"

****

Grace inhaled and jerked awake at Cricket's yowl. Her eyes flew open and her head reared back into the pillow as one tiny sharp claw caught in her cheek. She ignored the tiny pinprick of pain. She coughed until Cricket removed the foot from her throat. From Cricket's antics, she deduced something was very wrong. Without looking and from the coolness of the sheets, Grace knew Carmen was gone. Just to be sure, she slid a hand over the space without moving the rest of her body so as not to dislodge Cricket.

"She's off doing something reckless, isn't she? That's what you're trying to tell me."

In response, Cricket leaned close until she hovered inches away. Grace waited patiently as Cricket stared into her eyes. Breathing in slowly through her nose, Grace quieted her mind. A connection deeper than thought or emotion grew between them. Communicating in words with the cat wasn't a two-way street, but she could sense Cricket's concerns and feelings.

The love and affinity between them allowed Grace to sometimes even catch flashes of what Cricket saw. In this case, the strength of Cricket's disquiet transmitted readily. Grace saw through her eyes as Carmen dressed and left. Other images flashed. Blurry human forms laughed, discussing the dog ran down on the road. Metal coins clinked, landing in a heap. Fights erupted between people and Grace caught the flash of a steel blade. She gasped as the mental pictures stopped. The brief and intense connection loaded with so much imagery left a minor headache behind.

Grace needed a moment to catch her breath and process. Since kitten hood, Cricket had possessed a kind of precognitive ability that manifested during truly dangerous times. Once she had warned Grace of a house fire. Grace had immediately gone into the kitchen to find she'd left a dish towel near a lit stove. Carmen had avoided the fire and learned to listen to her feline companion in these matters. Of course, Cricket hadn't any idea who these people were. She conveyed only the belief they were bad. Considering how they laughed about running down Leyla, Grace agreed. Why Carmen had sought them out tonight was something Grace simply couldn't fathom.

All of the tales Carmen told of her exploits came to mind along with this latest development. She seemed to go from one catastrophe to the next without pause. If Cricket's instincts were sound, Carmen had just landed in another fix.

"What are we going to do with this woman?" Cricket offered a quiet purr to the question. "Let me guess. She doesn't have much time? Well, I hope you know where to find her."

Rather than attempt another link, Cricket sat on Grace's chest and cocked her head. Grace snorted, knowing Cricket had given every detail she could. The information was buried in Grace's head and she needed to sift through what her friend had shared. Sometimes that wasn't so easy. Maybe she could convince Cricket to find another way.

Rolling to her side, Grace gently shifted Cricket aside. She dressed while delving into recent memories not her own. Frustrated, Grace realized there wasn't time for her to dig out the information.

"All right, girl. Let's go find our friend." Grace grabbed her cell phone as she left the bedroom.

Once they located Carmen, Grace would determine whether she needed to call the sheriff's office. Sometimes a normal daily event seemed like a calamity to the cat. Until she was certain, Grace would hold off on that call. Just to be on the safe side, Grace paused long enough to reach into the bedroom closet. She pulled out a Mossberg pump action shotgun that she kept just for emergencies.

Grace hustled out the door, left the house and followed Cricket directly into the woods. Grace had lived in these woods most of her life. Exploring them after dark wasn't unusual for her so she didn't need any additional light.

"Just do me a favor. Keep in mind that your fur is the same color as the shadows. Stay where I can see you."

Cricket glanced up at her and then leaped over a fallen log. She picked up the pace when she hit the far side. Grace hurried after her, growing more concerned by the second. The two traipsed through the forest in a direct path for the row of cabins on the next road over. Before long, Grace spotted a light through the trees.

"Cricket, I hope you aren't planning to turn me into a peeping Tom.

There is absolutely no reason for Carmen to be here."

Intuition told Grace to keep her voice low. Somehow, she knew Cricket wasn't overreacting. From the moment she opened her eyes to find Carmen missing, Grace knew she was in trouble. The only thing she could imagine was it had something to do with her friend Katie. The possibility of Carmen in danger kept Grace going. Just as she emerged from the woods, Grace saw the car and her blood ran cold. Seconds later, a woman screamed.

Cricket turned on a dime and raced back into the woods while Grace stood frozen in place. Her mouth went dry in sudden apprehension, but she quickly thought of the cell phone. Grace dropped into a crouch and pulled the phone out of her pocket. She tried to dial the police, but realized she didn't have any reception.

For a long agonizing moment, Grace didn't know what to do. There wasn't time to run back to the house to make a phone call. Doubts rose in her conscience. Not about rescuing Carmen or anyone else if the need arose, but about harming another human being. Grace couldn't conceive of actually shooting someone. The shotgun, however, would make a great visual deterrent. If circumstances proved dire enough, she might even utilize the weapon as a club.

Grace took a deep, steadying breath. At least Cricket had run off in the direction of home. With her out of harm's way, Grace could focus on the situation. She knelt at the tree line nearest the cabin's front door. Now she could only wait and ask the Goddess to watch over Carmen. Grace fervently hoped Cricket's fears were unfounded. In the case that they weren't, Grace remained hyper-aware of every sound. She tuned in not only on the cabin, but also on the immediate woodsy area.

One after the other, Grace dried sweaty palms on her jeans and then tightened her grip on the shotgun.

Chapter Twenty-Seven

Some hazy sense of self preservation prevented Carmen from groaning in agony as she opened her eyes. Starbursts seemed to pulse in time with her heartbeat and the throbbing in her head. Carmen experienced the familiar sensation of dried, crusty blood caked against the side of her face, but only one smell stood out. The acrid, breath stealing stench of gasoline. Lots of it.

Blurry images of several people moved around the brightly lit room, but Carmen's gaze lingered on three five-gallon gas cans waiting in the corner.

"There you are. Welcome back. I was beginning to think that Leo hit you a little too hard. You really shouldn't go sneaking around peeking in your neighbors' windows. I'm glad you did though. I'd hate for you to miss the big finale."

Through a titanic effort of will, Carmen raised her gaze. Standing there with an incongruent smile stood Tiffany Nazem, showing more personality than she had during the entire disaster at Lucien Caisson's Swiss ski lodge. She positively glowed with satisfaction. Carmen couldn't find it in her to attribute the word happy to this unpleasant woman.

As her brain began to function normally once more, Carmen recognized a few others in the room. Sahari, Tiffany's husband, sat complacently on a wooden bench against the wall. Beside him stood Mike Doyle and the man who had struck Carmen with the tree limb. She didn't know his name or the other man who paced back and forth like a lion in a cage. The last man was the one she assumed had argued with

Mike near the car. This man carried an aura of anger clear to anyone who cared to look. His dark hair and mustache seemed the epitome of a classic villain. She tried not to stare at the wicked looking hunting knife sheathed on his belt. From a quick look around, Carmen saw that the other men carried dark pistols holstered to their sides. Sahari's suit concealed any signs of a weapon, but she figured he carried something for self defense.

"Carmen, are you all right?"

For the first time, Carmen noticed Katie. She sat only a few paces away directly beside Carmen. Both of them were tied upright in metal folding chairs, which did nothing to improve Carmen's outlook on the situation. Carmen's hands were tied to the front legs with a thin nylon rope. She couldn't pull very hard without tipping herself over.

"Katie, I see we have the upper hand as usual." Carmen coughed and directed her attention to the woman looming into her personal space. She attempted to project as much condescension into her tone as possible. "What do you want, Tiffany? Why are you even here?"

Tiffany chuckled and straightened up away from Carmen. She walked over to lean against a wooden desk next to her husband. Tiffany settled her rear end against the top edge and crossed her slim, elegant ankles. Carmen noticed the woman looked dressed for a night on the town, not for slumming it in the backwoods. The triple strand necklace of Cleopatra pearls along with the slim black evening gown seemed seriously out of place.

"Direct and to the point. I can do that. The truth is that we are here because you are here." Tiffany grinned like she'd just revealed some delicious secret, and maybe she had. Carmen was too groggy to keep up. "You see, when I learned you relocated here after our fun together in Switzerland, I knew this was the perfect opportunity to tie up loose ends."

Carmen glanced at Katie. "Us, you mean. You're the people Katie invested money with."

"Well, Mike is." Tiffany offered the man in question a somewhat predatory smile before resuming her diatribe. "See, Mike is very skilled at computers. Too bad for him that I'm better. Otherwise, I never would have discovered his penchant for embezzlement. After that, it was easy to convince him to join our group. Which is much smaller now, thanks to you."

Carmen didn't really care about Tiffany's need to outline her genius plan like every bad guy at the end of a *Scooby Doo* episode. Still, Carmen latched onto the maniacal monologue as a way to buy time. She mentally had her fingers crossed that Faye would roll in at any minute to make her threatened arrest.

"Kofi and Pymer worked for you and Sahari. With them gone, you'd need new henchmen. Is it hench people if some of them are women?"

"Please." Tiffany glossed right over the question and focused on the first part of Carmen's remark. "I am the leader of this organization. Everyone here answers to me."

Carmen noticed that Sahari sat quietly, apparently content to pick his nails. Maybe she could stir up a little resentment and set these two against each other. "Sorry, I don't mean to sound like a racist or anything, but I thought men in your part of the world preferred their women docile and easy to control."

To her surprise, Sahari cast adoring eyes on his wife before responding. "On the contrary, if not for Tiffany's brilliance, we would be as paupers in the streets. I am happy to follow where she leads."

So much for that. "So, who are the new kids on the block with Kofi and Pymer gone?"

"Why do you care?" Tiffany sounded suddenly suspicious. She glanced out the window quickly and then back to Carmen. "What are you up to?"

"Nothing. I mean, you're obviously going to kill us. Can't you answer a few simple questions first? What's it going to hurt?" Carmen continued tightening and loosening her fists, hoping to generate some slack in the ropes.

The short, squatty man next to Doyle took a step forward. He spoke with a heavy Spanish accent. "Go on, tell her boss. I'd like her to know how screwed they are."

"I'll decide that, Leo," Tiffany snapped, eyes flashing. "Fine, Leo and Eddie filled the void. Like our two deceased members, they enjoy the thrill of hurting people and making money. Satisfied? That's all we wanted you know. Just to make enough to live comfortably and then you came along and messed up everything. You weren't even a cop in Germany or Switzerland. Why did you have to stick your nose in my business?"

The proverbial light bulb went off in Carmen's head. "That was you in both places? You were running scams with werewolves and yeti?"

"Don't be ridiculous. There is no such thing as a yeti. I did find the whole werewolf at Oktoberfest quite original though. Between us, that was one of my more creative ideas. We made a lot of money all over Europe before you stepped in."

Tiffany sounded so pleased that Carmen finally reached her breaking point. The thought of buying time flew out the window. "Give it a rest, Tiffany. I'm not interested in your life story. The truth is simple. Greed. It always boils down to money. You're not exactly original."

Anger suffused her features and Tiffany lunged forward. Carmen flinched in surprise, but Tiffany stopped just short of striking her. Instead, she reached out to caress Carmen's cheek. Carmen shuddered at the cool fingers against her skin and the look in Tiffany's shark-like eyes.

"I do like the money, but I'm all about authenticity. For example, dear Katie is Interpol's prime suspect. I ensured that when I had Mike phone in the anonymous tip. He's also quite skilled at leaving cyber footprints of wire transfers and the like. Did you know that your friend Katie even has a Swiss bank account holding quite a substantial amount?"

Katie had remained silent throughout their entire exchange other than the occasional whimper. At this latest information, her outrage showed through as she said, "I don't have anything like that. Everything I own is legitimate."

"You do now."

"You set her up." Carmen strained against her bonds to no avail. She'd been right all along. Katie was nothing more than a trusting victim in all this. Too bad Faye wasn't around to rub her nose in it.

"Of course," Tiffany said. "It's the only way we all walk away and start over. The police will have their mastermind and all the little fish will swim away. No one will even look for them."

Carmen easily translated what Tiffany failed to say out loud. She only named names and gave details if she wasn't worried about witnesses. "So, you do intend to kill us."

"You really must stop getting hit in the head, Carmen. All that trauma is making you slow. But don't worry. I won't kill you. Katie will. It's the least you deserve for interfering in my plans."

"She's my best friend," Katie shouted, her face turning red as she struggled to reach Tiffany. "If I kill anyone, it'll be you. Please, just let us go. We won't tell anyone."

Carmen kept silent. She didn't believe Tiffany expected Katie to do anything. It would just look like she had. She watched as Tiffany's lip curled in distaste at Katie's pleas.

Tiffany's voice hardened. "Sahari, Mike, load the car. We're leaving tonight. The police will be here by morning. Leo and Eddie, douse the place. I want it reduced to ash."

"You intend to roast us?" Carmen swallowed hard. She through fast, trying to formulate any flaw in Tiffany's plans to make her rethink burning the cabin down. The thought of burning alive almost had her in a panic and Carmen grasped at straws. "It won't work. Any arson investigator will spot an accelerant in an instant."

Katie began to cry, but seemed past the point of actually fighting back. With her being so distraught, Carmen realized their only chance of survival rested with her. Faye and the cavalry clearly wouldn't ride in to save the day.

"I want them to find the gas," Tiffany answered. "How else would it explain your charred body? As for Katie, she's coming with us. I'm a little squeamish, so we'll wait outside while the boys do their work."

"You're letting me go?" Katie sniffled and sounded as disbelieving as Carmen felt.

Eddie snickered, the first sound he'd made since Carmen awakened in the cabin. "Who do you think is gonna take the fall for torching the place?"

"Yeah," Leo said, sounding angry and thrilled all at once. "Too bad you're not going far from here. They'll never find the body."

"Shut up you two, and get to work." Tiffany ordered Mike to release Katie from the chair before turning back to Carmen. "Oh, one more thing."

Tiffany drew back and slapped Carmen so hard that her ears rang. The blow combined with Carmen's recent concussion had her seeing stars again.

"I've wanted to do that for months. Goodbye, Carmen Bravo. I hope you die screaming."

Without another word, Tiffany turned on her heel and left the cabin, obviously expecting everyone to carry out her orders. She never looked back. Mike and Sahari followed her out the door while the Hispanic man and the snarky one headed to the corner to fetch cans of gasoline. They sloshed the liquid all around, soaking furniture and the floor around Carmen in a wide circle. Pungent, breath-stopping fumes made Carmen choke. She tried to bury her mouth and nose against the cloth of her shoulder, but her eyes streamed with tears. They alternated until Eddie held the final can. He spent most of the gas pouring along window sills and across the minuscule kitchen counters. As a final insult, Eddie held the can over Carmen and emptied the remaining bit it over her head.

Carmen choked until she retched. Gasoline soaked through her clothes and burned when it contacted her skin. Streams of fuel cascaded over her head and she clenched her eyes closed. By pressing her face tighter against her shirt, Carmen hoped to keep a fairly dry spot and protect her vision from the worst of the damage. Although there wasn't much left in the can, Carmen didn't think that really meant much in the long run. With the amount of gas and fumes scattered all around, she'd go up like a Roman candle as soon as someone lit the match.

Panic roared, a ravening beast in her mind that almost made her freeze. Self preservation quickly overrode the fear. Although birthed from the same primal instinct, the latter proved more useful. She focused and concentrated on freeing herself.

Desperately, Carmen twisted and struggled against the ropes. She succeeded in only further abrading her wrists. The two goons laughed as Eddie pitched the empty can into a pile with the others in the corner. Plastic containers bounced off one another and flew into a haphazard jumble.

Carmen swallowed hard, grasping that time had run out. The taste of fuel burned her throat and tears of a different sort streamed down her face. No one would come to save her and she couldn't wrestle free. Remorse and sorrow warred for dominance as she thought of Grace. She shouldn't have left without waking Grace, not telling her how much she cared. Most of all Carmen regretted dying without having the chance to see where this relationship might lead. She thought of Katie, too. Katie's gentle nature would cause her guilt over Carmen's death mingled with fear of her own fate. Right up until the moment these knuckleheads killed her.

Throughout it all, Carmen took solace in that she'd never given up on Katie's innocence. Too bad there wasn't anyone she could share the news with. Katie would die with the world thinking her the head of an underground criminal organization.

Carmen continued tugging so fiercely that she unbalanced the chair. It leaned to one side, but Leo caught her by the shoulder and shoved her upright. Both men continued chuckling at her antics. They seemed to find everything so amusing even though tears also coursed down their faces from the fumes. Neither seemed to mind. Leo suddenly coughed and spit onto the floor.

"Let's go man. My sinuses are burning. Time to end this."

"You go ahead," Eddie offered. "I'll light the fire."

Leo's eyes narrowed, from the gasoline or in suspicion Carmen couldn't tell. He finally shrugged and turned around. Over his shoulder, he said, "Just hurry up. You know she don't like to wait."

Despite her dour prospects, Carmen didn't have it in her to simply surrender. She intended to fight until the fire or the smoke took her out. "Why are you all so afraid of Tiffany?" Maybe getting him talking would keep Eddie from lighting the match for another few minutes. Hopes of Faye riding to the rescue lurked in the back of her mind.

"Ha, not me! The rest are just sniveling cowards where that crazy broad is concerned. Maybe because she'll slit your throat without thinking. Or set you on fire." A smirk twisted Eddie's lips as he squatted beside Carmen. He kept his gaze on her face as he unsnapped the sheath at his belt and withdrew the hunting knife. For a second, he pressed the tip to his lower lip, contemplating, before he raised the blade to her face. "Now, I figure we got about two minutes before she wonders why there ain't no bonfire. How's about we have some fun before then?"

The razor-sharp point of the knife pressed into Carmen's cheek just below her right eye. By the thinnest margin, she managed not to flinch. Eddie pressed hard enough that the knife tip pierced her tender flesh. Carmen felt the sting, amplified by the gas that slipped into the minor injury. Blood trailed down her cheek like a scarlet tear, but she took comfort in not reacting.

"How's about I pluck out an eye?"

He was teasing her, Carmen realized. Getting a thrill by driving up her terror and probably waiting for her to beg. No way. She wasn't about to give him that, even when he smiled and she had a clear view of his lack of oral hygiene. Blackened and missing teeth were covered with enough plaque to form tiny bridges between the remaining few. She fought the urge to retch again at the sight combined with the severe halitosis.

"Do whatever you're going to do. Anything has to be better than smelling your breath. You might want to find a good dentist."

Eddie's expression hardened and Carmen congratulated herself on making him angry. That lasted only as long as it took him to drop the hunting blade to her thigh. He drew the keen edge across her leg in one long, smooth stroke. The injury seemed only superficial, but the look on his face promised more to come.

"Just for that, I'm gonna do you slow."

Carmen clenched her teeth to keep them from chattering. A quaking sense of foreboding ratcheted her fear up another notch and caused her heart to hammer in her chest. Her heart beat so quickly that Carmen had an even harder time drawing breath.

"What would mommy say?" She grated.

Eddie drew back the hand holding the knife. Using the weapon as reinforcement, he drew back his fist.

A small troupe of four emerged from the cabin and onto the low-slung wooden porch. A strikingly beautiful woman with midnight tresses issued shouted commands that the men hurried to obey. The single naked overhead bulb illuminated the scene while casting more shadows around the group. Despite the woman's attractive features and stunning, albeit inappropriate, attire, a dark aura surrounded her. Even in the gloom, malicious energy flowed and shimmered around her like a malevolent beacon. Grace huddled closer to the ground as the evil streamed from her and drifted to the men, influencing their own malevolence. The men dragged a slightly built woman toward the car. The smaller woman struggled to no avail, like a fly resisting a hurricane. From everything she'd learned from Carmen over the last week, she guessed this must be the friend. Katie.

Grace swallowed against her grief for this stranger. All along, Carmen was right. In an instant and without ever meeting, Grace could see Katie would never willingly hurt another soul.

"No," Katie wailed. "Don't do this. You can't just burn her like that! You're nothing but a bunch of animals."

The evil woman chuckled and strolled ahead of the others, giving the appearance of striding down a fashion runway. Near the center of the clearing, she turned to survey the cabin while the men shoved the resisting woman inside the dark sedan. Once finished securing the prisoner, they joined the woman. Careful to maintain a respectful distance, they stood quietly waiting for something to happen. No one spoke. Anticipation filled the clearing.

Grace heard what Katie said, and could easily imagine why the group of miscreants lingered. The time had come to act. Quietly, she worked her way around the perimeter of the cabin. Grace took care to stay hidden, fearful that every second she wasted meant an excruciating death for Carmen. Grace had just reached the corner of the cabin leading around the rear when something dark and quick darted from the forest right toward her. Grace gasped and swung the shotgun around. She hadn't managed a quarter turn before she recognized the dark figure.

Don't scare me like that, she projected. *Where did you go?*

Cricket scrambled over and stood up to place her front feet on Grace's knee. The posture situated their faces close together. Suddenly, the image of a black canine pack flooded Grace's mind. She pictured shaggy animals with flashing teeth racing through the woods toward them. If Cricket hadn't broadcast reassurance as well as urgency, Grace's concern would have increased exponentially. Instead, she perceived help would arrive soon. What a pack of animals, a cat, and a lone woman armed with a shotgun she'd never used could accomplish, Grace had no idea. Options limited, Grace connected again with her friend to determine when reinforcements might actually arrive.

Chapter Twenty-Eight

This was it. With Eddie squatted so close, Carmen waited until he pulled his arm back as far as possible. Before he could let the punch fly, she reared back and struck the bridge of his nose with her forehead. She heard cartilage snap and saw blood spray onto the front of her shirt. The jarring movement from her assault toppled the chair sideways. Carmen grunted as she landed in a heap on top of Eddie, pinning him in place. Pain flared through her again, becoming a familiar ally in keeping her awake and fighting.

The knife spun from Eddie's hand and landed only inches away. Carmen ignored all the little hurts and scrambled to her knees with the chair still lashed in place. She felt like an elephant rode her back.

Eddie groaned and rolled onto his side as soon as she moved. He moved slowly, like a drunken beetle. Carmen took advantage and swung the metal chair around, clipping him in the temple. He lay still, but inertia carried Carmen forward and she fell atop the knife. Despite the pain of it digging into her arm, she lay there a moment to catch her breath. After only a second or two, Carmen tried to move. Someone would show up soon to check on Eddie's progress. Her head swam from recent trauma as well as the gas fumes. Ab muscles clenched. The flesh wound on her leg throbbed, but she struggled to rise.

With a sense of impending doom, Carmen inched off the blade and scootched down until she grasped the weapon at the tang. She sliced her fingertips trying to shift the weapon and managed to set the edge against the ropes on that side. Awkward didn't seem to describe the maneuver. Sawing through nylon cord binding her wrist with the same hand in which she held the knife proved extremely problematic.

Carmen fumed, cursed, and cut herself more than once. Red slicked the rope, but finally she sliced through a single strand. Carmen yanked her hand free and made quick work of the other rope. Her head swam as she stood upright for the first time in hours. Hands and fingers tingled as blood flow returned. She waited a second for full feeling to return, hunched over to inspect the injury on her thigh.

The front door bounced against the wall and Carmen's eyes flew up to identify the next threat. Mike Doyle took a step into the cabin.

"What the hell is taking so…" He stopped talking when he spotted Carmen standing free. Brown eyes drifted over to Eddie lying on the floor and the knife in her hand.

Mike reached for his sidearm at the same moment that the rear door to the cabin crashed open. Carmen gasped and dropped into a fighting crouch. She brought the knife up and pivoted on one foot to confront the dual danger. Grace raced into the room with an ancient looking shotgun at her shoulder.

To Carmen, Grace resembled an avenging angel. She had never seen anyone so lovely. That she would place herself in such danger or threaten another human with a weapon meant more to Carmen than she could express. Unfortunately, Carmen wasn't convinced she could actually pull the trigger. More than that, she wasn't convinced the weapon would fire if she did.

Horror caused her eyes to widen when she saw Mike lift his pistol and aim it at Grace. Grace's eyes closed as her finger tightened on the trigger. Carmen heard the click of the shotgun's hammer fall on an empty chamber. With only a split second to act, Carmen hurled the hunting knife at Mike. His shot went wide as the blade embedded in the upper right side of his chest.

An ebony streak shot across the floor and launched itself at Mike's face. He screamed in a combination of pain and shock. At the same time, he raised his left arm in automatic self defense. He couldn't seem to move his right arm. Mike fell backward with another shriek of fear as the object of fury and outrage struck him head on. Carmen lost sight of his face as Cricket went to work slashing and biting in a whirlwind of feline fury.

Carmen trailed the arc of movement as the handgun sailed into the air and landed beside the gasoline cans. Then Grace was beside her, one arm wrapped around Carmen's waist as she pointed the shotgun to the floor. Cricket didn't seem to notice that the immediate threat ended with Mike whimpering in a fetal position. Instead she growled and continued to slash in a flurry of teeth and claws. Mike tried to fend the cat off with one hand. Carmen heard him crying like a child.

"Come away, darling. I think you've made your point." Grace turned to Carmen. She sounded dazed. "Are you all right?"

"Better when we save Katie."

"She's outside. I saw some men put her in a car. Cricket, I said that's enough."

Reluctantly, the cat backed away from the cowering man. Her growl indicated her willingness to attack once more if he so much as twitched.

A fresh burst of adrenaline spurred Carmen into moving. Free and with reinforcements on site, she focused on getting Katie out of this alive. "Let's get something to tie them up. The others will show up in a minute wondering what's going on."

"I don't think we have time."

Carmen noticed a dazed, faraway look in Grace's eye. She appeared almost entranced. "What's going on?"

"They're coming. We have to get out of here. Now."

Grace grabbed Carmen by the collar and hauled her toward the back door. Carmen took a few hobbling steps, hissing at the pain in her leg. She tried to shuffle faster, calling to Cricket as they struck out for the rear door. They only made it half the distance before Carmen heard Tiffany's men on the front porch. A slug buried itself in the door frame as Carmen and Grace hurtled through. The sound of the gunshot reverberated in her head and caused her ears to ring. Wood from the pine walls splintered and peppered the air around them. Carmen hunkered over and dashed out of the cabin right behind Grace. They leapt off the back steps and onto the forest floor.

"That's far enough!"

Carmen slid to a stop with Grace beside her. Tiffany and Sahari stood a few feet away with weapons drawn. In seconds, Leo exited the cabin with Mike. They formed a loose semi circle around the two women.

Scratches and bite marks covered Mike's arms and face. One particular wound on his cheek sported clear bite marks that bled profusely. He looked seriously pissed. Eddie merely looked dazed. He swayed on his feet, but held tightly to the knife he'd recovered.

Tiffany's face twisted into a snarl. "I knew that idiot would make a mess of things. We'll just have to do this the hard way." She shifted her gaze to Leo and Mike. "Shoot them."

This is it, Carmen thought. No more chances. No other way out. She looked out over the treetops to see predawn streaks of red on the horizon. Carmen took Grace's hand. She smiled when Grace looked at her. "I love you. Close your eyes. You don't want to see this coming."

Grace's lips trembled. Tears welled in her eyes, glinting in the early light. Her lips parted, but before she could speak a terrifying din shattered the morning stillness. Snaps, yips, barking, and growls poured into the clearing along with a blur of snarling black wolves. Carmen spotted a white bandage around the lead animal's ribs. She watched helpless as Leo pointed his weapon at Leyla. Then she heard the sound of Grace racking a shell into the shotgun's breach. She felt like her eardrum exploded when Grace fired the weapon less than a foot away from her. Leo screamed and dropped to the dirt, holding his bleeding leg and no longer a threat.

Wolves attacked and brought men down. Leyla ignored the men and hurtled through the air directly toward Tiffany. Carmen saw her arms come up to hold the black wolf off, but she didn't stand a chance. She went down under lean muscle and snapping jaws.

Sahari raised a weapon Carmen assumed he'd kept tucked into a waistband. He aimed at the animal attacking his wife, but never got the shot off. Another lupine form latched onto his hand, crushing flesh against metal as Sahari screamed and struggled. Sahari let go of the gun and managed to wrench away, dropping onto his butt with a muted thump. Blood streamed from his mangled hand. He tried to scoot backward toward the woods, but froze when the wolf loomed over him. Again Carmen noticed the red of eyes in the moonlight.

In less than a minute, it was over. Carmen noticed that the animals didn't kill the men. They merely mauled enough to disarm. Two of the beautiful creatures, Leyla and another, guarded Tiffany. They showed their teeth to indicate she shouldn't move, but refrained from injuring her further. From what Carmen could see Leyla had merely used her weight and a show of force to subdue the hateful woman.

With Leo crying on the ground and wolves detaining the remaining criminals, Carmen thought it was finally over. Another blood-curdling scream made her whip around. Carmen threw herself in front of Grace, prepared to defend her to the death. She couldn't believe her eyes when Eddie stumbled around the fire pit near the back door. Cricket rode his back, claws buried in his neck and teeth latched onto one ear.

Carmen grabbed the shotgun from Grace and clubbed him in the head as he ran past. Eddie landed face first, unconscious before he slammed into the ground. Dried pine needles drifted up from the impact and drifted down over him. Cricket jumped away from him just before he landed. She moved a few paces away, sat down with her tail curled around her, and began licking one paw. A contented purr erupted loud enough for Carmen to hear from two feet away.

"Now what do you intend to do?" Tiffany asked. The snark still hadn't gone out of her.

"Good question," Carmen admitted. "I can't chance leaving one person to guard you while the other goes off to call the police. Even with these nice fluffy wolves as backup."

"I'll do it as soon as someone unties me."

Katie came walking around the side of the cabin. Her hair was mussed and a bruise had already purpled under one eye. Somewhere along the way, she'd lost a shoe, but she was whole. Carmen stifled the sob that rose in her throat and rushed to her friend. She hugged Katie tightly, eyes closed in gratitude that both had managed to survive the night. Carmen pulled away after a moment and returned Katie's grin.

"I'm so glad to see you."

"Same back to you. Carmen, I'm so sorry for not telling you everything. I'm supposed to be the expert on human behavior and I was duped. I was embarrassed."

Carmen shook her head. "Hush now, it's not important. We can talk later. Right now, someone needs to call Faye. I'll explain that later," she added when Katie frowned in confusion. Carmen propped the shotgun against her leg and untied Katie's hands while they spoke.

"Okay, I'll trust you on that. There's a phone in the bedroom. I don't think any of these geniuses ever checked the rest of the cabin once they broke in and tied me up. You go call and I'll help your friend keep watch."

Katie plucked the shotgun off the ground and limped over to stand beside Grace. She pointed the weapon at Tiffany's face. From the murderous look in Katie's eyes, Carmen seriously hoped Tiffany didn't test her.

"Hi, I'm Katie," she introduced herself without glancing away from the gang. "I assume these wolves and the cat are your doing? Sorry I called you a monster and thanks for saving us."

"Uh, yeah. Okay. Actually, I believe we all owe our gratitude to Cricket." Grace pointed at her feline friend. "She brought the wolves."

"Huh, isn't that something?"

Carmen left the women and animals in command as she scurried off to find a phone. Even without cell reception she could pull up Faye's number on her phone and make the call with the cabin's landline. Silent tears of relief and healing fell as she walked away and her heart rate finally resume something close to normal.

Pain lanced through every part of her body as Carmen shifted position on the cushions. Cricket's weight on her lap didn't make it any easier, especially when the cat dug her claws into Carmen's skin. Cricket hissed and stopped moving, the claws retracted and she resumed purring.

"She's comfortable where she is." Grace passed Carmen a glass of red wine and then settled beside her on the sofa.

"Yeah, I got that."

Sweet, comforting scents of damp earth and pine drifted in through the open window. Late afternoon sunshine warmed her neck. Carmen relaxed and took a small sip before reaching for Grace's hand.

"How are you feeling?"

"Better. I still hurt," Carmen admitted, "but at least I'm alive to hurt."

"And you don't smell like a filling station anymore."

Carmen chuckled. "There's that too. I'm just glad all this is finally over."

"I'm sure your friend Katie agrees. Do you think she'll be okay?"

"Katie is remarkably resilient. She'll be fine, especially since Tiffany and the others confessed. I think Faye is unhappy about how things panned out more than anyone, even Tiffany. She really was looking forward to arresting Katie."

Carmen remembered the set of Faye's jaw when she took the criminal mob into custody. She listened stoically to the tale adding few questions. Carmen recalled how she grew even colder upon meeting Grace. Carmen kept her arm around Grace throughout most of the questioning, happy to flaunt their relationship. In the end, Faye and the U.S. Marshals Service brought in a forensics team to mop up and released the witnesses. The Marshals were invited to the party since Tiffany turned out to be a fugitive they had an international warrant on. She left after gathering statements without any offer of keeping in touch. Carmen really believed Faye simply hated to lose, and even worse, hated being wrong.

"I think Agent Joubert was embarrassed at having her theory proven so wrong." Grace lifted their joined hands to kiss Carmen's knuckles. "She also wasn't very happy about us."

"Tough. She made her choice and I am glad she did. Otherwise, I'd never have met you."

Carmen released Grace's hand to slide her arm over her shoulder. She hugged Grace close and kissed her temple.

"Did you mean what you said? You know, when we thought they were going to shoot us."

Carmen nuzzled the top of Grace's head. "I have never meant anything more. Maybe I should have kept quiet since we haven't known each other long, but I can't regret telling you. Truth is, I just know you're the one I've waited to find." Carmen snorted lightly. "Sounds crazy, right?"

"No, it doesn't. Don't you remember that I've always known you were coming and that we belonged together?"

"That's right." Carmen felt more at ease about admitting the depth of her feelings. She should know by now that she could trust Grace with anything, including her heart. "By the way, I'm not sure I ever said thank you for coming to the rescue."

Grace stroked her fingertips lightly against Carmen's uninjured thigh. "Like I told Katie, the credit goes to Cricket. She woke me up and let me know you left. After taking me to the cabin, she went off to get Leyla. What did Katie mean when she apologized for calling me a monster?"

"Oh, that."

Carmen accepted Cricket's amazing talents easily. She'd seen too much to ever under estimate her new friends. Carmen stroked the soft fur and focused on Grace's question. She explained the argument with Katie that resulted in that minor bit of name-calling. "Katie was just upset at the time. She didn't really mean it. The true monsters are Tiffany and her thugs. *You* are nothing short of bewitching. Speaking of Katie, I'm glad she's staying the night at my place while I'm here."

"Oh really?" Grace interjected a playful note into her voice. She leaned close and planted a swift kiss on Carmen's cheek. "And why is that exactly?"

Carmen turned more fully toward Grace, relieved when Cricket hopped off her lap and left the room. She stroked Grace's forehead gently. "Because right now, I want to go to your bedroom." She brushed her lips to Grace's. "And feel my monster's touch in all the right places."

Grace's smile brightened the room and Carmen's heart soared.

"Deal, as long as you promise me one thing. Never attempt to solve another case. I don't think I can bear ever seeing you in danger again."

"Never again, my love. You and Cricket are all the mystery I need."

Cricket lay atop the empty dog kennel with her ears pinned back. The cries, gasps, and moans from the bedroom had drifted through the house for quite a while. She endured the commotion with feline reserve and outward detachment. No other being, not even the dog who was not a dog or the red-breasted bird, would ever know she secretly delighted in the sounds. Her person was happy and now Cricket had another person to feed and pet her.

About the Author

A decorated United States Marine and retired San Diego Deputy Sheriff, Susan dedicated her early life to public service. An on the job law enforcement injury pushed her into early retirement. These days, Susan resides in Murfreesboro, Tennessee. The lush surroundings help fuel her creative side to pursue another passion…writing.

This award winning author's other works include: *Under the Midnight Cloak, Now You See Me, Fractured Futures, Destination Alara, Under Devil's Snare, Woeful Pines, Illusive Witness, Beyond the Garden, The Flaw in Logic* and *Norwood Manor*. She has also published short stories in *Lesbians on the Loose, Crime Writers on the Lam* published by Jessie Chandler and Lori Lake, and *Our Stories* by Sapphire Publishing.

Acknowledgments

Heartfelt thanks to the following people for their continued support, knowledge and expertise. My publisher Flashpoint for taking the risk on this book. Kim Moore, whose knowledge of Denver, Colorado and the Police Air One Unit information proved invaluable. Love and special thanks to my friends Hobbes and Lola. The hours spent crunching ideas and the occasional kick in the pants to keep going were exactly what I needed.

Last, but not least, I wish to acknowledge my furry friends. Smudge, my snuggling purr-monster and Cricket whose mysterious feline ways ensured her inclusion in the latter third of this novel. I love you both.

FLASHPOINT
PUBLICATIONS

Bringing rainbow stories to life.

Flashpoint Publications welcomes submissions from writers of every color and books featuring characters of every color. In addition, Flashpoint Publications encourages job applicants of every color whenever a staff position becomes available. We believe that EVERYONE is entitled to a seat at our table.

www.flashpointpublications.com

CPSIA information can be obtained
at www.ICGtesting.com
Printed in the USA
JSHW010937140623
43144JS00004B/263